...AND THEIR

DREAM BECAME

A NIGHTMARE

Available now from bestselling author

ERICA SPINDLER

and MIRA® Books

CAUSE FOR ALARM

John sat on a park bench, the October day bright and mild. Before him lay Lake Pontchartrain, its diamond surface broken by the occasional swoop of a gull diving for food. A beautiful scene, John thought. Magnificent, calming. At any other time. But not now.

He breathed deeply, working to control his rage. He had followed Julianna. He knew where she worked, her hours, that she didn't associate with any of the other employees. He had learned that she'd given birth to a girl and that she had given her up for adoption. He knew to whom.

He knew everything. *Everything.*

Fury choked him. He had thought she was different. Special, more worthy than other people. How could he have been so wrong about her?

John stood. Above, a gull shrieked and circled, then dove for its prey. The man was to blame. The baby. The woman.

One complication had become three. The complications would have to be eliminated.

Dear Reader,

Adoption has come a long way in recent years. No longer is it considered something to be hidden, as if a shameful secret. It is acknowledged for what it is—an incredible act of love for all concerned.

As an adoptive mother myself, I know firsthand the immediate and overwhelming love and possessiveness an adoptive parent feels for their child. I understand the adoptive parents' irrational fear of their baby's biological family, and the uncertainty born of having opened life and heart to the unknown. And I know the lengths and depths they, like any parent, would go to keep their child safe from harm.

I used this knowledge as a starting point to create this work of fiction.

If you enjoy *Cause for Alarm*, please look for my other titles—*Red*, *Forbidden Fruit*, *Fortune* and *Shocking Pink*. And I hope you'll look for my next novel, *All Fall Down*, due out in March 2000.

Best wishes,

P.S. I love to hear from my readers. You may write me at: P.O. Box 8556 Mandeville, LA 70470

ERICA SPINDLER

CAUSE FOR ALARM

MIRA®

ISBN 1-55166-497-6

CAUSE FOR ALARM

Copyright © 1999 by Erica Spindler.

Printed in U.S.A.

ACKNOWLEDGMENTS

I wish to extend a special thanks to Detective Quintin Peterson, Metropolitan Police Department, Washington, D.C., for not only answering my questions about the M.P.D., but for bringing it to life. Special thanks also to Vicki and John Faivre for information on fly-fishing locales. A picture really is worth a thousand words. I'd also like to offer a huge hug of gratitude to Dianne Moggy and the amazing MIRA crew for helping me pull a rabbit out of a hat with this one. Time was definitely not on my side. Thanks also to Chuck and Evelyn Vagnier, Cover to Cover bookstore, Mandeville, Louisiana, for helping me locate all sorts of out-of-the-ordinary research materials. And finally, thanks to my incomparable agent, Evan Marshall, and my ever-helpful and always-understanding husband, Nathan.

For my sons

Prologue

The fashionable Washington neighborhood slept. Not a single light shone up or down the block of high-priced town homes, the only illumination the glow from the streetlamps and the three-quarter moon. The November night chilled; the air was damp, heavy with the scent of decay.

Winter had come.

John Powers climbed the steps to his ex-lover's front door. He proceeded purposefully but without fanfare, his movements those of a man who depended on not being noticed. Dressed completely in black, he knew he appeared more shadow than man, a kind of ghost in the darkness.

Reaching the top landing, he squatted to retrieve the house key from its hiding place under the stone planter box to the right of the door. During the spring and summer months the planter had been filled with vibrant, sweet-smelling blossoms. But now those same flowers were dead, their stems and leaves curling and black from the cold. As was the eventuality of all living things, their time had come and gone.

John slipped the key into the lock and turned it. The dead bolt slid back; he eased open the door and stepped inside. Easy. Too easy. Considering the parade of men who had come and gone through this door over the years, using this same key, retrieved from this same hiding place, Sylvia should have been more careful.

But then, forethought had never been Sylvia Starr's strong suit.

John closed the door quietly behind him, pausing a moment to listen, taking those valuable seconds to ascertain the number of people in the house, whether they were sleeping and where they were sleeping. From the living room to his right came the steady ticking of the antique mantel clock. From the bedrooms beyond, the thick snore of a man deeply asleep, a man who had probably drunk too much, one no doubt too old and out of shape to have spent the evening with the ever-enthusiastic and sometimes gymnastic Sylvia.

Too bad for him. He should have gone home to his fat, dependable wife and their ungrateful, cow-faced children. He was about to become a victim of being in the wrong place at the wrong time.

John started for the bedroom. He took his weapon from its snug resting place—the waistband of his black jeans, at the small of his back. The pistol, a .22 caliber semiautomatic, was neither powerful nor sexy, but it was small, lightweight and at close range, utterly effective. John had purchased it, as he did all his weapons, secondhand. Tonight he would give it a watery grave in the Potomac.

He entered Sylvia's bedroom. The couple slept side by side; the bed rumpled, the sheet and blankets twisted around their hips and legs, only half covering them. In the sliver of moonlight that fell across the bed, Sylvia's left breast stood out in relief, full, round and milky white.

John crossed to where the man slept. He pressed the barrel of the gun to the man's chest, over his heart. The direct contact served two purposes: it would muffle the sound of the shot and assure John a swift, clean kill. A professional took no chances.

John squeezed the trigger. The man's eyes popped open, his body convulsed at the bullet's impact. He gasped for air, the gurgling sound wet as fluid and oxygen met.

Sylvia came immediately awake. She scrambled into a sitting position, the sheet falling away from her.

The man already forgotten, John greeted her. "Hello, Sylvia."

Making small, squeaky sounds of terror, she inched backward until her spine pressed flat against the bed's headboard. She moved her gaze wildly back and forth, from John to her twitching, bloody companion, her chest heaving.

"You know why I've come," John murmured. "Where is she, Syl?"

Sylvia moved her mouth, but no sound escaped. She looked only a breath away from dissolving into complete, incoherent hysteria. John sighed and circled the bed, stopping beside her. "Come now, love, pull yourself together. Look at me, not him." He caught her chin, forcing her gaze to meet his. "Come on, sweetheart, you know I couldn't hurt you. Where's Julianna?"

At the mention of her nineteen-year-old daughter, Sylvia shrank back even more. She glanced at her bed partner, still and silent now, then back at John, working, he saw, to pull herself together. "I...I know...everything."

"That's good." He sat beside her on the bed. "So you understand how important it is that I find her."

Sylvia began to shudder, so violently the bed shook. She brought a hand to her mouth. "H-how...young, John? How young was she when you began leaving my bed to go to hers?"

He arched his eyebrows, amazed at her outrage, amused by it. "Are we feeling maternal suddenly? Have you forgotten how only too happy you were for us to spend time together? To let your lover play daddy? How eager to let me care for her so you could be free?"

"You bastard!" She clutched at the sheet. "I didn't mean for you to defile her. To...to take my trust and—"

"You're a whore," he said simply, cutting her off. "All you've ever cared about was your parties and men and the pretty baubles they could give you. Julianna was nothing but a pet to you. Another of your baubles, a means for the tired, old whore to buy a bit of respectability."

Sylvia lunged at him, claws out. He knocked her backward, easily, the heel of his hand connecting with the bridge of her nose. Her head snapped against the headboard, stunning her. He brought the barrel of his gun to the underside of her chin, pressing it against the pulse that beat wildly there, angling it up toward her brain.

"What Julianna and I share isn't about *fucking,* Sylvia. It's not so base as that, though I doubt you could understand. I taught her about life." He leaned closer. He smelled her fear, it mixed with the scent of blood and other body fluids, earthy but very much alive; he heard it in the small feral pants that slipped past her lips, the squeaks of a terrified mouse facing a python. "I taught her about love and loyalty and obedience. About commitment. I'm her everything...father figure, friend and mentor, lover. She belongs to me, she always has."

He tightened his grip on the gun. "I want her back, Sylvia. Now, where is she? What have you done with her?"

"Nothing," she whispered. "She...went on her...her own. Sh-she..." Her gaze drifted to the dead man beside her, to the ever growing pool of red, creeping across the white satin coverlet. Her voice shuddered to a halt.

With his free hand, John grabbed a handful of her hair and jerked her face back to his. "Look at me, Sylvia. Only at me. Where did she go?"

"I...I don't know. I..."

He tightened his grip on her hair and shook her. "Where, Syl?"

She began to giggle, the sound unnaturally high, otherworldly. She brought a hand to her mouth as if to hold the giggles back; they bubbled from her lips anyway. "She came to me...you wanted her to have an abortion. I told her...you're a...monster. A cold-blooded killer. She didn't believe me, so I called Clark." Her giggles became triumphant, bizarrely so, given her situation. "He showed her pictures of your handiwork. Proof, John. *Proof.*"

John froze, his fury awesome, glacial. Clark Russell, CIA grunt man, former comrade-in-arms, one of Sylvia's lovers. One who knew too much about John Powers.

Clark Russell was a dead man.

John leaned toward Sylvia, the gun forcing her head back, her chin up. "Clark sharing classified information? I guess you're a better lay than I thought." He narrowed his eyes, disliking the way his heart had begun to hammer, his palms to sweat. "You shouldn't have done that, Syl. It was a mistake."

"To hell with you!" she cried, her voice rising. "You won't find her! I told her to run, as fast and as far as she could…to save herself and the baby! You'll never find her. Never!"

For a split second he considered the horror of that possibility, then he laughed. "Of course I will, Sylvia. It's what I do. And when I find her, the problem will be eliminated. Then Julianna and I will be together again, the way we're supposed to be."

"You won't! Never! You—"

He pulled the trigger. Brains and blood splattered across the antique white headboard and onto the pretty rose-patterned wallpaper beyond. John gazed at the mess a moment, then stood. "Goodbye, Sylvia," he murmured, then turned and went in search of Julianna.

Part I

Kate and Richard

1

Mandeville, Louisiana,
New Year's Eve, 1998

Light blazed from every window of Kate and Richard Ryan's grand old home on Mandeville's Lakeshore Drive. The house had been built nearly a century before, at a time when gracious southern living meant something, a time before MTV and the breakdown of the American family, before it was okay for politicians to cheat on their wives and before the evening news calmly recounted grisly murders as if the daily occurrence of such events wasn't a horror in and of itself.

The house, with its double, wraparound galleries and floor-to-ceiling windows, spoke of wealth, of status, of solidity. Of family. The family Kate and Richard would never have.

Kate stepped out onto the house's upper gallery, shutting the French doors behind her, muffling the sounds of the New Year's Eve party in full swing inside. The January night, bitter cold and blustery for southern Louisiana, slapped her in the face. Crossing to the gallery's edge, she gazed out at the black, turbulent lake. She curled her fingers around the rail and leaned into the wind, unconcerned at the way it tore at her hair and cut through her thin, shirred velvet gown.

Across Lake Pontchartrain, connected by a twenty-six-mile causeway, lay New Orleans, a decaying jewel of a city, home to Mardi Gras and jazz and some of the best food in the world. Home, also, to the privilege of St. Charles Avenue, the poverty of the projects and the soaring crime rate that went with such explosive extremes.

Kate imagined the party happening on that shore, one celebrating not only the new year, but the last year in the century as well. A turning point, the end to an era, a door closing.

For her, too, she thought. And Richard.

Before the holidays, she and her husband had been forced to face the fact that they would never have children. The results of their last tests had been conclusive: Richard was sterile. Up to that point they had assumed their inability to conceive had been the result of her many, varied but correctable, problems. But when none of those corrections had done the trick, the doctor had insisted on testing Richard.

The results had devastated them both. Kate had been angry—at the world, at God, at all the people who had babies so effortlessly and with such little care. She had felt betrayed. Useless. Cast adrift.

And then she had felt better. For even though they hadn't gotten the answer they'd wanted, at least they had one. She could give up the exhausting and emotionally draining quest for pregnancy and get on with her life; they could get on with their lives.

Infertility treatments had taken their toll. On her personally. On her and Richard's marriage, on their professional lives. A part of her felt nothing but sweet relief at getting off that roller coaster, at being able to finally let it go.

If only she could let go of her longing for a child, her longing to be a mother. Some nights she lay in bed, staring at the ceiling, the ache inside her so great she couldn't sleep.

Strong arms circled her from behind. Richard's arms. "What are you doing out here?" he whispered, bending his head close to her ear. "And without a coat? You'll catch your death."

She shook off her melancholy and smiled over her shoulder at her husband of ten years. "With you to keep me warm? I don't think so."

He grinned, and his eyes crinkled at the corners. At that moment he looked as boyishly handsome at thirty-five as he had at twenty when she met him. He wiggled his eyebrows suggestively. "We could get naked and do the wild thing. Right here. Right now."

"Sounds kinky." She turned in his arms and looped hers around his neck. "I'm game."

He laughed and leaned his forehead against hers. "And what would our guests think?"

"Hopefully they're all too well-mannered to wander up here uninvited."

"And if they're not?"

"They'll see a side of us they never have before."

"What would I do without you?" He dropped a kiss on her mouth and drew slightly away from her. "It's about time for me to make my announcement."

"Nervous?"

"Who me?" He laughed and shook his head. "Never."

He meant it, Kate knew. Her husband's self-confidence never ceased to amaze her. Tonight, he was announcing his intention to run for St. Tammany Parish District Attorney, yet he wasn't nervous. He wasn't anxious or plagued by self-doubt and second thoughts.

Why should he be? He expected his announcement to be applauded by their family and friends, by his business associates and the leaders of the community. And he expected not only to win the race, but that the run would be nearly effortless.

Of course he did. Richard had always lived a kind of starred existence. Had always been the chosen one, the one voted most likely to succeed, the winner. He wore success as comfortably as others wore ten-year-old athletic shoes.

"You're certain Larry, Mike and Chas are one hundred percent behind this?" she asked, referring to his law partners at Nicholson, Bedico, Chaney & Ryan.

"Absolutely. What about you, Kate?" He searched her gaze. "Are you one hundred percent behind me? If I win, our lives will change. We'll be scrutinized, constantly under the magnifying glass."

"Trying to frighten me off?" she teased, leaning against him. "Well, it won't work. I'm one hundred percent behind you and your decision. And you might as well forget about 'If you're going to win,' because you are. I'm certain of it."

"With you at my side, how can I not?"

When she tried to laugh off his words, he cupped her face in his palms and gazed into her eyes. "I mean it. You have magic, Katherine Mary McDowell Ryan. You always have. Thank you for sharing it with me."

Tears stung her eyes. She chided herself for her earlier melancholy and silently counted her blessings. The girl who'd worn shoes with holes in the soles and hand-me-down school uniforms to St. Catherine's, the girl who had never known the security of a comfortable home, the one who had attended Tulane University on a scholarship, squeaking by borrowing books and waiting tables at night, had come a long way. In no small part because Richard Ryan, favorite son of one of New Orleans' first families had unbelievably, miraculously, fallen in love with her.

"I love you, Richard."

"Thank God." He leaned his forehead against hers. "Now, can we please go inside?"

She agreed and within minutes they were swept back into the party, surrounded, then separated by their jubilant guests. Richard made his announcement and, as expected, his news was greeted by those not already in the know with cheers of approval.

From that moment on, the party became almost manic. As if all in attendance had been struck by a strange sort of energy, a sense that life as it had been was about to change. The year 1999. The *fin de siècle*. The stuff of the future, of science fiction, of uncertainty and the unknown—not of the *now*. Not of everyday lives.

Midnight came. Confetti and streamers flew and horns sounded. Hugs and kisses were exchanged, more champagne drunk. The caterer served a buffet brunch. It was eaten and enjoyed then finally, one by one, Kate and Richard's guests began to leave.

As Richard walked the last out, Kate began picking up even though they'd contracted a cleaning service to take care of the mess first thing in the morning.

"God, you're beautiful."

She looked up. Richard stood in the doorway between the dining room and front parlor, watching her.

She smiled. "And you're flushed with success. Or alcohol."

"Both. But it's still true. You're gorgeous."

She wasn't, she knew. She was attractive, with an ageless, angular kind of face. Not gorgeous or sexy. Not a knockout. Classy, maybe. Solid, definitely. "I'm glad you think so."

"You never could take a compliment. Because of your old man."

"You have good bones, Katherine Mary McDowell," she said, imitating her father's slight brogue. "Never underestimate the importance of good bones and teeth." She laughed. "Like a work horse, for heaven's sake."

Richard grinned and as Kate had been earlier that evening, she was reminded of the fraternity boy who had swept her—and every other coed on the Tulane campus—off her feet. "Your father did have a way with words."

"That he did." She shook her head. "Come give me a hand."

Instead, he cocked his head studying her, a boyish, pleased expression on his face. "Kate McDowell," he said softly, "the one many wanted, including my good buddy Luke. But who I won."

As always happened at the mention of their mutual friend, Luke Dallas, the twin emotions of guilt and longing assailed her. Once upon a time, the three of them had been inseparable. They had been best friends at Tulane; Luke had been her confidant, the person she had turned to for comfort, advice, support. In many ways, she had been closer to him during those years than to Richard.

Then she'd destroyed their friendship with one thoughtless, reckless act of passion and grief.

Uncomfortable with the memory, she shifted her attention to collecting the soiled cups and plates. "You're drunk," she said lightly.

"So what? I'm not driving." He folded his arms across his chest. "Do you deny that Luke was in love with you?"

"We were friends, Richard."

"And nothing else, right?"

She met his gaze. "We were all friends. I wish that hadn't changed."

For a moment, her husband said nothing, just watched her. When he spoke, his mood had mellowed once more. "You're going to make the perfect politician's wife."

She arched an eyebrow. "Are you so sure of that, District Attorney Ryan? I don't have a pedigree, you know."

"Classy, beautiful, smart Kate. You don't need one, you're married to me."

She set the empties on a tray and began collecting more. He was right, she supposed. Marrying him had validated her in New Orleans society. She didn't need a good family, or to have come from money, she had been given his.

For the second time that evening, she thought of her blessings. She had many things to be grateful for, she knew. For her loving husband, their beautiful home. Her own business, a coffeehouse called The Uncommon Bean, which she loved; her stained glass work, plenty of money. All the things she had always told herself that she wanted. That she needed to be completely happy.

"I'm sorry if I upset you with that comment about Luke. I don't know what gets into me sometimes."

"It's been a long night, that's all."

Richard crossed to her and took the empty cups from her hands and set them back on the end table. "Leave the mess. That's what we're paying the service for."

"I know, but—"

"No." He took her hands. "Come with me. I have something for you."

She laughed. "I'm sure you do."

"That, too." He led her to the living room. There, before the still glowing fire, he'd placed two floor pillows. Beside them waited a chilling bottle of champagne and two crystal wine flutes.

They made themselves comfortable. Richard popped the cork on the champagne and poured. He handed her a glass, then held his out. "I thought we should celebrate privately."

She pinged her glass against his. "To your campaign."

"No," he corrected, "to us."

"I like that. To us." She smiled, then sipped.

For several minutes, they chatted about the events of the evening, sharing tidbits from conversations they'd had and chuckling over the antics of a couple of their less inhibited guests.

"You make me better than I am, Kate," Richard murmured, serious suddenly. "You always have."

"And you're drunker than I first thought."

"I'm not." He took the glass from her hand and set it aside. He laced their fingers. "I know how hard this last year was for you. Because of the...the infertility."

Her eyes flooded with tears. "It's okay, Richard. I have so much. It's wrong for me to want—"

"No, it's not. And if not for me, you could have it. You could have a baby."

"That's not true, Richard. I'm infertile, too, I have—"

"You have fertility *problems,* Kate. Hormones can be adjusted, endometriosis treated, ovulation stimulated. I'm *sterile.* Shooting blanks, as they say down at the firm." Bitterness crept into his tone. "How do you think that makes me feel? To not be able to give you what you want more than anything? To be less than a man."

It hurt to hear him express his true feelings, ones he hadn't before. She tightened her fingers on his. "That's bullshit, Richard," she said softly, fiercely. "The ability to sire children is not what makes a man. It's not what makes *you* a man."

"No? That's the way it feels."

"I know how it feels, because this is my problem, too. Bearing children is something all women are supposed to be able to do. It's a given, part of being a female. To not be able to without medical technology feels like a betrayal."

"I've let you down," he said quietly.

"No, Richard...that's not what I meant."

"I know. But that's the way I feel."

She turned fully to him, clasping his hands in hers. "Who's to say we're entitled to everything, anyway? Who's to say we're supposed to have all that our hearts desire? Look at us, at all we have. A beautiful home. Successful careers that we enjoy. Each other, Richard. Our love. An embarrassment of riches. Sometimes I have to pinch myself. I can't believe it's Kate

McDowell who's living this life. Sometimes I'm afraid I'm having a really good dream and that any minute it's going to turn into a terrifying nightmare.''

"I won't let it, sweetheart. I promise."

She brought his hands to her mouth, a sense of urgency tugging at her. "People have lied, cheated and killed to get what we take for granted, we have to guard what we have by appreciating it. We can't ever forget how lucky we are. The minute we do, the minute we get greedy, we could lose it all. We can't forget that, Richard. We can't. It's important."

He laughed. "And you still believe in leprechauns and fairies and the power of a four-leaf clover, don't you?"

"It could all be gone tomorrow." She tightened her fingers on his. "I'm serious, Richard."

"So am I. We *can* have it all, Kate. I want that for you." When she opened her mouth to protest, he shushed her with a finger to her lips. "I have something for you. A late Christmas present." He slipped a business-size envelope from its hiding place under one of the pillows and handed it to her. "Happy New Year, Kate."

"What is it?"

"Open it and find out."

She did. It was a letter from Citywide Charities, informing them that they had been accepted into the Agency's Gifts of Love adoption program.

Kate's heart began to hammer, her hands to shake. Citywide's program was the best in the area. They accepted only a handful of couples every year; at the end of that year, or shortly thereafter, those couples would have a baby.

She had studied up on adoption and on the programs

and options available in the area. She had looked wistfully at Citywide. But every time she had mentioned adoption to Richard, he had flatly refused to even discuss it.

She lifted her gaze to her husband's, overcome with emotion, eyes swimming with tears. "What happened? You didn't think adoption—"

"But you did."

Tears choked her, and she cleared her throat. "But we...if you don't really want to adopt, we can't. It wouldn't be right."

"I want to make you happy, Kate. This will be a good thing for us, I know it will. And it's the right time for us to start a family."

She couldn't find her voice, but even if she had she wouldn't have been able to find the words to express her joy. So she kissed him instead. Deeply and with the love and gratitude that filled her to near bursting.

They had kissed this way many times before, but this time was different, special. This time her heart felt fuller than it ever had before.

By this time next year they would have a child. They would be parents. A real family.

"Thank you," she whispered again and again as she kissed him. She removed his clothes, he hers. The remnants of the fire warmed them, as did their exploring hands, their exploding passion.

"This is going to be our most perfect year ever," Richard whispered as he positioned himself above her. "Nothing will ever come between us, Kate. Nothing or no one."

Part II

Julianna

2

The corner sandwich shop was located on one of the central business district's busiest corners. The shop, Buster's Big Po'boys, specialized in shrimp-and-oyster po'boys—huge sandwiches made on slabs of French bread and stuffed with fried shrimp, oysters or both. Most New Orleanians ordered them dressed—with lettuce, tomato and mayonnaise, the latter slathered on, good and thick. Of course, if fried seafood didn't appeal, Buster's offered all manner of other fillings and even a few nonsandwich specials, like traditional New Orleans red beans and rice on Mondays.

As corner sandwich shops went, Buster's was pretty run-of-the-mill for the Crescent City—housed in a century-old building, its plaster walls were cracked and peeling, the high ceilings dingy with God only knew how many years of God only knew what; and from June to September, the air conditioner ran full tilt *and* still couldn't keep up.

Anywhere else in the country, Buster's would have been closed down by the health department; New Orleanians considered Buster's a perfectly acceptable place to grab lunch while downtown.

Julianna Starr pushed open Buster's glass front door

and stepped inside, leaving the cold January day behind. The smell of frying seafood hit her in a nauseating wave, turning her stomach. The smell, she had learned over the past few weeks working as a waitress at Buster's, permeated everything—her hair and clothes, even her skin. The minute she got home from work, she ripped off her uniform and jumped into the shower to scrub the odor away, no matter how tired or hungry she was.

The only thing worse than the smell of the place, Julianna had decided, was its customers. New Orleanians were so...excessive. They laughed too loudly, ate and drank too much. And they did both with a kind of frenetic abandon. Several times, just watching someone tear into and consume one of the huge, sloppy po'boys had sent her scurrying for the john to throw up. But then, she was one of the lucky ones to whom morning sickness was confined to neither mornings nor the first three months of pregnancy.

Julianna quickly scanned the restaurant, heart sinking. Choosing today to oversleep had been a mistake; the lunch rush appeared to have started early. Only minutes after eleven and every table was filled; the take-out counter already stacked two deep. As Julianna made her way to the back of the restaurant, one of the other waitresses shot her a dirty look.

"You're late, princess," her boss called from behind the counter. "Grab an apron and get your tail in gear, you hear?"

Julianna glared at the man. As far as she was concerned, Buster Boudreaux was a grease-sucking pig with an IQ about the size of one of his stupid sandwiches. But he was her boss, and she needed this job, low as it was.

Without a word of explanation, she stalked past him and snatched an apron from the tree just inside the kitchen and slipped it on. The pink-ruffled atrocity rode up over her burgeoning belly, making her look like a pink whale. She muttered her displeasure under her breath, turned to the time clock and punched in.

Buster came up behind her, his expression thunderous. "If you've got a problem, why don't you say it to my face instead of under your breath."

"I don't have a problem." She stuffed her employee card back into its slot. "Where's my station?"

"Section one. Start servicing the tables as they open back up. In the meantime, give Jane a hand at the takeout counter."

Julianna didn't acknowledge him with so much as a nod, and he grabbed her elbow. "I've about had it with your attitude, you know that, princess? If I didn't need the help so bad, I'd kick your uppity butt out of here right now."

He wanted her to beg for her job, she knew. To plead, grovel before him like some sort of peasant. She would rather starve.

She looked pointedly at his hand on her arm, then met his gaze. "Is there anything else?"

"Yeah," he said, flushing and dropping his hand. "You're late like this one more time, and you're out. I'll get my grandmother to take your place, she'd do a better job anyway. Got that?"

Sure he would. Creep. "Got it."

She flounced past him and out onto the floor. As she did, she brushed past Lorena, a fellow waitress, who glared at her and muttered something that Julianna couldn't quite make out.

Julianna ignored her. It wasn't the first time she had

been the recipient of one of the other waitresses' barbs. They didn't like her, particularly Lorena. No doubt because Julianna didn't make a secret of the fact she hated working here, that she was too good to be serving these big sloppy sandwiches to people who barely looked at her. That she was too good for *them*.

They didn't understand, these rough-hewn, classless girls, that she wasn't meant to have to work this way, to have to be on her feet for hours, to be tired all the time, to be serving people. She had been raised for better things. To be taken care of, to be pampered and adored. Her entire life it had been so; all she'd had to do was smile, cajole or even pout prettily and whatever she had wanted had been given to her. Indeed, if she hadn't been running so low on the money her mother had given her when she left D.C., she wouldn't have lowered herself to their level.

She had been on the run for just over three months and in that time, had lived briefly in Louisville, Memphis and Atlanta. Until New Orleans, she had stayed in moderate hotels, eating her meals out, spending her time going to movies and wandering through shopping malls. Until New Orleans, she hadn't noticed the frightening rate at which her money was disappearing. She hadn't thought ahead to what being without money would mean or what she would have to do to get more of it. When she had finally realized it wouldn't last forever, she had been down to her last fifteen hundred dollars.

Wretched and demeaning as it was, Buster's was a necessity, at least for now.

Julianna sighed and glanced longingly toward the pay phone at the back corner of the restaurant, near the rest rooms, thinking of her mother. Her mother had always said that the power of a woman, one who knew how to use both her beauty *and* her brains, packed more punch than an atomic bomb. A beautiful woman could move mountains or level cities with nothing more than a carefully chosen glance or smile.

If only she could call her, Julianna thought, suddenly, achingly homesick. If only she could go home.

John, standing above her while she retched, his face pinched, white and terrible with fury. John warning her not to defy him again, telling her he would punish her if she did. Julianna drew in a deep breath. *The man and woman from Clark Russell's photographs, their throats slit from ear to ear.*

John was capable of anything. Her mother had said so. So had Clark.

She couldn't go home, maybe never again.

"Miss? Excuse me, Miss?"

Startled, Julianna blinked. A customer at the table to her right was signaling her.

"We need ketchup."

Julianna nodded and brought that table their condiment, another their bill, still another their sandwiches. That done, she ducked into the bathroom, something she had to do often these days.

She relieved herself, flushed the toilet, let herself out of the stall and stopped dead. A woman stood at the mirror, applying lipstick. She had hair the color of cinnamon; it fell in soft waves almost to her shoulders.

Julianna closed her eyes, her mind hurtling back fourteen years....

Her mother sat at her vanity, dressed only in her bra, panties and garter belt. Julianna stood in the doorway, watching as she leaned closer to the mirror and applied her lipstick. She drew the color evenly over her mouth, then pressed her lips together to smooth it.

Admiration and awe filled Julianna. "You're so pretty, Mama," she whispered, forgetting herself.

Her mother turned. And smiled. "Thank you, honey. Remember, though, when it comes to your mama, we say 'beautiful.' You're pretty. Mama's beautiful."

Julianna bowed her head. "I'm sorry."

"That's okay, sweetie, just remember next time."

Julianna nodded and inched into the bedroom, unsure if she was welcome or not. When her mother didn't protest, she sat gingerly on the edge of the big, satin-covered bed, careful not to crumple her dress.

She straightened her white pinafore and inspected her black patent shoes, looking for scuffs and finding none. Her mother had many rules she expected Julianna to follow, so many it was sometimes hard for five-year-old Julianna to remember them.

But Julianna never forgot that wrinkled, mussed clothing would be met with great displeasure and swift punishment. Especially when company was coming.

"Who's visiting tonight, Mama?" she asked, resisting the urge to rub her toes together, though she liked the squeaky sound the shiny leather made when she did. "Uncle Paxton?"

"No." Her mother took a stocking from the box on the vanity top. "Someone special." She eased the shimmery, silky fabric up her leg, then clipped a garter to it. "Someone very special."

"What's his name?"

"John Powers," her mother murmured, her expression growing faraway and soft looking. "I met him at that party at the Capital last week. The one I told you about."

"Where they had sandwiches shaped like swans."

"Canapés. That's right."

Julianna tilted her head, studying her mother. He must be special, she decided. She had never seen her mama look quite this way when talking about one of her visitors.

"I expect you to be on your best behavior."

"Yes, Mama."

"If you're a really good girl, I might buy you that doll you've been wanting. The one with the long brown curls, just like yours."

Julianna knew what her mother meant by being really good. It meant she was to be quiet. And cooperative. And what her mother called charming. Being really good would be rewarded. Not only by her mother, but by her gentleman friends, too. They brought her candy and small toys, they fussed over her, called her adorable, cute, pretty.

And then her mother sent her to her room.

Julianna figured that one of these days, if she was good enough, charming enough, she wouldn't be sent to her room. One of these days, when she was older, she would have very special visitors of her own.

"I will, Mama. I promise."

"Run along now and let me finish dressing, John will be here any moment."

"Miss? You okay?"

Julianna blinked, startled out of her reverie. "What?"

"You okay?" The woman at the mirror dropped her

lipstick back into her purse. "You were starin' funny at me, like you seen a ghost or somethin'."

Julianna blinked again, really seeing the woman before her for the first time. She had rough, pebbly skin and her cinnamon hair was obviously hers courtesy of a bottle. And a cheap one at that.

How had she ever thought this woman looked anything like her mother?

"I'm fine," Julianna whispered, crossing to the sink to wash her hands. "I just...I don't know what happened."

The woman smiled and patted her arm. "Had six kids of my own. Nothin' plays havoc with the mind like them hormones. It'll get better. Then it'll be them kids playin' havoc with your mind."

The woman cackled, patted her arm again and left the bathroom.

Julianna stared after her, unsettled by what had just happened. The memory had been so vivid; it had come upon her with such force and left her feeling so vulnerable. So alone.

She missed her mother, she thought, tears pricking her eyes. She missed Washington and her comfortable apartment. She missed feeling pretty and special. And safe.

The bathroom door swung open and Lorena stuck her head in, her expression annoyed. "You going to stay in here all day, or what? Your tables are lookin' for you."

Though the other woman was already gone, Julianna nodded in response and hurried back out to the dining room.

The remainder of Julianna's day passed minute by agonizing minute, hour by excruciating hour. As the lunch crowd thinned, then became nonexistent, Julianna became aware of how much her feet and back hurt, of how tired she was.

She worked alongside the other waitresses, refilling the condiments, wiping down the tables and putting up the chairs, preparing for the next day. Buster's stopped serving at three. Opening for dinner would be a waste of time and money—this part of the central business district became a graveyard at 5:00 p.m. when the law offices and other businesses let out for the day.

Julianna didn't listen to or participate in the other women's chatter. Every so often, she would become aware of one of them looking speculatively at her or making an ugly face in her direction. She ignored them and kept her attention fixed on her tasks so she could finish up and go home.

Finally, all the preparations for the next morning had been made, and she'd punched out. As Julianna reached for the door, Lorena stepped in front of it, blocking Julianna's way. The other three waitresses came up beside Lorena, flanking her, their expressions tight and angry. "Not so fast, Miss Priss. We've got a bone to pick with you."

Julianna stopped, glancing nervously from one to the other of the women. "Is something wrong?"

Lorena, obviously having been voted the leader of the pack, took a step toward her. "You could say that. We're sick and tired of your attitude. Of you thinking you're better than the rest of us. And we're sick and tired of having to cover for your lazy butt."

At the animosity in the older woman's tone and expression, Julianna inched backward, glancing over her shoulder, looking for Buster. He was nowhere to be seen.

"Where do you get off, thinkin' you're so much better than us?" Lorena took another step; the others followed. "Just 'cause you went and got yourself knocked up, you think you don't have to work? You think a bun in the oven makes you special or somethin'?"

Another one of the girls, Suzi, pointed a long, bloodred fingernail at her. "When you show up late, we've gotta cover your tables. That means we're working our tails off and getting crappy tips all around."

"And we're sick of it," Jane said.

"I overslept," Julianna said stiffly. "I didn't do it on purpose, for Pete's sake."

That, obviously, wasn't the response they wanted, because angry color flooded Lorena's round face. She looked like a bleached blond balloon about to pop. "I've got a question for you, princess. One we've all wondered about. If you're so frickin' high and mighty, why're you working in a dive like this? And if yours is so special it don't stink, where's your old man? Why'd he go and dump you the moment you got knocked up?"

"Yeah," Suzi added. "Or do you even know who the baby's father is?"

"Bet she doesn't," Jane taunted, before Julianna could jump to her own defense. "She's just a little slut who likes to put on airs."

Lorena laughed. "You're pathetic, you know that? I feel sorry for you. We all do." She leaned closer, smelling of Juicy Fruit gum and drugstore perfume.

"You're not going to make it, you know that? You or your little bastard. Come on, girls."

With that, the three turned and flounced out of the restaurant.

Julianna watched them go, tears welling in her eyes, threatening to spill over. Is that what they thought of her? What everyone thought of her? She brought her hands to her belly, self-conscious, humiliated. That she was pathetic? A woman rejected and without options? Lower, worse off than they were?

It had never occurred to her that others would look at her that way. That they would feel sorry for her.

Nobody had ever felt sorry for her before. She caught her breath and dropped her hands from her belly. She had never felt sorry for *herself* before. Not this way, not to the very core of her being.

She closed her eyes and thought of Washington, of the fine restaurants where she had dined on a daily basis, of the day spa where she'd had massages and facials and manicures, of her pretty apartment and closet overflowing with expensive dresses.

But mostly, she thought of John. She brought a trembling hand to her mouth.

Could he really be the monster her mother said he was?

From the kitchen, she heard Buster and the cook finishing up, preparing to lock up for the day. Not wanting them to catch her near tears, she hurried out of the restaurant and into the chill, late afternoon.

Julianna pulled her coat tighter around her. The sidewalks were crowded with workers heading home after the long work day. The St. Charles Avenue streetcar rumbled to a stop at the curb before her. Sun glinted off the glass, momentarily blinding her. A cloud drifted over the sun; the streetcar passed.

And she saw John.

He had found her.

She caught her breath, and took an involuntary step backward, panicked. He stood directly across the street from her, his head turned slightly away, as if gazing up St. Charles Avenue, looking for someone or something.

For her. Or for a place to take her and kill her.

Julianna froze, uncertain what to do—able to do little but stare, her heart pounding so heavily in her chest, she could hardly breathe.

The way it had fourteen years ago, when she had met him for the very first time. He'd been the most handsome man she had ever seen, tall and strong-looking and young, not shriveled and prunelike the way Senator Paxton was or fat and bald like Justice Lambert.

John hadn't been like any of her mother's other men friends.

Her mother had introduced her to him, calling her softly forward, letting her Alabama roots show in her gentle drawl.

"This is my baby," she said. "My Julianna."

Julianna curtsied, keeping her eyes downcast, the way her mama had taught her.

"Julianna, honey, say hello to Mr. Powers."

"How do you do," she said, her cheeks growing hot, wanting more than anything to really look at him.

"Hello, Julianna," he said, "It's a pleasure to meet you."

She dared a bold peek up at him, then another. She

made a small sound of surprise. "Your hair's white," she said. "Like snow."

"Yes, it is."

"But how come?" She drew her eyebrows together, confused. "You're not old and wrinkly like Dr. Walters and he has white hair." She tilted her head. "You've got lots more than him, too."

Her mother gasped, and Julianna knew she had made a mistake. But John Powers wasn't angry. He laughed, the sound deep and rich and really...nice. She decided she liked him better than all her mother's other friends.

He squatted down before her and gazed into her eyes—in a way none of her mother's other friends ever had. In a way no one ever had.

As if she were as important as a grown-up. As if she were special.

"It turned white overnight," he said. "I was on a mission. I almost died."

She widened her eyes. "You almost died?"

"That's right." He leaned closer and lowered his voice. "I survived by eating bugs."

She sucked in a sharp breath. "Bugs?"

"Mmm. Big, ugly ones."

"Tell me about them."

"Someday. Someday I'll tell you all about it."

"Okay," Julianna said, hanging her head, disappointed.

He gathered her hands in his and for long moments simply gazed at her, his expression serious. Then he smiled. "I have a feeling about us, Julianna. Do you want to know what it is?" She nodded eagerly, and he continued. "I have the feeling that you and I are going to be the very best of friends. Would you like that?''

She glanced up at her mother, saw that she looked pleased, then back at John Powers. ''Yes, Mr. Powers. I'd like that very much.''

The best of friends. The father she'd never had. Her protector. Her lover.

John Powers had become her everything.

And now he wanted her dead.

A horn ripped through air, followed by a shouted epithet. Julianna blinked, startled out of her reverie. She looked around her, disoriented. People, anxious to get home after a long day of work, streamed around her, a few sending her curious glances. John, if that had really been him, was gone.

Gone. She blinked again, despair rising up in her, stealing her breath. *The past, her former life. John. All gone.*

Pulling her coat tighter around her, she turned and walked away.

3

Julianna awakened with a start. She opened her eyes, instantly alert, though she couldn't say why. She darted her gaze around the dark room, looking for the shape that didn't belong, the one that moved slightly, listening for a breath, a stirring.

For the monster.

John. That had been him on the street. He had found her. He was with her now. Fear took her breath; it became a living thing inside her.

Inside her. She brought her hands to her swollen belly, half expecting to find it split wide, intestines and fetus and gore spilling out of her and onto the white sheets. Instead, she found herself intact, her belly round and hard and full.

Thank God…thank God… She closed her eyes and struggled to slow her ragged breathing. If John had been here, he would have killed her. He would have cut her open, punishment for her disobedience. Her defiance.

The way he had cut those other people open, the ones from Clark Russell's photographs.

"Don't cross me again, Julianna," John had warned. *"You won't like the consequences."*

She brought her fists to her eyes. He hadn't found her; how could he have? She had done almost everything Clark had advised her to do—she had run far from D.C., never stopping too long in one place; she hadn't used her credit cards for fear of leaving a paper trail, hadn't called or written home. She'd even had her car repainted in Louisville.

But not everything. He had advised her to change her name, take on a new identity. But that had been impossible. She'd tried, but hotels wanted identification; she needed a driver's license in case she was pulled over; Buster had demanded a social security number as a prerequisite for employment.

Julianna shook her head. It didn't matter that she hadn't changed her name—John was not going to find her, not all the way down here. That man on the street had been a trick of her imagination, just like the woman in the bathroom at Buster's.

Shuddering, Julianna fought to free herself from the sheets, tangled around her legs, encumbered by her ungainly size. She rested her head against the headboard. A part of her still couldn't believe John was a killer. Not John, who had showered her with affection, with gifts and attention and love. John who had held and stroked her, who had told her she was different, special, not silly, weak and stupid like so many other people.

A part of her couldn't believe it even after the nightmare of their last meeting.

She closed her eyes and remembered how it had been with them, not that last night, when John's face had been pinched and white with rage, his touch rough, his cruelty incomprehensible to her. No, she remembered how it had always been with them before, how gentle he had been as he held and petted her, how patient with her, how he had promised her the world.

For nothing more than being his good little girl.

His good little girl. Docile and sweet. The child who looked up to him as one would a parent, trusting, never questioning. The child who accepted his bidding as law.

Tears flooded her eyes. John had been her everything for as long as she could remember. Her tears spilled over and slipped down her cheeks. She needed him. To love her. To take care of her. The way he always had.

This was all a mistake; the events of the last months just a terrible nightmare. She could get rid of the baby, she thought, breath catching on a sob. As he had demanded she do. Go home and beg his forgiveness. For disobeying him. For taking his things. For going to her mother and believing her and Clark over him. She could promise to be his good girl again. He would forgive her, he would. He—

No, she thought. He wouldn't. He was angry with her. Furious. Julianna rubbed at her wet cheeks, shuddering, remembering that last night, the night he had discovered her pregnancy. He had been away on business for several weeks. She had meant to tell him that night, had planned every moment of the evening, wanting their reunion to be special, wanting to set the perfect stage for her announcement.

She had been so excited, so certain John would be thrilled with her news. Instead, he had become a man she hadn't recognized, coldly furious and cruel.

As was their custom, she had arrived at his apartment early so she could be waiting in bed for him, curled up under the covers like a sleepy child. Julianna leaned her head back, resting it against the cool plaster wall, remembering. She hadn't chosen a sexy, sheer nightie or provocative underwear to please her lover, but a long, pink floral gown with a high neck and white ruffle at the throat, wrists and hem.

The kind of gown a little girl would wear.

John's little girl....

She wiggled down under the covers more, and her soft flannel gown rubbed against her legs, fuzzy and re-assuring. She acknowledged excitement. Anticipation. Nerves.

She worked to quell the latter, though without much luck. Her heart beat almost out of control, her mind raced with what she would say to John and how he would respond, with thoughts about the future, their future.

Pregnant. Twelve weeks and one day. Though she had deliberately stopped taking her birth control pills in the hopes this would happen, she could hardly believe it was true.

She was a woman now, finally.

Julianna squeezed her eyes shut and took a deep breath, willing her runaway heart to slow. That's why she had stopped taking her pills without telling him. She was tired of being his little girl. She wanted to be a woman, was ready and anxious to have what other women had. She was certain she had done the right thing.

John would give her what she wanted. He always had.

She pressed a hand to her nearly flat stomach, imag-ining the future. She wanted her and John to be a real couple, like the ones she saw on TV. Real lovers, the way men and women were lovers in books and in movies. Passionate and committed. And...and adult.

Julianna didn't know how to put her finger on what

she wanted, what was missing from her relationship with John. It wasn't simply that she and John lived apart. It wasn't the difference in their ages or that he was the only man she had ever been with. It wasn't that she didn't love him—she did, with all her heart.

She rolled onto her left side and again the soft fabric of her gown tickled her legs. Sudden tears stung her eyes. She had prowled through the lingerie sections of the department stores, longing to wear the sexy, sheer clothes most women wore for their lovers; she had gazed with hunger at other men and women, other lovers, and the way they looked at and touched each other.

John treated her differently than that. Gently. With love, respect and tenderness. Which was good. But still… She wanted more. She wanted passion. Lust. Even the occasional argument.

She heard John at the front door. Quickly, she closed her eyes and breathed deeply, rhythmically, feigning sleep.

This was part of their game. One they had been acting out ever since the first time, so many years ago.

Only then, it hadn't been a game. It hadn't been an act.

Her bedroom door opened; light fell across the bed. A moment later the mattress dipped as he sat on its edge.

For long seconds he said nothing, and she knew he simply gazed at her. As always, she fought the urge to open her eyes and look at him, fought the urge to attempt to read what he was thinking in his eyes.

"Julianna," he said softly, "it's me, my sweet. It's John."

"John?" she whispered, letting her lashes flutter up, feigning sleepy confusion. "You're back?"

"Yes, love. I'm back."

"I missed you," she murmured and smiled at him. "Did you come to tuck me in?"

"Yes." He cupped her face and looked deeply into her eyes. "I love you, Julianna. I always have. Since the first time I met you. Did you know that?"

Even now, after all these years of playacting, she experienced a moment of alarm. A tiny explosion of panic in the pit of her stomach.

He bent closer and pressed his lips to her temple. "I brought you something."

"You did?"

"Mmm-hmm."

Feigning childish excitement, she scooted up in the bed. "What is it?"

He laid his hands on her shoulders. "Were you a good girl while I was gone?"

She nodded, the past and the present blending, creating a weird sensation of fear and excitement, discomfort and pleasure deep in her gut.

"Are you my good little girl now?"

She nodded again, beginning to tremble.

"I can't stay away, Julianna." He stroked her hair. "I've tried but I can't, not anymore. You're mine. You always have been. Always will be. Do you understand?"

"What...do you mean?"

"You'll understand. Soon." A smile played at the corners of his mouth. "You will, I promise."

He carefully drew the covers away, murmuring his satisfaction. "Pretty," he whispered, rubbing the fuzzy fabric between his fingers. "So pretty and sweet."

"John?" she said, working to sound young and frightened.

"It's all right, love. Show John how much you love him." He applied gentle pressure, forcing her back to the mattress. "Show him what a good girl you can be."

So, she did. She lay absolutely still, the way he liked it, as he ran his hands over her, gently at first, then with more urgency.

He didn't undress himself; he wouldn't penetrate her, she knew. He rarely did. Instead, he concentrated on gentling and pleasuring her, first with his hands, then his mouth.

Only when she had climaxed, arching up, crying out as with stunned uncertainty, then falling back to the bed and whimpering meekly like a kitten, did he press himself against her. He was sweating and short of breath, as if he had just finished a ten-mile run. He quivered with the force of his own unfulfilled needs, with excitement.

"My sweet, sweet Julianna. What would I do without you?"

She turned her face to his and kissed him, thinking of their baby, allowing herself a moment's fantasy about how John would take her news. "I love you, John." She smiled and kissed him again. "I love you."

"Show me how much, love." He caught her hand and brought it to his erection. "Show me."

Julianna did. She rubbed and stroked and massaged

him, curling her hand around his penis, pumping him to orgasm.

Julianna jumped as a burst of raucous laughter came from the apartment next door. She blinked, momentarily disoriented, then realized she had to go to the bathroom. Had to go so badly she wondered if she was going to be able to make it.

She dragged herself out of bed and padded to the john, the wooden floor cold and gritty beneath her bare feet. The mirror above the vanity was cloudy with age, a crack ran diagonally through its center, warping her reflection by causing the two sides of her face to not quite fit together.

She stared at her misshapen image, breath catching, hardly recognizing herself. She turned to the side, bringing her hands to her swollen belly. Pathetic, she thought, recalling what the other waitresses had said earlier that day. Rejected. Without options.

"You're not going to make it. You or your little bastard."

It hurt to look at herself, and Julianna turned away from her reflection. Why was she doing this? Why was she here, alone and pregnant? She didn't want to be a mother, did she? She didn't want to be one of those hollow-eyed women who came into Buster's, the ones who were always chasing after their children and wiping their running noses, the ones who always looked so tired. That's not why she had gotten pregnant.

Yet that's what lay before her.

She brought a hand to her mouth, realizing the truth. She should have done as John demanded, gotten rid of the baby. Even her mother had wondered if Julianna was certain she was making the right decision. Being on her own, keeping a step ahead of John, would be difficult enough without an infant to care for. She had offered to accompany her daughter to a clinic where the problem would be taken care of.

But Julianna had still been starry-eyed about the pregnancy. About being a grown-up. About her future.

With a moan, Julianna sank to the floor. She rested her cheek against the vanity's doors, the faux wood cracked and peeling. She didn't have any starry-eyed notions anymore. She saw the future—and it frightened her. Almost as much as the past.

She squeezed her eyes shut, tumbling back once more, back to that last night she and John had spent together....

They had lain facing each other on the bed, talking quietly. John had asked her about how she had spent the weeks he had been away. She had filled him in, barely able to catch her breath, going into great detail about the watercolor class she was taking and about her jazzercize group—when all she could think of, all she wanted to discuss, was her pregnancy.

John listened attentively, so attentively it was almost as if he knew she was keeping something from him. And while she spoke, he studied her with an intensity that was unsettling. He knew her so well. As no one else did or ever would.

Just tell him. Blurt it out—about how she had stopped taking her pills and about her missed period, her visit to the doctor, the urine test. Her excitement.

Not yet, she thought, a thread of panic snaking through her. Not yet.

"How was your trip?" she asked instead.

"Successful."

"Where did you go?"

He simply looked at her. He had a rule: she wasn't to ask him about his business, not ever. Julianna knew he worked for the state department, CIA, or somebody like that, and that what he did was classified. But that was all.

And for a long time, that had been enough. She hadn't cared what he did. But lately, she had been curious. Frustrated and annoyed by his secrecy. By feeling shut out of his life. Bored with her own.

So, even though she knew he would be displeased if he discovered what she was up to, she had started to snoop. The first time, he had just returned home from a trip and was in the shower. Heart thundering, she had rifled through his travel bag and jacket pockets.

She hadn't found anything suspicious that time, but in the many since she had unearthed several items that hadn't added up. In a coat pocket she had found a letter, its open envelope addressed to someone other than John, at an address other than his. The letter itself had consisted of a single line of gibberish. In the front pocket of his travel bag, she'd found an airplane ticket stub to Colombia, a place he professed never to have been, the passenger name on the stub a Mr. Wendell White.

Success had made her bolder.

When John was out of town and her nights seemed to stretch endlessly before her, she had gone to his place and searched it. Each drawer and every closet, every piece of furniture for a secret hiding place, baseboards and floorboards, behind framed photographs and the few pieces of art he had hanging on the walls. She had even checked the contents of his freezer.

There she'd finally hit pay dirt. Wrapped in white butcher paper, between two packages of frozen meat, she had found a small, spiral-bound, black leather book. Inside had been columns of dates followed by notations in some sort of code.

It was then that she'd figured out why John never spoke of his work; why he never mentioned an associate; why he flew all over the world, yet never left a number where he could be reached.

A spy. John was a spy.

Frightened, she had quickly returned the notebook to its hiding place.

"I have to leave again in the morning."

She propped herself on an elbow. "But you just got back!"

"Some unfinished business. Sorry."

"How long this time?"

"I don't know. A week or two. Maybe a month. Depends on how the assignment unfolds."

"At least tell me where you're going."

"I can't. You know that."

She did. But it didn't make it any easier. Pouting, she turned her back to him.

"Don't be like that," he chided. "You're too good for that kind of behavior."

She glared over her shoulder at him. "But I'm so bored when you're gone! There's nothing to do! And I'm lonely."

"Maybe this will help."

He had dropped his jacket beside the bed, and now he reached over the side for it. From one of the pockets he drew out a small, navy blue velvet box. He handed it to her.

"For me?" she asked, pleased.

"Who else?" He smiled. "Go ahead, open it."

She sat up and took the box eagerly from his hands, lifted the lid and gasped. Inside, sparkling against the blue velvet, was a pair of diamond stud earrings. She stared at them, stunned. They were huge—at least a carat each. She lifted her gaze to his. "John, they're beautiful."

"Not as beautiful as my special girl," he murmured, taking the box from her. "Here, let me put them on you."

She tucked her hair behind her ears, and he slipped the posts through her holes, then fastened on the backs. As soon as he dropped his hands, she bounded out of bed and to the bathroom. She flipped on the light and raced to the mirror. They were beautiful. Stunning. They sparkled like icy fire against her earlobes.

John followed her to the bathroom, coming to stand directly behind her. "They don't do you justice," he said. "They're not special enough. They don't have your warmth, your fire."

"Oh, John!" She whirled around and hugged him. "They're gorgeous! I love them!" She hugged him again. "Thank you. Thank you!"

"Silly." He laughed and smoothed her hair away from her face. "Don't you know you deserve them?"

"You spoil me."

"You were born to be spoiled." A smile tugged at his mouth. "To be mine to spoil." He kissed her. "I think I'll draw us a bath. Would you like that?"

She rubbed herself against him. "Sounds delicious."

He turned and began filling the big, old claw-footed tub. John loved to bathe her, the way he had when she was a child. He loved to wash her hair and body, to wrap her in a big fluffy towel, then pat and powder her and blow her hair dry.

The bath started off like the hundreds that had come before. He soaped a washcloth and began moving it over her body, murmuring softly to her. Suddenly he stopped, a frown creasing his brow. "You're gaining weight," he said after a moment, his tone one of reproach as he ran his soapy hands over her waist and belly.

Julianna stiffened. John loved her rail thin and girlish. What would he say when she told him she wouldn't be thin like that again for six more months?

"It's all right," he murmured, taking her silence for distress. "I'll work up a diet and exercise program for you to follow. Find you a personal trainer. You'll have those extra pounds off in no time."

He dipped the washcloth into the water and ran it over her back and shoulders. From there, he reached around her and ran the cloth over her breasts, softly rubbing.

Again, he stopped. She glanced over her shoulder at him. "John," she whispered, "there's something I have to tell you."

He met her eyes, then lowered his gaze to her chest. He smoothed the bubbles away, then cupped her breasts, as if weighing them.

She felt herself flush. *He knew. He could see and feel the changes in her body.*

Her words tumbled out in a nervous rush. She told him how she had stopped taking her pills, how she had missed a period, then gone to see the doctor. "I'm pregnant!" she finished excitedly. "We're going to have a baby. We're going to be a family."

He stared at her, his expression strangely blank, a muscle beginning to twitch in his jaw.

One moment became several. ''John?'' she whispered, a flicker of fear springing to life inside her. This was not going as she had planned it, as she had fantasized it.

He needed time to adjust, she told herself. Time to get used to the idea of being a daddy. That was all.

''And you want this?'' he asked. ''You planned it?''

''Yes.'' She looked pleadingly up at him. ''I hope you're not angry, but I wanted us to be a…a real couple. I love you so much and I…I wanted to be like other women.''

''Like other women,'' he repeated. ''You don't even know what that means.''

''I do. At least I think I do.'' She lifted her gaze pleadingly to his. ''Let me try, John. Please.''

''It's not going to happen, Julianna. This baby's not going to happen.'' He dropped the washcloth. ''So, forget about it.''

His words affected her like a blow. She reached up and caught his hand. ''Why not? You say you love me…you don't have to marry me, that's not what I mean. I just want…I want—''

''What?'' He shook off her hand. ''To be fat and stretched out and tired all the time? To be a doormat instead of a princess?''

''No!'' Tears flooded her eyes. ''It doesn't have to be that way. It wasn't that way with my mother.''

''Your mother's a whore. Is that what you want?''

Julianna stared at him in shock. How could he say that about her mother? They were friends. They had once been lovers.

''I won't share you with anyone, Julianna. Not another man. Not a career or a best friend. Not even a child. Do you understand?"

"But that's not fair!" Even as the exclamation passed her lips, she acknowledged that she sounded like a child, one who was petulant at not getting her way.

"No?" He laughed, the sound as cold and hard as ice. "Whoever said life was fair?"

"I want this, John."

"I'm sorry to hear that, but you'll get over it. Now, get out of the tub. Bath's over. When you're dressed, we'll discuss what you're going to do about this problem."

"What I'm going to do!" she cried. "You mean what you're going to tell me to do."

"That's right." He started toward the bathroom door. "I'll be in the kitchen."

"Why are you being this way?" She stood and grabbed for the towel, shaking with anger and indignation. It was so unfair! She was nearly twenty years old. Not a child, not a baby. "You treat me like I'm an infant! A two-year-old. I'm sick of it! I don't want to be a baby anymore. I don't want to be your *little girl*."

John swung to face her. He narrowed his eyes. "I recommend you stop this, Julianna. Now. Before it's too late."

She jerked her chin up, ignoring his warning though something in his tone and expression chilled her to her core. She held out her arms. "Look at me, John. Why can't you see me as a woman? The way you see other women? For once, why can't...you...why..."

Her words died on her lips as John's face transformed from the loving one she recognized into a

mask of cold fury. The face of a man without warmth
or humanity. One she didn't recognize. One that
frightened her. He started toward her and she shrank
back, feeling small and vulnerable suddenly, feeling
every bit the little girl she no longer wanted to be.
"John," she whispered, "please...don't be angry with
me. I just...I—"

He shot his hand out, catching her by the throat,
knocking her back against the wall behind the tub. Her
head knocked against the tile, and she saw stars.

"So, you want to be like other women, is that it?"

His hand at her throat constricted her windpipe and
she clawed at it, making gurgling sounds of terror as
she struggled to breathe.

"I spoil and pamper you. I treat you like a princess.
But that's not what you want."

She had never seen him like this, had never seen
anyone like this. He didn't raise his voice, and yet its
very evenness terrified her. *Where was the John she
knew and loved? The lover who was gentle, patient
and tender?*

He leaned toward her, the expression in his light
eyes glacial. "You want to be like other women? Like
your mother, the whore?"

He hauled her out of the tub and forced her onto
the floor. "Come on then, I'll treat you like other
women."

"No, John, I'm sorry. Please—" She tried to scram-
ble to her knees; he knocked her back to the tile, falling onto her, knocking the breath from her lungs.

"I'll treat you like other women," he said again,
unzipping his fly. "I treated you like you were special,
but you didn't like that. It wasn't good enough." He

forced her legs apart with his. "So be like everyone else, Julianna."

He rammed himself into her.

Julianna screamed.

He thrust into her again, then again. Pain tore through her. It felt as if he were trying to punch a hole into her uterus with his penis and hammer to death the baby she carried.

He pulled out, but the nightmare wasn't over. He flopped her onto her stomach and dragged her to her knees. Then he thrust into her from behind, holding onto her by her hips as she tried to crawl away, his fingers digging mercilessly into her flesh.

"You like this, Julianna? Doing it doggie style? My sweet girl? My princess?" He laughed, the sound colder, crueler than any she had ever heard. "Grunt like an animal for me. Be a rutting whore for me, it's so much better than being my special one."

He grabbed her tender breasts, squeezing and pinching them. "Do it, Julianna. Grunt for me. Squeal like a sow-whore you want to be."

Sobbing, she did, forcing the sounds past her lips, demeaned and ashamed, horrified. She wanted to shrivel up into a tiny ball, one so small that no one could see her. She wanted to die.

He climaxed, arching against her, his hands on her breasts tightening, the noises slipping past his lips feral, those of a beast who had dominated its foe.

He released her, and she collapsed to the floor. Her abdomen cramped, a gut-knotting pain, like a jagged blade ripping her delicate innards to shreds. Gasping, she curled into a fetal position, clutching her middle, tears coursing down her cheeks.

"Now you're like other women." She heard the

rasp of a zipper and the click of a belt being fastened. "Now you're like your mother. Happy?"

Her stomach clenched, then rose to her throat. She tried to hold her vomit back, but couldn't and turned her head to the side and puked.

He made a sound of disgust, then tossed her a towel. "You'll get rid of the baby tomorrow. Do you understand?"

She nodded.

"Until now, I've trusted you completely. Has that been a mistake?"

She whimpered and shook her head.

"Good. You'll never defy or disobey me again. Or you will be punished. Severely. Do you understand?"

She nodded. This time that wasn't good enough, and he asked her again. "Do you understand?"

"Yes," she whispered.

"Get rid of it tomorrow, or I'll do it myself."

And then he was gone.

Julianna's breath caught on a sob of despair, her thoughts racing back to the present. She realized she was huddled into a ball of misery on her bathroom floor, that she was sobbing. Cold and hurting.

John was the man her mother told her he was. A CIA assassin. The monster Clark Russell had described. The one who had killed those people in the photographs, and many others, according to Clark.

And he would kill her, too. If he ever caught up with her.

He wouldn't, she promised herself, using the edge of the counter for support and dragging herself unsteadily to her feet. She would stay a step ahead of him, even if she had to run for the rest of her life.

4

Julianna found a doctor through the New Orleans yellow pages. She had called a half a dozen obstetricians before she found one who would see her even though she didn't have insurance. The receptionist had explained that Julianna would be required to pay her bill in full after services were rendered.

Julianna's heart had sunk when she learned what the visit would cost. One hundred and thirty-five dollars—barring any unforeseen problems that might require special tests. Almost ten percent of what she had left of the ten thousand dollars her mother had given her. For one visit to a doctor.

But worth it, she decided. She didn't care how desperate she was, she simply could not bear the free clinic. She had taken one look inside and turned around and walked back out. It had been crowded with all manner of humanity, crammed one on top of the other in the hot, grungy-looking waiting room.

In stark contrast, Dr. Samuel's office was bright, sweet smelling and comfortable. The waiting room had been populated by a handful of other respectable-looking women, all noticeably pregnant.

Though everyone had gone out of their way to make her feel comfortable, she was nervous. Her palms were sweating, her heart beating fast. She didn't know what to expect; wondered what Dr. Samuel would be like and how he would take her request.

Julianna shifted on the examining table and the white paper beneath her crackled. *Hurry, Doc. Let's get this over with.*

She closed her eyes and breathed deeply through her nose. After today, she reminded herself, she wouldn't need any more doctor visits. It would be over. She shook her head. What had she been thinking for all these months? Being pregnant was a mistake. A big mistake.

The door opened and a man wearing a white coat walked through, the nurse who had taken Julianna's blood pressure, weighed her and given her a cup to urinate in, right behind him. He smiled and held out a hand. "I'm Dr. Samuel."

She took it. He was youngish and almost attractive, with a thin face and round, wire-rimmed glasses. He looked like someone who would be a good doctor—smart and kind. She relaxed a bit, slightly reassured. "Julianna Starr."

"Nice to meet you." He dropped her hand and turned to the nurse. She handed him a folder, no doubt the questionnaire she had filled out in the waiting room. "Blood pressure and weight look good. Urine checked out." He flipped forward a page. "No drinking? Drugs?"

"No, doctor."

"And you don't smoke. That's good." He smiled briefly. "Calculating from the date of your last menstrual cycle, you're 25 weeks, 3 days. That makes your due date May 11." He looked at her. "That sound about right?"

"I guess."

"Why don't you lie back and we'll take a look at how you're progressing."

Julianna did, and he measured her belly, from pubis to navel, manually examined her abdomen and breasts, then using what he called a Doppler, found and listened to the baby's heartbeat. It sounded like a tiny jackhammer inside her.

"Could be a girl," he murmured. "Girls' heartbeats are faster." He held out a hand to help her back into a sitting position.

"That's it?" she asked, surprised.

He smiled again and the nurse chuckled. "You want more? Most of my patients can't wait to get out of here."

"I just...I just thought there'd be...that you'd do more."

He glanced at her chart again. "You're young and healthy. It says here that money is an issue, and since I don't see any reason to do an ultrasound, I won't. They're expensive."

He met her eyes. "You're not having any problems you haven't mentioned, are you? Any bleeding? Pain? Anything like that?"

Julianna glanced at the nurse, then back at him. She wetted her lips, nervous again. "No, nothing like that."

"Good. Go ahead and get dressed, then meet me in my office. We'll talk about where we go from here."

Julianna nodded, grateful not to have to spill her guts in front of the nurse. There was something grandmotherly about the woman, and Julianna didn't know if she could have been completely honest in front of her.

Ten minutes later, Julianna was dressed and sitting across from Dr. Samuel.

"It says here that you're new in town?"

"That's right."

"We need to have your records sent to us. You don't list an obstetrician on the questionnaire."

"I don't have one." She looked at her hands, working to find the courage to say what she had to. "I went to my regular doctor for the pregnancy test and... and—"

"You haven't seen anyone since." She nodded. "So, I take it you're not taking prenatal vitamins?"

"No. I—"

"Not to worry, we'll get you on those right away." He took out a prescription pad and began to write.

"I want an abortion."

The doctor lifted his head. "Pardon me?"

"I don't want this baby. It was a mistake. The whole thing was a mistake."

For a moment he was silent, then he cleared his throat. "What about the father?"

"He's...no longer a part of my life. And he...he made it plain from the beginning that he didn't want this baby."

Dr. Samuel folded his hands on the desk in front of him. "Then you have a problem, young lady. First off, I don't perform abortions. Personally, I became an obstetrician to bring lives into the world, not to end them."

"But couldn't you refer me to someone who—"

He cut her off. "Secondly, you're no longer able to make that decision. An abortion isn't an option for you."

Her heart dropped. "I don't understand."

"You're too far along." She gazed blankly at him, and he shook his head. "In your pregnancy. The law allows abortions up until the twenty-fourth week after the date of the last menstrual cycle. You're past that. By a week and three days."

A week and three days. Hardly anything. Julianna shook her head, barely comprehending what he was telling her. It couldn't be. Her eyes filled with tears. "But you don't understand...I don't...I don't have...anybody. I can't take care of a baby, I don't know how." Her voice rose. "This was a mistake, you see. The whole thing was a mistake!"

"I'm sorry, there's nothing I can do."

He started to stand; she caught his hand and clutched frantically at it. "Couldn't someone... someone who does do abortions, just...fudge a little on the dates? I mean, don't they just suck it out with a little vacuum, or something?"

Color crept up the physician's cheeks, and he extricated his hand from hers, his dislike obvious. "You'd be asking a doctor to lie, Ms. Starr. To break the law. To put his or her medical license on the line. Not only that—" He made a sound of annoyance and checked his watch. "Let me show you something."

He crossed to his bookcase, selected a hardcover text and brought it back to her. He flipped it open, thumbed through, then set it open on the desk in front of her. It was a photograph of a baby in a womb.

"See that? That's two months' development." Julianna gazed at the photograph. It looked like every picture of an unborn fetus she had ever seen—like a little alien creature, with an oversize head and a network of spidery red veins showing through its translucent skin. Although humanlike, it was creepy looking. Foreign.

He flipped forward several pages, then stopped. "Here's your baby."

Julianna stared at the image, her heart in her throat. It was a baby. Not a nonrecognizable thing. Not an alien. It had hands complete with fingers, feet complete with toes. A face. It was sucking its thumb. She brought a hand to her abdomen even as she lifted her eyes to the doctor's. "Are you...sure? I mean, that I'm...that it's—"

"Positive." He cleared his throat. "Babies at this stage recognize their mother's voices from inside the womb, they respond to light and sound. You're far enough along that if you had this baby today, there's a slight chance it could survive outside your womb."

"I...didn't know." She lowered her gaze to the image once more. "I just...I thought..." Tears welled in her eyes, then spilled down her cheeks. "What am I going to do, Dr. Samuel? What am I going to do?"

He handed her a box of tissue, his expression softening. "Julianna, you say you can't care for this child, that you don't want to. Are you certain of that? When you see and hold your baby—"

"No," she said. "No, I don't want it. And I won't change my mind, I know I won't."

"Have you considered giving this baby up for adoption?"

"Adoption?" she repeated, knowing she sounded like an idiot. Feeling like one "No. I mean, I haven't...thought about much of anything but..."

But John. And about surviving.

The physician sat across from her once more. "There are thousands of infertile couples in this country, couples who are desperate to adopt healthy infants. These are nice, solid people. Committed couples. They would give this baby a good home, a loving family.''

He leaned toward her, his expression serious, earnest. ''You're already into your third trimester, Julianna. You don't even have that far to go. You've admitted you don't have the means or desire to care for a child. Abortion at this stage is out of the question. Adoption is the ideal solution.''

Julianna thought for a moment about what he was saying to her. ''But how...I mean, where would I find them? These couples?''

''There are several reputable agencies in the area as well as quite a number of lawyers who specialize in adoption. I work with one of the agencies, the finest, in my opinion. Citywide Charities.''

She hesitated a moment, then shook her head. ''I don't know.''

''It's a loving solution, Julianna. Your baby gets a wonderful life, parents who will adore and dote on him or her.'' He smiled. ''I should know, I'm an adoptive parent.''

He swung around and took a framed photo from his desk and handed it to her. ''My wife and I adopted all three of our children through Citywide.''

He named them, a girl and twin boys.

Julianna gazed at them, heart beginning to thunder. They were such cute kids; they looked so happy. So healthy.

''They're the light of our lives.''

Her eyes filled with tears again. ''I don't know what to do. I just thought...I thought that you...that after today...'' Her voice trailed off miserably.

''Think about it. Take a little time.'' He stood, went

around the desk and took a business card from his center drawer. "Here's a card with Citywide's number. Ask for Ellen. She can answer any questions you might have."

Julianna took the card and stood. "I will. Thank you, Dr. Samuel."

"I want to see you back here in three weeks." He must have seen by her expression that she had no intention of coming back, and he shook his head. "You need medical care, Julianna, insurance or not. You're not only putting the baby at risk, but yourself, too."

She caught her bottom lip between her teeth. "I know. It's just that it costs so much."

"If you do choose adoption, Citywide can help you with both your medical and living costs."

"You mean, they'll pay for my doctor visits and stuff?"

He smiled and stood. "And stuff. They base the amount of support on individual need, so I can't quote you exactly what they'll do for you. But I promise you this, you won't have to worry about any medical expenses. And, if you choose, you can continue to see me."

He walked her to the door. "Promise me you'll at least think about it."

She promised, then paid her bill and left the office, head spinning with what he had told her. As she did, she acknowledged that promise was one she would have no trouble keeping.

Part III

Luke

5

Houston, Texas, January 1999

Luke Dallas waited in a secluded booth of a dark, smoky bar. Over the drunken posturings of would-be cowboys, Tammy Wynette whined about true love with a untrue man. From the bar's far corner came the distinctive crack of pool balls connecting and the occasional throaty laughter of the big-haired women who circled the table, watching their men play.

Luke's lips lifted. The bar had been his contact's choice, but he rather liked it. It had a certain kind of style. An undeniable "Texas, Every Man," atmosphere. He could imagine his Alex Lawson at the pool table, pissing the local boys off by taking not only their money but their women as well. And not giving a shit that all hell was about to break loose.

That's what he loved about Alex, the character he had created in *Running Dead,* his first published novel. He had balls. He was arrogant, too smart for his own good and deeply scarred from a nightmare childhood. He was a man's man, but one women could love.

His editor had been so taken with Alex Lawson and his nemesis Trevor Mann, that she'd had him change the ending of *Running Dead* and reprise both men for his next novel. That had been three books, three consecutive runs on the *New York Times* bestseller list and a major motion picture deal ago.

Luke Dallas was publishing's new golden boy. His backlist was being repackaged and rereleased; his agent had scored him a fat new multibook contract and subrights agents were in bidding wars for both his new and old work.

Not bad for a guy who'd been tending bar to keep food in his belly and power flowing to his computer. Not bad at all.

Luke took a swallow of his tepid beer, turning his thoughts to his new novel, its new protagonist—and the reason he was waiting in this out-of-the-way, red-neck bar for a man who might or might not show.

His new novel's main character was a former CIA assassin turned vigilante, antihero. Luke had turned to Tom Morris, a contact he'd made at the Agency for some no-bullshit information. Tom Morris was a director of the Operations branch of the CIA, a man impressed by Luke's bestseller status and his Hollywood connections.

At first Tom had denied the existence of government assassins—laughable in the wake of documented accounts of the Agency's attempts to end the lives of political adversaries, including the many, infamous plots against Castro.

The documented cases weren't what interested Luke. No, what interested him was speculation. The things people talked and wrote about that were unacknowledged, undocumented and unadmitted by the Agency. Things even the president had no knowledge of—for his own good, of course. Mentions of The Farm. Of elite killing machines who served a specific, deadly purpose, who kept their country safe and on top through the process of eliminating ones enemies.

Luke was enough of a cynic to believe the speculation.

Finally, Morris had admitted the past existence of government assassins and the now defunct Farm. He'd insisted both had been the product of a now dead political climate—of the cold war and conservative, defense-minded administrations.

Luke thought that was bullshit, but he didn't argue. That was the great thing about fiction, he didn't have to prove something was true, only have the ability to make people believe it was.

Morris had agreed to set Luke up with a former Agency mechanic, code name Condor, though he had made no promises that the man would show. These guys were a special breed—loners, secretive—men who lived by their own code and on the fringes.

Condor. Luke brought his beer to his mouth once more. A bird of prey. Fearsome, majestic. A hunter.

A creature on the verge of extinction.

This man could provide Luke with a wealth of information—into the psyche of a paid assassin, a man who not only killed for a living, but for his country. A man who was a refugee of the CIA Farm, the elite training ground for government assassins.

In real life this man had been in the same spiritual place as Luke's fictional character. He had committed the same acts, had perhaps thought and felt the same things.

Perhaps. That's what Luke hoped to learn.

Luke checked his watch. Condor was late. Luke acknowledged a moment of anxiety. This meeting was a lucky break. Guys like Condor were near-impossible to find—there were damn few roaming the streets and even fewer willing to talk to a writer. He wanted this meeting to happen in a big way.

"Kate! Over here!"

In an instinctive reaction, Luke swung in the direction of the voice, his thoughts filled with her. His Kate. The woman he had once loved, the woman he had convinced himself loved him. Loved him enough to take a chance on a guy with nothing but his dreams and his belief in himself and his future.

Thoughts of Kate brought ones of Richard as well. Of the friendship which had degenerated into an ugly rivalry for Kate's affections. Of their last encounters, ones that had had nothing of the easiness and laughter they'd once shared, but were heavy with secrets, suspicion and resentments over things like social class and affluence. Things that shouldn't have mattered, that hadn't mattered to them once upon a time.

The better man had won, apparently. The one who could give Kate all her heart desired. The one who could make all her dreams come true. Or so Richard had said to him, that last morning, as Luke had stood in the cold sunshine in front of the student center, waiting to meet Kate. He had planned to tell her once and for all what she meant to him and to ask her to take a chance on him. To believe in him.

Richard had laughed at that.

The better man. Luke turned back to his beer, rolling the glass between his palms. The one with the money, the family connections and pedigree. The one with all the things Kate had never had. Not the would-be novelist intent on chasing an impossible and childish dream.

Not so impossible, after all. His lips lifted into a

grim smile. Not so childish. He wondered what she thought of his success. And of her choice. Did she ever wonder if she had made a mistake?

Obviously not. Four weeks ago he had received an invitation to Kate and Richard's annual New Year's Eve party, along with a chatty, happy-sounding letter from Kate.

Both had affected him like salt ground into an open wound. Even though he could now probably buy and sell Richard Ryan several times over. Even though he had proved to Kate and the rest of the world that his faith in himself and his talent hadn't been self-indulgent foolishness.

He supposed that was what really grated. That they were happy. That maybe she had done the right thing for her. That he had been a lovestruck, naive fool.

As he did every year, he responded to their invitation by making sure his publicist sent the couple his most recent promotional materials, news of his successes, updates on signings, personal appearances and so forth.

It was the only contact he'd had with them in years, and only because he took such perverse pleasure in rubbing their noses in his success. He understood Richard well enough to know that his onetime buddy's phenomenal success drove him crazy. As far as Richard was concerned, there could only ever be one king of the hill—and it had to be Richard Patrick Ryan.

Luke gave himself a shake. Kate and Richard were a part of his past. He was over his anger, his disillusionment. He was. The Ryans and their happiness had lost their power to hurt him.

"Luke Dallas?"

Luke swung back around. A man stood just behind

him, hands stuffed into the pockets of his corduroy jacket, gaze intently on Luke's. "That's me."

"Tom Morris sent me."

Condor. Luke motioned to the seat across from him. "I'm glad you could make it."

The man sat, his gaze still assessing Luke. Luke allowed him his scrutiny, using the time to do his own study. Condor looked nothing like Luke's fictional assassin. He possessed a kind of everyman face, with no visually outstanding features. He resembled a dozen other guys out there, medium brown hair and brown eyes, medium height, square jaw.

A nice face. Pleasant. Innocuous. He could be anybody's neighbor. Brother. Son.

Luke cocked his head. He found something almost disarming about the man. He had a lazy way about him, an easiness that suggested inattention.

That impression ended the moment you looked Condor directly in the eyes. The man was keen. Intelligent. He missed nothing, no detail, no matter how small or seemingly inconsequential. Of that Luke was certain.

"I like your books," the man said finally. "*Last Dance* kept me on the edge of my seat."

"Thank you."

"Let's take a walk."

Luke paid for his beer and the two men exited the bar. The night was cold; the neighborhood dicey. Luke figured he didn't have to be too concerned about thugs, considering the company he was keeping.

Luke hunched deeper into his bomber jacket. "Are you armed?"

His lips lifted. "Would your character be?"

"Yes."

"With what?"

"A .22 caliber semiautomatic. Secondhand."

"There are many ways for a man to be armed." He looked at Luke, then away. "A gun's not always the best way. Depends on the situation."

"Or the job."

"I'm not on the job tonight."

Luke inclined his head. "Morris told you I wanted to talk? That I wanted to interview you?"

"Your new character's a guy like me."

"Yes." They turned onto the block behind the bar. "Hero or villain?"

"Both. An antihero. This book is the first of a series like the Alex Lawson books."

"So, I'm not going to get whacked at the end?"

Luke laughed. "Nope. And you might even get the girl."

Condor smiled. "I like that. What exactly are you hoping to get from our interview?"

"I want to get into your head. Learn what makes you, guys in your profession, tick. I want to understand the way you think, how you view your profession. I want a look, a real look, into something most people know zero about. How you plan a job, what your day-to-day life is like, how you feel when you complete a mission."

"You want a lot," Condor murmured, glancing up at the black sky.

"Yeah, I do." Luke looked at him. "But I'll take whatever you're willing to give. As far as anyone will ever know, everything in my book is a product of my imagination."

Condor stopped. They'd circled the block and stood

just feet from the bar's entrance. "I'll think about it,"
he said. "I'll contact you."

"When?"

"You'll know when I know."

And then he was gone.

Part IV

John

6

John sat on an outcropping of rock, one hundred feet above the Merced River in Yosemite National Park. He breathed in the cold, crisp mountain air, letting it fill his lungs and rejuvenate his soul.

The beauty of this place called to him. The raw, undeniable power of it, of the river and the sequoias, the towering pines and flat blue sky. They hummed with life. They had been created by a force so much more powerful than anything man could hope to imitate.

John bent and scooped up a handful of rocks. They warmed in his hand, their smooth, hard surfaces a subtle symphony of color. Mankind preferred to destroy. Oh, the human animal made great noises about the things he created, but the fact was, human history had been built on war, on destruction and killing. Those were the things man had perfected over the course of civilization.

Nuclear power? He shook his head. What a joke. There was more power in these rocks than in the country's entire arsenal of weapons. When mankind succeeded in blowing himself into oblivion, the wilderness would still be here. In some form, it would live on.

John brought his binoculars to his eyes, training them on the lone figure fly-fishing at the river's edge. He watched as the man backhauled and fronthauled, watched as the fishing line floated and danced on the air, then spun far out into the river, the movement sheer poetry.

John smiled to himself. Clark Russell. Former comrade-in-arms. He had proved a hard man to get alone. But Russell, like all men, had a weakness. A place where he forgot safety to feed his desires. For some it was women, others drink or gambling. For Russell, it was fly-fishing.

John had never understood some men's fascination with fishing. What satisfaction was there to be had from hooking creatures by their mouths and pulling them from the water? He understood the enjoyment of quiet and solitude, of the communion with nature, even the satisfaction one might get from the repetitive motion of casting. But the other seemed unnecessarily cruel to him. Barbaric and pointless. He understand sport hunting no better.

He was a hunter, true. But of humans. This made sense. It completed the circle, kept order in the universe. Animals lived by instinct, not intent. They killed in order to survive. But humans destroyed for fun. They killed for pleasure. Or progress. Or out of arrogance.

Of all the living creatures on earth, only humans possessed an unending capacity for evil, for inflicting physical and spiritual pain. Theologians called that capacity sin; John called it a darkness of the soul.

The wind eased through the sequoias and lodgepole

pines; they swayed, their trunks groaning. John closed his eyes, taking in the sounds, the music they created. He believed in the soul, though not in the afterlife. He believed in the power of creation, though not in God, in the presence of evil, though not in the devil.

He reopened his eyes. Clark had caught a fish. It struggled desperately against its captor, arcing out of the water, the sun catching on its silvery scales, creating a small but brilliant flash of light.

Perfect and brilliant light. Like his Julianna's.

John fisted his fingers. Julianna's soul had held no darkness. She had been clean and without sin, emanating a true white light. With his mind's eyes, he saw her as he had that first time. Standing beside her mother, gaze cast downward, her long curls pulled away from her face with barrettes shaped like teddy bears, the same bears embroidered on the smocking of her jumper. Then she had lifted her gaze and smiled at him, purity and innocence radiating from her like the sun.

Her purity had called to him. Her innocence had fed his soul. Both had touched a place deep inside him, one that had all but shriveled and died. One that had stopped responding to all but the majesty of nature.

She had been an angel sent to earth and to him.

He had loved her, and only her, from that first moment.

He had tried to protect her from the corrosive influence of others, from the ugliness of a world gone mad, an ugliness that would spoil her as surely as the worm spoils the fruit.

So she would know what he never had, he had cherished her, had nurtured her bright inner flame.

Once upon a time, he, too, had had the special light.

But his had not been nurtured. It had been smothered, the darkness cultivated. He hadn't wanted that for his Julianna.

But her *mother* had seen fit to darken that soul. She had seen fit to frighten Julianna away, to introduce her to things she had been unaware of. Rage burgeoned inside him, icy cold and awesome.

Her mother and Clark Russell. Destroyers.

John lifted the binoculars once more. He scanned the river's edge in both directions, then the rocks and forest above, making certain he and Clark were alone.

It wasn't too late for Julianna. He knew it wasn't. He had to find her.

But first, Clark Russell would pay for his crime.

John stood and started down to the river. He picked his way effortlessly and nearly soundlessly over the rocks and through the dense underbrush. His breathing elevated, but only slightly; the oxygen fed and readied him, as did the adrenaline coursing through his bloodstream.

Killing wasn't personal. It shouldn't be. Get in, do the job as quickly, as impersonally as possible, and slip away. That was the way he had been trained; his ability to do just that had made him one of the Agency's most efficient specialists; it had earned him the code name Ice.

But this was different. John narrowed his eyes, closing the distance between himself and the other man, hatred burning in the pit of his gut. Clark had crossed the line; he had made this personal. A gunshot to the back of the head wasn't good enough; neither was the garrote or the blade.

No, John wanted him to know what was happening,

who was killing him. And why. He wanted to look into Clark's eyes as the life faded from them.

The rush of the water masked the last of his approach. John disabled Clark with a sharp, edge-of-the-hand chop to the back of his neck. A bird screamed overhead. The man dropped to his knees, then onto his side. John delivered another blow, this one with his heel to the solar plexus, followed by one to his kidneys. Sprawled flat on his back, Clark looked up at him, conscious but completely immobilized.

"Hello, Clark." John smiled at the fear that crept into the man's eyes. The fear of death, the certainty of it. "You crossed the line. You put your nose in my business. That made it personal. Now you have to pay."

He brought his heel down again, but this time in a crushing blow to the man's larynx, finishing the job. It took little more than a nudge with the toe of his boot to tumble Clark's remains into the water.

John watched the body bobble on the water as it was swept downriver.

Part V

The Open Door

7

Julianna kept her promise to Dr. Samuel. In fact, she had thought of little else for the next twenty-four hours. The way she saw it, her choices were slim and few. According to the doctor, she had to have this baby. She thought of seeing another doctor, or going to an abortion clinic and lying about the date of her last period. She figured it would be hard for them to tell, after all she wasn't *that* far past twenty-four weeks.

She had driven by one of the clinics, had seen the protesters out front, waving signs and holding up posters. Ones with pictures of mangled baby parts, pictures of bloody appendages and torn, mutilated flesh. The images had made her feel ill. They had frightened her. She had heard horror stories about botched abortions.

She had to have this baby.

But she didn't have to keep it.

So here she sat, in Citywide Charities' comfortable waiting room, hands clenched in her lap, silently rehearsing what she would say to the social worker she had spoken with on the phone.

She wouldn't tell her the truth, of course. Not the whole truth, anyway. She wouldn't tell her about John, or about planning to get pregnant, or about her mother.

No, her story would be a familiar one, one the woman had probably heard dozens of times before.

She had slipped up and gotten pregnant; she didn't know who the father was; she had no one to turn to for support and didn't want to be a mother. Period.

"Hi. You must be Julianna Starr."

Julianna looked up. The woman crossing the room had a perky, if not pretty face and she wore a welcoming smile. Slightly plump and motherly looking, her appearance instantly reassured Julianna.

"I'm Ellen Ewing, Citywide's director."

"Hi." Julianna stood.

"Why don't we go to my office and chat?" She motioned toward the hallway directly across from them. "Madeline," she said to the receptionist, "hold my calls, will you?"

Ellen made small talk, mostly about the weather, as they made their way down the hall. They reached her office, a peach-and-teal affair, and she motioned Julianna to one of the comfy-looking chairs in front of the desk.

"Juice? Soft drink? Bottled water?"

"Orange juice?"

"Got it." Ellen picked up the phone, buzzed Madeline and asked her to bring an OJ and a Diet Coke, then turned back to Kate. She laughed, only slightly self-consciously. "I'm addicted to Diet Cokes. I drink them all day, I'm afraid. With this figure, you'd think I was drinking the sugared variety." She sighed. "It sometimes seems that the less I eat, the bigger I get."

Madeline appeared at the door with the refreshments. While Ellen retrieved them, Julianna looked over the office. It was pretty, soothing and very feminine. The right side of Ellen's desk was heaped high with manila folders, the left with books. By the lamp sat a cut crystal vase filled with a bouquet of cheery flowers. Behind the desk, covering the entire wall, were pictures of children, from infants to school-age.

Ellen handed Julianna her juice, and smiled, following her gaze. "Those are my kids."

"Your kids?"

"In a manner of speaking." Ellen took her seat. "They're all Citywide adoptees."

"All of them?" Julianna moved her gaze over the wall, amazed. "There are so many."

Ellen smiled, skimming her own gaze over the wall of smiling faces. "They're all special to me. Almost as if they're part mine." She turned back to Julianna. "We take great pride in our maternity and adoption program, Julianna. Bringing families together is a special and completely rewarding endeavor."

She popped open her can of soda. "I don't want you to feel pressured. We don't just place children and babies for adoption here. Bringing families together also means helping women decide if they want to parent. If that's what you decide to do, we won't be angry or disappointed. We won't pull our support. Quite the contrary, we will do whatever we can to help you in your decision. We only ask that every step of the way you're honest with us about your feelings and plans."

"That sounds good to me." Julianna set her carton of juice on Ellen's desk. "But you don't have to worry, I'm not going to decide to parent."

"Your mind is made up? You want to give your baby up for adoption?"

"Yes. Definitely."

A small frown marred Ellen Ewing's brow, then disappeared. "Why don't you tell me a little about yourself."

So Julianna did, repeating the things she had re-hearsed.

"And the baby's father?" Ellen asked when Ju-lianna had finished. "What does he think about your being pregnant?"

"I don't know who the baby's father is."

Ellen was silent a moment. "You're sure? Because in this state, the father has to sign off on the adoption. Even if the baby's already been placed with a family, if a man shows up claiming and able to prove pater-nity, he'll have the right to the child. You can imagine how painful, how destructive that would be to all in-volved."

Don't defy me again, Julianna. You won't like the consequences.

Their throats slit, gaping and bloody, like perverted smiles.

"Honestly," Ellen continued, "getting sign-off is usually not a problem. In our experience, the last thing these daddies want is any kind of responsibility, fi-nancial or otherwise. And if you're uncomfortable talking to him, we will approach him for you. Take care of everything."

Julianna stared at the woman a moment, then shook her head. "I told you, I don't know who the father is."

Ellen narrowed her eyes slightly, studying her. "You're certain? This is important, Julianna."

"No, I mean...yes, I'm certain. I slept around...a lot." She hung her head. "I'm not proud of my be-havior."

"It happens, Julianna." Ellen's voice soothed. "To more girls than you imagine. But let's not focus on the past. The thing that's important now is deciding where you go from here. Deciding what's the best thing for you and your baby.''

Ellen went on to describe how Citywide worked— that they were a national organization funded by private donations, grants and fund-raising efforts. Maternity and adoption services was only one arm of the organization. She also explained what services they provided their birth mothers and how Julianna would choose parents for her baby.

''We work intensely with about a dozen couples a year. To put your mind at ease, we screen them very carefully. First and foremost, they are nice people and committed couples. They all have a great desire to be parents. All are now infertile and cannot conceive on their own, believe me they've tried. It's a painful and heartbreaking journey that brings these couples to us.

''They range in ages, up to forty. Their income level and educational backgrounds vary. We have several couples who are quite well off, a couple of modest means and the rest in between. Our couples all live in the region, though some in the country, some in the city. We have a variety of religious persuasions, women who plan to be stay-at-home moms and others who have demanding careers. Several couples already have one child, either adopted or biological.

''We want to offer our birth moms variety. You tell us what's important to you, what you envision as the perfect family for your baby. And we find them for you.''

The perfect family, Julianna thought with a wistfulness that surprised her. The one she had dreamed of for herself as a child. The one she had hoped for with John.

She looked up and found Ellen's gaze sympathetically on hers. Julianna thought of her confrontation with the other waitresses and of the word they had used to describe her. Pathetic.

Was that how this woman saw her, too?

Julianna stiffened her spine. Nobody needed to feel sorry for her. Whether they could see it or not, she had everything going for her. *Everything*.

"How do I pick them? Is it like an interview or a lineup, or something?"

A smile tugged at the social worker's mouth. "You can meet with the couple you choose, but that comes much later. Our couples complete extensive questionnaires. About their likes, dislikes, views on love, marriage, raising children. About their background, their families and childhoods. They put together a photo album of themselves and their family.

"From all that, we put together a packet about each couple. Each includes the couple's photo album, their essays and our synopsis, if you will, of the drier, more factual information about them. No identifying information is exchanged, and by that I mean last names, addresses and so forth. When you're ready, we select the couples who fit what you've told us you're looking for and give you their packets. You can take them home, study them, think it over. We won't rush you to make a quick decision. We know how important it is and above all, we want you to feel comfortable and happy with the family you choose."

Julianna thought for a moment, finding herself being drawn into the idea. "What if none of the couples you choose—"

"Seem right? You can look at all the packets, of course."

She went on to explain open and closed adoption.

Julianna was stunned to learn it was she, not the adopting couple or the agency, who made the decision of how much interaction there would be between her and the adoptive couple—anything from an initial visit or two before the baby was born, to continuing visits with the family after placement and for years to come. She could even choose a totally closed adoption, one that allowed no contact of any kind, not even the exchange of photographs and letters. It was completely up to her.

Of course, the couple would have to be comfortable with whatever arrangement she preferred, but Ellen assured her that if one couple didn't feel comfortable with a certain level of openness, another would.

"Perhaps you want to think all this over?" Ellen suggested, smiling gently. "I know it's a lot to absorb."

"No, thanks. I'm ready to do it."

"It's a big step. The emotional repercussions—"

Julianna looked her dead in the eyes. "There's nothing to think over. Getting pregnant was a huge mistake. I have no desire to be a mother. None. And it's too late for me to have an abortion."

"I understand."

"Good." Julianna took a deep breath, feeling completely in control now. "One more question. Dr. Samuel said the agency would be able to help with my medical expenses?"

"Absolutely. If you're without insurance."

"I am."

"We want, insist, really, that you have the best medical care. Whether you give your baby up for adoption or decide to parent, if you're in our program, you're guaranteed medical care. If you liked Dr. Samuel, you may continue seeing him. He's one of our regular obstetricians.''

"I liked him fine." Julianna cleared her throat. "He also said you...the agency sometimes helps with living expenses."

Julianna had thought the woman would balk at the question, that she might look at Julianna as a greedy opportunist. But she didn't. She answered the question as if she had been asked it many, many times before.

"We're able to help with living expenses, although to what extent and in what ways is not as clearly delineated as with medical assistance. Why don't you tell me what's going on with you in that area, then I can tell you what we might be able to do."

Julianna did. "I have no family to help me. Right now, I'm working as a waitress at Buster's Big Po'boys downtown. It's okay, I'm getting by right now. But some days I'm *so* tired. I'm afraid when I get farther along, I won't be able to keep up. And there's no way my boss is going to cut me any slack. He told me the minute I can't cut it, I'm out."

Ellen Ewing smiled at her. "If everything you've told me checks out, I don't see any reason we won't be able to help you. That's what we're here for, Julianna. We care about you and your baby."

Julianna smiled, feeling almost carefree. "So, what do we do next?"

8

Only those of the stoutest constitution had braved the outdoor café today, a collection of nearly deserted wrought iron tables huddled together just off Georgetown's busy Thirty-fourth street. Though the sun shone brightly, the breeze was stiff, cold and damp.

Condor made his way to where Tom Morris sat, sipping a latté. A benign-looking man, with round spectacles and balding pate, he reminded Condor of his slightly daffy uncle Fred. In actuality, as director of the operations branch of the CIA, the arm of the Agency responsible for all covert maneuvers including clandestine intelligence collection and covert paramilitary operations, Tom Morris was one of the shrewdest, most powerful and feared men in Washington.

"Morning, Tom."

The man looked up. Condor saw himself reflected in the other man's Ray-Bans, ones that were near replicas of his own.

Morris motioned to the chair across from his. "Have a seat."

Condor did, and the man didn't waste time getting to the point of the morning's meeting. "John Powers has become a problem."

"How so?"

"He's a loose canon. The Agency's at risk." Morris added a packet of artificial sweetener to his latté. "We have to be able to control him."

"Then keep him busy."

"Easier said then done."

Condor made a sound of disgust. "The man's a trained hunter, you can't expect him to suddenly become a lapdog. It doesn't work that way."

"Times have changed. You know that." Morris frowned into the distance. "Besides, we're beyond that."

"He's been freelancing a long time. Why the sudden concern?"

Morris took an manila envelope out of his briefcase and handed it to Condor. "Take a look."

Condor opened the flap and slid out two eight-by-ten glossies. Full color. A man and a woman. Very dead. Blood and other assorted gore sprayed across the wall and bed.

"Senator Jacobson," Morris supplied. "And his lover."

Condor studied the photos. "A professional job?"

"It appears so."

"Powers?"

"Possibly."

"Who ordered the hit?"

"I don't know. Maybe nobody."

Morris had his attention now. "I don't follow."

Morris sipped the coffee, made a sound of appreciation and set down the over-size cup. "There's a connection. Powers and the woman were once involved."

"Could be a coincidence." Condor dropped the photographs into the envelope.

"True. But there's more. Russell's dead. A blow to the back of the head, the kidneys and larynx. Definitely professional."

"Powers?" Morris lifted a shoulder. "Shit." Condor looked away, then back. "What's the connection?"

"Woman and Russell were also once…involved."

Condor frowned. "You think this is personal?"

"Yes. But we need to know for sure. A United States senator is dead. So is one of our division chiefs. If it was a hit, we have to know who ordered it. If it wasn't, and Powers was involved, we have a problem to be taken care of."

"What do you want from me?"

"Find him. Find out what we need to know. If need be, explain the Agency's position to him." He met Condor's gaze evenly. "Make certain he understands."

Condor nodded. "Whereabouts?"

"Unknown."

"Any specific instructions?"

"Your choice. Keep it low key."

"Of course." Condor stood. "By the way, I met with your friend, Luke Dallas."

"And?"

"I like him. Writes a hell of a book."

"He's a good guy."

"Can he be trusted?"

"I think so." Morris took a sip of his coffee. "You going to talk to him?"

"Maybe." Condor tossed the envelope onto the table. "I'll be in touch."

9

Sunlight spilled through the breakfast nook's bay window, falling over the antique oak farmer's table, warming its weathered top. The January day was brilliant but cold; the sky a postcard-perfect blue.

Kate sat at the table, one leg curled under her, hands curved around a mug of freshly brewed coffee. She brought the mug to her lips but didn't sip. Instead, she breathed deeply, enjoying the aroma almost as much as she would her first taste.

The beans were African, from the Gold Coast region. The roast was dark, the brew strong. The flavor would be bold, bright and complex. If it lived up to the roaster's claim.

She tasted, paused and tasted again. Smooth as well, she decided. She would add it to The Uncommon Bean's menu.

"Morning, gorgeous." Richard came into the kitchen, still straightening his tie. He crossed to her and she lifted her face for a kiss, then restraightened the knot of his tie, patting it when she had finished. "There. Completely presentable now."

He smiled. "I hate ties. A damn nuisance, I say."

"Poor baby."

"I'll bet our old friend Luke doesn't wear one of these boa constrictors." He went to the carafe and poured himself a cup of coffee, then popped a couple pieces of seven-grain bread into the toaster. "I went into the wrong line of work. I should have chosen something artsy-fartsy. Like writing."

Kate ignored his sarcasm and took another swallow of her coffee. She sighed with pleasure. "There's nothing quite as wonderful as a cup of hot coffee on a cold morning." She glanced over at him. "I'm trying out a new bean. Tell me what you think."

He took a sip. "It's good."

"Just good?"

"Really good?"

"How would you describe it?"

"Hot. Strong." He sipped again. "Tastes like... coffee."

She wagged her spoon at him in a mock reprimand. "Tomorrow you're getting instant."

"Okay." He laughed at her obvious dismay. "Sorry, sweetheart, I'm just not a coffee connoisseur, it all tastes about the same to me."

He carried his toast and cup to the table and sat across from her. Kate slid him the sports section of the *Times Picayune*.

"I read in the money section that Starbucks coffee is thinking of moving into New Orleans in a big way." She drew her eyebrows together in concern. "I hope they stay on that side of the lake. I don't need any more competition for this community's coffee dollar."

"How are things at the nuthouse?" he asked, unfolding the paper.

"Nuthouse?"

"The Bean."

"I don't know why you insist on calling the The Uncommon Bean a nuthouse. We're all quite sane."

He spread a bit of whole fruit jam on his toast.

"You're sane," he corrected. "I'm not nearly so confident of that crew you have working for you."

She laughed. Her crew was a bit unconventional; she couldn't deny that. "A coffeehouse is not a law office."

"No joke."

"My customers expect a bit of creative license. Besides, they're not nuts, they're characters. There's a difference."

"If you say so."

"I do." Kate poured herself a bowl of muesli, sprinkled on some fresh berries, then covered it with half 'n' half. "I also say you're a stuffed shirt and need to loosen up."

"I'm sure my clients would love that. Being a stuffed shirt is a good thing for lawyers. Inspires trust." He cocked an eyebrow as she dug into her cereal. "Cream?"

"Mmm." She licked her spoon, teasing him. "What's the matter? Jealous?"

"Not at all."

"Liar."

Richard was spartan in his tastes; she was excessive. He worked out religiously, ate low fat and whole grain and still had to fight acquiring a paunch. Kate ate sweets and fats and kept her workouts confined to long brisk walks along the lakefront—and still managed to remain slim and taut, her blood pressure and cholesterol ridiculously low.

It irritated him no end and he continually warned her that her life-style would catch up with her, that middle age would hit and she would have to suffer right along with the rest of the world. Kate laughed off his warnings. She came from a long line of people with uncommonly healthy hearts and in-the-cellar cholesterol and blood pressure. And if genetics failed her and Richard's predictions came true, well, she would cross that bridge when she came to it.

"Poor Richard. Want just a tiny taste?"

He eyed her bowl longingly, then shook his head. "I'm perfectly content with my toast."

"I can tell." She grinned, took another bite and washed it down with a sip of coffee. "I almost forgot. Last night you got in so late from your meeting, I didn't get a chance to tell you. Ellen called." He looked up from the sports page, obviously not following. "Ellen, from Citywide. It seems we get an A plus." Kate laughed. "We were the first couple in our group to get *all* our paperwork in."

"The first?" His lips twitched. "Leave it to us, type A overachievers."

She pushed her hair behind her ear, ignoring his sarcasm. "Determined. Enthusiastic. No way am I going to miss an opportunity due to procrastination."

"I'm just glad it's done."

Kate agreed. The adoption program's paperwork had been grueling. It seemed there had been a form that covered every aspect of their life: their family's history, their personal health, their financial and educational backgrounds. They'd even had to get fingerprinted and have a police background check done.

But by far the most difficult part of the packet to complete had been the personal profiles. The questions had been probing, requiring each of them to delve into their most intimate thoughts and feelings—about their marriage, about adoption and parenting.

They had been asked to search their hearts and souls, then spill their guts on paper. All the while knowing that a potential birth mother would read what they had written—knowing the words they chose would influence whether that birth mother would select them to parent her child.

The process had been made all the more nerve-racking for Kate because they had been told that the profiles were the most important component of all they would do. For the great majority of the birth moms, Ellen had explained, giving up their baby for adoption was an emotional decision, not an intellectual one.

So, Kate had sweated over her profile. She had poured out her heart and soul and longings—praying the whole time that something she said would strike a chord in one of the birth mothers. Praying that somehow, she could make the other woman see how much she longed to be a mother. And how much she would love her baby.

"The only thing left is our photo album. I finished it last night and planned to run it across to Citywide in the next couple of days. No chance you're heading to the south shore today or tomorrow?"

"No chance. Although I may go over on Friday."

"I'll keep that in mind, though I didn't want to wait that long."

"Type A," he teased.

"You think?" She laughed. "I just want it done."

"Ready to sit back, relax and wait for a baby to fall into our laps, huh?"

"Relax?" She cocked an eyebrow. "Maybe you can, but not me. I'm more excited and anxious than I was when we had all that paperwork stretching before us. Now it's real. Now it could actually happen, anytime."

"Take a deep breath, sweetheart. Remember what

Ellen said? It could take a year. Even longer. That year's going to pass pretty damn slow with your panties in a wad the entire time.''

He was right. She knew that. But knowing it didn't change the way she felt. Kate sighed. "I know, Richard. I remember what she said. It's just that I've…that we've—"

"Waited so long already." He reached across the table and covered her hand with his. "I know, sweetheart."

She curled her fingers around his, grateful for his understanding. "Love you."

He smiled. "Love you, too."

From outside came the squeal of the school bus's brakes, coming to a halt at the stop at their corner. It came every day at 8:10 sharp. Richard looked at his watch and swore. "I've got to go. I'm late."

"Me, too." They both stood, carried their dishes to the sink, grabbed their things and hurried for the door. There, Richard kissed her. "You haven't forgotten our dinner with Sam Petrie and his wife have you?"

"Of course not. Dakota's, 7:00 p.m."

"You got it. Why don't you wear your red silk? I love that on you."

She laughed. "That's a pretty sexy choice for a weeknight, counselor."

"And Sam Petrie could be a major supporter in my run for D.A." At her shocked expression, he grinned. "Just kidding. You're beautiful in anything. Wear whatever you like." He kissed her again, then stepped out onto the lower gallery. "I'll call you later."

She watched him go, then grabbed her coat and purse and headed out after him.

10

One of the many pluses of owning her own business, Kate had decided within her first month in operation, was the location she had chosen. Just three blocks down Lakeshore Drive from their home, most days she was able to walk to work.

Once upon a time the structure had been a guest house for the large home on the adjoining property. Both had been built well before air-conditioning or the Causeway, when wealthy New Orleanians had escaped the stifling heat of summer by trekking to the north shore of Lake Pontchartrain and the fabulous homes they had built along the lake.

She had found and fallen in love with the dilapidated cottage, and bought it—despite Richard's argument that it would cost too much to build out, that a location more on the beaten path, in one of the shopping areas or strip malls, would attract more patrons.

Kate had stuck to her guns and as she had known they would, customers had found her. None of the other coffee cafés had what she had: a panoramic view of Lake Pontchartrain, century-old live oak trees in whose high, thick branches egrets roosted at dusk, a feeling of history, and an undeniable charm that was the Old South.

Her regulars weren't the strip mall types. They weren't the two-point-two kids, minivan-and-dog types that heavily populated Mandeville. No, The Uncommon Bean seemed to draw the North Shore's uncommon residents. Artists and writers, college students and misfits, retired professionals, freethinkers, debaters and loners.

Even her employees were unique. Sometimes too much so, Kate thought as she stepped through The Bean's front door only to discover her two managers, Marilyn and Blake, deep into one of their famous discussions. She shook her head. Anyone who didn't know them would swear not only that they were arguing, but that they hated each other as well.

And no wonder; the two couldn't be more different. Marilyn was a blond bombshell with a Minnie Mouse voice and an IQ to rival Einstein's. At twenty-five, she was working on her fourth college degree, this one in ancient religions. Blake, on the other hand, at twenty-eight, was still on his first go-round at college. Gay and proud of it, he was outspoken, funny and a bit too flamboyant to be living comfortably on the rather conservative North Shore. But he did anyway, he said, because he liked the trees.

Their heated discussions had become legendary with the regulars. Some swore they came in not for the coffee, but to witness the fireworks. Even so, the two never got truly angry with one another and made a good working team.

"Honey," Blake drawled to Marilyn as Kate approached, "I'm telling you, when it comes to size, all races have not been created equal."

Marilyn made a sound of disgust. "Not only are you gross, but you're playing to cliché and racial stereotype. A civilization that depends on stereotypes—"

"Excuse me," Blake interrupted, placing his fists

on his hips and cocking his head at her. "But just how do you think clichés get started?"

"Usually as a form of hatred and oppression." Marilyn swiped at a spot of water on the counter, her cheeks pink. "My God, as a gay man, I'd think you'd be more sensitive to this sort of thing."

"Exactly. I mean, just for argument's sake, how many big, black—"

"Enough, guys!" Kate said, stepping in. "This is inappropriate. We have customers."

"S'okay with me," called Peter, a regular sitting in the booth closest the register. "I was kind of getting into it."

"Me, too." Joanie, a romance writer and another regular, said as she sauntered to the counter for a refill. "Grist for the mill and all that."

"No," Blake murmured. "Kate's right. But before we move on to a less...controversial subject, I feel obligated to say one more thing. Anyone who says size isn't important, either has a teeny little wienie or is having a relationship with one."

Marilyn gasped, Joanie nearly choked on her refill, and Kate fought back a laugh. Before Kate could reprimand her employee, Peter chimed in, "I've never said that, Blake. Believe me. Quite the contrary, I always say size is the most important thing."

That brought a fresh round of giggles and groans from the group. Just as it looked as if the conversation were going to slip back into the realm of the totally inappropriate, a mother and her two young children entered The Bean. Marilyn and Blake became instantly professional.

Kate shook her head, fighting a sound of amused exasperation. She could imagine Richard's reaction if he'd witnessed the goings-on at The Bean. He already thought the place a nuthouse; no doubt he would judge them all, including her, certifiable.

She glanced at Marilyn and Blake, chatting with the woman as they filled her order, then smiled. She enjoyed The Uncommon Bean. She enjoyed the people, the ones who became regulars and the ones who only stopped by occasionally. She enjoyed her employees, their eccentricities, being involved in their lives.

Though her first love was art, she had decided early on that she was *not* going the starving artist route. She had grown up with that. Living hand-to-mouth, from sale to sale, watching her parents wait with growing bitterness for the recognition that had never come. Seeing how disappointment had sucked the life out of their marriage.

They had divorced the year Kate graduated from Tulane. The year after that her mother had been killed in a traffic accident, and her father had left New Orleans to become artist-in-residence at an art colony north of San Francisco. Though they spoke often and affectionately, geographical distance kept them from spending much time together.

No, after watching her parents Kate had decided on a degree in business and had relegated her beloved art to a hobby. Now, instead of on gallery walls, her stained glass creations hung in every window of The Bean. She created them because she loved the craft. Not for money. Not for recognition. Now and then she sold a piece, and when she did she was pleased. It was freeing not having to deal with the pressure of *having* to sell.

Kate knew how lucky she was. She could have been stuck working nine to five, pushing papers in a job she derived little pleasure from. And doing it day after day, just to keep a roof over her head.

And she would have, and made the best of it, because she was a practical person.

Something Luke had never been able to understand.

Funny, she thought, picturing him in her mind's eye. They had both come from low-income homes, both had attended Tulane on scholarship. Yet Luke had been determined to stick to his dream of being a novelist. He had refused to even consider journalism or copywriting. He had believed in himself that much.

What would it be like to have that kind of confidence? she wondered. To have that much courage?

The woman and her children served, Kate motioned to her managers. "If I can trust you two to keep your conversation respectable, I'll be in my office working on payroll." Kate looked from one to the other. "That is, if you want to get paid today?"

"Go...go." Blake waved her toward the back. "I'm broke."

Marilyn clucked her tongue. "You need to manage your finances better. There will be a tomorrow, you know."

He sniffed. "Words of wisdom from the queen of the college loans."

"Screw you."

"Sorry, darlin'," he drawled, "but you're not my type."

"You don't have to worry about *me* keeping it respectable, Kate," Marilyn said, looking pointedly at Blake. "*I* have the ability to think about other things."

Kate threw up her hands. "You two will never change. I'm going to stop trying, just don't scare all the customers away. Okay?"

Not waiting for a response, Kate made her way to her office, checking supplies as she did, making notes of what she needed to order. The time cards were stacked neatly on her desk, waiting for her. With a sigh, she took a seat and got to work.

She had only been at it a few minutes when Blake tapped on her open door. "We have a problem."

She looked up and motioned him in. "What's up?"

"It's the baker. Again. He didn't show Saturday. Consequently, we were out of half our pastries before the after-movie crowd even arrived."

"Did you call?"

"Of course." Blake frowned. "I got the machine. Twice."

"And he still hasn't called back." She made a sound of disgust. "How many times does this make?"

"Four. The jerk." Blake lifted the heart-shaped paperweight from her desk, weighed it in his hand and set it back down. The Baccarat crystal heart had been a gift from Richard last Valentine's Day. "I really hate irresponsibility."

Kate smiled. That's what made him such a good employee. "I'll take care of this, Blake. There are other bakers in town, and we're going to find ourselves one."

"Thank God." He wagged his finger at her. "And this time you're not going to listen to any sob stories, right? It doesn't matter if his dog died or his wife left him, he has a commitment to us and our business. You're much too nice, you know."

A notorious soft touch, that was what Richard called her. Con men and door-to-door salesmen could see her coming. She smiled. "No hard luck stories, no excuses. That Pillsbury Dough Boy is history."

That brought a smile to his lips. "Good. Thank you."

Blake started out of the office. Kate stopped him. "How was business this weekend?"

"Excellent. Though it would have been even better if we'd had a full stock of desserts."

"How did the new kid do?"

"Beanie?" Beanie, so nicknamed because he wore a different hat every day, was the newest member of her crew. And the youngest. She had hired him because she thought he would do a good job and because she feared she might be his only chance at gainful employment. "He did okay. I had Tess stay right with him. Consequently, he made no major goof-ups that I saw and the customers seemed to like him. Not bad for his first shift."

Tess, Kate's other employee, though a good worker, tended to be a bit of a flake. Kate arched an eyebrow. "Tess? Training?"

Marilyn popped her head into the office. "Kate, telephone. It's Ellen. From Citywide."

Kate nodded, catching her breath. "Thanks." She picked up the phone. From the corner of her eye, she saw Marilyn nudge Blake. The two eased out of the office, closing the door behind them.

Kate smiled. All her employees and most of the regulars knew she and Richard were adopting. They also knew what she had been through and how badly she wanted a child.

"Hi, Ellen," she said. "What's up?"

"Good news."

"Good news?" Kate repeated, her heart beginning to pound.

"We've got a new birth mother in the program.

She's beginning to review profiles. Yours is one of the ones I've selected for her. But before you get too excited," she added quickly, "you and Richard are only one of several couples she's initially considering. Although I see you as a good fit, she might not. Be prepared, before this is all over, I'll probably be showing your profiles to a dozen birth mothers."

"Oh." Kate took a deep breath, so disappointed she hurt. "I understand."

Ellen laughed, but with sympathy, not amusement. "No, Kate, *I* understand. You have every right to be excited. But I feel obligated to warn you, adoption can be every bit the emotional roller coaster of infertility treatments. You have to pace yourself.

"I know it's hard," Ellen continued before Kate could respond. "The waiting is hell and the ups and downs are worse. Knowing that, the best you can do is strap in for the duration."

"Pace myself." Kate laughed, a bit self-consciously. "You sound like Richard. Relax, he says. All things in their time."

"He's a wise man."

"I know, it's just that…that—" To her embarrassment, tears flooded her eyes and when she spoke, her words came out soft and broken. "We've waited so long, Ellen. I've…we've wanted a child for such a long time." Her voice cracked, and she cleared it. "I'm sorry. You must think me a complete dope."

"Far from it," the other woman murmured. "I think anyone who wants a child as much as you do is going to be a very good mother."

Kate regained a modicum of composure, grateful for the woman's understanding. "Thank you."

"I'll tell you this, Kate, from speaking with this

birth mother several times now, I believe she's committed to adoption. I sense no conflict in her over whether to parent or give up her baby. And,'' Ellen added, ''she *is* interested in you and Richard. You have many qualities that are important to her. With that in mind, I was wondering when you could get your photo album to me.''

''I finished it last night and planned to run it over in the next few days.''

''The sooner the better.''

''I'm bringing it now. See you in forty-five minutes.''

11

Julianna sat on her bed, back propped by pillows, legs stretched out in front of her, the Citywide profiles stacked on what was left of her lap. She gazed at the typewritten words of the profile on the top of the stack, her vision blurred with tears.

I've loved Kate since the moment I laid eyes on her. She's my partner, my lover, my best friend. I can't imagine my life without her.

Julianna drew in a ragged breath, rereading the words, an ache of longing, of hunger, in the pit of her gut. She wanted that. To be loved and needed so ferociously. To be someone's everything.

She closed her eyes, her thoughts whirling. She had planned to pretend to have considered all the profiles and just randomly pick one of the couples. After all, she didn't want this baby, and Ellen had assured her that every couple had been carefully screened as to their worthiness for parenthood. Any one of them would have done.

Then, for no particular reason, she had begun to leaf through the first of the profiles Ellen had given her. Something about that couple had jumped out at her. A tone underlying the words, a kind of sanctimony. As if they thought themselves a bit too good for this whole thing. Too good for Julianna. And her baby.

Taking an immediate dislike to them, she had tossed

the profile aside and selected another. The next couple had seemed nice enough. Sincere. Eager to be parents. She was a homemaker, he an accountant.

They had bored her silly. Their life-style, what they'd had to say about parenting, their hopes for their child's future.

She had tossed them aside as well.

Then, on Saturday, she had found Richard and Kate. Everything about them had called to her—their life-style, beliefs, hopes and dreams and plans. Theirs was the life, the relationship, she had always fantasized as her own.

Now, on Monday, after having read their profiles a hundred times, she realized she had found so much more than just a couple to adopt her baby. The man she had been waiting for all her life. The one she was meant to be with.

Julianna drew in a ragged breath, struggling to get ahold of her runaway thoughts, denying them even as she was drawn back to his words, ones she knew now by heart.

We met at the university. She was so alive, so bright and eager and smart. I looked at her and saw the future in her eyes. My future.

What had John seen when he'd looked into her eyes? A child who needed protecting? An innocent who could be molded to his liking? Julianna swallowed hard. What had anybody ever seen in her eyes?

At the answer, the tears welled and spilled over, trickling slowly down her cheeks. Her mother had treated her like one of her expensive accessories, no different than a Hermés scarf or Gucci handbag. John, too, had had a narrow space for her in his life. And although he had professed to love her and had treated her well, he had wanted her to conform to that space and fill no other.

She wanted more now. She wanted what Kate had.

Angry, Julianna swiped at her cheeks and lowered her gaze again to the profile on her lap. She read about Richard's childhood and family, his dreams and aspirations. He shared his hopes for the future; his views on love, marriage and parenting.

She turned the last page, realizing only then that she was trembling. His words were her thoughts. Her hopes and dreams and prayers. This man, though they had never met, had reached into her head and heart, touching her in a way no one ever had.

It was as if he knew her. As if they were connected somehow, one person separated by time and fate.

Brought back together by the same.

Richard. And Julianna.

She tested his name on her tongue, saying it aloud, mating it with her own. Their names sounded…right together. They felt right together. As she said them, repeating them over and over, it was as if a bell went off in her head, a sort of chime, ringing out the beginning of her life. The real beginning, one that had nothing to do with her physical birth. Nothing to do with her past.

She was new now. Reborn. All the pieces had fallen into place. It all made sense. This was why she had gotten pregnant. Why John had driven her away. This was what every event of her life had led her to.

She believed in fate. In destiny. She had found hers.

Richard. And Julianna.

Julianna laid the profile aside and picked up its accompanying photo album. She ran her fingers over the embossed leather cover, heart beating uncomfortably fast, almost afraid to open it, though she didn't know why.

Perhaps because what she was feeling was so potent, so new and frightening. Perhaps because of the feeling in the pit of her gut—that she had just run headlong into her future.

Her future. Theirs. Richard and Julianna's.

With trembling fingers, Julianna opened the photo album. She went from one page to the next, turning them almost reverently, breathless at the enormity of what was transpiring, how her life was changing.

He was as she had pictured him through his words. Tall and dark-haired, with broad shoulders and an enticing, boyish smile. He looked strong and confident. A man a woman could lean on. One who loved deeply, passionately.

The man she had been waiting for.

Richard and Julianna.

And Kate. A problem.

Julianna drew her eyebrows together. She bore the woman no ill will. How could she? After all, she was a part of this, too, one of the pieces that had drawn them all together. If not for Kate's desire for a child, how would Julianna have found Richard?

Julianna skimmed her gaze from one photo in the album to the next, reading the accompanying inscription. Richard and Kate skiing in Aspen. Sailing on Lake Pontchartrain. Vacationing in the Tropics. Arms around each other. Smiling and gazing into one another's eyes.

Julianna stared at the photos, a knot in her throat. Kate wasn't gorgeous. She wasn't even beautiful, not really. But she looked smart. She looked classy. Not like a little girl. Not dependent. Not an over-sexed glamazon.

She touched one of the photographs, stroking her finger over Kate's glossy image. Kate was someone a man like Richard would fall in love with, she thought. Someone who would be this man's lover and partner.

Someone who deserved all the good things that had come to her.

Julianna frowned. At the tug of jealousy she felt. At the pang of insecurity.

She shook the emotions off. Those wouldn't do. She was prettier than Kate, younger and sexier. Class could be acquired, education feigned.

If she chose, she could be everything Kate was, have everything Kate had.

If she chose.

Julianna returned her attention to the album, to the photos of Richard and Kate. As she gazed at them, Kate disappeared and Julianna became the woman on Richard's arm, the woman he looked at with such love. The one to whom all the good things had come.

Yes, she thought. She chose to become the woman Kate was. To have what she had; to live her life.

All she had to do was make it happen.

12

The Saturday morning crowd at The Uncommon Bean consisted almost exclusively of college students and singles. The former came to visit with friends or to study, the latter to meet other singles, a healthy alternative to the bar scene.

This was the double-cappuccino, café-mocha crowd, and business had been brisk. Neither Kate, Blake nor Tess had been away from the counter except to bus tables since they opened up.

"We're out of scones," Blake announced, placing the last one on a plate. "And if this crush keeps up, we'll be out of croissants and muffins, too."

"What gives this morning?" Tess tucked her blond hair behind her ear. "Is it a holiday, or something? I've never seen it quite this busy."

"The weather, I think," Kate replied, smiling and thanking a customer as she counted out her change. "Everybody wants out of the house when it's this pretty."

"Not me." Tess passed a hand across her eyes. "I'd love to be home, in bed, the curtains drawn. I'd sleep 'til at least three, I swear I would."

Kate shot the other woman a part sympathetic, part exasperated glance. From the looks of her employee this morning, she had been out partying the night before, no doubt stumbling in sometime around dawn.

Tess smiled at the couple who approached the counter, took their order and called it back to Blake, who was manning the espresso machine. She glanced at Kate. "I met a guy last night. I think I'm in love."

Here we go again. Tess, an art student at Southeastern Louisiana University in Hammond, was pretty, vivacious and smart—but an absolute dope when it came to men. She believed every line she was tossed and fell for every guy in a tight pair of jeans. Blake, not the most sexually conservative himself, said Tess had the morals of an alley cat. Kate was of a different opinion—she felt Tess used men and sex as a way to feel good about herself.

That kind of thinking and behavior was not only self-destructive, it was downright dangerous, and Kate used every opportunity to try to counsel the girl. If only she could see how terrific she was. She didn't need a man, or anything else, to validate her.

Kate shook her head. "Oh, Tess."

The young woman frowned. "I don't know why everyone always says that to me."

"Honey," Blake drawled, his back to them as he frothed milk for a cappuccino, "consider your track record. You fall in and out of love daily. Like a rabbit."

"I wouldn't talk, Mr. Monogamy."

"Yeah, but I don't call it love."

"Okay children," Kate murmured, using the sudden lull to refill the pastry trays. "Let's not fight."

"Besides this is different. He's different. Special. Older, more sophisticated." She looked pleadingly at Kate. "You believe me, don't you?"

"It doesn't matter what I believe, Tess." She

crushed an empty bakery box and stuffed it into the trash. "It's what you believe that matters."

"See?" She made a face at Blake, who only shrugged and went to chat with a couple of the regulars. Tess leaned against the counter, her expression dreamy. "You know how you can just look at someone and *know?*"

"Know what, Tess?"

"That they're special. Different. That they're the one for you."

An image of Luke popped unbidden into Kate's head. As he had been that first time she saw him, standing outside the student loan office, looking defiant and proud, yet somehow vulnerable, too.

Kate shook her head, as much, she realized, to expel his image as to differ with Tess. "But can't that feeling translate to friendship? Just because someone is attractive to you, or thinks you're attractive, or makes you smile or whatever, that doesn't mean you have to fall in love with him. It doesn't mean you have to become sexual with him."

Because sometimes when you do, it ruins everything.

"It doesn't work that way." Tess drew her eyebrows together. "I only know how I feel, you know? It's like..." She hesitated before beginning, as if to gather her thoughts. "It's like, if I don't have him I'm going to go crazy or die. And when I get that way, I'll do anything to be with him."

"Do anything to be with him?" Kate repeated, arching an eyebrow. "Even lie? Even cheat or hurt someone you care about? Even lose your self-respect?"

Tess met Kate's eyes, her cheeks pink. "Yeah. Yeah, I think I would."

Kate was taken aback. She hadn't expected that answer. Truthfully, she was shocked by it. "You can't mean that, Tess. And if you do, don't you think that's a problem?"

"A problem? No." The younger woman looked dumbfounded at the suggestion. "Why should I?"

"Tess, you're telling me you'd lie to be with a man. That you'd hurt yourself or a friend. In my book, that's a problem. It's not healthy."

"You don't get it. It's because the feeling's so strong. And that's love. I know it is."

"How?" Kate challenged. "You've been in love dozens of times in the past year, it's never lasted. If it were really love, it would."

Blake finished with his customer and crossed to where they stood. He nodded his head. "I've been in love like that. The way Tess is describing. A couple of times."

"Really?" Tess turned to him. "What happened?"

He was quiet a moment. "Let's just say, I never want to feel that way again." Kate opened her mouth to console him, but he shook his head. "I'll clear the tables."

Kate watched him walk away, heart breaking for him. Blake had not had an easy life, she knew. He'd had to battle discrimination and intolerance, even from his own family. He longed, like all people did, for love and acceptance, yet had had his heart broken time and again. And despite his acerbic sense of humor and oftentimes sarcastic tongue, Kate knew that deep down he was a softy with a heart of gold.

"Don't you feel that way about Richard, Kate?"

Kate turned back to the other woman, thinking back fifteen years, to her first meeting with Richard. To how she had felt during the first weeks and months of their love affair. Giddy. Flushed. Over the moon.

She smiled at the memory. "I suppose I did. Once."

Tess looked so disappointed for her, Kate laughed. "Nobody died, Tess. What you don't understand yet is that love and marriage are about so much more than what you're talking about. They're about commitment. And sharing. And trust. They're about working together to build a good life. And a family. What you're describing is new and exciting. But it's fleeting."

"That makes me so sad for you."

"Don't be. It's incredibly rich and satisfying." Even as she said the words, meaning them with her whole heart, she felt a tug of dissatisfaction, as if indeed, something were missing from her life.

The feeling unsettled her, and she reminded herself that there was something missing from her and Richard's life—children. But they were remedying that.

"You'll see, Tess. It's good. Really good. I promise."

The conversation with Tess nagged at Kate for the rest of the day and into the evening. Even during dinner with Richard at their favorite restaurant, she had found herself going over each part of the conversation in an attempt to figure out what had triggered her melancholy. She had found herself thinking back, remembering their courtship, her feelings. Attempting to analyze his.

From their first date, Richard had made her feel like a princess. Like the poor, plain stepsister who had somehow won Prince Charming. He had taken her places she had only dreamed of, had shown her a way of life so far out of her league she had been left wide-eyed with wonder. She had fallen madly, wildly in love with him. He had seemed to be just as in love with her.

Seemed. She shook her head at the thought. Like all young couples, they'd had their troubles. He had been young, used to getting his way, to being the center of attention. He had been something of a ladies' man; when they'd begun dating, he had been up-front about that. He didn't plan to get serious about one girl, he'd said. But they had become serious. And when they had, she'd demanded he choose.

He had chosen her. And even though a half dozen times he had broken up with her to date someone else, he had always come back.

"Kate?" Richard waved his hand in front of her face. "Did you want coffee?"

She blinked, then flushed, realizing that she had been so engrossed in her own thoughts she hadn't even noticed the waiter approach their table. She smiled at the young man. "Yes, coffee. Thank you."

"Bad day?" Richard asked as the waiter walked away.

"Not really."

He arched his eyebrows. "Then why so quiet?"

"Have I been?"

He smiled. "Let's just say, the coroner keeps livelier company."

She laughed. "Sorry. I guess I'm not much of a date tonight."

He leaned across the table and covered her hand with his. "Want to talk about it?"

"It's silly." She laughed again, this time sheepishly. "You'll laugh, I know you will."

"Try me."

So she did, relaying her conversation with Tess. "The way she looked at me, as if she felt sorry for me, as if she thought our marriage was bloodless—" she lifted a shoulder "—it's left me feeling strange all day. Out of sorts."

Richard made a sound of disbelief. "You're not letting her dingy notions about love bother you, are you?"

"No, it's just that…" She looked away, then back. "Did you ever feel that way about me? Like you couldn't eat or sleep for thinking about me? Like you would die without me?"

"Kate, listen to yourself. Tess is what? Nineteen? Twenty? From what you've told me, she's never even had a committed relationship." He leaned closer, a smile tugging at the corners of his mouth. "Face it, when it comes to love, she's clueless."

"I suppose." Kate gazed out at the lake a moment, then looked back at him. "But did you? Ever feel that way about me?"

"I still do."

He leered at her, and she frowned. "Stop it. I'm serious about this."

He sat back. "I can see we're having one of those kinds of conversations."

"And what kind is that?"

"One where no matter what I say, I'm damned."

"That's not true. I'm trying to be serious and you're clowning around."

"Serious about what?" Richard leaned toward her, catching her hand and drawing it toward him. "Tess has more mileage on her than the Oscar Mayer Wienermobile, and you're letting her opinions on love, on our marriage, bother you? You don't think that's just a little irrational?''

Amused, Kate curled her fingers around his. "When you put it like that, it is pretty silly. Great image, by the way. The Wienermobile.''

"Thanks." He flashed her a smile. "Ever have one of those little wienie whistles?''

"What kid didn't?''

"Tess, probably. That's why she keeps looking for Mr. Good Wienie.''

Kate grinned despite the flash of sympathy she felt for her employee. "As simple as that, you think?''

"I do." He brought their joined hands to his mouth, kissed her knuckles then released them. "Just think where you might have ended up if not for the Wienermobile visiting your local grocery store.''

"Just think." She sobered. "Richard?''

He glanced up from perusing the bill. "Hmm?''

She ran her finger along the edge of the table. "You don't...there's nothing missing in our marriage for you, is there? I mean, you're happy, aren't you?''

"What a question." He shook his head as he dug his wallet out of his inside jacket pocket. "I'm completely happy, Kate.''

"Me, too." She made a sound, part contentment, part relief. "I just wouldn't want anything to happen to us.''

"Nothing will, love." He tossed his credit card onto the bill, then smiled at her. "That I can promise you.''

13

Julianna caught the streetcar at the stop outside Buster's and headed uptown, to Citywide's office. She took the last remaining seat, vacated as she boarded by a hugely obese man wearing clothes that smelled vaguely of beer, tobacco and sweat.

The smell lingered as did the warmth of his body and repulsed, she scooted forward on the seat until she was perched on the very edge. She longed for the days when she had zipped from destination to destination, without a thought to anything but her own convenience.

Now, she was forced to use public transportation. To travel on someone else's schedule. With people she didn't know, most of whom she wouldn't want to know. Now, she was forced to endure screaming children and constant stops, the crush of bodies at rush hour and the occasional burp, fart or halitosis that went along with that crush.

She found it irritating and distasteful. But it was cheap. She hadn't been in New Orleans twenty-four hours before she learned that the cost of parking in any of the lots in the central business district or French Quarter was outrageous. Working at Buster's certainly didn't allow her such luxuries, so when she had found one of the rare, free parking spots on the street near her apartment, she had maneuvered her car into it and hadn't moved it since.

Julianna turned to the window and gazed out at the waning afternoon, trying to ignore the greasy smear on the glass. This wasn't forever, she reminded herself. Soon she would have all the things she loved and needed. Soon, she would feel like her old self again.

Richard.

And Julianna.

She closed her eyes and pictured her future, imagined her days, how she would spend them, what her life would be like. Her life with Richard.

It would be perfect, everything she ever longed for.

She smiled to herself. Last night Richard had come to her in her dreams. He had whispered in her ear. That *she* was his everything. His lover and partner. His best friend.

He'd told her he couldn't live without her.

And they had been together. Sexually. Spiritually. Two souls made one, bodies entwined in an act of love so pure, so perfect, it defied the physical plane of existence.

Kate had come to her as well. She had been smiling. Holding a baby in her arms. Completely content.

Giving her blessing to the union of Julianna and Richard.

The baby stirred inside her, and she brought a hand to her belly, pleased. The dream had been a sign, a marker sent by the universe for Julianna to follow. She was meant to be in Richard's arms, to fill his life. To be the one he counted and depended on.

And Kate was meant to have a baby in her arms. Julianna's baby.

She would give her baby to Kate, Julianna had decided. And in return, she would take Kate's husband.

The streetcar rumbled to a halt. Julianna opened her eyes. They were stopped in front of a school. Through the wrought iron gates she could see a lovely courtyard; at its center, a fountain and a statue of the Blessed Virgin. A symbol of goodness and purity, one that guarded all against the encroachment of evil.

Another sign. An assurance. She brought a trembling hand to her mouth. *Destiny.*

The vehicle began to move, leaving the school and the statue of the Blessed Mother behind. Julianna twisted in her seat, craning her neck to keep it in sight as long as possible.

When it had completely slipped away from her, she faced front again. She laid her hands across her swollen belly and smiled. Today she took the first step toward her future. Today she would tell Ellen that she had chosen Kate and Richard to be her baby's adoptive parents.

The streetcar squealed to a stop at the corner of St. Charles and Sixth Street, her stop. The charity's office was located just off the Avenue, in a big old home that had been gutted and turned into an office complex, housing several small businesses.

Julianna left the vehicle. The day, unseasonably warm for early February, had cooled with the descent of the sun, and Julianna hunched deeper into her coat. The weather report had promised falling temperatures—the result of a cold front that had already moved across much of the country.

From overhearing hundreds of conversations at Buster's, she had decided that New Orleanians were obsessed with the weather. She figured that was because it not only changed frequently, but ran the gamut, from flooding rains, to unexpected freezes, to temperatures hot enough to boil seafood. One of her customers had proclaimed that anybody who lived in a place that got as hot as hell's kitchen deserved to obsess about the weather a bit.

She supposed he was right.

Julianna reached Citywide's office and let herself in. Madeline, the receptionist, was not at her desk, and Julianna took a seat, figuring the woman was either in the common kitchen area down the hall or using the rest room and would be right back.

Several minutes passed. From down the hall, the direction of Ellen's office, she heard the sounds of conversation. Ellen was in. Bored and antsy, Julianna stood and followed the sounds, stopping outside the social worker's partially open door. Judging by the one-sided conversation, the woman was on the phone. Julianna lifted her hand to tap on the door, pausing when she heard Ellen say the name Kate. Then the name Richard.

Julianna caught her breath. *Her Kate and Richard?*

Heart beginning to thunder, she dropped her hand and leaned closer, straining to hear more clearly. At that moment, Ellen hung up the phone.

Julianna sprang back from the door, cheeks burning. Afraid Ellen was going to catch her lurking outside her office, she quickly stepped forward, knocked, waited a split second, then poked her head inside.

"Hi, Ellen. Madeline wasn't at her desk, so I came back. I hope that's okay?"

The woman smiled warmly. "Of course. Come on in, Julianna." She motioned to the two chairs facing her desk, closing the manila folder on top of the stack in front of her. "Have a seat."

Julianna followed the movement with her eyes, the blood beginning the thrum in her head. Could that be Richard and Kate's folder? If she had just been on the phone with one of them, it seemed likely.

She had to get a look at it. There had to be a way.

"Thank you," she murmured, dragging her gaze back to the other woman's. "I was afraid you'd be too busy to see me."

Ellen smiled again. "Actually, your timing couldn't be better. I was going to call you this evening."

"You were?" Julianna settled into a seat. "What about?"

"I have some good news for you." Her smile widened. "Your expenses have been approved. Medical and living."

"Oh, my God." Julianna brought a hand to her chest. "You're serious?"

"Dead serious. Dr. Samuel has been notified. You need to call his office for an appointment. Before you leave, remind me and I'll give you one of his cards. As for your living expenses, you'll receive your first check at the beginning of next month and every month thereafter until the birth of your child."

For a moment, Julianna simply stared at the woman, unable to believe it was true. No more waiting on ungrateful slobs. No more aching feet and back or going home at night reeking of fried food.

Another sign.

Tears stung her eyes. "Thank you, Ellen. Thank you so much. This is going to make things so much easier for me."

"That's what we're here for. Now—" she folded

her hands on the desk in front of her "—what can I do for you?"

Julianna drew in a careful breath. Ellen, she was certain, would not believe in destiny. Or fate. She would not understand how Julianna and Richard were meant for each other. And, Julianna was certain, if she even suspected what Julianna was up to, she would toss her out of the program so fast her head would spin.

She needed to play this just right.

Julianna lowered her eyes for a moment, then returned them to Ellen's, hoping to appear hesitant and unsure of herself. "I've...I've come to a decision. About which couple I want to adopt my baby."

"Have you?" Ellen leaned slightly forward, beaming at Julianna.

"Yes, I...it wasn't easy. I sympathized with every couple. I almost feel bad that I can't...choose them all."

"But one couple jumped out at you." Ellen smiled encouragingly. "One couple seemed perfect."

Julianna returned her smile. "That's exactly right. How did you know?"

"It always works that way. I think of it as part of the miracle of adoption." Again the woman beamed. "So, who have you chosen?"

"Before I—" she took a deep breath "—before I tell you, I have a few questions. About how openness works."

"Certainly." Ellen folded her hands on the desk in front of her and went on to explain Julianna's different options, from a closed adoption to a completely open one and the many choices in between. The former being no contact between her and the adoptive parents, the latter including regular postplacement visits with both the baby and its new family.

When Ellen had finished, Julianna said nothing for several moments, pretending to take in all the woman had told her. "But...how will I know if the couple I choose will agree to the arrangement I want?"

"Truthfully, most of the couples are quite flexible. After all, they're all anxious to be parents."

"But what if the couple I choose feels differently?" Julianna caught her bottom lip between her teeth. "What if...I mean, I would hate to get my hopes up only to have them dashed."

"I can understand that. Let me reassure you, however, that's never happened."

"But still..." Julianna wrung her hands. "If I tell you who I chose...could you tell me what they've agreed to?" She met the other woman's eyes pleadingly.

Ellen hesitated, but only a moment. "I guess so. Who's the lucky couple?"

"Richard and Kate."

"Richard and Kate," Ellen repeated, looking pleased. "You've made a wonderful choice, Julianna. They're a lovely couple and have so much to offer a child. Their folder is right here." She tapped the folder on top of the stack in front of her. "Just give me a moment and I'll check the degree of openness they selected."

She opened the folder and flipped through a few pages, finally stopping on one. Julianna watched her, heart pounding, fingers itching to get her hands on that folder.

"They're open to meeting you," Ellen murmured. "They've agreed to postplacement letters and pictures and quarterly visits for the first year." She met Julianna's eyes. "How does that sound?"

"It sounds...good," Julianna murmured. "It gives me a lot of options." She looked down at her folded hands a moment, then back up at Ellen, her expression as earnest as she could make it. "I haven't completely decided what I want yet. There's so much to consider. I want to do the right thing. The best thing."

Ellen nodded. "I appreciate that and so will Kate and Richard. Just remember, Julianna, you're already doing the right thing for your baby. He or she will have a wonderful life with the...with Kate and Richard."

Julianna dropped her gaze to Ellen's desk and Kate and Richard's folder, scrambling for a way to get her hands on it. Suddenly, inspiration struck.

Julianna got to her feet. "Thank you so much for your time and...your...your—" She brought a hand to her head. "I don't feel so well."

Ellen jumped up. "What's wrong? You're not...is it labor?"

"I don't know. I don't...think so. I feel—" Julianna fluttered her eyelids and swayed slightly. "I feel a little...a little...faint."

"Oh, dear." The social worker rushed around the desk and took her arm. "Come, let me help you. There's a sofa in the waiting area. You can lay down there."

Julianna shook her head. "No...really. I don't...just let me sit here. A glass of water or...juice. Could you...please?"

"Of course." The other woman nodded and helped ease her back into the chair. "I'll be right back. Just call out if you need me."

The minute Ellen cleared the door, Julianna launched to her feet. She grabbed the folder and flipped it open. "Ryan," she whispered, reading the information. "On 361 Lakeshore Drive. Mandeville."

She repeated the information silently, committing it to memory, even as she shut the folder and laid it back on Ellen's desk, careful to return it to the exact spot she had found it.

No sooner had she settled back in her chair, than the social worker rushed back into the office with a glass of orange juice. "Here you are."

Ellen handed the glass to Julianna and hovered over her while she sipped the juice, making sure she drank the entire glass.

"How do you feel?" she asked when the juice was gone.

"Better." Julianna smiled weakly and handed the glass back. "Much better. Thank you."

The woman seemed unconvinced. "Have you eaten? I could get you some more juice. I think Madeline has a stash of cookies around here someplace, I could get—"

"I'm fine now. Really." When Ellen opened her mouth as if to argue, Julianna hurried to reassure her more. "I had a peanut butter sandwich and glass of milk just before I left Buster's. Sometimes I just get a little dizzy."

"It's called being pregnant." Ellen smiled, obviously relieved. "But you need to mention it to Dr. Samuel anyway."

"I will." Julianna looked at the floor, thinking of the future, of her and Richard and how it would be between them. "To tell you the truth," she said, meeting Ellen's eyes once more, "I'm looking forward to not being pregnant anymore."

"It won't be long now." Ellen laid a reassuring hand on Julianna's shoulder. "Kate and Richard, may I tell them the good news? They'll be thrilled. Over the moon, really."

"Not yet, please. I want to live with my decision awhile." Julianna clasped her hands together. "And I need to decide what I want, in terms of openness. I need to decide what's going to feel right to me. Do you understand?"

"Of course. And that's absolutely what we want you to do. Believe me, it will save a lot of heartache and confusion later."

"Thank you again, Ellen. For everything." Julianna stood and slipped into her coat, anxious now to be on her way. Anxious to decide her next step, to decide what to do with the information she had learned today. "I should go."

"Are you certain you feel well enough? Perhaps you should stay? Madeline will be back any moment and I'm sure—"

Julianna cut her off. "I feel fine now. And I'd like to get home before dark."

Ellen nodded and walked her to the door. There, she gave her a light hug. "Congratulations on your decision, Julianna. You've made a wonderful choice."

"Yes, I have," she murmured. "A wonderful choice. And now everyone will have the thing they want most."

"Julianna?" She met the woman's gaze. "May I ask, why did you choose Kate and Richard?"

"Excuse me?"

"Was there something special about them that firmed your decision? I'm sure they'd love to know."

Julianna gazed at the woman a moment, then smiled. "I fell in love with them. If they ask, tell them that."

14

Julianna didn't waste any time. The next day, after gleefully telling Buster she quit, she drove across the Causeway to Mandeville.

She hadn't known what to expect of the North Shore community, having never ventured over before, but she found it lovely. Small and charming, almost like a resort town. She decided right away that she liked it and would enjoy living there.

Finding Lakeshore Drive proved to be a no-brainer. Finding Richard and Kate's home was only slightly more difficult, and only because she initially turned the wrong way on Lakeshore Drive.

When Julianna located the address, she pulled up in front of the house and simply gazed at it, awed. It reminded her of a home she had once seen in *Southern Living* magazine, or one she might find in *Architectural Digest*. She wondered at its age, its history, if it had always been in Richard's family.

She moved her gaze over the house and grounds, drinking in every detail. The sweeping double galleries with their floor-to-ceiling windows. The four white wicker rockers that graced each gallery, two on either end. The deep front yard dotted with massive live oak trees, their branches laced with Spanish moss. The swing that hung from the huge, twisted branch of the tree closest to the front gate.

A sense of déjà vu, of *rightness* settled over her. She was meant to live here, in this community, this house. It called to her, just as Richard's words had.

Smiling to herself, she rested her head against the seat back and closed her eyes. A series of images formed in her head. Of her on the swing, wearing something filmy and white, laughing back at Richard as he pushed her. Of her, on the lower gallery, entertaining friends and sipping something cool and frothy.

Of her and Richard making love on the upper gallery in the dark, the sounds from the lake mingling with their sighs of pleasure.

A knot of emotion formed in her throat. She loved him. Deeply. Passionately. In a way she had never loved before. Not even John. Especially not John.

A laugh bubbled to her lips. She could imagine what others would think if she shared her thoughts with them. They would think her crazy, ridiculous. A silly girl with an even sillier crush. But they didn't know. They hadn't been in her head as she had read and reread his words, as those words, his thoughts, had mingled with hers; they hadn't been with her as she had lain night after night, gazing at the photographs of him, recognizing him not just with her eyes, but with her heart as well.

They would be one. They were destined to be. Soon, he would see as she did, feel as she did. He would understand.

And he would be grateful, so grateful, she had brought them together.

The blare of a horn followed by a shouted greeting startled her out of her reverie. She realized how odd she must look, sitting in her car, staring at the Ryans' house. She glanced around her. On the lake side of the street was a waterfront park, complete with tables and benches, children's play equipment and farther down, a small gazebo.

The park was busy. Couples walked hand in hand along the bulkhead; children played while their mothers watched, chatting with each other; teenagers huddled together, laughing and sharing cigarettes.

No one would notice her there.

Julianna restarted her Miata, drove up a half block to a public parking area, drew to a stop and climbed out. After locking her car, she walked back to the busy part of the park and chose a bench that afforded her a clear view of Richard's house.

Minutes ticked past. The day began to fade, the sun with it. The park emptied; the air grew colder. Julianna clutched the collar of her coat, her hands and ears beginning to tingle from the cold.

Still, the Ryans' remained dark. Julianna checked her watch. Nearly six now and except for the occasional jogger who passed, she was alone in the park.

Julianna shifted on the hard bench, a kind of panic coming over her. What if they didn't come home? What if they had gone out to dinner or worse, were out of town? She had come so far, she had to see them. She had to see *him.*

Her stomach began to hurt. She curled her arms around her middle, wishing she had brought along something to eat. Something warm to drink. She hadn't been thinking clearly; she hadn't been thinking of anything but finding Richard.

Julianna glanced longingly toward her car. She could run up to the convenience store she had passed on her way here and get a sticky bun and a hot chocolate. It would take her ten, fifteen minutes, tops.

And in that time she could miss them. Coming and going would draw attention to her. No. She forced away her hunger and the cold by closing her eyes and imagining Richard and Kate arriving home, imagining her first real glimpse of them.

Her mind wandered. She thought of her mother and of John. She wondered if he had come looking for her, wondered what he would do when he learned that she had fallen in love with another man.

Would he be jealous? Angry? She supposed so.

She would be more worried if she wasn't so certain he wouldn't find her. As her mother and Clark had advised her, she hadn't written or called home; she hadn't used her credit cards, though many times she had longed to, and she had kept on the move, not stopping until far from the D.C. area.

But what if he did find her?

She shuddered, then shook her head, forcing away the fear. Richard would send him packing. He was a lawyer; he knew people who could catch and punish John. He would see to it that John never bothered her again.

A light popped on in the Ryans' house. Julianna straightened, her heart leaping to her throat. A figure moved across the lit window, then another light glowed from behind sheer drapes.

Kate, Julianna realized. She held her breath, hardly able to believe the other woman was only a few hundred feet away.

As Julianna watched, Kate moved from room to room, flipping on lights as she went. Julianna imagined her touching this and that, checking the answering machine, sorting through the day's mail, glancing at the clock and wondering what time Richard would be home.

Just as Julianna wondered. Just as Julianna waited—impatiently, heart thundering in her aching chest.

They both loved the same man.

The truth of that affected her like a shock to her system. She and Kate shared that; it connected them. Just as her unborn baby did. They were bound by something important, elemental and potent. She felt its pull, its power.

In some ways, they were the same person.

One of the upper gallery doors opened. Kate stepped out and crossed to the rail. Julianna strained to see her, though she could make out little but her silhouette.

Julianna tilted her head. Kate was taller than she looked in her photographs. Slimmer. Julianna hugged herself, longing to have her own rail thin figure back. Even though she had only gained nine pounds since becoming pregnant, her body was immeasurably changed. She felt huge in comparison to Kate.

She dropped a hand to her swollen belly, feeling the baby stir, unable to quell the quick kick of resentment she felt toward it. She squeezed her eyes shut, reminding herself that without the baby she wouldn't have found Richard. She wouldn't have the gift that would draw them all together.

But she couldn't fool herself, either. To compete with Kate for Richard, she would have to be firm and lithe. She would have to be sexy.

Kate walked to the driveway end of the gallery and peered over the side, though Julianna couldn't see at what. She moved gracefully, Julianna thought studying the other woman, recalling Kate as she had been in the photos. Fluidly. Everything about Kate Ryan was graceful, classy.

But not cold. No, Kate was warm. Approachable. Julianna had seen that warmth in her photos, her eyes and smile had radiated it. And she had read it in her words—ones about motherhood, love and trust, about life.

Tears stung Julianna's eyes. Kate was a nice person. An emotional one, one who felt things keenly.

Julianna was going to hurt her; what she planned would hurt her. Terribly. Julianna hated that, she did.

She sucked in a ragged breath, forcing back her remorse, the pinch of guilt. It was for the best, she reminded herself. Kate would forget Richard, forget her hurt as she held her baby in her arms, as she watched it grow.

A car pulled into the driveway, its headlights arcing light across the face of the house, bringing Kate briefly into clear view.

Richard. Julianna stood. She brought a hand to her chest, to her runaway heart. It hurt to be so close to him, yet so far. She longed to go to him, longed to feel his arms around her, to hear his whispered greeting in her ear.

What would he do if she approached him? Would he recognize her the way she had recognized him? As his soul mate? The one he was meant to love? To be with?

She sank back to the bench, knowing he would not. He was a man of logic. Of reason and of commitment. Because of his commitment to Kate, he would deny he felt anything for Julianna.

Until he could deny it no more.

Her mother had taught her that no man was ever

really married. She had taught her that deep down, in every man, there lurked a need that went unfulfilled. A secret longing so potent, that once realized, they would leave family, country or God to have it fulfilled.

She would find Richard's secret longing. The universe, the benevolent gods, would lead her to it.

A car door, his car door, slammed shut. From the upper gallery, Kate called out a greeting and waved. He looked up and called back to her. The sound of his voice floated on the evening air, reaching Julianna and wrapping around her like a lover's arms.

He came around the front of the house, then stopped suddenly and turned toward the lake. Toward the park, the bench—toward her. She felt his gaze upon her as tangible, as real, as a caress.

She brought a hand to her heart. *He sensed her presence. He felt the connection between them. Like a spark of light in the darkness, like heat in a vast, cold wasteland.*

A moment later, he disappeared into the house.

Julianna didn't move. Time passed, though she didn't know how much. The cold slipped over and around her, seeping through her coat, then skin, numbing her. As her body ceased to exist, her mind took flight.

She knew what she had to do to win Richard.

She had to become Kate.

It was so obvious. Richard loved his wife. Deeply. Everything about her. It was one of the reasons Julianna had fallen in love with him.

If she became like Kate, a younger, sexier Kate, he would love her, too. He would love her more. He would see that they were meant to be together.

She would watch them, study and learn. And he would be hers.

Smiling at the future she saw unfolding before her, Julianna stood and left the park.

15

Saturday morning the phone rang, just as Richard was leaving for the gym. "Could you get that, Kate?" he asked. "I forgot my gym bag upstairs, and I'm already running late."

"Sure, hon." She shut off the kitchen faucet and grabbed the dish towel, drying her hands as she crossed to the phone.

"And if it's my mother, she's missed me. I'll call her back later."

Kate nodded and picked up the receiver. "Hello?"

Not waiting to see who it was, Richard hurried from the kitchen. He had a 9:00 a.m. session with his personal trainer, and the man did not appreciate waiting. Nor did he refund lost minutes if a client was late.

Richard grabbed the gym bag from his walk-in closet, quickly checked its contents, then jogged downstairs. He popped his head into the kitchen. "I'll be back after...Kate? What is it? What's wrong?"

Pale, visibly shaking, Kate met his gaze. She opened her mouth as if to reply, but no sound came out.

He crossed to her, heart in his throat. He cupped her elbows and shook her lightly. "Has there been an accident? Kate, has one of our parents—"

"That was Ellen," she whispered, eyes flooding with tears. "We've been...a birth mother..." The tears choked her, and she struggled to clear her throat. "A birth mother...she picked...us."

Richard took a step back, stunned. It couldn't be. They couldn't have been chosen so soon.

Richard searched his wife's gaze, looking for amusement, laughter at having successfully pulled one over on him. He saw neither.

But he wasn't ready.

He fought for composure, for the cool that rarely escaped him. "You're sure we've been chosen? I mean, you're certain it's not that we're just being considered, seriously considered, but not—"

"No, I'm sure. Positive. Ellen wants to meet early next week to go over what to expect."

"But..." Richard dragged a hand through his hair, shocked to realize it shook. "But we only signed on with Citywide, not even two months ago. It's not supposed to happen this fast. They said a year, maybe more. They said—"

"I know." Kate brought her hands to her mouth. "The baby's due soon. Early May. That's less than three months away."

Early May?

Dear God, what did he do now?

Kate put her arms around him and pressed her cheek to his chest. "We're going to be parents, Richard. We're going to have a baby."

He held her to him tightly. He could feel her happiness, her complete and utter joy, in the way she trembled, in the way she clung to him. He saw it in her eyes and heard it in her voice.

So, why did he feel nothing but trapped?

She tilted her head back to meet his eyes. "How do you feel?" she asked, as if reading his thoughts.

The truth would never do. He couldn't hurt her that way. He wouldn't, no matter what it cost him. "Happy, I guess."

She laughed. "You guess?"

"Yes, definitely happy." He searched her gaze looking for a hint of hesitation, of the weakness and fear that milked him dry. He saw none. "It's just...I can't believe this is happening."

"Me, either. It's a dream come true."

A dream come true. For her.

Hating his thoughts, he drew her against him once more. He was happy, he was. He just wasn't as starry-eyed as Kate. He wasn't as adventurous. As trusting. He was a lawyer, for God's sake. He saw possible complications, legal entanglements.

This could blow up in their faces. Kate could have her heart broken.

"You're quiet," she murmured.

"I'm thinking."

"Uh-oh." Again she tipped her head back and laughed up at him. "Stop that. Stop looking for problems. You're going to be a great daddy, Richard Patrick Ryan."

He smiled, drawn into Kate's joy. "What makes you think so?"

"I just know so." She cupped his face in her palms and gazed into his eyes. "You're going to be the best daddy ever."

16

Kate and Richard met with Ellen at the Citywide offices first thing Monday morning. The meeting fulfilled a two-fold purpose: it was an opportunity for them to discuss their pending adoption; and it would serve as their first home study interview. The law in Louisiana required that a home study be completed before a child could be placed in an adoptive home. Due to the circumstances, Kate and Richard's would have to be rushed through.

Richard shifted in his seat, anxious for the interview to begin. He had a luncheon meeting scheduled with a potential campaign contributor, a midafternoon pow-wow with his law partners, and he was due to go to trial next week with a defense that had more holes in it than a block of aged Swiss cheese.

None of those weighed as heavily on him at that moment as the reason they were in Ellen's office.

Since the call from Ellen, Kate had talked of little but the fact that a birth mother had chosen them. She had hardly slept; she had called both their families, had even browsed through a couple of baby stores.

Her excitement concerned him. His lawyer's instinct found the whole thing damn suspicious. He reviewed the facts. Some woman they didn't know had chosen them to be her child's parents. A stranger was asking them to make a lifetime commitment to her offspring.

He and Kate knew nothing about the woman, not her life-style or her genetic history. It wasn't safe. Or smart.

He had tried to present his concerns to Kate; she had laughed them off. All she could see was the carrot, not the string attached.

Richard passed a hand across his forehead. The fact was, he had agreed to adopt to please Kate. Because he had wanted to give her the one thing she desired more than any other. He had felt guilty; it had seemed simple enough, the idea of having a child rather pleasant.

Now, it didn't seem simple at all. Now, he saw the string. He saw the monster attached to the end of it.

He wasn't sure he could go through with this.

If he backed out now Kate would never forgive him.

"Good morning." Ellen hurried into the conference room, balancing a cup of coffee and a sweet roll on top of several file folders. "Sorry I'm late. One of our mothers went into labor just before midnight."

She set her breakfast on the table, pulled out a chair and sank onto it with a sigh. "Finally." She took a swallow of her coffee, sighed again, then looked at them, smiling widely. "I bet you two had a good weekend."

Kate beamed at the woman. "I've been too excited to sleep. It's all so amazing."

"I'm very happy for you." She smiled again, moved the sweet roll and flipped open the top folder. "And how about you, Richard? Stunned or what?"

"It came up awfully fast, that's for sure."

"It happens sometimes," Ellen replied. "We call them 'fall out of the sky' babies."

He frowned at the description. "I don't imagine falling out of the sky is all that healthy for an infant."

She started to laugh, then realized he might not be making a joke. She drew her eyebrows together in question. "I'm sorry, I don't get your meaning."

"I'll speak plainly, then. Is there something wrong with this baby?"

Ellen straightened slightly. "Not that I know of."

Kate made a sound of shock; Richard ignored her. "So there's a possibility?"

Color crept up the woman's cheeks. "The mother and child have been thoroughly examined by a doctor and will continue to have the best medical care. Everything looks normal, the mother is young and healthy. Of course, something could have gone wrong in utero, something all the exams and ultrasounds in the world couldn't pick up. The same as if Kate were pregnant. Babies are a crap shoot, Richard. A game of Russian roulette."

"This game of roulette is our lives, Ellen. I don't take that lightly."

"Nor do I," she said stiffly. "If I could promise you this baby will be perfect, I would. If I could promise you that this birth mother won't change her mind, I would. But I can't. The best I can do is assure you that I believe those things to be the case."

"Of course that's all you can do," Kate murmured, looking at Richard, a frown marring her brow. "We're thrilled at having been chosen. Aren't we, Richard?"

"Yes, thrilled." Richard shifted in his seat. "Though I do have one last question before we move on. Why didn't this birth mother pick one of the other couples? One who had been in the program for some time?"

Ellen looked from one to the other of them. "Am I hearing some hesitation on your part, Richard? If so—"

"No!" Kate covered his hand with hers. "Of course not."

"Richard?" Ellen persisted, shifting her gaze to him, not looking at Kate. "Just as I wouldn't place a baby in a home if I thought the birth mother had doubts, I won't place a baby in a home where the parents aren't totally committed to adoption. It wouldn't be fair, not to the child, the birth mother, or the dozen other couples on our list."

Kate's fingers were cold; they trembled. He understood how much this meant to her. He curled his fingers around his wife's. "I'm a lawyer. I'm suspicious by nature, and I ask a lot of questions. It's what I do." He forced a laugh. "I do wonder though, why us?"

"Yes." Kate leaned forward, the relief in her voice audible. "Did she say why? I'd love to know."

Ellen hesitated, then inclined her head. "She said she'd fallen in love with you. Her words."

"In love with us?" Kate repeated. She looked at Richard, and he grinned.

"I always said we were lovable. This confirms it."

Ellen laughed. "I know that probably sounds odd to you, she's a complete stranger, after all. But you have to understand, the process for these girls is intensely emotional. I'm sure what she meant is that she's fallen in love with your lives. With the picture she has of the life you will give her child."

Ellen folded her hands on the desk in front of her. "Many of these young women are desperately lonely. Or coming from a really bad situation. Some of them have been deserted by a lover, some kicked out of the house by their parents, some are bucking intense family disapproval of their decision to place the child for adoption. Add to that a fear of making the wrong decision. Believing in the adoptive couple she's chosen is more than important for her. It's essential. And this birth mother believes in you, simple as that.''

''When will we meet her?'' Kate asked, her voice thick with tears. ''I want to thank her for this.''

The woman glanced away, then back. ''At this point, you won't be meeting her. She wants the adoption to be completely closed.''

''Completely closed,'' Kate repeated, making a sound of distress. ''But I...I'd really hoped we could at least meet her. And all the literature on the subject says it's best for everyone, especially the baby.''

''We do prefer it.'' Ellen looked from one to the other of them. ''But ultimately, it's the birth mother's choice.''

''I don't understand,'' Richard murmured, frowning. ''Why does she get to choose? It seems to me we're a fifty-percent partner in this deal.''

''Quite simply, because she has something you, and thousands of other couples like you, want. She's in the driver's seat, Richard. Like it or not, that's the facts.''

Richard looked at Kate, then back at Ellen, frown deepening. ''This doesn't feel right to me. Is there something she's trying to hide? Some reason she prefers not to meet us?''

Ellen flushed. ''She has nothing to *hide*. And if she did, we would discover it and ask her to leave the program. We screen everyone involved in this process very carefully. Nothing gets by us.''

''We have complete confidence in you and the program." Kate squeezed his fingers in warning. "Don't we, sweetheart?"

"Complete confidence, of course. We're simply disappointed with her choice of a closed adoption."

Ellen inclined her head. "As I said before, this is an intensely emotional experience for these women. Some choose to distance themselves from it any way they can. Depersonalize it. Some change their minds when they realize the tactic doesn't work."

"Can you at least tell us her first name?" Kate asked. "What she looks like or how old she is?"

"At this point, she doesn't wish for you to know even her first name. I can tell you, however, that she's nineteen and quite attractive. In fact, her coloring and build is similar to yours, Kate. I know that doesn't quell your curiosity, but it's the best I can do right now."

Kate looked at Richard, then back at Ellen. "Could you talk to her? Tell her how eager we are to meet her?"

"I'll try," Ellen murmured, "but I don't think it'll do much good. She's a very determined young woman. From what I've observed about her, when she sets her mind on something, she can't be dissuaded."

"What she wants, she gets," Richard murmured.

Ellen smiled. "And in this case, she wants you."

17

Julianna moved to Mandeville to be near Richard and Kate. She found an apartment, half of what New Orleanians called a shotgun double. Small, shabbily furnished and more expensive than other, nicer apartments available in the area, she'd chosen it for its location—in old Mandeville, only six blocks from the Ryans'.

Renting in their neighborhood made perfect sense to Julianna. Living within blocks of them, it wouldn't be odd for her to be seen hanging out at the waterfront park, it wouldn't be unreasonable for her to walk or drive past their house several times a day, or to frequent the restaurants, shops and other places Richard and Kate enjoyed.

And frequent them she did. Julianna spent her days watching the Ryans. Following them.

She found doing so surprisingly easy. They came and went, blissfully unaware of her presence. She quickly learned their schedule, their likes and dislikes, who they associated with for work and who for pleasure. Richard enjoyed golf and Kate reading, most often mysteries. Richard ordered fish more than meat when out to dinner; Kate preferred shellfish and loved desserts. The list of Julianna's discoveries went on and on; each new fact she committed lovingly to memory, a sort of mental scrapbook or family album. Every so often, she would open the album and wallow in what she had learned, stroking and holding each fact, getting to know her new family, growing to love them more each day.

After the first two weeks, Julianna focused most of her attention on Kate. She studied her—the way she moved and gestured, how and when she laughed, her expressions. She discovered the scent she wore, the coffee she preferred, studied the cadence of her speech.

Julianna had gone to The Uncommon Bean, careful to choose times Kate was away, eavesdropping on conversations as she pretended to read, staying as long as she could without drawing attention to herself. She learned that the other woman was both liked and respected by her employees. She discovered she had a sense of humor and seemingly boundless energy, that she was an all-around nice person.

Everything about the other woman inspired Julianna. But of all her qualities, the one that impressed her most was Kate's artistic ability.

Her first time in The Uncommon Bean, Julianna had gazed in awe at the stained glass creations that hung in every window, dappling the café's interior with colored light.

Julianna had looked at the creations and ached with longing, with envy. Once upon a time, Julianna had fantasized about being an artist. She had fantasized about going to Paris or New York to study art. John had forced her to face the truth—she had neither the talent nor the discipline to succeed as an artist.

Kate did. Kate, it seemed to Julianna, had everything.

But not for long. February had become March,

March became April. Dr. Samuel said she was close now, that it could happen anytime. She had begun to dilate, he'd said. The baby had dropped and was in position.

The baby was as ready as she, Julianna thought, standing before her bathroom mirror, naked save for her bra and panties. Her face was as naked as she, freshly scrubbed, devoid of expression. She turned this way and that, studying her reflection, studiously avoiding looking at her bulging belly, hating it.

Finally, she could ignore it no longer. Purposefully, she turned sideways and gazed at her body's profile. She splayed her hands over the tightly stretched flesh. It was smooth and hard, extended to its limit.

She smiled suddenly, taken aback by the sense of wonder that filled her. Maybe Kate could mold glass and lead into amazing images, beautiful *things,* but she couldn't do this. She couldn't create life.

Beneath her palms, the baby stirred, then kicked. Julianna laughed and pressed her hands closer, for the first time delighted with the discomfiting sensation, with her pregnancy.

Kate was smart and classy. Kate lived in a beautiful home and owned her own business. She had inspired the love of a wonderful man.

Julianna could be like her, she could have all those things. She *would* have them.

But the thing Kate longed for most, she couldn't do on her own. She needed Julianna for that.

Julianna laughed again. That made her feel good. Made *her* feel important. And special.

Time to get started.

Julianna closed her eyes and breathing deeply, cleared her mind and pictured Kate. She pictured her talking, then tipping her head back and laughing; she pictured her smiling at her husband or daydreaming when she thought no one was looking. Minutes passed; the Kate images filled her head, crowding out all others.

Julianna opened her eyes and smiled—Kate's smile. Quick, broad and warm. It transformed Julianna's face, changing it subtly. She did it once more, repeating the motion until it felt natural not forced, never letting go of the images in her head.

"Hi," Julianna said, "welcome to The Uncommon Bean. What can I get for you?"

That wasn't right, she realized, frowning. That wasn't the way Kate spoke. Kate had the habit of lifting her voice slightly on the consonants, lending it a musical quality.

Julianna said the words again. And again. She practiced tirelessly, working to mirror the other woman's speech pattern. As it became more natural to her, she added Kate's smile, her laugh; she tucked her hair behind her ear, as Kate was wont to do, she gestured with her hands, copying the other woman's small, fluid movements.

The light streaming through the bathroom window changed, becoming harsh with midday, then mellowing as the day began to fade. Still, she practiced. Hunger pulled at her; so did fatigue. Her back ached; her head pounded. She broke for food and drink, but propped a hand mirror up on the kitchen table so she could use the opportunity to imitate how Kate ate, how she took small bites and chewed slowly, how she patted her mouth with a napkin and sipped her water.

When she had finished her meal, Julianna forced

herself to her feet and to the bathroom's big mirror, though her body screamed for rest.

She switched on the overhead light, then opened the vanity's center drawer. She removed a photograph of Kate, a close-up shot she had stolen from the couple's photo album, and the bag of cosmetics she had purchased the day before—cosmetics in the warm earth tones Kate preferred.

Julianna taped Kate's photo to the mirror, then gazed at it, noting each shadow and curve of the other woman's face, analyzing the way she wore her makeup—subtly, artistically, in a style that heightened her assets.

Imitation in mind, Julianna selected the foundation and applied it, smoothing it carefully over her face and neck. From there she applied blush, powder, eye color.

Each step of the way, she paused to compare her reflection to Kate's image, looking for differences or imperfections and eliminating them.

She knew she would never be Kate's twin. The shape of their faces was different, their features. Her aim was to create the other woman's look, her style, on her own face.

Finally, she had it. She had Kate. A facsimile of the woman stared back at Julianna from the mirror. Julianna made a sound of triumph; it came out in a twisted gasp. She doubled over and clutched her middle as a thin, sharp pain speared through her.

Julianna sank to the floor, to the puddle of liquid pooling around her feet. She looked at it in amazement, realizing her water had broken, realizing what it meant.

The baby was here.

18

After fifteen hours of labor, Julianna gave birth to a baby girl. A week and a half early, she weighed a mere five pounds, two ounces, but what she lacked in size, she made up for in lung capacity.

Julianna had held her briefly in the delivery room, though not because she wanted to. Without asking, the nurse had laid the howling infant on her chest, beaming ridiculously at Julianna, babbling about how beautiful her daughter was. As far as Julianna had been concerned, the baby looked like a red-faced frog, and she hadn't wanted to have anything to do with her.

She'd turned her gaze away and asked the nurse to take her. Ellen, who had stayed with her during the entire ordeal, had stepped forward, eager to hold the child. Julianna had watched the woman cradle the baby, tears streaming down her cheeks and had wondered what the big deal was.

She still did.

Ellen popped her head into the room. "Hi," she said softly. "How are you?"

"Tired."

"I'll bet. Can I come in?"

"Sure. Is that for me?" Julianna indicated the bud vase containing a single pink rose surrounded by white baby's breath.

"Of course." Ellen set the vase on her bed table. "Congratulations, Julianna. You did great."

Just then the nursery attendant entered the room, pushing a bassinet. The woman smiled brightly. "I thought you might like to spend a little time with your daughter."

She scooped up the sleeping infant, careful Julianna saw, to support her head. She placed the baby in Julianna's arms. "Just ring the nursery when you need us to come get her. Congratulations again. She's just precious."

"Everyone keeps saying that," Julianna murmured when the nurse was gone.

"What's that?"

"Congratulations."

"That's because the birth of a child is something to celebrate."

"I suppose." Julianna lowered her gaze to the bundle in her arms, swaddled in a pink receiving blanket, her moon-shaped face overwhelmed by the knit cap covering her head.

Julianna studied the sleeping child. The infant's chest rose and fell with her rapid breathing; peeking out from above the blanket, her hands were squeezed into fists, her puffy eyes shut tight.

An unfamiliar ache in her chest, Julianna shifted her gaze to Ellen, hovering at the foot of the bed. "She is beautiful, isn't she?"

"Yes," Ellen said softly, "she is."

Julianna returned her gaze to the baby. She traced a finger across the infant's cheek, finding her skin almost unbearably soft. "I did this," she murmured. "I made her. All by myself. And she's perfect. Absolutely perfect."

"That she is." Ellen cleared her throat. "A tiny miracle."

"Yes." Julianna smiled and looked at Ellen once more. "I didn't understand that before. I didn't know. But I do now."

A look of distress crossed the other woman's features, then just as quickly disappeared. "How are you feeling? It was rough going in there."

Julianna agreed, though after a point in the labor she didn't recall anything. The pain had been unbelievably intense, building, cresting, then retreating. After a time, one crest had led directly to another. The best she had been able to do was suck in a lung full of air before the next contraction had racked her body.

Even so, she had refused the epidural block and welcomed the pain, finding it almost pleasurable. Cleansing. Affirming. It belonged to her and her alone.

She hadn't been about to let anyone take it away from her.

"At one point you passed out. Believe me, you gave us all a scare."

"Did I?" she murmured, still gazing at the baby. "I don't remember."

"Julianna?"

"Yes?"

"Now that she's been born, how do you feel about giving her up? Are you having second thoughts?"

"Why would I be?"

Ellen hesitated a moment, then lifted her shoulders. "The baby's real now. You've held her in your arms. This is when some women realize they can't go through with the surrender."

"I'm not like that. I know I'm not meant to be her

mother.'' Sudden, sharp emotion welled up inside her, taking her by surprise. She tamped it back. ''Kate is.''

''Are you certain? If you have any misgivings, now's the time to acknowledge them. Afterward… after placement, it's hard on everyone. Even the baby.''

She hesitated a moment. ''I don't have any misgivings.''

How could she? This moment, Julianna Starr ceased to exist. Her old life was gone, her new one beginning. Starting this moment she became the woman Richard would love.

''Buzz the nursery and tell them to come get her. Then call Kate and Richard. Tell them their daughter's been born.''

19

Kate gazed at her new daughter, cradled in her arms for the very first time. A bundle of pink and white, she had been born two days before, on April twenty-ninth.

Kate and Richard had named her Emma Grace. Emma after his grandmother and Grace at Kate's insistence because she believed it had been only through God's perfect grace that Emma had come to them.

She moved her gaze over her sleeping daughter's face, taking inventory of every feature: the turned up nose, the tiny rosebud mouth, the eyes, still puffy from birth and squeezed tightly shut, the cap of silky dark hair, skin as fine, soft and white as a gardenia petal.

Kate trailed a finger across Emma's cheek. As she did, the infant turned her head slightly, following Kate's finger, instinctively seeking a nipple.

Kate drew in a shuddering breath, a tidal wave of love and protectiveness rising up in her. Before now, this moment, she hadn't had a clue what a mother's love really meant. Now, she knew. It was an awesome thing, all-encompassing, powerful. She would go to any length to protect her child, she realized. She would face and beat back any who meant her harm, she would give herself, her own life if she had to.

Kate lifted her swimming gaze to Richard's only to

find his on her, damp with his own tears. In that moment she loved him more than she ever had.

"She's so beautiful," Kate whispered. "So perfect."

"You're perfect. You're beautiful together."

Emotion choked her. For long moments she couldn't speak. When she found her voice, all she thought of to say was thank you.

20

Kate's first six weeks as a new mother were confusing and exhausting. Caring for Emma consumed her every waking moment—and then some. The infant needed to be fed every few hours; she cried often and it seemed to Kate, for no reason at all.

Those times, Kate walked the floor with her, bounced her or sang softly as she rocked her in the big chair Richard had bought her. Still Emma cried.

Frustrated and insecure, Kate wept with her. She wasn't meant to be a mother, she thought. There was something wrong with her, something missing in her womanly makeup that left her unable to nurture a baby. Maybe that's why she had been unable to conceive. Maybe nature had been telling her something.

Then, as suddenly as it had begun, Emma's crying stopped. And she smiled. Not just any smile, not just at anything. Or anyone. No, she had gazed into Kate's eyes with total trust and presented her with a beautiful and adoring smile.

A smile meant only for Kate.

In that moment, everything changed. Kate had become Emma's mother, for real and forever. In that moment it was all worth it—the sleep deprivation, the hours walking the floors, her haggard appearance and the self-doubt. In that moment, they all melted away.

Kate gazed down at her sleeping daughter, heart

filled to near bursting. She trailed her fingers softly, rhythmically over her silky head. She never got enough of looking at Emma, of holding and touching her. All else in her life slipped away, and she found herself mesmerized by the tiniest changes in the infant's expression.

From downstairs, came the sound of the front door opening, then snapping shut. Richard was home. Doubting that it could be that time already, Kate checked her watch and saw that it was.

She eased out of the rocking chair, careful not to disturb Emma. After settling the baby in her crib, she headed downstairs to greet her husband.

He was in the kitchen, leafing through the day's mail. "Hi, hon," she said, crossing to him.

"Hey." He stopped what he was doing, bent and kissed her. "How was your day?"

"Great. How was yours?"

"Okay. Really busy."

She poured them both a glass of wine, and set his on the counter beside the mail. "Hungry?"

"Starved. I missed lunch."

"That's too bad." She flashed him an apologetic smile. "Hope you don't mind reheated pizza."

"Do I have a choice?"

"Sure." She went to the refrigerator, pulled out the remainder of the previous night's supreme. "A tuna fish sandwich. But I think the bread's growing something fuzzy and green."

Richard said nothing and she went about getting together their meal, meager though it was. "Emma did the most amazing thing today. She laughed out loud." He didn't look up from the mail. "I wish you could have been here. It was so great."

Kate slid the cookie sheet with the pizza on it into the preheated oven. "It wasn't a gurgle or a coo, but a real honest-to-goodness laugh."

He still didn't respond and from the corner of her eyes, she saw him rip open an envelope, scan its contents then frowning, cross to the trash and toss it in.

Kate watched him. "What was that?"

He met her eyes, then looked away. "From the Alumni Association. About an alumni *celebrity* event."

The way he said the word told her who the celebrity was. She asked anyway. "Who's the star?"

"Who else? The great Luke Dallas. He's giving a lecture and signing copies of his new novel. Pompous prick."

Luke didn't have a pompous bone in his body. She may not have seen him in ten years, but she knew that anyway. "What's eating you?"

He looked up, spoiling, she saw, for a fight. "Excuse me?"

"You heard me. Why the attitude?"

"Leftover pizza."

She narrowed her eyes. "Sorry, I didn't have time to go to the grocery. I've been a little busy."

"No joke."

"Meaning?"

"That maybe you should make the time."

"It's not as easy as that."

"No?" He folded his arms across his chest. "We could have gone out."

"Not with Emma."

"They do allow babies in restaurants, you know."

"I know. But this is her nap time. I don't like to disturb her. She gets cranky." Kate sucked in a deep breath, working to make light of his comments even though they had angered her. "When your nap is interrupted, you get a little cranky, too."

He made a sound of disgust. "I'll tell you when I get cranky, when I'm fed leftover pizza two days in a row. I get cranky when my wife greets me in the evening in a bathrobe or when the only thing she ever talks about is *the baby*."

Kate stared at him, so furious suddenly, she wanted to hit him. "You think I like going around all day like this?" She motioned to the baggy sweats and old shirt she had thrown on that morning. "Maybe if you helped out once in a while, I'd have the time to go to the grocery or get dressed in the morning."

"The baby's your responsibility. That's what we decided."

"My responsibility?" She arched her eyebrows. "Oh, I see. What you're saying is, since I'm the primary caregiver, I should never ask you to watch her for a few minutes while I do something else, like take a leisurely shower or run to the market? That I should never hope you'll take one of the 2:00 a.m. feedings so I can get more than three hours of uninterrupted sleep a night?" Her voice cracked. "Or that I should never expect you to want to spend time with her? She's your daughter, too, Richard."

"Is she?"

Kate caught her breath. "What's that supposed to mean?"

He ignored the question, crossed to her and caught her hands. "How about a date, Kate? You know, you and me, candlelight and kisses."

"And sex."

"Since you brought it up, yeah, a little sex. When's

the last time we made love? Two weeks ago? Three?''
He lowered his voice. "I've missed you. I've missed
us."

Tears stung her eyes. "I'm just so tired, Richard.
So damned tired all the time. It's hard to feel sexy
when—"

The baby monitor crackled as Emma stirred in her
crib. Once Emma stirred, Kate knew, she was awake.
In a minute she would begin to howl, demanding to
be fed.

"Damn," Kate muttered and crossed to the refrigerator. She took out a bottle of formula, loosened the
top and popped it in the microwave to warm it. Sure
enough, just as the microwave dinged, Emma began
to cry.

"Great." Richard dragged a hand through his hair.
"Just fucking great."

"What do you want me to do?" she asked, snatching out the bottle and tightening the lid. "Let her
cry?"

"Yeah, maybe I do."

Kate sucked in a shocked breath. She met his eyes.
"I'm going to try to pretend you didn't say that. Excuse me."

Bottle in hand, she strode from the room.

"Kate, wait!" He caught her arm. "I'm sorry. I
didn't mean that."

She looked at him. "No?"

"It's just that I'm...I'm missing you. Missing the
way we were. Our life."

Tears flooded her eyes. "Like I said, if you'd help
out a little, maybe I'd have a little more time for us."

"Hire someone. It's not like we can't afford it."

She stared at him in disbelief. "I don't want to do

that. We've waited too long to be parents to turn over her care to a stranger. Besides, I want you to help out. To hold and feed her, to play with her. You're missing out, Richard. You need to get to know your daughter, she's pretty great.''

"I don't have time.''

"But you have time for us to go on a date? For us to go out to dinner or away for the weekend?'' Upstairs Emma's cries took on a hysterical edge. "Let me go. She needs me.''

"I need you.''

"You're an adult, Richard. You're—''

Suddenly, she realized the truth. It wasn't just feeding time and diaper duty that Richard didn't participate in. The events of the past weeks ran through her head, like one of the filmstrips they used to show in history class. He'd hardly even held Emma. He didn't go to her when he arrived home from work, didn't inquire about her day or her many firsts.

Kate brought a hand to her mouth. He hardly ever even looked at her.

Stunned, hurt beyond words, Kate turned and ran up the stairs to the nursery. She scooped up Emma and cradled her in her arms. The minute she did, the infant's cries lessened and she began rooting for a nipple.

"Here's Mommy,'' Kate murmured, carrying her to the rocker and settling into it. "Everything's okay now. Everything's going to be fine.'' She offered the bottle, and Emma latched on, sucking vigorously, gluttonously, as if she had been deprived of food for days instead of just hours.

After a moment, Kate looked up. Richard stood in

the doorway watching her, his expression so lost it hurt her to look at him.

"What's going on with you, Richard? Don't you—" Tears choked her and she fought them back, fought to clear her throat. "Do you wish...do you regret us having..."

She couldn't say the words. She feared the answer.

He said them for her. "Do I regret us having adopted her?"

"Yes."

He looked away, then back. "How could I? It's just that...this is a huge adjustment. It's..." He took a deep breath. "Suddenly you're completely involved with the baby and I'm...I'm just hanging out here. Taking up space."

"Because you're not involved with the baby. You need to be. If you were, you'd feel differently. You'd feel a part of her and what's happening to our lives."

"I know." He passed a hand wearily across his face. "I've been so busy, with new cases at the firm, with the campaign." He swore softly. "I'm sorry, Kate. You know I don't take change well. And this one's been a doozy."

She laughed at that. It was true; he didn't enjoy change. She, on the other hand, welcomed it with open arms. He would come around. Of course he would.

"I suppose that's why God gave most couples nine months to adjust to impending parenthood."

He crossed to the rocker and knelt down beside it. "Thanks for being so great." He kissed the baby's head, then Kate's hand. "It's going to get better, love. I'm going to hire someone to help me with campaign work, I'm going to adjust." He lifted his face to hers. "Never stop loving me, okay? Not even when I'm behaving like a horse's ass."

She smiled through her tears. "Not even then."

21

Long after Emma had fallen asleep and Kate had gone to bed, Richard sat in the rocking chair in Emma's nursery, staring at the crib. The room was dark save for the soft glow of the night-light, and every so often the infant would stir and whimper, then fall silent again.

Richard passed a hand over his brow, weary and disheartened. Tonight, for Kate, he had gone through the motions with Emma. He had held and rocked her; he'd given her her bedtime bottle and even changed her diaper. Or tried, anyway; he had been all thumbs at that.

Kate had watched him, flushed with pleasure. With happiness and pride. Emma, too, had seemed pleased with his attention. She had kicked and gurgled and waved her arms. And when he had fed her, she had looked up at him with wide, trusting blue eyes.

With eyes, a gaze, designed to melt the coldest heart.

It hadn't melted his.

What the hell was wrong with him?

Richard stood and crossed to the crib. He gazed intently down at the child for long moments. His daughter, he reminded himself. His. And Kate's.

So, why didn't he feel anything but anger? Anything but resentment and failure?

Because he had always gotten everything he wanted. Had always been the one in control, the one who made things happen. It had been the way of his life; was the way he expected his life to be.

Not this time. This time he hadn't gotten what he wanted, he hadn't been able to control the situation, mold it to his liking. He'd been told no. And he didn't like it. Not one damn bit.

Unable to look at the child a moment more, he left the nursery. After making certain Kate was still asleep, he retrieved the bottle of Jack Daniel's and a glass from the bar and went to his study. There, he poured himself a shot, tossed the drink back, then poured another.

Richard crossed to the French doors that led out to the first-floor gallery, pushed aside the drape and gazed out at the black night. He swore under his breath. At first he'd watched Kate and Emma with pleasure and affection. They made a charming picture; he had been warmed by Kate's obvious happiness.

But as the days and weeks had passed, he'd found himself becoming resentful and jealous. Of the time Kate devoted to Emma. Of her obvious and complete love for the child.

He had found himself wishing the baby would just…disappear. That he would wake up one morning and find that adopting Emma had been nothing but a disturbing dream and that he had his old life back. His wife back.

What did those thoughts say about him? About his character?

He pressed the heels of his hands to his eyes, disgusted with himself and his thoughts. With the answer.

He felt like a snake. A loser. A failure.

He could never tell Kate the truth. Not about this. It would devastate her. She wouldn't understand. She would never look at him the same way again.

He couldn't bear to lose her.

He dropped his hands. If only he felt like a father. If only he looked at Emma and got all gooey-eyed with love or puffed up with pride. If only he didn't look at her and remember his own failure. That he hadn't been able to impregnate Kate. That he hadn't been able to give his wife the one thing she'd wanted more than anything.

He shot blanks, he reminded himself bitterly. He was half a man.

Unable to bear his own thoughts a moment more, he opened the French door and stepped out onto the gallery. The midnight air was cold; it went straight to his head, clearing it. He breathed deeply, several times, releasing the pent-up breath in a rush.

It was the change in their lives causing him to feel unsettled and resentful, he told himself for the umpteenth time. The alteration of their life-styles. His feelings for Emma would deepen. Soften. They would. He was an adult, a good person; he could make that happen.

He *would* make it happen.

And when he did, everything would once again be as it should be between him and Kate. He would be in control of their lives.

And he and Kate would be happy again.

22

From her vantage point at the sidewalk café across the street, Julianna watched the employees pour out of Nicholson, Bedico, Chaney & Ryan. They laughed and joked with one another, some paired off, obviously heading for an after-work get-together, others called cheery good-nights as they hurried to their cars.

In the ten weeks since the baby had been born, Julianna had been busy. She had mastered Kate's smile and laugh, the cadence of her speech. She had practiced her walk until it had become second nature, had shopped for clothes and accessories Kate would choose, scouring the discount store racks until she found a few good, select items. She'd had her hair cut and styled to replicate Kate's. She had worked out until ready to drop with exhaustion, firming muscles gone slack during pregnancy.

Now she was ready for the next step, the one that would take her that much closer to her destiny.

That much closer to Richard.

Julianna's heart began to pound with anticipation. These past weeks, keeping her distance from him had been agony. Waiting for the right moment to meet him, using caution and reason when all she had wanted to do was throw both to the wind and be with him, had been the hardest thing she had ever done. She loved him beyond reason. Desired him in a way that left her weak and trembling and desperate.

In her dreams they had been together. She had spent her nights making love with him, acting out her every fantasy of their future together. In the mornings she had awakened with the sheets tangled around her legs, her pillow wet with tears of longing.

And regret. That the night had ended. That once again Richard would be away from her, in her heart but not her arms.

Though it had been agony, reason had won out. Julianna had played it smart, had held back, carefully weighing the pros and cons of where they should meet the first time. A chance meeting in a bar, through his country club or at the health club, had all been considered and discarded. None of those would allow her the opportunity to insinuate herself into his life and his affections.

No, she and Richard had to meet through the professional arena, she had decided, most likely through his law firm. To do that, she needed an ''in'' at his firm. Someone who would vouch for her; someone he trusted who would introduce them.

That's where *she* came in. Her girl.

Julianna returned her attention to Nicholson, Bedico, Chaney & Ryan and the employees emerging from the building. This was the five o'clock crowd, the secretaries, assistants, and other clock-punching, working stiffs.

Richard never left work at five. None of the partners did. They either left early or much later. It was a sign of their status within the firm, of their importance.

Julianna had quickly learned the firm's hierarchy. It hadn't been difficult. Most people didn't realize how much they revealed to the world without saying a word. Things like, what their station in life was. How they felt about themselves. Whether they were liked or loners, meek or aggressive.

The partners strode with purpose; they held themselves in a way that shouted their exalted place in the world. They wore expensive, impeccably cut suits; gold glinted at their wrists. The partners, she had learned, either left work with one of the other partners or an overworked assistant, one frantically scribbling notes while struggling to keep up with their boss's long, purposeful stride.

Julianna sipped her soft drink, searching for her girl. Finally, she spotted her. She emerged from the building and scurried down the front steps. As if eager to catch up with her co-workers. As if afraid that if she didn't she would miss an invitation to an after hours tête-à-tête.

She caught up with the group; none seemed to notice.

Julianna felt almost sorry for the young woman. It was pathetic, really. To be so hungry for attention. To be so obvious about it.

Julianna took another sip of her drink, studying the other woman. She didn't appear to be that much older than Julianna. She had straight, brown hair of a medium length and wore wire-rimmed glasses. She carried a briefcase in an attempt, Julianna suspected, to look like a higher-up instead of an underling. She wore ill-fitting suits, ones she had no doubt chosen to look more professional, older and smarter. Instead, they emphasized the opposite. She looked woefully out of place, like a lost little girl wearing her mother's clothes.

Pathetic, Julianna thought again. A dowdy-looking wanna-be. Wanna-be more than the secretary she was. Wanna-be liked. Accepted. Part of the group. Popular. *No doubt about it. She was the one.*

For days now, Julianna had watched her. She always left the firm alone. As the others streamed around her, chatting and making plans, she kept her head down save for the surreptitious, hungry glances she sent them. Glances the others either didn't notice or chose to ignore.

Julianna laid two dollars on the table, stood and left the restaurant. She followed her girl at a comfortable distance, unconcerned with hurrying—she knew she parked her car in the lot around the corner, that she lived in an apartment in Covington, and that she spent almost every evening alone at a coffee café called Bottom of the Cup.

That's where they would become friends, Julianna had decided. Best friends. Starting tonight.

23

Bottom of the Cup was one of those places where singles went to meet each other, the nineties version of the pickup bar. The specialty of the house was caffeine instead of alcohol, the music folksy rather than frenetic, and smoking an absolute no-no.

It was also a place where the terminally unlikable could sit alone but hopeful without seeming too out of place or too desperate.

In the time Julianna had been tailing her girl, the closest the woman had come to meeting someone had been when a guy at the next table had asked her to pass a couple packs of sugar.

Julianna smiled. Her girl's luck was about to change.

"Hi," Julianna said, stopping beside her table. "How do you like it?"

The young woman looked up from her book, her expression stunned. "Are you talking to me?"

"Of course I am, silly." Julianna held up her copy of *Dead Drop*, purchased an hour ago and in anticipation of tonight. "I'm reading Luke Dallas's new book, too. What do you think?"

Color crept up the other woman's cheeks. "I like it a lot. Though I don't usually read this kind of fiction. I like books that are a little more substantial."

Julianna didn't have a clue what she meant by that, but smiled brightly. "Me, too. Can I join you?"

"Sure."

Julianna set down her coffee and book, then took the seat opposite the other woman. "I'm Julianna."

"I'm Sandy Derricks. It's nice to meet you."

Julianna reached for a packet of sugar and added it to her café mocha, then glanced at Sandy's cup, feigning surprise. "Look, we like the same coffee." She leaned toward her conspiratorially. "We're practically sisters. So tell me, Sis, what other books do you like to read?"

Looking embarrassed but pleased, Sandy rattled off a list of authors and books, none of whom Julianna recognized. She sipped her coffee, pretending interest, her mind running ahead to what she would say next and how she would work Nicholson, Bedico, Chaney & Ryan into the conversation.

She found her opportunity a short time later. "I really appreciate your letting me sit with you," she said. "I'm new in town and don't know anybody. I haven't even found a job yet."

"Really? I've lived here all my life. Well, not here. In New Orleans. I moved over here because of a job opportunity."

"No kidding." Julianna brought the cup of oversweet coffee to her lips. "Where do you work?"

"At a law firm. Nicholson, Bedico, Chaney & Ryan." She sat up a bit straighter, obviously proud. "I'm Chas Bedico's assistant. He's one of the partners."

Julianna widened her eyes. "Wow, lucky you. I'd kill for a job like that." She sighed with exaggerated frustration. "I sure hope I find something soon."

After that, they chatted about nothing for a long time. Finally, her coffee long gone, Julianna glanced at her watch. "I can't believe the time. I guess I'd better go." She stood. "You want to meet again tomorrow?"

"Tomorrow?" Sandy repeated. "Me and you?"

The other woman looked so disbelieving, Julianna had to force back a smile. "Why not?" She lifted a shoulder. "What do you say we meet here, at eight o'clock? We'll talk about the book some more."

24

Kate sat in her office at The Bean. Though still on maternity leave, she had popped in to tally the time sheets and do payroll. On the desk in front of her lay the Tulane Alumni Association's invitation to Luke's lecture and book signing. Unbeknownst to Richard, she had dug it out of the kitchen trash. She wasn't sure why she hadn't told him. Perhaps because she had known he wouldn't understand, that he would react with unreasonable and unsubstantiated jealousy, that he would claim Luke's friendship didn't matter to him and try to intimidate her into letting it die.

But Luke's friendship did matter to her. She missed it. She missed him. She wanted the opportunity to patch things up. She wanted the opportunity to tell him how sorry she was for...everything.

She reached for the phone, thought better of it and drew her hand back. She had already called him three times, had already left three messages, the last pleading with him to meet with her and Richard when he came to town.

He'd returned none of them.

His silence was her answer. Luke didn't want her friendship. He didn't need it, or her, anymore. He didn't want her in his life, he had made that clear.

Let it go, she told herself. *Let him go.*

She pushed away from her desk, and crossed to

Emma, asleep in her car carrier in the corner. Kate smiled, feeling lucky—not to have to choose between a job and motherhood, not to have to leave her child every day. She would have hated that, would have hated missing her smiles, her many firsts, seconds and thirds.

The way Richard did.

She thought of Richard. Since their argument over leftover pizza and Emma a couple of weeks ago, he had been away in the evenings much more than usual. But when he'd been home, to her great relief, he had doted on Emma. He seemed to finally be taking pleasure in his daughter, in being a father.

Becoming parents had been a huge adjustment for them both. Stressful. Anxiety producing. She shook her head. Even wonderful life changes caused stress. She knew that. The problem was, she'd had her eyes focused for so long on the dream of becoming a mother, the ramifications of the actual event had blindsided her.

Kate returned to her desk and the waiting time sheets. Her gaze fell once again on the invitation. As it did, her thoughts returned to Luke. Would he enjoy being a father? she wondered. She knew from the bio on his books that he was still single. Had he ever wanted to marry? Did he long to be a parent, to share his life with children, as she and Richard had?

Fat chance, she decided, smiling to herself. A big success now, brushing elbows with Hollywood, no doubt the last thing he wanted was a wife and kids. He was probably dating some twenty-year-old starlet, for heaven's sake.

"Kate?"

She lifted her gaze. Marilyn stood grinning in the doorway. "What's up?"

"Not a thing. While we were in a lull, I thought I'd come and chat. I've missed having you around."

"Come on in." Kate smiled and pushed aside the time sheets. "I wasn't getting much done anyway."

"I saw that." Marilyn made herself comfortable in the chair in front of Kate's desk. "You looked like you were a million miles away."

"I confess, I am a little preoccupied." Kate glanced down at Luke's invitation, then back up at the other woman. "Have you ever lost a really good friend? Someone whose friendship was important to you? Really important?"

"Yeah, I suppose. I had a couple really good girlfriends in high school. We were as close as sisters. But we drifted apart after graduation."

"Do you miss them?"

"Not them, no. But I do miss what we had."

"Ever thought of calling them, of getting together again?"

"We actually did. We met and had lunch." One corner of Marilyn's mouth lifted in a rueful smile. "It wasn't the same. We didn't have anything in common anymore." She shrugged. "We kind of sat there, wishing we had something to say. Struggling to find some common ground to latch on to."

"Did you ever find anything?"

"The past. That's all there was." Marilyn met Kate's eyes. "Why the trip down Memory Lane?"

"An old friend," she said, picking up the invitation and handing it to Marilyn. "He's going to be in town, and I'd love to see him."

"You know Luke Dallas? *The* Luke Dallas?" She

tipped her head, studying his press photo. "He's so cute."

"We went to Tulane together. He, Richard and I were really good friends. The best of friends."

She handed the invitation back. "So, what's the problem?"

"We had a fight right before graduation and haven't spoken since." Kate sighed. "I don't know if it's becoming a parent or what, but it's been gnawing at me lately. I want to try to repair the rift. I need to."

"And since he's going to be in New Orleans, you see it as the perfect opportunity."

"I do. He, obviously, feels differently. I've left three messages, he hasn't returned one of them."

Marilyn said nothing for a long moment. She sat, eyebrows drawn together in thought. Finally, she met Kate's eyes. "If this is that important to you, why are you asking his permission?"

"What do you mean?"

"You've got an invitation. It's a free country. Just go."

"You mean, just show up at the signing?"

"Why not? Force a confrontation. Get right in his face and make him listen to you."

"But what if he—"

"Blows you off?" she supplied. "Sends you on your way?"

"Yes." Kate clasped her hands together, feeling like a kid instead of a grown woman with a child. "I'd hate that. It'd be so...humiliating."

"At least you'd know you tried. At least you could say you did all you could to repair the friendship." Marilyn stood and started toward the door. When she reached it, she stopped and looked back at Kate. "Think about it. After all, what do you have to lose?"

25

_____

She had nothing to lose, Kate decided, and the following Saturday morning, after Richard left for his golf game, she got herself and Emma dressed and off to Luke's signing. Forty minutes later she was back home, juggling a squirming Emma in her arms as she fumbled to fit her house key into the front door lock. She finally did, opened the door and stepped inside.

Emma squealed in delight, and Kate made a sound of exasperation. "Why today, you little stinker? Are you deliberately trying to make me miss the signing?"

The infant beamed at her in response, and Kate shook her head and hurried to her bedroom. That morning, in anticipation of seeing Luke for the first time in more than ten years, she had taken extra care with her appearance. She had chosen a chamois-colored linen jacket and trousers and a short-sleeved silk shirt.

She had been halfway across the Causeway when Emma had thrown up. Not any old puke, but a major, bypass the bib, all over her clothes, upchuck. Always prepared for this not unusual occurrence, Kate carried an extra set of clothes for Emma everywhere she went. She had swung into one of the crossovers, and gone around to change Emma.

One small problem. She hadn't brought another set of clothes for herself and just as she had gotten Emma looking picture perfect again, her daughter had decided once was not enough and had decorated the front of Kate's blouse.

She'd had two choices: go to the book signing wearing a blouse with baby puke stains decorating the front or turn back.

So, here she was.

Kate reached the bedroom and laid Emma on the bed. The infant smiled and waved her arms and legs in delight. "Oh sure, now you're happy, troublemaker."

Emma's response was her rendition of a laugh, a kind of low hum followed by a popping sound.

Kate couldn't help but laugh. "Okay, so we're going to be late. Big deal. Less time waiting in line."

After slipping out of her jacket, she crossed to the closet, unbuttoning her blouse as she went. The mirrored doors were slightly ajar; she slid them the rest of the way open. As she reached for another blouse, she caught a glimpse of the bed, reflected in one of the doors.

It was slightly rumpled, as if someone had lain on it. She moved her gaze to the pillows. Both bore the imprint of a head.

She frowned. *That wasn't right.*

She had made the bed moments before hurrying out of the house. Hadn't she? She searched her memory. Admittedly, she had been flustered. Nervous at the prospect of seeing Luke again, worrying about what she would say to him when she did. Richard had already left; she remembered fluffing the pillows and tossing them into place, then rushing out the door with Emma.

She hadn't even sat on the bed after she'd made it. She certainly hadn't lain down.

Someone had been in her house. Someone who had not been invited. A stranger. They had reclined on her bed, had pressed their face into her pillow, into Richard's.

Kate shuddered, surveying the room. Nothing else appeared out of order. She shook her head, feeling slightly off-kilter. She had to be imagining things. Why would someone break into her house and take nothing? And how could they have gotten in and out so quickly? She hadn't even been gone an hour.

She crossed to the bed, bent and ran a hand over the spread, smoothing it. As she straightened, her gaze landed on an edge of something shiny and pink peeking out from underneath the bed.

One of her padded, satin hangers, she realized. One of the ones she hung her good lingerie on. She frowned. Now, how had that gotten there? She retrieved it and started for the closet.

Again she stopped, a sensation like ice water sliding down her spine. She turned back toward the bed, staring at the space between the floor and the edge of the frame.

A space deep enough for a grown man to hide under.

Even as she told herself to grab Emma and run, Kate walked toward the bed, heart pounding. She glanced at the now quiet Emma. The infant watched her every move, her gaze wide and solemn, as if she, too, felt something was amiss.

Kate reached the bed. She bent and reached for the dust ruffle. She lifted it and peered underneath.

The phone rang.

Kate screamed and sprang away from the bed. Startled, Emma let out a wail of terror. Kate scooped her up, cradling her to her chest and cooing softly.

The recorder answered on the fourth ring; a moment later Richard's mother's voice echoed through the house. Kate let out a breath she hadn't even realized she held and rested her head against Emma's. No one like Mom Ryan to bring her back down to earth.

Kate laughed self-consciously. What an imagination. There had been nothing under the bed but a couple of dust bunnies and a pair of Richard's socks.

Of course, there hadn't been. What had she expected to find? Or who? The bogeyman? A murderer or rapist? This was Mandeville, for Pete's sake. What was wrong with her?

It was nerves. Over seeing Luke. Over what she would say and how he would respond.

She glanced at her watch and muttered an oath. If she didn't leave soon, her worrying would be for naught—the signing would be over and Luke long gone.

Emma calmed, Kate hurried to the closet. She grabbed the blouse hanging smack in front of her, slipped it on, fastened the buttons and tucked it into her linen trousers. With one last look at the bed, she lifted Emma and hurried out of the house.

26

The Tulane University bookstore manager ushered Luke and his publicist to a table set up in the middle of the store. A wide path had been cleared from the table to the store's double glass doors. Copies of *Dead Drop* were stacked on and under the table and racked on the surrounding displays. Off to the right, a book cart was weighted down with several dozen cartons stamped with Luke's publisher's name and the book's title.

Luke stared at their number, aghast. He'd never seen so many copies of one of his books in the same place.

"I hope we ordered enough," the manager said, looking flustered. "Some of those people have been waiting two hours already. They're not going to be happy to leave with an IOU."

Luke shifted his gaze to the bookstore's glass front and the mob of people waiting outside. All those people were here for him? He had thought they were here to buy concert tickets or something.

"Hot damn," Helena, his publicist, muttered. "I think I just creamed my jeans."

Luke laughed. The ever-raunchy, slightly cynical publicist was gazing at the glass doors and the crowd beyond, all but gloating with pleasure.

"You know what this means, don't you?" She

squeezed his arm, not taking her eyes from the throng of readers. "You've *arrived*, Mr. Dallas. This kind of crowd only shows for a brand author—Clancy, King— those guys. Or for celebrities. This is better than sex, I swear to God."

Luke shook his head, too amazed to speak. It wasn't so long ago that he'd sat in a mall bookstore, copies of his novel piled on the table in front of him, signing one or two during the entire two-hour event and being grateful for it. It wasn't so far in the past that he couldn't remember the rush of anticipation when a customer would approach his table; then the disappointment when they'd asked him if he knew where the bathroom was. Or where Clancy was shelved. Or if the new Grisham was in.

"Play it as cool as you want, Mr. Macho," she whispered as they took their seats behind the table. "I know you're so pleased you could piss your pants about now."

Luke sent his publicist an amused glance from the corners of his eyes. "Piss my pants? Helena, isn't that a bit crude, even for you?"

She leaned toward him, eyes alight with humor. "I'm a New Yorker. So fuck off."

He laughed. Crude or not, it was true. For a writer, nothing could compete with the high of knowing your books were being read and enjoyed. Not even a fat royalty check was as satisfying as a glowing letter from a fan, though he had to admit, the checks didn't hurt a bit.

The store manager opened the door; the crowd descended. For the next hour and a half, Luke signed one book after another. Helena and the store manager assisted him by handing him books, already opened to the title page.

The crowd was friendly; Luke's only regret was not having time to chat with each reader. There was no time for such pleasantries, not if he didn't want a riot at the back of the line.

Which was in sight. Luke glanced up, trying to calculate whether there would be enough books to go around and how long it would be before he could give his hand a break. His fingers had begun to cramp.

The line shifted, moved forward, parted. And there she was, the most beautiful face in a sea of faces, instantly recognizable to him even though it had been at least ten years since he had last seen her. He caught his breath; his mind went momentarily blank, then flooded with but one thought, one stunning realization: *Kate was here.*

Helena leaned slightly toward him. "God, I need a cigarette. Mind if I slip away for a minute?"

Luke blinked, crashing back to the moment, where he was, what he was supposed to be doing. A reader stood in front of the table, her expression expectant. He smiled, asked her name, autographed a book to her, then greeted the next reader in line.

He looked at his publicist. "What did you say?"

"A smoke. Mind if go for one?"

"Not at all." He shook his head and returned his gaze to the end of the line and Kate. He saw that she wasn't alone. She had a baby on her shoulder. A girl, judging by the pink romper she wore. *Richard's baby.* He steeled himself against the way that made him feel, against the quick kick of resentment. Against the something that smacked of jealousy.

He drew his eyebrows together, mustering indignation and what he told himself was anger. Didn't she get it? There was a reason he hadn't answered any of her messages. He hadn't wanted her here. He didn't want to see her.

Liar. He'd wanted to see her too much.

Luke forced himself to focus not on her, but on the job he had to do. On this triumphant moment. He smiled, signed his name and told himself Kate was just another reader, that he would treat her as such. When she reached the front of the line, he would sign her book and send her on her way.

That moment came sooner than he would have liked. She stood before him, looking flushed and nervous and hopeful. It was the last that affected him most.

She smiled. "Hello, Luke."

"Kate." He kept his tone impersonal. The store manager slid him a copy of *Dead Drop*. "How would you like this inscribed?"

Her smile faltered, the baby squirmed in her arms. "To Kate and Richard, whose friendship once meant the world to me."

She had never pulled her punches; had never danced around the truth or issues. It was one of the many things he had admired about her. Now, he found himself angry at her brass. He did as she requested anyway and handed her the book.

"I'd hoped we could talk," she said, dropping the book into her stroller and jiggling her baby, who had begun to protest in earnest now.

"This is hardly the time or place."

"I know. There's a la Madeline at the corner of St. Charles and Carrollton Avenue. Could we meet there, after the signing?'' The line stirred behind her, growing impatient. ''Please, Luke.''

Refuse and send her on her way.

He expelled a quick, frustrated breath instead. ''I'll be a while yet. Another hour, maybe more.''

''I'll wait for you.''

He looked away from her, then back. ''I'll try. No promises, though.''

She nodded, and he watched her walk away, thinking of the past and promises and a time when he'd thought he couldn't live without her.

In the end, Luke couldn't not meet her. He told himself he was doing it for closure, so he could get her out of his life and system, once and for all. He told himself that after today, Kate Ryan would be a permanent part of his past.

That wasn't the way it felt, however, when he walked into the French bakery-café an hour and a half later. It wasn't the way *he* felt. No, as he stepped into the restaurant and sought her out with his gaze, he felt twenty again and madly in love with a girl who didn't love him in return.

The feeling rankled, and Luke stiffened his spine and crossed to where she sat, feeding her baby a bottle.

Kate lifted her gaze. ''I didn't think you'd show.''

He slipped into the booth across from her. ''I wasn't going to.''

''But you're here.'' She eased the empty bottle from her baby's mouth, then brought the infant to her shoulder and began patting her back. ''Why?''

''Morbid curiosity.''

''Funny.''

''I'm not laughing.''

For a moment she sat frozen, then a ghost of a smile touched her mouth. "You always were brutally honest."

"I'm thirsty," he said, standing. "You want anything?"

"A coffee refill. Thanks."

He went to the counter, got Kate's coffee and a Coke for himself, then returned to the table. She had burped her baby and was carefully transferring the now sleeping infant to the car carrier. That done, she snapped the child's harness into place, then tucked a soft-looking blanket around her.

"She's beautiful," he said, setting the drinks on the table. "Congratulations."

"Thank you." Kate's lips lifted. "Her name's Emma."

"Motherhood suits you." Though he said the words easily, he felt like he would choke on them, they were so bitter, so grudging. "Richard must be...pleased." *More like, so puffed up with pride he resembled one of the Macy's Thanksgiving Day parade balloons.*

She hesitated. "Of course he is."

"In that chatty Christmas letter you sent, you didn't mention being pregnant."

"I wasn't." She paused. "Emma's adopted."

The words landed between them, begging an explanation, begging for him to ask what had led her and Richard to adoption. Instead, he looked her dead in the eyes. "What do you want, Kate?"

"To see you. Is that so strange? We were once the best of friends."

"Years ago. A lifetime ago. We're not a part of each other's world anymore."

"I know. I—" She bit the words off and fussed

with her baby a moment, smoothing and retucking the blanket. Then she met his gaze once more. "I regret that. I miss you, Luke. I miss our friendship."

He felt her words like a kick to his gut. "Stop it, Kate."

"It's true. You don't know. You—" She drew in a deep, shaky breath. "I wanted to see you. I wanted to try to make you understand how it was. What happened."

"I know what happened. I was there, Kate." He flexed his fingers, furious suddenly. So angry he shook. "Or have you forgotten?"

She swallowed hard but didn't look away. "I haven't forgotten anything, Luke. Not one moment."

Her words stung. As did the rush of hope. He hated that she could still affect him this way, after all these years.

"What are you telling me?" he asked, his voice hard, insulting. "Richard's not enough anymore? That you need a good screw with somebody else?" He leaned toward her, shaking with anger. "That you feel like repeating the past?"

She recoiled at his words, her expression wounded. "You know better than that. You know *me* better than that."

"Do I?"

"I'm sorry, Luke. I'm sorry I hurt you." Her eyes flooded with tears. "I'm sorry I killed our friendship."

"I'm sorry, too." He stood. "But you did. And it's too late to go back."

"Wait! Please!" She caught his hand. "That night…when we were together…it wasn't a ruse. I was devastated. Richard had broken up with me again. I'd vowed it would be for the last time. I'd vowed that

I wouldn't take him back, not again, no matter how many flowers he sent. We were through, I believed that. I turned to you because—''

"You used me. To make Richard jealous. To get back at him for the blonde. The many blondes." He shook off her hand. "Well, it worked. I hope you're happy with the life you angled for."

"That's not true! None of it." She lifted her face to his. "Please, Luke, just hear me out."

Emma stirred and released a small, whimpering cry. Luke sank back to the booth and nodded tersely. "Say your piece, but do it quick."

"The next morning, Richard came to see me. The way he always did, tail tucked between his legs. I told him we were through, that I'd had enough. He begged me to forgive him, Luke. *Begged me*. And he cried. He loved me, he said. He wanted to marry me. He wanted us to be together forever."

"And you crumbled?" Luke snapped his fingers. "Just like that?"

"I loved him, had loved him for years. Marrying him was what I'd dreamed of for so long. How could I not forgive him?"

"How?" The word roared past Luke's lips. "By remembering where you'd spent the night before. By remembering the promises you made to me."

"I didn't make you any promises. I—"

"That's bullshit, Kate. You slept with me. That meant something. To a girl like you, it meant something. We talked about Richard. The past, our future."

"I'm sorry." She clasped her hands together. "If I could take that night back, I would. Don't you know how often I've wished I could? I wasn't thinking clearly—I acted irresponsibly. I hurt you, our friendship. Richard.''

Luke made a sound of fury. ''Don't tell me how you hurt Richard. Did it ever occur to you that Richard knew where you were that night? That he knew about us? Didn't you ever wonder why he asked you to marry him that morning?''

''What are you saying? That Richard proposed to me to spite you? To beat you?''

''Think about it. Richard was obsessed with winning. He couldn't bear to lose, not ever. But particularly to me.''

''No.'' Kate shook her head, the color draining from her face. ''That's not the way it was. He proposed because he loved me. Because, just like he said, he didn't want to…to…''

Her words trailed off; Luke smiled. ''He didn't want to *lose* you. Isn't that what you had been about to say?''

''That's not what I meant.''

''Think back to the times Richard and I almost came to blows over things as inconsequential as tennis matches or hands of poker—to the competition over grades. He was not about to be bested by me, poor scholarship student, worthless dreamer. I know how he laughed about my dreams of being a novelist.'' Luke leaned across the table, eyes narrowed. ''Who's laughing now?''

''It's not true,'' she whispered, eyes bright with tears. ''That's the way *you* might have felt, but not Richard.''

''How can you look me in the eye and lie this way?''

''He's my husband. We have a good marriage. A

happy one. Marrying me had nothing to do with some adolescent competition with you.''

''Whatever gets you through the night, babe.''

This time it was Kate who stood, who prepared to leave. And Luke who grabbed her hand, stopping her. He looked her dead in the eyes. ''And what about you, Kate? Did you say yes to Richard because you loved him? Or because you loved the cushy future you would have with him?''

''Let me go.''

''Not until you answer me.''

''Why are you doing this?''

''You wanted honesty, sweetheart. You wanted to dredge up the past. Well, here it is, in all its glory.''

For a moment she simply stared at him. In her eyes he saw her hurt, that he had wounded her deeply. He felt a moment of regret. In that moment he wished he could take it back, all of it, every word.

Then he reminded himself of the way she had used him, and he firmed his resolve. He dropped his hand. ''See, sometimes the past is better left alone.''

''Yes,'' she whispered, ''I do see now. I won't trouble you again.'' She collected her things, then lifted her baby carrier. She met his eyes once more. ''You never used to be mean, Luke. You are now. I'm sorry about that.''

''Haven't you heard? Nice guys finish last.''

''You were never last in my book, Luke. *Never.*''

And then she walked away, out of his life, head held high. Luke watched her go, ignoring the feeling of loss that settled over him, the urge to chase after her.

Kate Ryan was now a permanent part of his past.

27

Late that afternoon, exhausted and heartsick, Kate arrived home. Richard was still out, thank goodness. She didn't know what she was going to say to him about today, about her meeting with Luke.

She sighed and dropped her keys onto the entryway table, shifting her sleeping daughter in her arms. Richard had assumed she was going into The Bean; she hadn't told him otherwise. If he had known about her plans, he would have been angry and jealous, he would have insisted she not go.

Kate sighed. She had been so certain she was doing the right thing, so certain that tonight she would be telling Richard how she had repaired the rift in her, Luke's and his friendship, certain that she would be feeling so pleased and proud of herself.

Now, she wished she had told him. Now, she felt like a fool. An optimistic, naive idiot. Some things couldn't be changed. They couldn't be made better by time or good intentions. Just as some wounds never healed, they festered instead.

Emma whimpered and snuggled closer to Kate's shoulder, trying to get comfortable. It had been a long day for them both, Kate thought, carrying Emma to her nursery. She laid her carefully in the crib, then as quietly as possible, raised the guard rail. Through it all, Emma didn't even stir.

Kate drew in a deep, shuddering breath and curled her fingers around the crib rail, gazing down at her sleeping daughter, at her beautiful, peaceful face. It wasn't true, what Luke had said to her about Richard's reason for proposing to her. They had been married for ten years. They were happy. They had a good marriage. The kind built on love, not on some juvenile competition. He took his wedding vows seriously, just as she did.

Kate turned away from the crib and busied herself straightening the nursery. She had left in such a hurry that morning, she hadn't had a chance to clean up from her and Emma's play.

She bent, collecting the rattles, shakers and stuffies from the play mat, then carried them to the basket she kept for them next to the rocking chair. Her mind drifted once more to her confrontation with Luke, to the things he'd said. And what of herself? she wondered. Had she been motivated by something other than love? By greed, as Luke had suggested?

She dropped the toys into the basket. He thought she was a gold digger. That she had married Richard for his money, for his standing in the community.

Tears pricked at her eyes, and she made a sound of annoyance, struggling to remember, to go back to that thrilling but tumultuous time of her life. To recall her feelings and examine them. All of them. Honestly.

She had loved Richard. She had loved him from the moment she met him. Sure, he had behaved badly sometimes. He'd been young and cocksure and accustomed to having his way. And yes, he had broken her heart more than once.

But even with his faults, she had longed to marry him; she had prayed he would ask her. Because dating

him had been thrilling. Because most of the time, he
had been charming and attentive, fun-loving and gen-
erous. He had made her feel special. And cared for.

Had his money, his affluence and influential family
colored her feelings for him? Sure they had, Kate admitted. How could they not? They were a part of who
Richard was. That didn't mean she hadn't loved him.
It didn't mean she was a gold digger.

Kate crossed to the baby's dresser and began
straightening the framed photos and knickknacks that
decorated its top. She frowned. Her favorite photo was
missing. The one of Richard holding Emma her first
day home.

She looked on the floor, behind the dresser, in the
crib. When she didn't find it in any of those places,
she stopped in the middle of the room, hand on hips,
frowning. It had to be here. She had looked at it this
morning, after Richard left for the club.

She brought a hand to her head, trying to remember.
She and Emma had been in here, playing on the quilt.
Richard had come in to say goodbye; she had stood
and kissed him. As she had turned to return to Emma,
the photograph had caught her eye, and she'd smiled.

So, where was the photo now?

From the hallway outside the nursery came the
creak of a floorboard. A soft whoosh, like a soft breath
being expelled.

Kate froze, suddenly, completely terrified. She
brought a hand to her throat, her mind filling with the
image of her bed from that morning, of the indenta-
tions in the pillow. Of her lingerie hanger peeking out
from under the bed.

She turned slowly to face the doorway. And found

it empty. Legs shaking, she crossed to the door and peered out into the hallway. It, too, was empty.

"Richard?" she called. "Is that you?"

Silence answered her. She held her breath, straining to hear the slightest sound, a stirring or a rustle, even as she told herself she was being silly. Old houses creaked. They groaned and sighed.

But photographs didn't go missing on their own. Hangers didn't walk from the closet to the bed.

She wasn't alone.

Heart thundering, Kate crossed to the crib and picked up her daughter, careful not to jostle her. The infant moaned and stirred, then snuggled into Kate, still deeply asleep.

Kate carried her out of the room and toward the front of the house, moving as quietly as she could. She had left the car carrier and diaper bag in the foyer. She reached it and hands shaking, squatted beside the carrier and gently laid Emma in it. She snapped the harness, then stood and turned toward the door.

A man stood just beyond the beveled glass, a dark silhouette against the gathering dusk. She made a sound, high and surprised, and took an involuntary step backward.

"Kate?" The man rapped on the door. "It's Joe, from around the corner."

She brought a trembling hand to her mouth and laughed, feeling both relieved and foolish. Old Joe, as everyone in the neighborhood called him, was eighty if he was a day and more than a bit of a busybody. He was also about as harmless as a person could be.

"You startled me," she said, crossing to the door. She opened it. "I was just leaving."

"Sorry about that." He glanced past her, into the house. "Nothing wrong, is there?"

As he asked the question she realized how silly she had been behaving, how she had let her imagination run away with her. The house creaked and she'd been ready to run for the hills. "Of course not." She laughed again, her cheeks warming. "Come on in."

He stepped across the threshold and glanced around. "Richard's not home from his golf game yet?"

She bit back a smile. "Not yet. He was going into work straight from the course. Did you need to speak to him?"

"Nope." He drew his bushy eyebrows together. "How's the baby?"

"Fine." She motioned toward the carrier. "Sound asleep."

"Sorry to hear the pretty little thing was ill. What did the doctor say?"

Kate shook her head, confused. "She hasn't been... Where'd you hear that, Joe?"

"From your friend. This morning. She said you'd gone to the doctor with the baby."

"Friend?" Kate repeated, searching her memory. "Someone from The Uncommon Bean?"

"The friend who was visiting. She was on your swing, waiting for you to return."

The hair on the back of Kate's neck stood up. "There was a girl on our swing?"

"A pretty young thing. Maybe twenty. She looked mighty surprised when I called out to her." He cocked his head. "I asked her what she was doing in your yard."

The missing photo. The tousled bed.

The sense of being watched. Of not being alone.

Kate began to shake. She worked to hide it from Joe. "What did she say when you confronted her?"

"That she was a friend of yours, visiting from the city. Said you'd taken the baby to the doctor. She didn't say her name, and I figured it was none of my business and didn't ask." He frowned. "Maybe I should have?"

"She wasn't a friend of ours." Kate swallowed hard. "About what time was this, Joe?"

"I was walking Beauregard." He scratched his head. "It was about noon, I suppose."

By noon, she had been in the city and Richard deep into the second nine.

Joe made a sound of frustration. "I knew something about her wasn't right. At the time, though...I mean, she knew your names and that you had a baby. So, I figured she was on the up-and-up. Sorry I didn't do more."

She forced a smile, not wanting to worry him. "I'm sure it was nothing."

"That's what I thought. But I just wanted to let you and Richard know, just in case."

"Thank you. I'm glad you did." Kate walked him to the door. She saw Richard's Mercedes pull into the drive. "I feel safer knowing you're in the neighborhood, Joe."

He beamed at her, pleased with himself. "I'll keep my eyes open and let you know if I see her hanging around again."

Kate thanked him once more and said goodbye, then waited at the door for Richard. From down the walk, she heard Richard greet Joe; a moment later he appeared at the door. "Hi, hon." He bent and kissed her. "How was your day? Everything go okay?"

She looked at him, surprised. "Excuse me?"

"The Bean, was business good?"

She stared at him, heart beginning to thrum. She opened her mouth to tell him about her meeting with Luke. Instead, she murmured, "You know The Bean, Saturdays are always good."

As soon as the evasion, the lie it represented was out of her mouth, she regretted it. But to take it back, she feared, would be worse.

Let sleeping dogs lie, she told herself, even as guilty heat crept up her cheeks. Why upset Richard over something that was done and over with?

"Are you all right?" he asked, crossing to the refrigerator for a beer. "You look a little strange."

Tell him about Luke. Tell him now. "Do I?"

"Mmm." He popped the top and brought the beverage to his mouth. "What did Old Joe want?"

Joe. The woman on the swing. The missing photograph. Coming home to change; the feeling of being watched. It all came tumbling out. As she filled him in, her unease returned, her feeling that something was terribly wrong.

"I thought I heard someone in the house, Richard. I'd convinced myself my imagination was playing tricks on me, but now..."

"Is anything besides the photograph missing?" he asked, frowning with concern.

"I...I don't know." She hugged herself. "I was too spooked to look around. Then Old Joe arrived."

He set down his beer, went to his golf bag and pulled out his new Ping putter. He met her eyes, the seriousness of his expression sending a chill down her spine. "If you ever even suspect there's a stranger in the house, get out. Do you understand, Kate? Take

Emma and leave. Go to The Bean or a neighbor's and call me or the police.''

She nodded, her mouth desert dry, her pulse fast. She was more frightened now, by his concern, than she had been before, alone in the house. ''I understand.''

''Good. Now, let's take a look around.''

Richard, armed with the putter, Kate with Emma in her carrier, they made their way through the house. They went from room to room, looking under beds and in closets, checking the silver, Kate's jewelry, Richard's office.

They found nothing missing or out of place.

Back in the kitchen, Richard slipped the golf club back into the bag. ''Well, nothing looks amiss. Was the side door locked when you got home?''

''I don't know.'' Emma began to stir, sucking in her sleep—a sign that she was not only about to wake up, but that she was hungry. Kate went to the pantry for a can of formula. ''I came in the front.''

''I'll check it.''

A moment later he returned. ''Door's locked. Key's in its hiding place.''

Kate filled a bottle with the formula, popped it in the microwave, then turned to Richard. ''Why would anyone break in only to steal a photograph?''

''Good question. Could you be mistaken? I mean, a hanger on the floor, a few wrinkles in the bed, none are particularly sinister. And we both know, this old house creaks and groans more than a ninety-year-old spinster.''

Kate frowned, frustrated. The truth was, at the time it had seemed so real, so chilling. Not at all like her imagination running away with her. But now, it all seemed rather far-fetched. "I'm not usually flighty like that, Richard. You know I've never been one to let my imagination run away with me."

"I know. But you've had a lot on your mind lately. Sleep deprivation has been known to cause some pretty far-out behavior."

Emma picked that moment to wake up and fret; Kate lifted her out of her carrier and crossed to the microwave to retrieve her bottle. He had a point, no doubt about it, though something kept nagging at her as she fed Emma her bottle. Something dark and disturbing. A thought, a fear, more terrifying than any she had ever experienced before.

As she rocked her daughter, gazing down at her perfect face, it grew, took shape. And then she saw the fear for what it was.

That Emma's birth mother had somehow sought them out. Because she wanted Emma back.

By the time she had finished giving Emma her bottle and had changed her into her pajamas, Kate had worked herself into a state of complete terror. Afraid the child would pick up on her distress, she tucked her into her swing, then went in search of Richard.

She found him in the kitchen, seasoning a steak for the grill. "Richard?" She stepped into the room, hands clasped in front of her, barely able to speak so great was her fear.

He looked up, his smile dying when he saw her expression. "What's wrong?"

She hugged herself. "I...I have this terrible feeling, Richard. What if...what if Emma's birth mother has found us? What if she's the one...the one who—" Kate bit the words back, unable to verbalize her darkest fear. The one that fueled her nightmares and kept her up nights.

"Who what? Broke in and stole the picture of Emma?"

"Yes," she whispered, her voice shaking.

"And why would she have done that?"

"You know." Kate's eyes flooded with tears. "Because she's changed her mind. Because she wants Emma back."

"And she came here today in a bizarre quest to steal Emma away?"

"I couldn't bear to lose her, Richard." Her tears brimmed, then spilled over. "I couldn't."

"Come here." He held out his arms and she moved into them, pressing her cheek to his chest, and he folded his arms tightly around her. "You're being silly, love. That's not going to happen."

"How do you know?" She tilted her head back to meet his eyes, her vision blurred with tears. "How?"

"Because it's not logical." He smiled. "First, she chose a closed adoption. She knows nothing about us, not our names or where we live. Second, if she wanted the baby back, she would go through Citywide. She'd call Ellen, she'd hire a lawyer. Not sneak into our house and lurk about, for God only knows what reason."

He was right, she knew he was. So, why didn't she feel reassured?

"Where's the picture, Richard?"

He chuckled and shook his head. "It got knocked into a drawer. The cleaning service moved it."

"But I looked at it this morning! I know I did."

"You could be mistaken." As she opened her

mouth to protest, he laid a finger against her lips. "It'll turn up, Kate."

"What if it doesn't?"

"We'll take another," he said, amusement coloring his tone. "Or get a copy made of that one. Buy a new frame."

"Very funny." She rested her forehead against his chest a moment, then met his gaze once more. "Earlier today, when I had that feeling I was being watched, that I wasn't alone, it was so creepy, Richard. And then, when Joe told me about that woman..."

She drew in a shuddering breath. "She was the right age. And it just seems like such a coincidence...I mean, what was she doing inside our gate?"

He cupped her face in his palms. "Don't read so much into this, Kate. It could have been anyone. The gate's not locked, we live on a well-traveled street. There's a park directly across from our house, for heaven's sake. Someone saw our swing, thought it looked inviting and helped themselves."

"But she knew our names. She knew we had a baby."

"So do a lot of people in the area. Could be someone we knew who was embarrassed at having been caught. Who was afraid Joe would tell us." Richard bent and dropped a light kiss on her mouth. "Your imagination is running away with you. Trust me, love. There's no cause for alarm here. None at all."

28

Luke spent the hours after his meeting with Kate wandering through the French Quarter, refamiliarizing himself with the sights, sounds and smells that were New Orleans. He enjoyed beignets and café au lait at the Café du Monde, walked along the moon walk, sat on a bench in Jackson Square and studied the people who passed.

As he did, he was swamped with memories of his days at Tulane, of the young man he had been back then, of the force of his dreams. Kate resided at the heart of each of those memories: the things they had done, the way they had laughed, how she had made him feel without doing anything but being at his side.

A part of him regretted the things he had said to her earlier that day, the way he had hurt her. That same part had longed to chase after her, apologize, make some hollow excuse for his behavior and beg her forgiveness.

He had quelled the urge, reminding himself that she had come to him for an airing out of the past. That she had come to him for honesty, and he had simply and frankly given her what she wanted.

His publisher had booked him into a suite at the Royal Orleans Hotel, one of the French Quarter's grandest establishments, built and maintained in the tradition of the Old South.

When he entered the hotel, he was struck by both the cool and the quiet. Out on the street, the shift in the French Quarter crowd had begun, the day-trippers being replaced by the night owls, the shoppers by the partiers.

Luke crossed the sweeping lobby with its massive crystal chandeliers, heading toward the front desk. Helena had arranged a dinner at Commander's Palace with the company's regional sales rep and the local book distributor. She had promised to leave a message at the front desk confirming the place and time they would meet. He glanced at his watch. If he was lucky, he could take a quick shower, change and still put in two hours at the laptop.

He stopped at the desk. The clerk, an exotic-looking woman named Aimee, greeted him by name. He smiled. ''Any messages for me?''

She returned his smile. ''I think so, Mr. Dallas. Let me check.'' She crossed to the message center, then looked over her shoulder at him. ''Yes, you do. There's also a package for you. It's in the back. I can have it sent up, or if you have a minute, I'll get it.''

''I'll wait. Thanks.'' She handed Luke an envelope, then disappeared through a door at the back of the registration area. Luke ripped open the envelope to see that he did, indeed, have several hours before his dinner engagement.

Aimee returned with a small shopping bag. She handed it to him. Inside was a copy of *Dead Drop,* autographed by him that very day, inscribed to Bird Man.

Luke frowned. He had signed so many books that morning, had seen so many faces. There had been at least a dozen Marys, a handful of Stevens and

Daves—but only one Bird Man. He remembered signing the book—why couldn't he recall the man? With
a name like that, he should be firmly fixed in his memory.

Luke drew his eyebrows together. He had been mid-
dle-aged and rather nondescript; Luke remembered
looking right at him. But now, no matter how he tried,
he could recall nothing else about the man's appearance.

"Mr. Dallas?" Luke looked up from the book,
meeting exotic Aimee's eyes. She flushed. "I just
wanted you to know, I love your books. I can't wait
to read your new one."

He grinned, pleased. "Thanks. By the way—" he
held up the bag "—did you see who left this for me?"

"Sorry, I just came on."

"There was no note with this? No message?"

"Not that I saw. But I'll double-check for you."

There wasn't, so Luke headed up to his room. The
phone was ringing as he let himself in; he hurried to
catch it before the hotel message service. "Hello."

"Meet me in the bar of the Vieux Carré Gun Club
in twenty minutes."

"Who is this?"

"Twenty minutes," he repeated. "If you still want
to talk."

The line went dead, and Luke held the receiver for
a moment before dropping it into the cradle. Condor,
he realized, a smile tugging at the corners of his
mouth. Bird Man. Of course.

The Vieux Carré Gun Club was a private organization and judging by the building's address and facade, catered to an extremely wealthy clientele. The

doorman allowed Luke in, directing him to the receptionist's desk. The woman, a beautiful blonde, immaculately dressed in a Chanel suit, stood as he approached, greeting him by name. She asked him to sign the guest register, then led him to the lounge.

Luke spotted Condor immediately. He sat alone at a corner table, his back to the wall.

"Bird Man, I presume?"

Condor smiled. "Corny, but I couldn't resist." He motioned to the chair across from his. "How long did it take you to figure it out?"

"Too long, I'm embarrassed to say." He settled into the leather tub chair. "That was you at the signing? I never would have guessed."

Condor signaled the waitress. "Look at the eyes, they always give the man away."

The waitress arrived to take his order, and Luke glanced at the other man's drink. As if reading his thoughts, Condor said, "I never consume alcohol. It dulls the senses and impairs reaction time."

"Precisely why most people do drink it. Personally, I like the taste." Luke smiled at the woman, ordered a beer, then turned to Condor. "Pretty fancy digs."

"It ain't shabby, that's for sure." The man raised his glass of tomato juice to his lips.

"And you're a member?"

"Let's just say, I have friends in high places."

They chatted about nothing for a few more minutes; Luke sensed Condor was still sizing him up. Testing the waters.

"I'm curious," he said, "why did you decide to talk to me?"

Condor shrugged. "I like your books. My wife likes your books."

"You're married?"

"You sound surprised. Aren't I allowed?"

Luke took a swallow of his beer. "I suppose. It just doesn't fit the image of the hired killer."

"Your image," he murmured, a smile tugging at the corners of his mouth. "Hollywood's."

"Does she know what you do?"

"Of course not. I'm a software salesman. I travel a lot."

"You have kids?"

"Two. Age six and eight. Boys."

Luke thought about that a moment. "Do you ever imagine how she would feel, if she found out? If your kids found out?"

"That's not going to happen. There's no reason they would."

"And if you're killed on assignment?"

"The Agency would take care of my cover from there." Condor stood. "You shoot much, Dallas?"

Luke followed him to his feet. "Enough to write about it with some authority."

"Good." Condor smiled. "Let's go have some fun."

The glitz and glamour of the gun club's common areas ended as they entered the indoor range. Garage-like, windowless and well insulated, it was outfitted with six firing stations, each with a mechanical pulley used to move paper targets forward and back.

They were alone in the range. On the table at station one sat two boxes of ammo and a gun.

Condor crossed to the table and picked up the weapon. "Beretta 9mm, semiautomatic."

While he spoke, he examined the gun, checking the magazine, pulling back on the slide, then releasing it, tipping it from one side to the other, running his fingers expertly over the metal. He handled the weapon with reverence and familiarity. Like it was an old friend.

"Fifteen round magazine," he continued, "weighs 2.52 pounds, fully loaded. Muzzle velocity 1280 feet per second, rivaling the .357."

He loaded three clips, then slid one into the magazine. "You own any hardware, Dallas?"

"A .44 Magnum."

Condor met his eyes. "That's a lot of firepower. More than I would have thought an author would need."

Luke laughed. "I bought it when I was writing *Last Dance*. What can I say? I like Dirty Harry movies. I saw my lead character as a kind of Harry Callahan, a rugged loner. A renegade."

Condor shook his head, disagreeing. "A renegade's an outlaw. Callahan was the ultimate lawman. He lived by a code of justice. Of an eye for an eye. Fight firepower with firepower, violence with violence. Simple."

"Is it simple? Is that the code you live by?"

"Basically. We live in a violent society, Luke. No matter how big and bad someone is, they're made vulnerable by the same fragile physical shell as everyone else. Think of death as the ultimate problem solver."

"And that's what you do? How you think of yourself, as a problem solver?"

"And a patriot, yes. Let's see what this baby can do." He clipped a paper target, a black silhouette of a human torso, onto the pulley, sent it back fifty or so feet and slipped on a headset. He aimed and fired, one shot after another, the explosions near simultaneous, emptying the magazine.

Condor flipped the pulley switch, retrieving the target. He had blown away the target's head and riddled its heart with holes. He replaced the target with a new one, then turned to Luke, gun butt out. "Your turn."

Luke took the weapon and reloaded. The gun felt heavier in his hands than the two and a half pounds Condor had quoted; it felt colder. He stepped up to the firing line, adjusted his target, aimed and fired, neither as quick nor, he knew without looking, as accurately as Condor.

He emptied the magazine and checked the target, grateful to see that it looked like most of his shots had at least hit the target.

"Not bad. For a civilian."

Luke's lips lifted and he handed the weapon to the other man. "Thanks."

"All that fancy hardware you see guys like me using in the movies," Condor murmured, jacking another clip of ammo into the magazine, "that's strictly Hollywood. For the professional, simple is best."

He slipped on his headset and approached the firing line. As before, he aimed, emptying the magazine in a matter of seconds. He slid the headset off and crossed back to Luke. "A gun, a knife, a garrote. Simple, effective, quick."

He reloaded the clips, his movements economical, automatic. He had done the same thing so many times, Luke saw, he didn't even have to think about what he was doing.

"The thing is," Condor continued, "the pro has to weigh firepower and effectiveness against practicality, traceability and cost. That .44 of yours has way more punch than I'd need, but it's not such a bad choice for you, if you can handle its kick. There's an intruder in your house, you want to blow as big a hole in him as you can. You might only have one shot, and who knows where you're going to put it.''

''Thanks for that vote of confidence.''

Condor laughed, then continued. ''A weapon is a tool and nothing more. Not a lover or a pet. You can't get attached to your weapon—you never use one twice.''

''Never?''

''Never. The same weapon would link the hits. Any mechanic worth his salt disposes of his weapon after each hit. In the case of a gun, when possible, I dismantle it first. The pieces are disposed of in a variety of locations, the butt in a Dumpster, the barrel down a storm drain, you get the picture. That way I know the weapon will never be recovered.''

''Why not dispose of the body?'' Luke asked. ''That's evidence. No body, no crime to investigate.''

''Yeah, but tougher to get rid of, wouldn't you say?'' He handed the Beretta to Luke. ''Remember, all police adhere to the same theory of crime solving. Motive, means and opportunity. Statistics show that most violent crimes are committed by people who know one another, so that's the first place the local boys look. Get rid of the weapon and all of a sudden you have a crime, but no motive and no weapon. I'm long gone before the local boys have even finished interrogating the wife, business partner, best friend.''

Luke took the gun, replaced the clip and stepped up. He took aim, then fired. This time more confidently and with more accuracy. He slipped off the headset and handed the gun to the other man.

"Before the hit, what goes through your mind?"

"Getting in, getting the job done and getting out. The professional has two goals. Kill the target. And walk away. That's it."

"What about after the hit?" Luke asked. "You don't think about the victim's wife or kids? You don't question whether you're doing the right thing?"

"They're not people to me, Dallas. They're targets. A name and a face on a piece of paper." He laid the gun on the table. "I'm not a murderer. I'm not some amoral psycho. Those guys make me sick. They have no loyalty or self-control. They're selfish little bastards who act on whim and without honor.

"I'm a patriot. A soldier. I work for my country, and I don't question my orders." At Luke's expression he laughed. "Don't be naive, every government in the world employs men like me. We're a political necessity.

"I love my country and my family. Just like any other man, I'd do whatever's necessary to protect them. To keep them safe."

It astounded Luke to hear this man talk about honor and loyalty and patriotism. To see the tenderness in his eyes when he spoke of his wife and children.

A part of Luke realized that he should be afraid. This man could kill him in a dozen different ways, and would do it without second thought. He was a man who operated outside the law, yet within in, too.

And he was telling Luke his secrets, sharing his innermost thoughts. Making himself vulnerable to Luke. And that would be an unsettling thing for a man like Condor.

But Luke wasn't afraid. He felt in his gut that he had nothing to fear from the other man. In a weird way, he respected him. Even liked him. In any other profession, his loyalty and code of ethics would be laudable. His love of his family—and his desire to protect them—admirable.

"What you do, is it ever personal?"

"Personal?" Condor frowned. "No, not ever. You never cross that line."

"But what if a guy like you did? What if something happened, and suddenly the pro turned vigilante?"

Condor paused, as if carefully considering. "That'd be bad news, Dallas. You're talking about a killing machine. It's what he's been trained to do." Condor leaned toward him; the cold in his eyes sent a chill down Luke's spine. "He can kill a man in a hundred different ways, and he will do so without compunction. He doesn't concern himself with the moral issues that you might. He doesn't think about heaven or hell, right or wrong. He doesn't believe in someone's right to life or their humanity.

"People are targets. Pure and simple. The only thing that keeps the assassin in check is his honor. His code of ethics." He looked Luke dead in the eye. "Take that away or twist it, and you've got a veritable killing machine roaming the streets. A man to whom vengeance is just another word for justice."

29

Julianna and Sandy met at the coffeehouse every night for a week. At the end of that week and at Julianna's suggestion, they graduated to a Friday night dinner and movie, from there to shopping and lunch on Saturdays.

They became the very best of friends.

And, as Julianna had known she would be, Sandy was grateful for her friendship. So grateful, she never stopped to question Julianna's devotion to her, never wondered why, after having had to struggle to be liked for so long, Julianna liked everything about her so easily.

Julianna decided it was time for her to make her next move.

She chose to make it during one of their Friday nights out. They had just shared a salad and a dessert at a local café known for both and were making plans to shop the next day.

Julianna counted out the money for her half of the bill and sighed. "I really need to find a job."

"No luck yet?"

"Not unless I want to sling burgers at McDonald's."

"Bummer."

"No kidding. I never thought it would be this hard to find a decent position." She looked away, then back at Sandy, as if inspired. "What about where you work? Is there anything available there?"

Sandy shook her head. "I don't think so. Nothing you'd be qualified for, anyway."

"How do you know?" She leaned toward her. "I can do lots of things."

"Both openings require a college degree and experience at a law firm. Sorry."

Julianna was crestfallen and didn't hide it. She had been sure, at a place as big as Nicholson, Bedico, Chaney & Ryan, there would be something, *anything,* she would be qualified for. Maybe Sandy wasn't being honest with her. Maybe she needed more of an incentive. "That's all I've been hearing." Julianna looked at her hands, her eyes filling with tears. "I'm afraid I'm going to have to go back."

"Back?" Sandy repeated. "You don't mean back to D.C.?"

When she nodded, Sandy made a sound of distress. "But you can't go! We're...we just became friends."

"I don't want to, but what am I supposed to do? I can't seem to get a good job here. I have connections in D.C., but you're the only one I know here and you can't..." Her voice trailed off miserably. "It sure would have been nice to work together. We could have had lunch together every day. Passed notes when the bosses weren't looking. Like back in high school."

"I really would have liked that," Sandy whispered, her longing palpable. "I really would have. You're the...you're the best friend I've ever had, Julianna."

"And you're the best friend I've ever had. I'm going to miss you."

They fell into a miserable silence. Sandy slumped down in her seat, looking ready to cry. Then, suddenly, she straightened and met Julianna's eyes. "Wait, I just thought of something. Another opening."

Quickly, the words tumbling past her lips, Sandy relayed how she had overheard Richard Ryan's secretary complaining about her workload. "He's running for local District Attorney and she's threatening to quit because of the increased workload. I heard her say that he promised to hire an assistant to handle the secretarial and gofer work associated with his campaign."

Richard needed an assistant? Another sign. "When was this?"

"Just this week." Sandy paused, thinking back. "Tuesday, I think. Yes—" she nodded "—definitely Tuesday. In the break room. Though I don't know if he's run an ad yet or if he has someone in mind already."

Julianna brought a hand to her chest, so excited she could barely breathe. *Work directly with Richard? It would be too good to be true.*

"This is perfect." She leaned toward the other woman, reaching out and capturing her hands. "You have to introduce me to Mr. Ryan. You *have* to, Sandy!"

Sandy froze, her expression alarmed. "I don't know about that, Julianna. I mean, an introduction is…it would be—"

"A vote of confidence in me," Julianna supplied. "You do believe in me, don't you?"

"Well, sure. It's just that—"

Julianna tightened her fingers over the other woman's. "I need that job, Sandy. I have to have it. Do you understand? I *have* to have it."

"You're hurting me, Julianna," she whispered, tugging on her hands. "Let go."

Julianna backed off, trying to look repentant. "I'm sorry, Sandy. It's just that…" She drew a deep breath. "I'm getting desperate. You can understand that, can't you?" Sandy nodded, squirming in her seat. "And this job it…it sounds perfect for me. I lived in D.C., remember? I moved in political circles. Politics are second nature to me."

Sandy gazed at her expectantly, waiting. More, Julianna thought, she had to have more. She scrambled around for something that would convince Sandy she was qualified for the job. She thought of her mother, then her mother's lover.

Senator Jacobson. Of course.

"I was one of Senator Jacobson's campaign assistants." A tiny lie—she had stopped by his election headquarters several times; his campaign manager had shown her and her mother around and explained the duties of the various volunteers.

The other woman perked up. "You were?"

"That's right." She smiled. "He'd give me a recommendation, I know he would."

For a long moment, Sandy said nothing. She gazed at Julianna, her face an open book. She wanted to do it, but she was afraid of sticking her neck out. Of hurting her reputation, of getting in trouble with the bosses.

All she needed was another little push. "Just think, Sandy. If Mr. Ryan hired me, we'd be working in the same building. We could have lunch together every day. Take our coffee breaks at the same time…go out for drinks after work."

She looked Sandy in the eyes, her expression as

earnest as she could make it. "I've never worked with a best friend before. It'd be so cool."

"It would be fun," Sandy said softly, hesitantly.

"So, you'll do it?" Julianna caught the other woman's hands once more. "You'll introduce me to Mr. Ryan? You'll put in a good word for me?"

Sandy caved in with a sigh. "All right, Julianna. I'll do it."

30

Sandy agreed to give Julianna's resumé to Richard first thing Monday morning. Julianna spent the entire weekend preparing it, taking as much creative license as she thought she could get away with. She changed her age to twenty-two. She listed her mother's contacts and former lovers as references, hoping Richard wouldn't check them. And finally, she claimed to have been one of Senator William "Billy" Jacobson's campaign assistants.

The people at the copy store had helped her with the format. She had rented time on a computer and printed out the final copy on their laser printer. The end result looked pretty darn good, if she said so herself. She especially liked the part where she had outlined the duties she had been responsible for in her job with the senator. Who would have thought years of listening to her mother's men friends talk and a couple of tours through campaign headquarters would yield such bounty?

Julianna had decided that after she interviewed with Richard, depending on how it went, she would break the silence and call her mother to set everything up with the senator. That way she would be covered if Richard checked her references.

Monday morning Julianna called Sandy to wish her luck. "Hi, it's me."

"Hi."

"Are you ready?"

"I guess."

Julianna frowned. She and Sandy had met the evening before so Julianna could give Sandy the resumé and coach her on what she wanted her to say. Then, the other woman had been upbeat and excited. Now, she sounded nervous and more than a little reluctant to carry through on her promise.

Julianna tightened her grip on the receiver. "Sandy, you're not having second thoughts about helping me, are you?"

"Of course not," she said after a moment, the way she dragged the words out belying their meaning.

If she thought Julianna was going to let her off the hook, she was in for a big surprise. "Good," she said, "because you don't sound too upbeat this morning. And if I'm going to get the job, you have to be enthusiastic. You've have to present me positively."

"I know. It's just that—" Sandy hesitated, then sighed again. "It's just that Mr. Ryan...he's a *partner*. If this backfired...it could cost me my job."

"What could backfire?" Julianna lowered her voice, softened it. "You know me, Sandy. We're best friends. And I'm telling you, I can do this job and do it well. If Richard Ryan hires me, he'll be so happy you'll probably get a raise *and* a promotion."

"And we'll be able to have lunch together every day. Right?"

"And coffee breaks, too." Julianna smiled, knowing she had won. "I'd never do anything to hurt you, Sandy. If I didn't know I could do the job, I wouldn't ask you this favor. You've got to believe me."

"I do." Sandy made a sound of relief, then giggled

as if drawn into Julianna's excitement. "I'm just being a jerk."

"Be sure to mention what good friends we are and that I worked for Senator Jacobson."

"I will."

"You're sure? You won't forget and let me down?"

"Of course not."

"And don't tell him where we met or when. Unless he asks."

"Got it."

"Remember," Julianna said, suddenly so nervous she felt ill, "you're doing him a favor. I'm perfect for this job. If you believe it, he will, too." As Sandy prepared to hang up, Julianna stopped her. "And call me the minute you know something. I won't stray from beside the phone until you do."

Sandy's call came at four-thirty that afternoon. "He's agreed to interview you," she said, sounding excited. "Tomorrow morning at eight sharp."

31

"Mr. Ryan," Julianna said, stepping into his office and holding out her hand, "it's a pleasure to meet you."

"The pleasure is mine." He took her hand, then indicated the leather chairs facing his desk. "Have a seat."

"Thank you." Julianna sat, working to quell her nerves, her runaway heart. Richard Ryan would not be compelled to hire a nervous girl. She had to present herself as a collected, intelligent and savvy woman.

She had to be like Kate.

To that end, she had worn her best "Kate suit," had applied her cosmetics with extra care and stood in front of the mirror for long, precious minutes, practicing Kate's hello, her smile, her gestures.

The transformation had been startling.

Richard cleared his throat, lifting his gaze from her resumé. "It says here that you worked for Senator Jacobson. You seem a bit young to have been on his staff."

She straightened. "Twenty-two. Not that young."

One corner of his mouth lifted. "Wait ten years," he murmured, then returned his attention to the paper before him. "I'm surprised he hired you without a college degree."

Fighting panic, she folded her hands in her lap.

"Billy was a family friend. He was kind enough to take a chance on me even though I had no experience." She met Richard's eyes. "I didn't let him down. And if you hire me, I won't let you down either."

Again, Richard's lips lifted in a half smile. "You seem confident. Self-possessed. That's important."

She leaned slightly forward, her heart in her words. "If you hire me, I'll work hard for you. It wouldn't be just a job to me. I believe in your platform. Your policy of being tough on first timers, on using plea bargaining as a last resort, on the three strikes rule."

He smiled, obviously pleased, and she went on, hearing the passion in her own voice, the excitement. "It would be an honor to work with a man like you, Mr. Ryan. A man of integrity and intelligence. It would be a thrill to help you become St. Tammany Parish's next District Attorney."

For a moment he said nothing, simply gazed at her, then he glanced back at her resumé. "I see you performed a variety of tasks for Senator Jacobson. Donation solicitation, mailings, public relations and canvassing." He lifted his eyebrows. "That's quite a broad spectrum of duties."

She scrambled for an explanation, suddenly realizing she might have claimed too much. "I was one of the underlings, no doubt about it. Basically, I filled in where I was needed. One notch above a gofer."

She looked at her clasped hands a moment, then back up at him. "I'll be honest, at the time it was a bit of a pain, but now I realize that having experience in so many areas is one of my assets."

"I agree, Ms. Starr." He cocked his head, studying her. "You look familiar to me. Have we met?"

"No." She shook her head. "At least I don't think so. I haven't been living in Mandeville that long."

He leaned back in his chair. "What brought you all the way down here from D.C.?"

His question surprised her. It was one she hadn't prepared for. She groped around for an answer that would make sense to him. She lowered her eyes a moment, then returned her gaze to his. "My mother passed away last year after a..." she cleared her throat "...after a long battle with cancer. I have no other family and after she died, I just didn't want to stay."

"I'm sorry."

She inclined her head in acknowledgment of his sympathy. "Anyway, I'd always heard about New Orleans, about Mardi Gras and the French Quarter and had always dreamed of visiting." She smiled. "So, here I am."

"But now you're in Mandeville."

She smiled. "New Orleans wasn't quite as I imagined it to be. Then one Saturday, I drove across the lake—and fell in love."

He returned her smile. "I can understand that. I grew up in New Orleans, but now I wouldn't live anywhere but the North Shore." He stood and held out his hand. "It was a pleasure meeting you, Ms. Starr, and I will definitely keep you in mind for the job."

She worked to hide her disappointment. She had fantasized that he'd offer her the position right off. "Do you have any idea when you'll make a decision?"

"Soon. If you haven't heard from me in a week, give my secretary a call. Her name's Nancy."

After shaking his hand, she started toward the door, then stopped and turned back to him, heart pounding, desperation tugging at her. "I want this job, Mr. Ryan. I need it. If you give it to me, I'll work hard. I'll perform any task, no matter how menial. If you give me this job, I won't let you down. I promise."

He looked pleased with her speech. "I'll keep that in mind. Oh, and Ms. Starr?" She stopped again and turned expectantly toward him. "My condolences on the Senator's passing."

"Excuse me?"

"Senator Jacobson. I was a fan of his policies. His murder was more than an outrage. It was a real loss for America."

Julianna stared at him, the room starting to spin. A tingling sensation started at the top of her head and inched downward. "Murder?" she whispered. "Billy's...dead?"

Richard came around the desk; he took her arm. "You're white as a sheet. Come, sit down. I'll get you a glass of water."

He led her to the chair she had occupied only moments before. She sank onto it and lowered her head to her knees and breathed deeply and slowly through her nose. After a minute the dizziness passed. But not her shock.

Billy was dead. Murdered.

Dear God, her mother.

"I'm so sorry," he said, handing her the water. "I never would have said anything...I thought you knew. It was in all the papers."

She shook her head and took the glass, hand shaking. She sipped, then met his eyes. "I haven't...with the move..." She took another sip. "When did it...how...?"

"About four months ago. He was shot, though I

don't remember all the details. I don't think they ever caught the killer. Or if they did, I didn't hear about it.''

Her mother's lover was dead. Murdered.

They hadn't caught the killer.

John.

She began to shake, though she tried to hide it. She got to her feet, forcing a semblance of calm, though she could see by Richard's sympathetic expression she wasn't doing all that good a job of it. She held her panic at bay by telling herself over and over that Billy's death had nothing to do with her or John. Why should it? People were murdered all the time, it was a tragic fact of modern life. Hadn't John always said so? Hadn't he always said that death was a bullet that couldn't be dodged, not forever anyway?

Richard walked her to his office door. ''Sorry I can't give you any more details. You could go to the library and check the back issues of the *Times Pica-yune.*''

The library. Of course. ''Thank you, Mr. Ryan, I think I will.'' She smiled weakly at him. ''I look forward to your call.''

Somehow Julianna managed to make it from Richard's office to the Covington branch of the St. Tammany Parish library. There, the librarian helped her find what she was looking for on the microfilm, then left her alone.

Julianna scanned the article. It had happened November sixteenth. The senator, the paper reported, was found shot to death in his Washington hotel room. He had been shot at point blank range; he died instantly.

At the time the article was written, the police had no suspects though they were following several leads.

Julianna stared at the screen, her vision blurring with tears, her teeth beginning to chatter. She hugged herself. Something didn't sound right, she thought. Why had Billy been in a hotel room? Sure, he lived with his family in Virginia, but whenever he was in town he stayed with her mother.

"Are you all right?"

Julianna lifted her gaze. The librarian had returned and was looking at her with concern. "I'm sorry," Julianna whispered, "what did you say?"

"Is there anything I can do for you?"

"No, I—" Her tears threatened to spill over, and she fought them back. "You said I could make a copy of this?"

"That's right. They're a quarter a page."

Julianna dug two quarters out of her purse, one for the front page and headline about Billy's murder, the second for the rest of the story, buried at the back of the paper. She handed them to the woman, who made the copies for her.

Julianna thanked the librarian and left, clutching the copies to her chest. She made it home, though she had no recollection of climbing into her car, let alone driving, and raced to the phone. Heart thundering, she dialed her mother. The phone rang once. Then twice. While she waited, she told herself over and over that her mother was safe and unharmed. That Billy's death had nothing to do with her or her mother, nothing to do with John.

On the third ring a recording informed her that the number was no longer in service. The receiver still clutched in her hands, Julianna sank to her knees. It couldn't be, she thought. She had dialed incorrectly; that was all. She tried it again, paying closer attention this time.

The same recording rang in her ears.

Fighting complete hysteria, Julianna dialed long distance information and asked for a listing for Sylvia Starr. The operator informed her there was no such listing in the D.C. area.

No listing for her mother. Billy was dead.

Julianna bent at her waist, phone cradled to her cheek. Dear God, what did she do now? She had to make sure her mother was all right. She had to find her.

Clark Russell. Of course.

Swiping at her tears, she called information, then dialed the CIA in Langley, Virginia.

"CIA. How may I direct your call?"

"Please, could you…" Julianna whispered, choked with tears. "I need to speak—"

"You'll have to speak up," the woman said, "I can't understand you."

She cleared her throat. "Clark Russell. Please."

"May I tell him who's calling."

"Julianna Starr."

There was a moment's silence on the other end of the line, then a series of clicking sounds. A moment later a man came on the line. "This is Todd Bishop. May I help you?"

"I was…I need to speak with Clark Russell, please."

"I'm sorry, Mr. Russell is no longer with the Agency. May I help you?"

"No longer with—" Julianna struggled for an even breath. "But where…when did he—"

"He retired this past January, the lucky guy. Is there something I can—"

Julianna slammed down the receiver, a low moan escaping her lips. She sank to the floor, drawing her knees to her chest and wrapping her arms around them. She pressed her face to her knees and rocked, struggling to get a grip on herself, on her fear.

Billy was dead. Murdered just three weeks after she had run away. Clark was no longer with the CIA. Her mother was missing.

John was cleaning house. He was exacting revenge. *Her mother was dead, too.*

No. She brought her hands to her ears as if by doing so she could block out the sound of her own thoughts. It wasn't true. Her mother was fine, living on a yacht with that Arab millionaire, the one she had met shortly before Julianna left, the one she hadn't been able to stand. He had made himself more attractive to her mother by sweetening the pot. It had happened before.

That was it. Julianna swiped at the tears on her cheeks. Her mother had ended her relationship with Billy, taken the millionaire's offer and closed up the brownstone. That's why Billy had been staying in a hotel. That's why her mother's number was no longer in service. As for Clark Russell, he had retired, just as that man had said.

It all made sense. More sense than believing John was out exacting revenge on anyone who had known her.

Calm stole over her. She smiled and stood, chiding herself for letting her imagination run away with her. Learning of Billy's death had been a shock, of course, but from now on, she would keep her attention fixed firmly on Richard and the future they would have together.

32

As Richard drove home that evening, his thoughts were on the girl he had interviewed in the morning. He had thought about her on and off all day, though he couldn't say for certain why.

She had given a good interview, no doubt about it. She was as qualified as anyone else he had interviewed; he liked her determination and ambition, appreciated the hunger for the job he had heard in her voice, the hint of desperation.

He had decided against her anyway. She was too young for the job, too pretty, too inexperienced.

But still, he couldn't stop thinking about her. And the more he thought, the more he wavered in his original decision against her. She possessed a kind of determination that he hadn't seen in the other applicants, a kind that made him believe she would do a good job, a better job than the others he had interviewed.

She also possessed a kind of social confidence and savvy that suggested a woman older than her years, one who had seen more of the world than one would expect of a twenty-two year old.

Richard turned onto Gerard Street, heading toward the lake. He smiled to himself, remembering the way she had looked at him, the way she had looked *up* to him. As if she believed in him one hundred percent. As if she didn't have a doubt about his abilities or the fact that he would win the race for D.A.—or any race he ran in, for that matter.

He shook his head, amused with his own thoughts. When she'd looked at him that way, he had been reminded of the young man he had been back at Tulane. Unstoppable. Cocky and without doubts—about himself, his abilities or his golden future. He had been reminded of the way it had felt to snap his fingers and whatever he had desired would be his.

Richard grimaced. A pretty young thing, one more than ten years his junior, gazed up at him in awe and he'd puffed up like some damn peacock.

Reason enough not to hire her.

He sobered, remembering her surprise and devastation at learning of Senator Jacobson's death. Poor kid, she'd been really upset. He had felt bad for her.

He drew to a stop as the light ahead turned red, his thoughts drifting to Kate. She used to look at him the way Julianna had today—as if she believed he not only hung the moon, but that he could do no wrong as well. She used to make him feel all puffed up and invincible.

He drew his eyebrows together in thought. When had she stopped? he wondered. When had he ceased being a hero to her?

The baby, he thought, unable to quell a stab of resentment. Since Emma nothing had been the same between them.

The light changed, and he turned onto Lakeshore Drive. He waved at their next-door neighbor, out pruning her crepe myrtles, as he swung into his drive. Kate sat on the upper balcony, reading while the baby slept in her swing. He pulled his car to a stop, collected his briefcase and climbed out. Kate saw him and called a greeting.

That was it, he realized as he waved to his wife. Something about Julianna Starr reminded him of Kate, though they looked nothing alike. Kate possessed a classic, quiet kind of beauty. Julianna Starr reminded him of the supermodels made so popular by designers like Calvin Klein—waif-Madonnas, somehow child-like and sensual. Despite those differences, he saw something in Julianna's manner that reminded him of his wife—the way she moved and spoke, her smile.

He let himself into the house. He found Kate in the kitchen opening a bottle of merlot. He crossed to her, closing his arms around her from behind. He bent and pressed his lips to her ear. "Hello, beautiful."

She turned in his arms, looping hers around his neck, smiling up at him. "Hello to you, too."

He kissed her, then moved his gaze over her face, taking in the shadows beneath her eyes. "You look tired."

She grimaced. "I am. Emma had a fussy day."

He released her and went to the cabinet for a couple of wineglasses. "She's quiet now."

"Thank God. Nothing I did today made her happy. I swear I spent most of the day walking the floors with her."

He poured them each a glass of the mellow, red wine and brought her one. "I guess you didn't get to The Bean the way you hoped to?"

"Not a chance. Emma would have lasted about two seconds." Kate brought the glass to her lips, sipped, then sighed. "I needed that." She took another sip, sighed again, then put down the glass. "How are the interviews going?"

"Funny you should ask that. I interviewed someone interesting today. A woman."

Kate glanced at the baby monitor to make sure it was on. "Tell me about her."

So he did. When he had finished, Kate looked at him. "She sounds like a dream. Are you going to hire her?"

"I don't know. She's young. Not experienced enough." He eyed his wife's expression, then laughed. "I can see you take umbrage with something I just said."

"It's not that, it's...do you think she can do the job?"

He considered the question a moment, then nodded. "Yeah, I do."

"And you think you could work with her?"

"No doubt, though—" he cut his wife an amused glance from the corners of his eyes "—all that hero worship could get a little old."

"Hero worship?" Kate laughed and tossed the dish towel at him. "Give me a break."

He laughed and leaned against the counter. "So, what are you saying? That you think I should give her the job?"

"It's your decision, of course." From the monitor came the sounds of Emma beginning to stir. Kate straightened. "But she sounds great. And after all, you said she reminds you of me. She has to be good, then."

This time it was he who tossed the towel. She sobered. "Think about it, Richard. We were both young and untried once. Why not give her a chance? Hire her on a trial basis, see what she can do. Tell her you'll evaluate her performance in thirty days."

He thought a moment, then nodded. "I think you're right, I should give her a chance. I'm going to offer her the job."

33

Over the next two weeks, Julianna threw herself into her new job, anxious to impress Richard. The work was deadly dull—making speaking engagements, contacting supporters, running errands—but working with Richard was heaven on earth.

She used every opportunity to worm her way into his affections. Her plan of attack was two-fold. She chose every day's attire with care, endeavoring for a balance between sexy and professional. She purposely wore her skirts a bit too short and when she could, left an extra button of her blouse unfastened—neither being overt enough to cause talk or arouse suspicions, but with an eye to being sexy, womanly. Inviting. The second part of her plan involved being completely accommodating to him, making his every wish her command.

She wanted him to grow to depend on her, to look forward to seeing her, to desiring her. She wanted him to realize he couldn't live without her.

Some days, when he smiled at her in that special way of his, or when he laid a hand on her shoulder or cast a furtive glance at her legs or breasts, she would think she was winning. Other days, when she hardly saw him or when he barely acknowledged her presence, her confidence would sink, her spirits with it.

On those days, she reminded herself that they were

meant to be together, that Richard was her destiny. Then she would double her efforts.

"Julianna?"

Receiver propped between her ear and shoulder, Julianna lifted her gaze. Sandy stood in the doorway to her closetlike office, her expression hopeful. "Yes?" Julianna asked, frowning.

"I thought…maybe, we could have lunch?"

"Sorry." Julianna shook her head. "Mr. Ryan and I are having lunch today."

"You and Mr. Ryan? Your boss, Mr. Ryan?"

"Yes, Sandy." Julianna sighed. "We have business to discuss."

"Oh." She cleared her throat. "So, when can we have lunch together? Tomorrow?"

"I don't know. Maybe."

"That's what you told me yesterday," Sandy said, her tone that of a petulant child. "And the day before, too."

Julianna narrowed her eyes. "Your point?"

"We haven't had lunch once since you came to work here. And it's been two weeks."

"I've been busy. Work comes first."

"I understand. I… How about dinner, then? Or coffee at the Bottom of the Cup? We never see each other anymore."

"Sorry. Can't."

Julianna returned her attention to the call she needed to make, dismissing the other woman without a word.

Sandy didn't budge. "I saw you with Laura and Bruce yesterday. You weren't too busy to have lunch with *them*."

Julianna made a sound of impatience. Sandy was proving to be an annoying drag. The little mouse was the *last* person she wanted to be associated with at the firm, the last person she wanted Richard to associate her with. But still, it seemed unwise to make an enemy of her.

"Geez, Sandy, you sound almost jealous. Like I'm cheating on you or something."

Hot spots of color flew into the other woman's cheeks. "I don't mean to, but...when I got you this job, you promised—"

"Wait a minute, you didn't *get* me this job. I got it. For myself. On my own merits. What would people think if they heard you say that?"

The woman took a step backward. "I'm sorry. It's just that—" She twisted her fingers together, eyes sparkling with tears. "It's almost like you're... dropping me or something."

Julianna closed her appointment book, bent and fished her purse out from under her desk. She slipped the strap over her shoulder and met the other woman's eyes once more. "You're imagining things. I'm just so busy now. In fact—" she glanced at her watch "—I've got to run. Richard is waiting."

For a moment, Sandy simply stared at her, then something crossed her face, a kind of dawning realization. "You used me," she whispered, voice quaking. "To get this job. So you could get next to Mr. Ryan."

"Don't be ridiculous." Julianna battled to conceal her unease. "I didn't know anything about you when we met. Including where you worked."

Sandy shook her head. "How do I know that? You could have been following me around for weeks, learning everything you needed to in order to get close to him."

Julianna stood, alarmed. She hid it as best she could. "And why would I do that?"

"Because you're in love with him. I see the way you look at him. Everybody does."

"You need to get some professional help, Sandy. That or a life." Julianna crossed to stand directly in front of her. "You're really pathetic, you know that? I feel sorry for you."

Julianna slipped past the other woman, leaving her standing in the office doorway, her shoulders shaking with the force of her tears.

34

Julianna and Richard went to the café across the street from the firm. The hostess led them to a table by the windows, and Julianna gazed out at the patio. She looked back at him and sighed. "I love dining alfresco."

Richard laughed. "That's right, this is your first August in southern Louisiana. What do you think? Hot enough for you?"

"What do I think? That I'm going to melt, it's so blasted hot."

She propped her chin on her fist, something that Kate did often and Richard was struck by how much she reminded him of his wife.

"Is it ever going to cool down again?" she asked.

"We usually see some cool days in October."

She picked up her menu, her lips curving into a shy smile. "You're teasing me."

"I wish I were." He smiled. "Just imagine the days before air-conditioning."

That was too horrible to even contemplate, and they fell silent as they studied the menu. No sooner had they laid them aside, than their waitress appeared to take their lunch orders.

Richard watched Julianna while she ordered, thinking again of the similarity between her and Kate. He cocked his head and drew his eyebrows together. It was almost uncanny.

She caught him staring and flushed. "What?"

"You remind me of someone," he said.

"Who's that?"

"As crazy as it sounds, my wife."

"Why would that sound crazy?" she asked.

He laughed. "Because you look nothing alike." The waitress brought their iced teas. He watched as Julianna added two sugars, and he shook his head. "She adds two sugars to her tea, too."

"I don't mind being compared to her," Julianna said softly. "Judging by the picture of her on your desk, she's very attractive."

"Yes, she is." He took a sip of his tea. "You'll have to meet her sometime. I'm sure you'll like her."

"You don't have any children?"

"Pardon?"

"I didn't notice any pictures—"

"I have a daughter," he said quickly. "She's three months old." Even as he said the words, they sounded awkward on his tongue, cumbersome, as if he were telling an untruth. "Emma Grace, that's her name."

"You need to put a picture of her on your desk." She smiled. "Show her off a bit. I'm sure she's gorgeous."

"Of course she is." He cleared his throat, anxious to get off the subject of Emma and down to business. "I'm going to be tied up at the courthouse all afternoon with pretrial motions and thought we'd better go over a few things before it gets too crazy."

"Fine with me." She bent to retrieve her notebook and pen from her purse on the floor. She flipped it open and laid it on the table. "Shoot."

"You've called the local Shriner's and confirmed my speaking engagement?"

"Done." She referred quickly to her notes. "The president, a Jay Summers, will introduce you. I sent over a brief bio. I also reconfirmed the content of your speech, that you would be discussing the district attorney's place in the legal system and your platform. He asked me to remind you to leave twenty minutes at the end for Q and A."

"Good." Richard took another sip of the tea. "As you know, I go to trial next week. It's going to be nuts, you probably won't see me at all. I'll check in with you as I can, but I'll mostly go through Nancy. If anything urgent comes up, let her know."

Julianna nodded, taking notes as he went on. He asked her to contact the people in charge of several upcoming festivals and to reserve a booth at each. He also asked her to query printers about bumper stickers, refrigerator magnets and flyers.

"Got all that?" he asked, when he had finished.

She nodded. "One question, though. How long do you anticipate the trial lasting?"

The waitress brought their sandwiches. When she walked away, Richard began again. "My guess is two to three weeks. There's a lot of evidence to be presented, some of it tricky DNA results."

"So, no speaking engagements, dinners or anything until the trial concludes?"

"Exactly."

She took a bite of her chicken salad sandwich, then washed it down with a swallow of tea. "It must be difficult having to review all the evidence for a crime like this." She shuddered. "I mean, isn't he the one accused of hacking his girlfriend to pieces?"

The media had dubbed his client Dr. Death because of the nature of the crime and because Dr. Robert Wellever was a renown New Orleans surgeon. "Some of it is pretty gruesome," he agreed. "But it's my job and it has to be done."

"Do you think you'll get him off?"

"I hope so. He's an innocent man."

"But what if—" She bit the words back, shaking her head. "Never mind."

"Go ahead, Julianna. What were you about to say?"

"But what if he isn't innocent? Or rather, what if you thought he was guilty?"

"I'd still represent him. In this country, you are innocent until proven guilty. Every American has the right to a fair trial and unbiased representation."

He met her eyes and saw the eagerness there, the admiration and awe of youth. He had to admit, he liked seeing it directed at him. It made him feel young again and on top of the world. "All that said, that's precisely the reason I'm running for D.A. I want to be on the other side of the courtroom for once. I've defended guys who were guilty as sin, I knew they were because they'd confessed to me. Even so, I presented the smartest case I could, given the evidence, and I got them acquitted.

"I didn't like the way that made me feel. Like maybe I needed a bath." He laughed a bit self-consciously, surprised at the way he was confiding his thoughts to her. "A couple times I wished I could turn the sick bastards in myself. Just walk up to the jury and tell them the truth."

"Wow." She leaned toward him, eyes sparkling. As she did, the front of her blouse parted slightly, revealing the curve of one breast. Desire kicked him square in the gut, and he dragged his gaze away, guilt rushing over him in a storm. She lowered her gaze, then looked up at him through dark lashes. "It's such an honor to be working for you."

He laughed. "That makes me sound like some ancient Supreme Court justice. Wrinkled and arthritic."

She joined his laughter. "You're not like that at all. You're the sexiest man—" She brought a hand to her mouth, embarrassed color flooding her face. "I can't believe I...that I said that. I am *so* sorry."

"Don't apologize, for Heaven's sake. I may be old, but I'm not dead. A compliment like that from a beautiful woman is damn nice." Better than nice, he admitted silently. Exciting. Exhilarating. It seemed ages since anyone had looked at him the way Julianna did. Even Kate. These days his wife looked at him as a father first, husband second. He wasn't sure if sexy would even make the top ten.

"Thank you," she murmured. "For the beautiful part."

"You're welcome." He grinned, realizing that he was flirting with her. And not in a small way. Even as he told himself to steer the conversation back to professional matters, he angled his body toward hers. "Tell me about yourself, Julianna. You've been working for me for two weeks and I know nothing more about you than I did the day we met."

She pushed her half-eaten sandwich away. "What do you want to know?"

Everything, he realized. The things she liked, the ones she didn't; what her childhood had been like, the qualities she looked for in a man.

He swallowed hard, uneasy. He hadn't had thoughts

like these about a woman since he had said "I do."
Sure, he had admired a woman's chest or ass, had
wondered, briefly, what she would be like in bed.
There wasn't a heterosexual man, married or not, who
didn't do the same from time to time.

But this was different, he acknowledged. This was
real interest—in Julianna, the person. This was an at-
traction that went deeper than a tickle of arousal over
a short skirt or a glimpse of skin.

Interest in a person—who just happened to be a
pretty secretary—wasn't a crime. It didn't mean he
was a snake or a sneak. It didn't mean he was going
to *cheat*.

He wasn't that kind of man anyway. He was the
kind who loved his wife and believed in the sanctity
of his marriage vows. The kind who had sown all his
wild oats *before* taking the nuptial plunge.

And it was a good thing, too, he thought. Because
if he hadn't, being around Julianna Starr day in and
day out could prove to be dangerous.

35

"Come on, sweetheart," Kate murmured to Emma, who was swinging her arms and legs for all she was worth. "We want to be pretty for our company, don't we? And for Daddy?"

In response Emma kicked harder and squealed louder, laughing at her mother's attempts to dress her. Kate shook her head in amused exasperation. "I guess not, you little stinker."

Kate bent, pressed her lips to the child's bare belly and blew, giving her daughter a raspberry. Emma froze, then let out a gurgle of delight. Kate used the moment to slip the garment over Emma's head, then ease her arms in. Before she could protest, Kate snapped up the legs and crotch.

She grinned at her daughter. "Gotcha."

Aware of time passing, Kate checked her watch and saw that Richard and his new assistant would be arriving in minutes—and she wasn't even dressed yet. After lifting and locking the crib rail, she wound Emma's colorful mobile, which the child would watch for as long as Kate could keep it moving, and dashed to her bedroom to throw on something she wouldn't be embarrassed to be seen wearing.

Sure enough, as she fastened the last button at the neck of her soft, swingy dress, she heard Richard arrive home. "Be right out, hon," she called from the bedroom door. "There's a bottle of white in the fridge and a red in the rack. Pour me a red, will you?"

Kate went to the mirror to check her appearance one last time. She confessed to being a little nervous at the prospect of meeting Julianna. Richard had done nothing but sing the young woman's praises, and when he had mentioned needing to put in some late hours, she had suggested they come to the house. They could all have dinner together, then he and Julianna could get to work while she cleaned up and tended to Emma. After all, she had teased, she wanted to meet this prodigy. He had teased right back, accusing her of being jealous of all the time he was spending with another woman.

She had laughed and kissed him.

She wasn't laughing a few minutes later when Julianna turned, smiled and held out her hand. "You must be Kate," she said softly.

Kate shifted Emma in her arms and took the woman's hand. From Richard's description she had expected a young, eager and unsophisticated woman. She had expected her to be pretty.

But not beautiful. Not mysterious and sexy-looking. She hadn't expected her to be so poised and self-confident.

And she certainly hadn't expected the almost possessive way Julianna looked at her husband.

"And you're Julianna," she said. "It's good to finally meet you."

The young woman shifted her gaze to Emma. Her lips curved into a small, knowing smile. "And this little beauty is Richard's baby. Emma Grace."

Kate bristled. "Yes, this is Emma. *Our* daughter."

Julianna looked at Richard. "I'd love to hold her."

He smiled. "Go ahead."

"No." Kate drew back instinctively as the girl reached out. Embarrassed by the involuntary action, she cleared her throat. "Sorry, but sometimes Emma doesn't react well to strangers. She needs time to warm up."

"Since when?" Richard said with a laugh, on his way out back to light the grill. "Let Julianna hold her. I'm sure she'll be only too happy to give her back if she starts fussing."

He was right. She was behaving like an overprotective idiot.

Kate handed Emma over, a lump forming in her throat. As she watched the younger woman cuddle and coo to her daughter, Kate fought the urge to snatch her back.

What was it about this woman that affected her like fingernails dragging across a chalkboard? Kate wondered. Why had she taken such an immediate and overwhelming dislike to her?

She was acting petty and jealous, Kate decided. A form of dementia brought on by an adult spending all her time alone with an infant.

Be that as it may, when Emma began to squirm, Kate used the opportunity to take her back. "You know babies," she said lightly, forcing a smile, "no one will do quite like their mothers."

"Richard tells me she's adopted."

Kate turned and looked at the other woman. Again, she wore that small, knowing smile. Not a smile, Kate decided, gritting her teeth. A smirk. As if she knew a delicious secret and it made her feel really superior.

Kate wanted to snap that adopted or not, she was still Emma's mother. But she didn't, managing to hold her tongue by reminding herself that this girl was one of Richard's employees. "That's right," she said coolly. "If you'll excuse me, I'll get the appetizers."

Much to her chagrin, Julianna followed her into the kitchen. "You must feel really lucky. I hear it's hard to find babies to adopt."

Kate counted to ten. Normally she didn't let people's well-meaning but sometimes hurtful questions about Emma's adoption get to her. Kate accepted the fact that her daughter was adopted as simply a part of who Emma was, one of the many things that made her special and unique. When someone made a stupid or offensive comment it was because they didn't know any better, and Kate always used the opportunity to educate them.

But Kate found something about this young woman sly. And smug. Julianna's comments rang not of naivete but of nastiness. Kate decided she didn't like Julianna Starr at all.

"We didn't *find* her, Julianna. We adopted her through a very reputable agency."

"Grill's hot," Richard announced, rubbing his hands together as he entered the kitchen. He crossed to the platter of Brie, strawberries and crackers and sliced himself a wedge of the cheese.

"Kate and I were just talking about adoption. I think it's so wonderful that you were able to adopt Emma."

He beamed at the young woman, and Kate nearly choked on a strawberry. Obviously, her husband did not feel the same way she did.

"We think so, too," he said. "In fact, we consider it a kind of miracle." Richard turned to her. "Don't we, hon?"

Kate smiled at her husband, loving him so much in that moment it took her breath away. "That we do."

"Why don't you give Julianna a tour of the house while I cook the steaks?"

Giving Julianna Starr a tour of her home was the last thing Kate wanted to do, but she saw no graceful way out of it. As they moved from room to room, Kate had the strangest feeling that Julianna had been here before, that she knew the layout of the house already, that she was familiar with the room designations, the decor.

Unsettled, Kate hung back slightly to see what Julianna would do. As Kate had suspected she would, Julianna took the lead, and Kate experienced the oddest sensation that *she* was being given a tour of her own home. The sensation made her skin crawl.

"And this is Richard's study," Julianna murmured. She moved into the room, and closing her eyes, breathed deeply through her nose. "It smells like him."

The hairs on the back of Kate's neck stood up. "Excuse me?"

"He's a wonderful man," Julianna said, looking at Kate. "You've been very lucky."

"You make that sound like my luck's about to change," Kate murmured, forcing lightness into her tone.

"Did I? Sorry." Julianna moved her gaze over the room, then fixed it on Kate once more. "I'd love to see the nursery. It's just down the hall, I'll bet."

"It is. But I'm sure there's nothing of interest—"

"Don't be silly, Kate. I have to see precious Emma's room."

She smiled at the infant, and Kate shifted her daughter to her opposite shoulder, the one farthest from Julianna. "All right, then. It's this way."

Kate led her down the hall to the nursery. When they reached it, Julianna rushed into the room, making a sound of pleasure. "It's a little girl's dream room," she said. "All pink and pretty."

She crossed to the dresser and the framed photographs that decorated the top. She inspected each, unabashedly curious. After a moment, she looked over her shoulder at Kate. "There are none of Emma and her daddy."

Kate stared at her, a chill moving up her spine. "We had one," she murmured, her mouth dry. "It was stolen."

"Stolen?" Julianna repeated, bringing a hand to her chest, looking horrified. "You mean someone broke into your home? How awful."

Kate laughed a bit self-consciously. "I should say, maybe stolen. Maybe misplaced. Suddenly, it was just gone."

"That happens to me all the time. I just hate it." Julianna shook her head. "I'm sure it'll show up."

Kate said she hoped it did, then having finished the tour of the upper floor, which served as the main residence, led the other woman downstairs to her studio. Julianna wandered through, touching this and that.

Kate let her wander, using the moments to study her. Richard had said that Julianna reminded him of her. At first, she hadn't seen it. But now she did. Gazing at Julianna was like gazing at a distorted image of herself in a fun house mirror. Julianna wore her hair the way she did; her dress, though made of different fabric and in different colors, was the same style as hers; Julianna's smile, laugh, the way she gestured, all reminded Kate of herself.

Kate swallowed hard, unsettled. It was almost as if the woman had crept into her bedroom in the middle of the night and borrowed her identity.

She wondered what else of hers the young woman might want.

She glanced at her watch. "I'll bet the steaks are almost done. Why don't we go check on Richard?"

Julianna acted as if she hadn't heard her. "I wanted to be an artist," she confided. "But I..." She let her words trail off and picked up Kate's autographed copy of *Dead Drop*. "I just read this. Have you?"

"Not yet, no."

She opened the book and read the inscription. Again Kate had the urge to snatch something of hers out of the girl's hands.

"You and Richard know the author?"

"Yes. He's an old friend of ours." Kate crossed to her and held out her hand for the book. Julianna handed it over, and Kate laid it back on the shelf. "Now, we really must go upstairs. I'm certain Richard's waiting."

Hours later, after Julianna had left and Emma was soundly asleep, Kate stood in front of the mirror in their master bathroom, thinking of Julianna Starr. Richard was already in bed, going over his notes for court the next day.

She glanced his way. "I don't like her, Richard."

He looked up. "You don't like who?"

"Julianna."

He looked completely astounded. "Why on earth not?"

"There's something about her…" Kate looked from him to her own reflection, recalling the sensation of Julianna having stolen her identity. "A secretiveness. I don't think she's told you everything about herself."

He chuckled and shook his head. "Of course she hasn't. I'm her boss, remember?"

Kate frowned. "That's not the way she looks at you."

"For Pete's sake, Kate. She's—"

"You don't see it." Kate squeezed toothpaste onto her brush, then waved it at him. "She looks at you like she'd like to eat you up."

He burst out laughing. "Now there's a thought."

She glared at him. "I'm serious about this. Did you see the way she looked at Emma. As if Emma was hers, not ours." She began to scrub her teeth, then stopped. "When I walked her through the house she all but drooled." At his amused expression, she added. "She acted like she had been here before. Like she knew this house."

"She probably has been, Kate. In her dreams." At her look he lifted his shoulders. "What kid starting out hasn't looked at what we have and drooled? Or maybe fantasized about how someday this would all be theirs? A beautiful home, nice things. A great marriage, successful careers." He smiled softly to take the sting out of his words. "Instead of being suspicious, maybe you should be flattered."

Flattered? She felt threatened. "It wasn't like that," she said, frustrated. "You didn't see it."

"No, I didn't." He patted the bed beside him. "Come to bed. You're exhausted and overwrought. In the morning you're going to feel pretty silly about being so suspicious."

* * *

But in the morning, Kate didn't feel silly. She felt uneasy and unsettled. She hadn't slept well, tormented by dreams of being stalked by a creature she couldn't see but knew was deadly. A creature who threatened to consume her and all she held dear.

As Kate sat in her kitchen sipping her coffee and trying to shake the cobwebs from her head, she acknowledged that urging her husband to hire Julianna Starr might have been a mistake.

36

In the two nights since her dinner with Richard and Kate, Julianna hadn't been able to sleep. Both nights she sat on her bed, knees drawn to her chest, eyes wide and mind racing. Whirling with what she had learned about Kate, Richard and their relationship.

She saw now. She understood. What Richard needed. How she could win him from Kate. It had been so obvious, once she had spent an evening with them.

Julianna worked to slow her breathing, to calm herself. Her mother had been right. Every man had a place inside him, a well that needed to be filled. She had found Richard's.

Kate didn't love him enough.

Not the way she, Julianna, loved him. Not enough to sacrifice her own needs for his, not enough to lay herself adoringly at his feet. Richard needed a woman who made him feel strong and sexually potent. A woman who leaned on him, who not only asked for his opinion, but depended on it.

Kate was too strong-willed, too independent for that. She was too focused on Emma's needs to cater to her husband's. Julianna made a sound of disgust. Kate had hardly put the infant down all night, even bouncing her on her knee during dinner. She had stroked and kissed her, had cooed to her and attended her needs. In contrast, she had simply raised her mouth for a kiss from her husband.

Kate was making it easy for her.

Destiny.

A giggle bubbled to Julianna's lips and she brought a hand to her mouth to stifle the sound, as if someone might hear. Kate's inattention to her husband's needs was only one of the weapons available to her—Luke Dallas was the other. At dinner, Julianna had brought up the author and Kate's autographed copy of his latest book.

Richard had stiffened at the mention of the other man, an angry flush staining his cheeks. Kate had become defensive; she'd lied about where she had gotten the book. A friend had gone to his signing, she had said, and had gotten them a book. He remembered Meg Martin, didn't he?

Julianna knew the truth. She had been at The Uncommon Bean that Saturday morning, had overheard Marilyn tell Blake where Kate had gone. Kate had driven to New Orleans to be with Luke Dallas. She had lied to her husband about it.

Julianna could use that against the other woman. She could use that and Richard's jealousy as a wedge to drive them apart.

And once she did, she would make her move.

What she had to do was so simple. Be there for him. Cater to him, look up to him. Make him feel like a man. Smiling to herself, she scooted down under the covers. Be ever understanding and adoring. Richard would begin to confide in her, small confidences would lead to big ones. Each would bind him to her. Each would solidify their relationship.

And when the rift between the husband and wife grew too great, she would be there, waiting with open arms.

37

John stood on the sidewalk outside Buster's Big Po'boys. His heart raced; a line of sweat formed on his upper lip, another trickled down his back. He closed his eyes and breathed deeply through his nose, working to overcome the slight trembling in his limbs, the excitement. It had taken him eight months, but he had finally found her. His Julianna. His angel.

He double-checked the address he'd gotten from his source at the IRS, saw that it matched Buster's, then moved his gaze over the restaurant's dumpy facade. He couldn't believe Julianna worked here, couldn't believe how low she had sunk. But she did work here— her employer had filed a 1099 under her social security number.

Lucky for him.

A smile touched his mouth. Eight months of waiting was over. Six months of following each lead that surfaced, of frustration when the lead fizzled. Of wondering, worrying and longing—all were over.

John entered the shop. A waitress with a blond beehive hairdo sailed past him, snapping her gum loudly as she did. "Hey, dawlin', sit anywhere. I'll be right wit' you."

Like he would ever sit in a place like this, let alone choose to eat in one.

Well after lunchtime, the restaurant was nearly

empty. John crossed to the cash register and smiled at the girl who sat there, looking bored out of her mind. "Hi, is the owner or manager in?"

The girl looked him up and down, then nodded. "Buster!" she called, "somebody's here to see you."

A moment later a man in a filthy apron emerged from the kitchen. "I'm Buster Boudreaux. What can I do for you?"

"I'm an attorney with Reed, Reed and White." John handed him a business card. "I represent the estate of the late Jonathan Starr and am looking for his daughter, Julianna. Does she work here?"

The man studied the card a moment, then looked up at John, his expression openly curious. He was wondering, John had no doubt, if this situation might yield anything for him.

John smiled. "Ms. Starr has inherited a great deal of money, Mr. Boudreaux, and we're trying to locate her. There's a hefty finder's fee for anyone who provides information that leads to her location."

With a look of disgust, Buster pocketed the card. "She did work here," he said. "Up until four or five months ago. She up and quit without so much as a moment's notice."

"Do you know where she went?" John asked, excited. He was so close, he could all but smell her now.

"Sorry. She didn't leave a forwarding address. Hold on, let me ask one of my girls if they know. Lorena," he called, looking past John, "come here a minute, would you?"

John turned to the waitress who had sauntered over, the bleached blonde who had greeted him when he walked in.

"This guy's lookin' for Julianna. Says she's inherited a whole bunch of money. You have any idea where she went?''

"I don't know and don't care." The woman curled her brightly painted lips with derision. "Little princess thought she was better than everybody else. And there she was, no better than a whore, pregnant and with no man at all."

Anger was swift and white-hot. John narrowed his eyes, holding on to it, though it burned brightly in the pit of his gut. He couldn't allow this piece of human refuse to talk about his Julianna this way. He wouldn't allow it.

"I could give you the address she used when she worked here."

"Thank you. That would be helpful."

The man went in back and returned a moment later with a business card. He'd written Julianna's address on the back. "You did say there'd be a finder's fee in it if I helped you locate her?"

"Absolutely." John plucked the card from the man's fingers, then shifted his gaze to the blonde. "I'll see to it that you get a little something, too, sweetheart. Trust me."

The hour grew late; the French Quarter street gradually emptied. John stood in the shadows across from the hole-in-the-wall bar, watching the lights go off inside, one-by-one.

Finally, his patience was rewarded. Two figures emerged from the bar, a man and the blonde from the po'boy shop, the one with the big mouth. The two said their goodbyes then parted, heading in different directions.

John stepped out of the darkness and started after the woman. He kept his distance, his footfalls silent.

She looked back only once, when he was almost upon her. She started to run then, but it was too late. He caught her on the back of the head and she flew forward, sprawling face first on the damp, filthy street. Where she belonged, he thought, circling her, disgusted.

While she lay there, sobbing into the muck, begging for her life, he kicked her, placing the blow dead to her ribs. The impact lifted her slightly off the ground. He delivered another blow, this one slightly lower.

He hadn't killed her. She would only wish he had.

"Next time," he said softly, "I suggest you show a little respect for your betters."

38

Richard sat across the café table from Julianna. Her head was bent as she studied the menu, and he took the opportunity to enjoy gazing at her. Lately he had been noticing things about his young assistant, nice things. The dewy freshness of her skin, the melodic quality of her laugh, the way she looked up at him, admiration and awe shining from her eyes.

He shook his head, thinking of Kate and the things she had said about Julianna. Manipulative? Secretive? He had spent a good bit of time with her, and he had found her to be sweet, forthright and completely genuine.

Richard took a sip of his iced tea, fighting back a grin. No doubt Kate would hotly deny it, but he suspected the green-eyed monster had something to do with her opinions of his assistant. Who could blame her? Julianna was young, attractive, unencumbered.

It made sense. Although Kate loved Emma and being a mother, it had been an adjustment. The 2:00 a.m. feedings. The fussy spells. The lack of personal freedom. She wasn't even back to work yet, and he couldn't remember the last time she had been down to her glass studio.

"I think I'm going to have the grilled chicken Caesar," Julianna said, closing the menu and lifting her gaze. She found his upon her and blushed. "Is something wrong?"

He couldn't remember the last time he had made a woman blush. He smiled, unreasonably pleased. "Not a thing."

"Then why—" Her blush deepened. "You're staring, Richard."

He propped his fist on his chin. "Am I?"

"You know you are! You're—" She made a sound of exasperation. "Stare all you want, it doesn't bother me."

He laughed and set aside his menu. He and Julianna had gotten into the habit of having lunch together every day he was free. It had proved a good time for them to go over his campaign calendar and discuss his progress.

"Have you talked to Leo this week?" she asked after the waiter had taken their drink orders and walked away.

Leo Bennett was a political consultant Richard had hired to manage his run for office. At this point, still a year and a half out, Leo was serving strictly as a consultant and leaving the actual day-to-day business of "Ryan for D.A." to Richard and Julianna. When they were six months out and all hell was about to break loose, he would step in to take a more active role in the campaign.

"He's out of town. He sent me a list of nonprofit groups he thought we should contact to offer my services as a speaker." He took the list out of his pocket and handed it to her.

She scanned the list, then refolded it and slipped it into her appointment book. "I'll get started this afternoon."

The waiter arrived with their drinks, then took their lunch orders. When he walked away, Richard turned his attention back to Julianna. "How was your weekend?"

She shrugged and added two packets of sugar to her tea. "Okay."

"Just okay?" he teased. "No hot date?"

"Not a one. How about you?"

"Another quiet weekend home with the baby."

She made a sympathetic sound. "Kate still won't leave her with a sitter?"

A week back, he had confided to Julianna his frustration with Kate over her refusal to leave Emma. He had been surprised at himself, breaching their professional relationship with something so personal, but Julianna had been great about it, offering her support and understanding.

Since then, he had confided a dozen other things to her, hopes for the campaign, worries over his parents' health, frustrations with a judge, his paralegal's bumbling incompetence. He had grown to look forward to their talks. Unlike Kate, Julianna always seemed to have time for him. She always understood.

"She will, but it's a fight. She won't use a teenager, not even one from the neighborhood. They're too young, she says. She's found two women she likes very much, but they're always booked. Calling them at the last minute is impossible, and Kate has gotten so she won't even try. I just don't understand it." He expelled a weary-sounding breath. "I don't understand her."

"Not understand her?" Julianna repeated, incredulous. "Surely, that's not true, Richard. She's your wife. You've been together for years."

"She's changed," he said after a moment. "We used to go out. We entertained. Now, she only has time for—"

He bit back the words, flushing at the way he sounded. Petulant and self-absorbed. "Becoming a parent is an adjustment," he said. "It takes time for everything to fall into place."

"Of course it's a big adjustment," she said softly. "But I wonder…how old's Emma?"

"Four months."

She pursed her lips. "Oh."

"What is it?"

She lifted a shoulder. "I've never been a parent, of course. But I have heard that some women…" She shook her head. "Never mind. It's really none of my business."

"Nonsense." He leaned toward her. "I've made it your business by bringing it up. Tell me what you've heard."

"That some new mothers become terribly depressed. It gets to the point that their spouses hardly recognize them. Could that be what's going on with her? I mean, do you think she's happy?"

"You had dinner with us." He frowned. "What do you think?"

She hesitated, as if choosing her words carefully. "She seemed…devoted to Emma."

But not to me. Julianna didn't need to tell him that. He knew it already.

"Be patient," she murmured. "I'm sure this will pass."

But what if it didn't? he wondered as the waiter delivered their food. What if he and Kate kept drifting farther apart until they neither understood each other nor had anything in common?

He and Julianna ate in silence for several moments. She broke it first. "Richard?"

He glanced up, and Julianna reached across the table and covered his hand with her own. He lowered his gaze to their joined hands, surprised by her gesture and by the jolt of awareness that shot through him.

He told himself to draw his hand away. He didn't move a muscle.

"There's something I've wanted to tell you, but I...I—" Her voice faltered, but she cleared her throat, seeming to marshal her courage. "I've been going back and forth, trying to decide if I should tell you, but now, with Kate behaving so strangely..."

"This is about Kate?"

"Yes." She looked away, then back. "And...and Luke Dallas."

Richard stiffened. "What are you talking about?"

"That night, at your house...she didn't tell you the whole truth about that autographed book. I saw her, Richard."

He shook his head. "What do you mean? You saw her where?"

"At Luke Dallas's book signing. She had Emma with her. The line was really long, and I remember looking at her with the baby and feeling sorry for her. She looked so tired."

Richard struggled to hide his fury. His embarrassment. The betrayal that rushed over him in a hot, bitter wave.

She sat back in her chair, her expression distressed. "I shouldn't have said anything. I'm sorry, I just thought you'd want to..."

That he would want to know. That his wife was chasing all over the countryside after an old boyfriend when she didn't have time to go out to dinner with her own husband. That she had lied to him.

"I'm sorry," Julianna said again, eyes filling with tears. "I can tell that you're upset, and I don't blame you." She leaned forward, her tone pleading. "Please, forget I said anything. I probably was mistaken and I'd...I'd hate if you and Kate argued over this."

"Nonsense," he said stiffly, forcing a smile. "I'm glad you did bring it up. It's no big deal. The three of us were good friends back at Tulane, and I'm sure she simply forgot to tell me."

"I'm sure that's it."

They both knew that was a lie. He checked his watch, then signaled the waiter to bring the bill. Their server brought the check; Richard paid with cash. "We'd better get back. It's going to be a busy afternoon."

"That it is."

Julianna eased her chair back from the table, preparing to stand. He stopped her.

"Julianna?" She looked at him. "Thanks for listening. I know it's not exactly in your job description."

Her lips curved into a sweetly sad smile. "I'm always here for you, Richard. No matter what you need. Don't forget that."

39

Richard was late. Kate checked her watch for about the hundredth time in the past hour. Ten o'clock, she saw. *Where was he?* When she'd spoken with him right before lunch, he had said he'd be home early.

She caught her bottom lip between her teeth, worried. It wasn't like him not to call. If he'd had a last-minute dinner appointment or meeting, he would have let her know.

Kate began to pace, nearly hysterical with worry. She had called everyone she could think of—his partners, golf buddies, even his parents—had checked the health club and country club bar. She had tried the police and local emergency rooms. Nobody had seen him.

She drew in a shuddering breath, imagining him at the side of some road, bleeding or unconscious, his car a heap of twisted metal and broken glass.

Ten became ten-fifteen. Became eleven. Still no Richard.

When she finally heard his key in the lock, she flew to the door and yanked it open. "Richard, thank God! I've been worried sick. Where have you been?"

"Well, if it isn't my devoted and loving wife."

He lurched past her, and she brought a hand to her nose as the smell of liquor and cigarettes hit her in a nauseating wave. "You've been drinking."

"Give the little lady a gold star."

He tossed his briefcase toward the couch and missed. It hit the floor with a loud thump. Kate glanced nervously toward the nursery. "Careful, you'll wake the baby."

"The *baby*," he mimicked, his tone snide. "It's always about the baby, isn't it?"

He hadn't just been drinking, she realized, a sinking sensation in the pit of her stomach. He'd been bingeing. And brooding. The way he sometimes had in college, the way that had always brought out the person she didn't like.

"Where have you been, Richard?"

"Out." He swung to face her. "The more appropriate question is, where have *you* been?"

"Here. Waiting for you. Worried out of my mind."

"I need a drink."

He started past her; she stopped him with a hand to his arm. "I think you've had enough."

"You don't tell me what to do." He shook off her hand roughly. "Nobody does."

Kate took a step back, shocked. This was a Richard she had only seen a couple of times, years ago. Still, she knew from experience that being confrontational when Richard was in this mode was counterproductive. When he was like this he had a hair-trigger temper, and when it snapped, it was terrifying.

She took a deep, calming breath. "Talk to me, hon," she coaxed. "Tell me what's happened."

"Why don't you tell me?" He took a step toward her. "Let's talk about the book, Kate. Tell me about *Dead Drop*."

"Luke's book?" She shook her head. "I don't understand."

"Sure," he sneered. "How'd you get that auto-graph?"

Her heart began to rap against the wall of her chest. The last thing she wanted to bring up was her visit with Luke, not while Richard was already half crazy. "I told you how I—"

"That's bullshit!" he shouted. "You went to New Orleans to see him. Behind my back." He took an-other step closer. "What did you do? Dig that fucking invitation out of the trash?"

She lifted her chin, meeting his eyes evenly. "As a matter of fact, I wanted to see him. I wanted to try to repair our friendship."

He released a short bark of laughter. "Friendship my ass."

"It's true. I wanted us all to get together. I called him several times, and when he didn't call me back, I decided to go see him."

"And because it was all so perfectly innocent," he said slurring his words, "you lied to me about it."

She clasped her hands together, wishing she could go back, take back the lie, hating herself for it. "At first I didn't tell you because I knew you'd react like this. Then the other night, I didn't want us to get into it in front of your assistant. I'm sorry, Richard. Believe me, I wish I had been honest with you from the be-ginning."

"Sure you do." He took a lurching step toward her. "You lied to me. So you could see him. That bas-tard."

"I'm not going to talk with you about this now," she said, hanging on to her temper by a thread. "You're drunk."

She tried to duck by him; he blocked her exit, face

twisted with rage and jealousy. "You don't have the time or energy to devote to me when I need you, yet you have enough of both to drive into the city with Emma and wait hours in line so he could sign his precious, fucking book."

"You're drunk," she said again. "We'll talk about this in the morning."

"The hell we will, we'll talk about it now!" He dragged a hand through his hair. "She saw you there. That night, she knew the truth about you and Dallas. You can't imagine how humiliating, how—"

"Who saw me there?" she demanded. "And what truth are you talking about? That Luke and I were friends and now we're not?"

"You know what I'm talking about." He leaned toward her, swaying drunkenly. "You know."

"Who saw me?" Kate demanded again. "Your assistant?" His expression said it all, and Kate felt sick. No wonder the young woman had been so interested in the book, no wonder she'd brought Luke up that night at dinner.

"She's a snake, Richard. You're just too smitten to see it."

"You wish you'd married him, don't you? Now that he's Mr. Big and Famous Author. Now that he has more money than I do."

Kate recoiled from his words, even as they tore at her heart. "How can you say that? How, after all these years together?"

"That's why you went to see him, isn't it? To tell him you made a mistake. That you wished you'd married him."

"That's ridiculous," she said stiffly. "You're being

ridiculous. And I'm not going to listen to one more word.''

She began to turn away; he stopped her, catching her by her upper arms. "Why'd you marry me, Kate? For my money? So you could be Mrs. Richard Ryan and live in a big, fancy house?''

"Stop it!'' she cried, losing her tenuous grip on her emotions. First Luke, now Richard. Didn't the men in her life know her at all? "Stop before this goes any further. Before we both say more that can't be taken back.''

From the baby monitor clipped to her belt came the sound of Emma stirring in her crib. A moment later the harmless snuffling became whimpers, then mewls of discomfort.

Kate yanked free of her husband's grasp. "Emma needs me.''

"I need you, too. What about me, Kate?''

She looked at him, incredulous. "She's an infant, Richard. Not an adult.''

She started for the nursery.

"Go on, then,'' he called after her. "Like you went to Luke. You have time for everyone but me, don't you? Luke Dallas. The Bean. Your daughter.''

She stopped, turned and faced him. "Our daughter,'' she murmured, voice shaking. "*Ours*. Though for all the time you spend with her, no one would ever know it.''

"Why should I? You're already spending twenty-four hours a day with her. What's left for me, Kate?''

Kate was stunned by his jealousy. His feelings toward Luke and Luke's success were bad enough. But to be jealous of his own daughter, a helpless infant? It made her sick.

"Grow up, Richard. Act like an adult instead of the spoiled little rich kid who always got his way."

Kate hurried to the nursery, Emma's mewls full-fledged cries now. Richard followed. Before she could scoop the child up, Richard caught her by the arm and yanked her back against his chest. "You're mine, Kate. I won you and I won't let Luke or anybody else take you away."

"Won me?" she repeated brokenly, remembering what Luke had said to her. "Is that what our marriage is about? Some sort of competition?"

He didn't answer, and she began to struggle against his grasp. "Let me go, Richard! Emma's crying."

"Mine," he said again, tightening his grip on her.

A moment later his mouth crashed down on hers in a bruising kiss. He ground his lips against hers, forcing them open, shoving his tongue inside. She gagged at the sensation and at the sickly sweet smell of bourbon.

She wrenched her mouth free, heart thundering, Emma's cries ringing in her ears. "Let me go! Richard—"

He brought a hand to the back of her head to hold her immobile as he found her mouth again. This time, as he forced his tongue into her mouth, he ground his pelvis against hers, his erection—and intention—obvious.

Hysteria rose up in her. She struggled, pushing against his chest, twisting and kicking. Dear God, who was this man? What had happened to the loving and gentle man she had been married to for ten years?

She jerked sideways and wedged her arms between them, then brought her heel down hard on his instep. With a grunt, he released her and stumbled backward, the pain seeming to penetrate his liquor-induced frenzy.

He looked at her, his bleary-eyed expression becoming one of dawning horror at his own actions.

She spun around, snatched up Emma and cradled her to her chest, talking softly as much to calm her own fears as Emma's. Tears burned her eyes and throat, choking her.

"Kate?" he murmured brokenly. "Kate?"

She couldn't bring herself to acknowledge the anguish in his voice, couldn't bring herself to even look at him—not now, when her mouth still burned from his brutal attack, when her limbs still trembled from the effort expended fighting him off.

"She's not even ours," he whispered. "And still you love her more than me."

Kate felt as if her world were crumbling around her. She'd never been so angry, so hurt, in her life. She looked at her husband then, acknowledging that he was a total stranger.

"What's wrong with you?" she asked, voice quavering. "How can you say that? She is ours. Parenting is about loving and nurturing. Not about a physical act of copulation." She struggled to speak around her tears. "I thought we both believed that, Richard."

When he said nothing, just simply stared at her, her tears welled and spilled over, her heart hurting so badly she feared it would break. She bent and pressed her head to Emma's. "Get out," she said. "Get out because I don't want you around Emma. And I can't bear to look at you."

Without a word, he turned and left the nursery. A

moment later, the sound of the front door slamming echoed through the house.

Emma snuggled safely in her arms, Kate sank onto the rocking chair and sobbed.

40

Richard found himself at Julianna's front door. For long minutes, he simply stood there, staring at the door, wanting to knock but knowing he shouldn't. It was late. He was her boss. Being here crossed an invisible line, one that separated employer from employee, professional from personal.

Richard told himself to turn away, to head home, tail tucked between his legs. He stood frozen to the spot instead. He closed his eyes, imagining Julianna opening the door, ushering him in. She would gaze up at him in the way she always did, the way that made him feel ten feet tall and invincible. She would listen and understand.

Julianna believed in him. She thought he was special.

The way Kate used to.

He lifted his hand and rapped lightly on the door. The moment he did, twin emotions of exhilaration and panic coursed through him. Panic won, stealing his breath, bringing him to his senses. What the hell was he doing? He was a married man. Julianna was his employee. Forget the moral ramifications of his behavior, what about the legal ones? This could surely be labeled sexual harassment. He was a lawyer, for God's sake. He hoped to be St. Tammany Parish's next district attorney.

He took a step backward, then swung around and started down the steps, grateful some sense had wormed its way into his booze-fogged brain before it was too late.

Not before it was too late. Her door opened; light spilled out into the night. "Richard? Is that you?" He turned and met her eyes, and she made a sound of surprise. "What in the world are you doing here?"

He flushed, wishing he could think clearly, wishing he had not had so much to drink. "I'm sorry, Julianna. Kate and I...we had a fight, and I didn't know where else to—" He drew in a deep breath. "I feel like a total ass about this. I hope you can forgive me this horrible breach of professional etiquette."

She opened the door a bit wider and stepped more fully into the rectangle of light. "You and Kate had a fight?"

Backlit that way, her gown became nearly transparent. Even as he told himself not to, Richard lowered his gaze. His mouth went dry; the blood began to pound in his head.

"Yes." He dragged his gaze back to hers, both embarrassed and aroused. "I needed someone to talk to, and I...I thought of you."

She pushed the door the rest of the way open. "I'll get my robe."

Her apartment was small and shabbily furnished but neat as a pin. Even exhausted and inebriated, he noticed expensive, elegant touches here and there: a vase of exotic flowers, a shimmery, soft-looking throw on the couch, groupings of scented candles of varying sizes and shapes.

She returned several moments later, wrapped in a

white chenille robe and carrying two steaming mugs of coffee.

"Have a seat," she murmured, a smile tugging at her mouth.

Richard realized he hadn't moved from just inside the door and crossed to the couch and sat down. "I shouldn't be here. I feel like a jerk."

"We're friends. I'm glad to be here for you."

She bent and handed him his coffee. As she did, the front of her robe gaped open, giving him a view of her breasts, clear to their tight rosy nipples.

Arousal hit him, taking his breath. He jerked his gaze up to hers. "Thank you."

She straightened; the flaps of her robe fell back into place. "Do you need cream or sugar?"

He looked blankly at the mug in his hand, then back up at her. "Black's fine, thanks."

She took a seat at the opposite end of the couch, curling her legs under her. "Tell me what happened."

He hesitated a moment, then began to speak. "You weren't wrong. She lied about the book." He wrapped his hands around the mug. "She went to see Dallas."

Julianna was silent for a moment, then she made a sound of regret. "I'm sorry."

He shook his head. "Back at Tulane, we were all friends. Or so I thought. Then I discovered Dallas was in love with her. All along, while he pretended to be my friend, he schemed to steal my girl. The bastard."

"Yet you remained his friend?"

"It wasn't until right before graduation that I found out what he'd been up to. He told me, flat out." He looked at Julianna. "That's some balls."

"It is," she murmured. "I'm sure Luke Dallas meant nothing to Kate. After all, she chose you."

Richard thought of his and Kate's fight, of the question he had asked her. *Why did you marry me, Kate? For my money?*

She had denied it, of course. She had been indignant, incensed. He wanted to believe her, but a voice of doubt buried deep within him taunted that was exactly why she had married him.

"In college, Luke didn't have a pot to piss in. Now look at him, rich and famous. Brushing elbows with celebrities."

Even without family money or connections Luke had bested him, Richard thought angrily. Just like he had always said he would. Cocky bastard, he hated him. Hated him with a fire that burned deep inside him, raging nearly out of control.

"He got lucky," Richard said, setting aside his coffee and launching to his feet. He began to pace. "Lucky," he repeated. "That's all. It could happen to anyone. To hear Kate talk, you'd think he was the second coming. Selling a couple of books certainly doesn't mean he's special. Or that he should be put up on some goddamn pedestal."

"Of course not," she cooed. "And I know some women find all that fame and money a powerful lure, though I don't understand it." She hesitated, as if choosing her words carefully. "I'm sure Kate wouldn't be swayed by such superficial things."

He stopped pacing and looked at her. "You really think so?"

"I do. Besides, so what if Dallas had a thing for Kate? It would be different if they had been lovers. But they weren't. Right?"

It would be different. It would make all the difference in the world.

He sat back down, his legs refusing to hold his weight a moment more. He flopped against the sofa back, resting his head against the cushion and staring up at the ceiling. All these years a suspicion that something physical had happened between Luke and Kate had burned in the pit of his gut. More than a suspicion, really; a kind of awful certainty. But he had been able to shrug off the suspicion by reminding himself that he, not Dallas, had won the prize.

Kate had lied to him. So she could see Dallas.

"Richard?"

"Right," he said. "No sex. They were just friends."

"Then you have nothing to worry about. Be patient. I'm sure she loves you very much."

"I don't know." He shook his head. "Just a few months ago I believed that. I believed I had the perfect marriage. Now I...now it seems like everything's falling apart."

Disgusted with himself, with his self-pity and whining, he stood again and crossed to the window. Julianna's street was dark, deserted. Not a light shone down either side; Richard realized how late it must be. Was Kate still awake? he wondered. And if so, did she worry where he was?

Julianna came up behind him. She laid her hands on his shoulders and began to massage them, working at the tight, aching muscles. It felt great, and a sound of pleasure slipped past his lips.

"I should go," he murmured, though leaving was the last thing he wanted to do.

"Yes."

He turned and faced her. "Thank you for tonight. I

don't know what I would have done without you to talk to.''

She smiled sadly. "How could she not love you? You're everything a woman could—'' Her throat closed over the words, and she looked quickly away.

"Julianna?'' He brought a hand to her face. "Look at me.''

She did and he saw that she was crying. He made a sound of surprise. "Baby, what's wrong?''

She shook her head and took a step away from him. "Nothing. Just go.''

He caught her hand, stopping her from leaving. "You're crying. Something must be wrong.''

A single tear rolled down her cheek. "It's not right for me to say. You're a married man.''

"I'm not leaving until you tell me what's wrong.'' He brought both hands to her face, cupping it. "Talk to me, Julianna.''

She drew in a shuddering breath, tipping her face into his palm, rubbing herself against him like a cat. "All my life I've...I've waited for a man like you. And Kate, it's like she's just tossing...doesn't she see...doesn't she know how special you are?''

Warmth for this girl, this innocent, swelled inside him. "Sweetheart.'' The endearment slipped from his lips, as naturally as his breath. She lifted her gaze to his again and his heart turned over. Her eyes were filled with longing—and with regret, that it was not to be.

At that moment he could think of nothing but her lips, their color, how they would feel against his, how they would taste. Giving in to the questions, his longing, he bent and ever so lightly brushed his mouth against hers.

Her lips trembled, then parted. With a groan, he deepened the kiss, spearing his tongue into her mouth, tasting, exploring. Conquering.

She curled her fingers around his shoulders, clinging to him for one perfect moment, then flattened her hands and pushed him away.

"No, Richard." She sucked in a shaky breath. "We can't. You have a wife. A child."

Richard struggled to get ahold of himself. Struggled for the equilibrium that until tonight had rarely escaped him.

"I'd give anything to be with you," she said softly, "but not like this. You'd hate yourself later. And I couldn't bear that."

"Julianna—"

"No." She placed a finger against his lips. "Don't say anything. Just go home, Richard. To Kate. To your baby daughter."

She was right, he knew. His responsibilities lay elsewhere. But still, he was torn. There was such a sweetness about her. Such vulnerability.

It called to him. She called to him.

He opened his mouth, though he hadn't a clue to say what. Nothing seemed adequate, everything meant nothing. Would change nothing.

He was a married man.

With one last look at her, he walked away.

41

For a long time after Richard left, Julianna sat alone in the dark, reliving Richard's visit, their kiss. She brought a hand to her mouth, still feeling the imprint of his lips against hers. Hot. Searching. Desperate.

Julianna shuddered at the memory. She had wanted him just as desperately. Pushing him away had been one of the hardest things she'd ever had to do. She had only found the strength of will to do it by reminding herself of the things her mother had told her over the years about winning a man. To reel him in slowly. To never give in to sex too quickly. That nothing would send a man scurrying back to his wife faster than guilt. That a man had to feel his behavior justified, even when he was cheating. He had to feel righteous for having held out as long as humanly possible.

Julianna smiled. Richard had tumbled once, he would again, falling deeper under her spell. How could he not? Now that he'd had a taste of what he could have with her, Kate's distracted kisses and hurried lovemaking would be less satisfying than before. More frustrating.

Besides, she simply couldn't lose. She had destiny on her side.

Richard didn't know it yet, but he was already hers.

42

The next morning, Richard was contrite. Distraught. He begged Kate's forgiveness and cuddled Emma to him, saying how much he loved her. He blamed his behavior on stress and booze; he must have been out of his mind, he said and promised it would never happen again. During the day he sent Kate a huge bouquet of flowers; that evening he came home from work with a stuffed bear for Emma.

Kate agreed to forgive him. How could she not? He was her husband; she had made him a promise of for better or for worse, had made it in front of their family, friends and God.

And this was definitely one of those times in the "worse" category, she thought later that night as she stood on the upper gallery, gazing out at the dark lake. She lifted her face to the starless sky. She had said she would forgive him and she would. Forgetting would be the problem. For as hard as she had tried, she'd been unable to put out of her mind the way he had forced himself on her, the things he had said. Especially the ones about Emma.

And she couldn't shake the feeling that something had gone terribly awry in their marriage, that they were being manipulated by forces outside themselves.

She had felt that way for weeks.

Kate frowned, thinking back. Since the day of

Luke's book signing, she realized. The day the photo of Richard and Emma had disappeared, the day Old Joe had told her about the girl on the swing.

The girl on the swing.

Julianna. Emma.

Kate rubbed her arms, chilled despite the warm night, her head whirling with thoughts of Emma falling into their lives so suddenly. Of Richard's new assistant and of the surprising and intense dislike she had taken to her. Of Richard's behavior and the missing photograph. Of her own feelings of helplessness.

One had nothing to do with the other. Nothing except swirling together to create an unsettling brew, one that had knocked both her and Richard completely off balance.

"Kate?"

She turned. Richard stood in the doorway, his expression boyish and guilty. She couldn't control the anger that speared through her, though she tried.

"Trouble sleeping?" he asked.

"Yes."

He crossed to her, but didn't touch her. She glanced at him, then back out at the lake. Had things gotten so bad between them that he was afraid to touch her? And that she didn't care if he did?

"I'm sorry," he said. He turned to her. "I really am, Kate."

She had heard those words from him, said in exactly that way so many years ago. She sighed. "I know."

"Will you ever forgive me?"

"I'm trying." *But it wasn't as easy as it had once been. And that frightened her to her core.*

He caught her hands. "Come to bed. Let me make love to you. Let me prove how much I love you."

When she hesitated, he brought her hands to his mouth. "Everything's going to be okay with us, Kate. The way it's always been. Trust me."

She acquiesced and he led her to their bedroom, to their bed. They made love and she clung to the familiar, to the Richard she had known and loved for so long. The Richard she had been happy with.

But even as she did, she feared that nothing would ever be the same between them again.

43

Richard lay on his side and watched Kate as she slept. Two weeks had passed since the night he and Kate had fought. Two weeks since he had run to Julianna and held her in his arms. Two weeks of hell.

He moved his gaze over his wife's face, knowing each curve and hollow, each line and shadow by heart. They had been together long enough to know each other inside and out. He loved and admired her. He wished he had her goodness, her strength. He couldn't imagine his life without her.

Yet even as he lay beside her on their bed, he felt himself slipping away from her and toward Julianna. It was wrong. He knew that. Each day he headed to work armed by a night with Kate, by a night spent reminding himself of his responsibilities, his moral obligations, that a man was only as good as his word.

The minute he saw Julianna, reason, reminders and moral responsibilities flew out the window. She made him feel young again. Sexually potent. She awakened in him feelings, urges, he hadn't had in years.

He had become obsessed with the other woman. With thoughts of sex with her—how she would taste, how it would feel to be inside her, the sounds she would make when she climaxed.

It had been two weeks of hell, of being torn between

two different women, between right and wrong, love and lust.

Richard rolled onto his back and stared up at the ceiling and the gently whirling fan. Only an hour ago he and Kate had made love. When he'd climaxed he'd thought of Julianna. He had pictured her writhing under him, bucking against him with her own release, crying out his name.

But it had been his wife crying out his name, and his guilt had been a bitter, sobering brew.

He threw his arm across his eyes, disgusted with himself. What was wrong with him? He loved Kate. He loved their life together.

But he wanted Julianna. So much, he sometimes thought he would go mad if he didn't have her.

Julianna hadn't encouraged him. Quite the opposite, she had held him at arm's length, seemingly more conscious of his responsibilities and moral obligations than he.

They'd talked about their kiss, agreed it had been a mistake and that it would never happen again.

Easier said than done, he thought, stifling a groan. The air between them was electric; it all but crackled with awareness and unrelieved arousal. During the middle of a meeting he would find himself staring at her mouth, remembering and becoming aroused. While working, their hands or shoulders would brush; they would both look up at the same time and their gazes would lock.

And he would see his own longing mirrored back at him from her eyes.

If it were only sexual, he thought not for the first time, his head beginning to hurt, he could deal with it, could somehow conquer it. But everything about her called to him. When he looked at her he felt a deep urge to hold her close, to protect and possess her, the way men had been protecting and possessing women throughout time. She was everything a woman should be—sweet, vulnerable and bright, sexy as hell.

She had offered to quit. Had urged him to find someone else for the job. His family, she'd said, came first. They had to be strong, had to do the right thing.

He had refused. He couldn't do that to her; it wouldn't be fair or right. Besides being good at her job, she needed it.

No, it was up to him to be a man. To be strong; to exert self-control. It wouldn't be easy—for either of them—but they could do it.

The jangle of the phone startled him out of his musings. He grabbed it before it could ring a second time, not wanting Kate or Emma to be awakened.

It was Julianna. She was crying. Nearly hysterical.

"What wrong?" he asked alarmed.

"I don't know what to do. I'm so frightened."

He glanced over his shoulder at Kate. She stirred, but didn't awaken. He sat up and pressed the phone tighter to his ear. "Tell me what's happened?"

"Someone tried to break in. I was sleeping and—" she sucked in a broken-sounding breath "—he rattled the doorknob and I...I saw someone...a figure at the window."

"I'll be right there. Make sure all your doors and windows are locked, and just sit tight."

He hung up the phone and climbed out of bed.

"Richard?" Kate mumbled. "What's going on?"

"The office," he said. "There's been a break-in."

The lie slipped so easily, so convincingly, past his lips it frightened him. He wished he could call it back.

But he couldn't, he realized, stomach sinking. Now spoken, he was stuck with it.

"A break-in?" She eased up on an elbow, her expression concerned.

"I'm going to check it out." Unable to look her in the eye, he turned his back to her and pulled on a pair of khakis and a golf shirt.

Fully awake now, she sat up, pushing the hair out of her eyes. "Are you sure it's safe? I don't know if it's such a good idea for you to—"

"The police are there. They need one of the partners to come down and look the place over, reset the alarm, things like that." He looked over his shoulder at her, smiling reassuringly. "Lucky me, my number must have topped the list."

She frowned. "If you're sure it's safe?"

"I am." Blood pounding in his head, Richard went around the bed, bent and kissed her. As he did, he was struck with what a big part of his life she was, how long they had been together, how much he loved her. And how close he was to losing it all.

No. He wouldn't allow that to happen. He was letting his imagination run away with him. He was going to help a friend in need. A woman who was alone and terrified. He'd lied about it because...because it was late and he'd wanted to avoid a scene. That was all.

He bent and kissed Kate again, this time more deeply. "I love you, Kate," he murmured, his voice catching. "Believe that."

When he broke away, she clung to him a moment. She searched his gaze. "I'm scared, Richard."

He knew she wasn't talking about tonight or about his going down to the firm to check out an attempted robbery. She was talking about them, the forever they had taken for granted for so long.

He kissed her one last time. More, he acknowledged, to reassure himself than her. ''There's nothing to be scared of,'' he said, forcing an easy smile. ''I'll be back before you can say Jumpin' Jack Flash.''

44

Julianna opened the door and Richard stepped into her apartment. He closed and locked it behind him, then turned and met her eyes. They were both adults; they knew exactly what they were doing—why he had run right over, first lying to his wife, then kissing her three times before leaving.

They didn't speak. Julianna moved into his arms and pressed herself against him. Through her sheer gown he felt every curve and hollow of her body. He dropped his hands to her backside and pulled her closer, wanting her to feel how desperately and completely he wanted her.

At the contact, the breath shuddered past her lips. She rubbed herself against his erection, clinging to him, trembling.

He stripped off her gown; she his clothes. Naked they sank to the floor. She took him first in her hands, then her mouth, doing things to his body he had only dreamed of before.

Gasping, he rolled onto his back, lifted and impaled her. She thrust her hips forward and back, driving him to a fever pitch. And when she arched her back and screamed, he orgasmed violently.

Still shuddering with his release, realization set in. He'd fucked another woman, had broken his wedding vows, every promise he had ever made to his wife.

Only this time he couldn't blame his actions on booze or Kate's inattention; he couldn't blame Luke Dallas. What he had done had been with a clear head and full awareness of the consequences.

The consequences. He sucked in a choked breath.

Dear God, he'd ruined his picture-perfect life. He'd thrown it away. On a woman, on a quick, sweaty roll in the hay.

Julianna purred and rubbed herself against him, and he felt sick. At what he'd done. That, God help him, he wanted to do it again. Now. Tomorrow. The day after that.

His body cooled. He tightened his arms around her. Even as he scrambled for a way out of what he'd done, a way to return to the honorable man he had been a minute before he'd succumbed, he realized he couldn't go back. That he didn't want to.

Now that he'd had Julianna, he couldn't imagine not having her again. She was in his blood now.

Part VI

Cause for Alarm

45

John stood at the center of Julianna's tiny apartment. He smiled. With satisfaction. In anticipation of their reunion. It would be good, he decided, unable to suppress a shudder. Very good.

He moved his gaze over the room, curious yet repelled. There were no signs of a baby here, no toys or playpen or crib, no cloying smell of formula or powder. As he had known she would once she'd had time to consider her options, she had seen things his way and aborted it.

After all, Julianna was spoiled. She was accustomed to being taken care of, to having her way, to having nice things. Caring for a howling infant night and day, changing soiled diapers and messy bibs was not her style.

Not that one would know it from this hovel of an apartment, he thought, disgusted. Or the jobs she had taken in the past months. He shook his head. He supposed nothing she had done, no depths to which she had sunk since leaving his care, would surprise him anymore.

She would already be home with him if not for her mother and Russell. They had frightened her. They had told her things about him that weren't hers to know; she was confused and afraid. By what they had said. And by her own disobedience. Her disloyalty.

He closed his eyes and drew in a deep, cleansing breath. His angel had fallen from grace. She had paid the price, living like this. But only part of the price. The rest was to come.

At his loving hands.

John crossed to the desk, shoved into a corner of the living room, and began leafing through the pile of mail on its top. Sale circulars and advertisements, the utility and phone bill. He opened the latter and scanned the register of long distance calls. There were several to New Orleans, all to the same number, two charges for long distance information and one call to Langley, Virginia.

The Agency. John frowned, staring at the familiar number. Why had she called CIA headquarters?

John slipped the bill into his pocket, the call a reminder of the other reason he had tracked Julianna here. His book. It contained information that was important to him. Names and dates. Places. Amounts. He had kept the record as a bargaining chip, a sort of "Get Out of Jail Free" card.

Quite a number of people would love to get their hands on it, including his former buddies at the Agency. He wanted it back.

When he had discovered the book missing, his fury had known no bounds. He'd been furious at her for her willfulness and at himself for underestimating her. For trusting her too much.

He wouldn't make that mistake again.

John began his search, starting with the desk and living room, then moving on to the kitchen and bathroom. He worked methodically, checking both the obvious places and those she might consider clever. He inched along the baseboards, looking for one that was loose, the same with the floorboards; he went through the contents of her freezer, the pantry; he checked the toilet's water tank and between the stack of bath towels on the rack above it.

He finally reached her bedroom. He searched from one end to the other, saving the dresser for last. He worked from the bottom up; he opened the top drawer and froze. It contained sheer nighties and skimpy underwear. He stared at them, disoriented, light-headed. He lifted a pair of the thong panties. Made of black nylon and polyester lace, they were the type worn by a woman who fucked freely, indiscriminately. The kind of woman who's soul had been fouled, her light extinguished.

Not his Julianna. Not the sweet girl he had loved so well and for so long.

He curled his fingers into the fabric, the blood pounding, drumlike in his head. It made him sick, the thought of her, his special girl, in these whore's clothes. And if she wore them, who did she wear them for?

Rage swelled inside him, stealing his breath, his ability to reason, to think. One by one, he destroyed the offensive garments, using his teeth and hands to snap elastic and lace, to tear flimsy nylon.

She had not learned from his lesson that last night. He would have to give her another. He would show her the error of her ways. Every child chafed under the restraints of the older and wiser. This was her rebellion.

He drew a calming breath, flexing his fingers, steadying himself. He would punish her and they would go on as before. Better than before.

He would wait. Bide his time. Toy with her; rock the safe little world she had created for herself.

But first, a gift.

He went to the bed and pulled back the coverlet and top sheet. He knelt on the edge, unzipped his pants and took himself in his hand. Closing his eyes, he stroked himself, imagining, remembering—skin, as smooth and white as new silk; tiny buds of breasts, pink-tipped and tender, a pubis as smooth and moist and new as the rest of her. He stroked faster, harder, his breath coming in pants. With a groan, he ejaculated on her sheets.

He fastened back up, then extracted a folding knife from his pocket. He swung open the blade, honed to a razor sharp edge. Without flinching, he ran the blade across the top of his hand. The skin parted, a line of red chased the tip of the blade.

Satisfied, he held his hand out, watching the blood trickle from his hand to the bed—blood meeting sperm, mingling with it. Life. And death. Beginnings and endings. Now and forever.

She would understand.

46

"What do you have for me?" Tom Morris asked Condor without preamble.

They sat on a bench in the main hall of D.C.'s busy Union Station. People streamed by, commuters and tourists and businessmen like themselves. The sound of so much bustling humanity echoed through the great hall, bouncing off the spectacular ninety-foot barrel-vaulted ceiling.

"Not much," Condor answered, brushing at a cookie crumb that had landed on his lap. A vendor in the food court one level below sold the best chocolate chip cookies on earth. Condor had bought himself a dozen of them.

He held the bag out to Morris. "Cookie?"

The man eyed the bag, then helped himself. "Thanks."

"Powers hasn't been back to his apartment," Condor continued, scanning the faces of the people around him. "He hasn't traveled under any of his known aliases. I've made all the right inquiries and come up with nothing. The man's gone under."

"I don't think so."

Condor glanced at the older man. "No?"

"No." Morris broke off a piece of the cookie. "A call came in to the Agency a couple months ago.

Caller identified herself as Julianna Starr. She was looking for Clark Russell.''

"Julianna Starr," Condor repeated. "Any relation to the stiff?"

"Her daughter. I would have passed this along sooner, but the agent who took the call was new, and it fell through the cracks."

"What did she want with Russell?"

"Good question. One I'd like the answer to." Morris cleared his throat. "Here's the interesting part. This Julianna didn't show for her mother's funeral, and she hasn't collected her inheritance. None of her mother's neighbors or acquaintances have seen her for a while. Curious, considering the circumstances."

Condor drew his eyebrows together in thought. "Could be she doesn't know her mother's dead. Or, could be she saw her mother and the senator get whacked and is running for her life. Called Russell for help. Or information."

"My thoughts exactly."

"A couple months is a long time. This Julianna could be to hell and gone by now." Condor tipped back his head and squinted up at the magnificent ceiling. "You got an address?"

"And a picture." Morris handed him a manila envelope. "Ever been to southern Louisiana?"

"As a matter of fact, I just got back."

"I hope you liked the weather, my friend, you're making a return visit."

47

Julianna unlocked her apartment door and hurried inside. She and Richard had managed to sneak away for a leisurely lunch. Lunch at her apartment. In bed. But first they would make slow, delicious love.

She closed the door behind her but didn't bother to lock it—Richard was only minutes behind her, charged with the job of stopping for sandwiches at the café down the street.

She would be waiting for him in bed, she had decided. Naked, trembling with excitement and anticipation.

These past three weeks as Richard's lover had been perfect. Everything she had dreamed of and planned for. He treated her like a woman and as an equal. He encouraged her to express her opinions and wasn't angry when those opinions differed from his own.

The sex had been glorious. Hot. Fulfilling. Unlike anything she had experienced with John. At first she had been hesitant to tell him what she desired. But now she knew he enjoyed when she took charge, when she boldly explored his body, when she called out to him, and when she told him how she wanted him to touch her.

It was so freeing. She felt alive and for the first time in her life, like a real woman. She initiated lovemaking everywhere, anytime she thought they could get away with it—in his office between meetings, parked in his car at the lakefront, the windows open to let in the cool fall air, in a restaurant's bathroom, once in his and Kate's bed while Kate was out.

When they were together, they didn't talk about Kate. Or Emma. They didn't talk about his marriage or what the future would bring. That was okay with her, for now. Her mother had taught her well, and she knew better than to rush him. He needed to come to the realization that he couldn't live without her on his own.

Besides, she didn't need to talk about something she already knew the outcome to. She and Richard were meant to be together. And they would be. Forever.

Crossing to the bed, Julianna stripped down to her bra and thong panties. She jerked back the coverlet and sheet, then stopped dead, a small sound of surprise slipping past her lips. She stared at the gory-looking mess in the center of her bed, her stomach rising to her throat.

What was it? She reached a hand out, snatching it back as realization dawned.

A cry raced to her lips, and she swung away from the bed. Her gaze landed on her dresser, on the garments spilling out of her top drawer. Heart pounding, she inched slowly across the room, picking her way, as if the carpet itself might be contaminated.

Not garments, she saw. What was left of her underwear and nighties. They had been ripped to pieces.

John. He'd found her.

"Julianna?" Richard called out. "Babe, I've got lunch."

"Richard!" She scrambled for the door, yanking it open, then slamming it shut behind her, not wanting him to see what John had done. "Richard!" she cried again when she saw him. He turned and she launched herself into his arms. "Thank God you're here."

"You're trembling." He held her away from him, searching her expression, his concerned. "What's wrong? What's happened?"

She shook her head and pressed herself close again, unable to look him in the eyes. She longed to tell him about John, longed for him to comfort and reassure her. She didn't dare. If he knew the truth—about her, about John—he might not want her anymore. And she couldn't bear to lose him.

A partial truth, she thought, clinging to him, working to calm herself.

"Julianna?" he prodded. "Babe?" Again, he eased her away from him, forcing her to look into his eyes. "Talk to me."

Julianna's eyes flooded with tears. "Back in D.C., there was this man, an awful man. He's the real reason I came down here. To get away from him." Her throat closed over the words, and she struggled to clear it. Richard waited, watching her intently. "He's a bad person, Richard. If he finds me, he'll hurt me. I know he will."

"And you think he's found you?"

"Yes. I...I came home and I—" She caught his hand and led him to the bedroom. She showed him the bed, then the lingerie drawer.

As he surveyed the damage, Richard's expression became thunderous. "How do you know this old boyfriend of yours did this?"

"I don't, I just assumed... Who else would do something like this to me?"

"It could have been any sick bastard off the street.

Some guy who's seen you around, followed you home and broke into your place. I don't like this."

Her teeth began to chatter. She grabbed her robe off the hook on the closet door and slipped into it.

"Were your doors and windows locked?"

"I think so...I don't know. The front door was, because I unlocked it when I got home."

They checked them all and though the rear door was locked tight, they found several windows unlocked. Richard took care of them, then they returned to the living room. "From now on, I want you to be really careful. Get yourself a can of mace, and don't go out alone at night. Be aware of anyone who seems to be following you, or anyone who seems to be hanging around. Let's say you notice a guy at the market, then see him again at the gas station, report it to the police."

"The police?" she repeated. "Do I have to?"

"Yes." He looked her in the eyes, the expression in his deadly serious. "I'm going to leave, Julianna. Then I want you to get dressed and call the police."

Her eyes filled with tears. "You're going to leave?"

"I can't be here when the police arrive. Considering the circumstances. You understand, don't you?"

She nodded miserably and hugged herself. "I'm scared, Richard."

He drew her back into the circle of his strong arms, fitting her cheek against his chest. He kissed the top of her head. "We'll get this worked out, babe. I'm not going to let anyone hurt you."

"Promise?" she whispered, lifting her gaze to his.

Richard cupped her face in his hands. "You have no reason to be afraid, Julianna," he murmured, bringing his mouth to hers. "Never again."

48

"Welcome back, Kate!" Blake, Marilyn and Tess called in unison as she walked in The Bean's front door early Monday morning. The maternity leave she had given herself was officially over and although she had continued managing from a distance and had even worked an occasional day here and there over the past six months, today marked her first day back full-time.

Kate stopped dead, surprised and overwhelmed. Her employees had strung a banner above and behind the counter area that announced She's Baaack! A Mylar balloon decorated each table, a bouquet of them bobbled beside the register.

Her three employees hurried across to greet her. Marilyn took Emma, Tess grabbed the overflowing diaper bag and Blake took her arm. "Come on in, honey," he said. "The surprises have only just begun."

They led her to the back of the café. They had turned the furthermost corner into a play place for Emma, cordoned off with accordion-style baby gates and filled with bright-colored toys. The tile floor had been covered with a big patchwork rug; above the area hung a sign that read Baby Central in primary colors.

All three of her employees starting talking at once.
"We all went together—"
"Some of the regulars, too—"

"—and bought the baby gym, fun saucer and Johnny jump-up."

"I made the sign," Tess said.

"We wanted to do something for you and Emma and thought this way—"

"Working would be so much easier—"

"For both of you." Marilyn beamed at her. "We're so happy you're back, Kate. We've really missed you."

Kate turned to her employees, tears stinging her eyes. "I don't know what to say. You guys are the best."

"Glad you think so," Blake said, grinning, "because we're not done yet." He caught her hand. "Now, for your office."

"My office," she repeated weakly.

Giggling like kids, they led her to her office. There, they'd installed a portable crib and a big, old rocking chair.

"The chair was my sister's," Marilyn murmured. "She said you could use it as long as you like."

Kate shook her head. "This is too much, guys. Really, it is."

"Richard helped us."

"He knew about this?"

"Oh yeah." Tess laughed. "He gave me and Marilyn carte blanche at the baby store. It was *really* fun. I was born to spend other people's money."

From out front came the sound of knocking. Then a call of, "Hello. Anybody here?"

Blake looked at his watch. "Oh, man, look at the time. We opened ten minutes ago."

"Should have opened ten minutes ago," Kate corrected, already heading for the front of the café.

"Please tell me the menu boards are done and that the coffee's already made." They weren't. From that moment on, they played catch-up. As the day progressed, many of the regulars made an appearance to welcome Kate back and make a major fuss over Emma. Deliveries ran late, the cappuccino machine went on the fritz, and a mother-and-toddler group came and let their children run amok.

In other words, business as usual. Kate decided it was really good to be back.

When they had a quiet moment, Marilyn sidled up to her. "How are things with Richard?"

Kate considered all of her employees friends, but she and Marilyn were particularly close. They often discussed their lives, using one another as a sounding board. Some time back, Kate had confided to the other woman that Richard was having trouble adjusting to parenthood.

Kate smiled, happy that she could honestly answer that things were good. Though he had been gone from home a lot—frantically busy between securing support for his bid for D.A. and handling several weighty cases at the firm—when he was home, he was attentive and loving. To her *and* Emma. She had found it heartening to see him finally responding to his daughter. Being affectionate with her. More often than not he came home with some trinket for the child, a stuffed toy or bow for her hair, a rattle or picture book. Kate smiled to herself. He had even taken to bringing his wife a little something—flowers, a special bottle of wine or dessert she enjoyed.

It was as if their last, awful fight had changed not only his attitude but in some fundamental way, his feelings as well. He was like a new man.

"I'm so glad," Marilyn said when Kate finished. She gave her a quick hug, then grinned wickedly. "Nothing like a guilty conscience to straighten a man right up."

Blake wandered over, a carton of napkins hooked under his arm. He caught the last of Marilyn's comment. "Straighten a man up?" he repeated, his expression deadpan. "Honey, you're entitled to your orientation, but don't go and ruin it for the rest of us."

"Why is everything with you always about sex?"

Blake smiled. "You know what they say, girlfriend, everybody's good at something. I just happen to be the prince of peni—"

Kate held up her hands to stop them. "No doubt about it, I'm back now."

"Then you're ready to be brought up to speed?" He stowed the carton under the buffet, then turned back to the two women. "It's been a regular Peyton Place around here."

"Peyton Place, huh? Since we're in a lull, fill me in."

"Ralph and his wife split," Tess said, referring to one of the regulars. "She got custody of the Jeep and the cat."

"He was devastated," Blake added. "He loved that vehicle. And he'd just made the last payment, too."

They went on to tell her about a surprise pregnancy, that their resident writer finally sold a book, and that Big Burt Beals had lost twenty-five pounds on the Sugar Busters diet. "Not to mention," Blake added, "Tess's five new love-of-her-life boyfriends."

"It was six, I think." Marilyn laughed.

"I heard that." Tess bopped up behind them, carrying Emma. Obviously fascinated by Tess's blond hair, the infant had a fistful of it. The young woman seemed not to notice. "Can I help it if so many guys are fatally flawed?" She turned to Marilyn and Blake. "Did you tell her about the new guy?"

"She's referring to our newest regular," Marilyn offered from the counter where she had gone to take an order. "Actually, we have three."

"All men," Tess murmured. "Though only one's a hunk-a-hunk of burning love. Nick Winters."

Kate freed Tess's hair and took Emma from the other woman. "Tell me about them all. Nick Winters first."

"He's really cute." Tess crossed to the counter to help Marilyn, took an order, then glanced back at Kate. "And single."

"And too old for you." Marilyn rolled her eyes. "But she's right about him being attractive. He's rugged but also an intellectual. Up until recently he was a professor of philosophy at Cleveland State College. He inherited some money, sold everything he owned and hit the road."

"What's he doing down here?"

"Just one of his stops on his Tour of America."

"Then there's Steve Byrd," Blake said, "my personal favorite. A real flashback to the sixties kind of guy, complete with a ponytail. He followed the Grateful Dead for the past twenty-five years, making a living selling Dead paraphernalia at the concerts. Says since Jerry Garcia died, life has no meaning."

"I don't think there's much doubt that this guy all but fried his gray matter with drugs." Marilyn shuddered. "I never could understand that whole scene."

"Sounds like he'll add a little color to our motley

crew.'' Kate laughed. ''So, what about our last new guy? You said there were three.''

Her employees exchanged glances. Blake cleared his throat. ''He's a little scary. Ex-military. Doesn't talk much. Comes in every day and glares at Steve. And everyone else who looks a little counterculture. Including me and Beanie.'' Blake shuddered. ''He's got gay-basher written all over him.''

''What's his name?'' Kate asked.

''Don't know. I told you, he doesn't talk much.''

''I tried,'' Tess said. ''He was really ugly to me, so I backed off fast.''

''For once I agree with Blake,'' Marilyn said. ''Something about this guy is as cold as ice.''

As cold as ice. Kate frowned, unsettled. Why would someone like that even choose to hang around a place like The Uncommon Bean? She couldn't think of any reason except one—he was looking for trouble.

She would just have to make sure he didn't find it.

49

John sat on a park bench, the October day bright and mild. Before him lay Lake Pontchartrain, its diamond surface broken by the occasional swoop of a gull diving for food. Above him, the branches of a centuries-old live oak spiraled toward the sky, a majestic and awe-inspiring work of nature.

A beautiful scene, John thought. Magnificent, calming. At any other time. But not now.

He breathed deeply, working to control his rage. He had followed Julianna. He knew where she worked, her hours, that she didn't associate with any of the other employees. He had learned that she'd given birth to a girl and that she had given her up for adoption. He knew to whom.

He knew everything.

He lifted his gaze to the perfect, Easter egg blue sky. *Everything.*

Julianna was fucking someone else. *His* Julianna. His special girl. He flexed his fingers, understanding now the drawer full of cheap undergarments, picturing her in them, writhing under the man's hands.

Like her mother, she had become a whore. She had forgotten his lessons about loyalty and commitment.

A *whore.*

Fury choked him. He had thought she was different. Special, more worthy than other people.

She had been. Once upon a time.

A sound slipped past his lips, low and feral, like an animal in pain. A sound of grief, of mourning. For the girl he had known. For the purity and light that had been lost.

He closed his eyes, seeing her with his mind's eye, as she had been that first day, radiating goodness, an innocence that had touched the cold places inside him, warming them.

John brought his hands to his face, shocked at how they trembled. How could he have been so wrong about her? He dropped them to his lap. And now, how could he say goodbye?

A mother and her daughter strolled past. The little girl looked to be about the age Julianna had been when they first met. The child peered flirtatiously over her shoulder at him as they drew away, already the coquette.

He stared back at her, unmoved. She didn't have Julianna's inner light. Her beauty of spirit that made her different from others. No one did.

He hadn't been wrong about his Julianna.

John sucked in a sharp breath. She was special. But she was also young, still a child—if not in years then in her heart. Her youth made her reckless, easily influenced.

She hadn't been raised to take care of herself. In confusion, she had turned to this Richard, this *nothing*. Without John to guide her, she had succumbed to the ways of her mother.

John stood. Above, a gull shrieked and circled, then dove for its prey. The man was to blame. The baby. The woman.

One complication had become three. The complications would have to be eliminated.

And once eliminated, he would know if Julianna was as worthy as he had thought her to be.

50

The next few days were busy and exhausting for Kate. Being back at The Uncommon Bean after so many weeks at home was a major adjustment. For Emma, too. The constant noise and parade of new faces overstimulated the infant, which led to fussiness, especially at night. By the time Kate got her daughter rocked to sleep and tucked into her crib, all she had the energy to do was change into her nightclothes and fall into bed.

Add to that all manner of small annoyances that she'd had to deal with on the home front—crackling on the phone line and the repairman who'd shown up needing to check the inside wiring; lack of rain necessitating constant watering of her lawn and flower beds; a refrigerator that had decided after only six years to call it quits.

But even with all that, something Marilyn had said kept tickling at the edges of Kate's thoughts.

Nothing like a guilty conscience to straighten a man right up.

Did Richard have a guilty conscience? Kate wondered as she bussed The Bean's outdoor tables. Was that why he was being so attentive? So thoughtful? Was that what the constant stream of gifts had been about?

She could understand if he felt bad about the things

he had said to her. About Luke. And Emma. She supposed he cringed when he remembered how he'd tried to force himself on her that night. She still did.

But was there something else? Something more?

She cleared the table, collecting the used napkins, empty sugar packets and creamers, stuffing them into an empty coffee cup before she wiped the top down with a damp cloth. She was being paranoid. Letting her imagination run away with her. She had been ever since the day Old Joe had seen the girl on their swing.

The girl on the swing. Kate didn't know why, but it always seemed to come back to her.

As if her thoughts had conjured him, Kate looked up to find her neighbor approaching, his Shih Tzu prancing ahead, tugging at the end of its leash.

She held a hand to her eyes to shield them from the sun and waved with the other. "Joe," she called, "come have a cup of coffee with me."

He waved back and started up The Bean's front walk. Several minutes later, they were both seated at one of the tables on the porch, coffees in front of them and a bowl of water at their feet for the panting Beauregard.

They exchanged pleasantries for a few moments, then Kate got right to the point. "I've been wondering about the young woman you saw on our swing. Do you remember what she looked like?"

Joe appeared unsurprised by the question. He scratched his head. "Now, let me think," he murmured. "It's been a while, and she and I weren't eye-to-eye, you know."

He looked at Kate, forehead wrinkling in thought. "She had hair the color of yours, cut in about the same style. She was youngish, like a college girl. And she was wearing a short skirt.''

He shook his head and snorted with disgust. ''She had no business swinging in an outfit like that, if you know what I mean?''

Kate agreed that she did. ''Is that all you remember about her, Joe? Was there anything else about her appearance or behavior that struck you as odd or outstanding?''

He thought a moment, then shook his head. ''Sorry, Kate. Wish I could be more help.''

They chatted a few moments longer, then he thanked her for the coffee and left. Kate stared after him, her thoughts whirling with the little bit he had told her.

Brown hair. Medium-length page boy. Youngish. That description could belong to hundreds of women in the Mandeville area. It also matched the one Citywide had given them of Emma's birth mother.

Dear God, Emma's birth mother.

Even as she told herself she was once again letting her imagination run away with her, she jumped to her feet and hurried to her office. She picked up the phone, dialed Citywide's number and asked for Ellen. A moment later, the woman was on the line.

''Ellen,'' Kate said, sounding breathless even to her own ears. ''It's Kate Ryan.''

''Kate,'' she said warmly, ''it's nice to hear from you. How's the baby?''

''Wonderful. She's getting so big, you wouldn't recognize her. She rolled over yesterday, and she was so proud. Just beaming, the little stinker.''

''Bring her by, we'd love to see her.'' The social worker's tone changed, becoming all business. ''I'm 'guessing you didn't call to talk about Emma's many accomplishments. Am I right?''

''Right.'' Kate cleared her throat, nervous about how to approach this. She didn't want the social worker to think she was paranoid or to start having doubts about the stability of the couple who were now Emma's parents. But she had to know if she thought Emma's birth mother could be having second thoughts about giving her baby up. If she couldn't have somehow found them.

''I was wondering...have you heard from Emma's birth mother?''

''No,'' Ellen responded, ''not at all. Why do you ask?''

''I'd still like to meet her. We both would.''

''I'm sorry, but she was adamant about keeping the adoption completely closed.''

''I see.''

''I know you're disappointed, but hang in there, she may change her mind yet.''

She wouldn't, Kate knew. Maybe that was just her paranoia thinking for her, but she didn't think so. She had this awful feeling the woman didn't want to meet them because...what? She had plotted some diabolical scheme, one designed to ruin their lives?

Right. That kind of scenario didn't happen in real life—only in Hollywood screenplays.

Even as she told herself she was losing it, Kate asked, ''This may sound crazy, but is there any way Emma's birth mother could have found us? Could any of our identifying information been inadvertently included in our profile packet?''

''Absolutely not.'' Ellen drew a cautious sounding breath. ''Is something wrong?''

Kate sighed. "It's silly, but I...I have this terrible feeling that—"

"Emma's birth mother has changed her mind and wants to steal Emma away from you."

"Yes." Kate brought a hand to her chest, both relieved and horrified. "That's it. How did you know?"

The social worker laughed lightly. "Because it's such a common fear among adoptive parents, especially ones involved in a closed adoption. In a closed adoption, the birth parents remain big question marks. The adoptive parents don't understand why they gave their baby up. They wonder, how could they? After all, to them the baby is the most wonderful, perfect creation in all the world, and they love her so much, they can't image life without her."

She had wondered those things, Kate acknowledged. In just that way, too many times to count.

"Actually," Ellen continued, "your fear of losing Emma shows me how completely you've bonded with your daughter. You're a family now and the thought, even unfounded, that someone might have a claim to a piece of that family is, well, it's terrifying. As time passes, it'll get better." Kate heard the smile in the woman's voice. "I promise."

Kate laughed self-consciously, somewhat comforted, but she couldn't help thinking there had to be something about Emma's birth mother that even Ellen didn't know. "She never expressed any second thoughts? She hasn't called and asked about Emma? Nothing?"

"Nothing. Kate, I promise you, Emma's birth mother was totally committed to placing Emma. She was as at peace with her decision as any birth mom

I've worked with. Trust me on this, you will not be hearing from her.''

Moments later, Kate hung up the phone, the social worker's reassuring words ringing in her ears. But even so, Kate couldn't shake the uneasy feeling that it was too late—they had already heard from her.

51

It didn't take long for Kate to begin meeting The Bean's newbies. The first was Mr. Military, as Blake had dubbed him. Kate was dismayed to see that for once her melodramatic employees had not exaggerated—he was a very scary guy, cold as ice.

Kate approached him, introducing herself as The Bean's owner, intent on learning his name and what he was doing in Mandeville. She failed miserably. He made it clear that he had paid her exorbitant price for a cup of coffee and that he would like to enjoy it in peace.

She granted him his request, though not without a measure of dismay. Why, she wondered, had he decided to frequent her friendly little establishment?

The Jerry Garcia groupie strolled in next, her third morning back, reeking of incense and saying things like "cool" and "far-out." Marilyn got into a lively no-nukes discussion with him, and Tess took a break to hear about his days traveling with The Dead.

Kate wandered over after getting Emma fed then down for her nap. "Hi, Steve," she said and held out her hand. "I'm Kate."

He smiled and shook her hand. She noticed that his skin was unusually smooth for a man's. "Figured as much," he said. "Love your place. It has great vibes."

"Thank you."

"The stained glass is awesome, really. Tess tells me you're the artist."

"Thanks again, and yes, I am." She narrowed her eyes, studying him. Something about him seemed awfully familiar. "Have we met before?"

"Don't think so." He sipped his latté. "Haven't been in town that long. You ever see The Dead in concert?"

She shook her head. "No, though I have a few of their CDs."

They chatted some more, mostly about the Grateful Dead's music. After a few moments, she excused herself to return to the counter to help Blake with the group of college students that had just come in. When they had serviced the group, she leaned toward Blake. "Something's wrong about that guy," she murmured.

He followed her gaze, then frowned. "Are you talking about Steve?"

"Mmm-hmm. Ever heard the expression, crazy like a fox?"

"Him?" Blake made a face. "No way. The guy's a Jell-O-head."

"I don't think so." Steve looked up suddenly, and Kate quickly averted her gaze. "Check out his eyes. I'm telling you, that whole hippie thing's a put-on. That guy's sharp as a tack."

Blake shook his head. "Get real, Kate. First off, why would anyone actually want to pretend to be a seventies drug casualty? And second, the guy's a complete stoner. Pure and simple."

Kate let it drop, though she didn't buy it. And she still felt certain that she and Steve Byrd had met before. She resolved to keep a close eye on the man.

* * *

Later that day, The Bean's last newbie made an appearance. If she hadn't already guessed by the man's Cleveland State T-shirt, Tess's *"Oh, my God, it's him,"* would have given it away. The young woman practically drooled in his double espresso.

"You must be Nick," Kate said, holding out her hand. "Welcome to The Uncommon Bean."

He seemed completely immune to Tess's reaction to him, and smiled at Kate, revealing the most beautiful, whitest teeth she had ever seen. He had a movie star's smile, she decided, disarmed. Tess was right—Nick Winters was quite an attractive man. She would bet the coeds at Cleveland State had lined up to take philosophy.

He took her hand. "And you must be Kate. Your employees have told me all about you."

"Really?" She laughed a bit self-consciously and eased her hand from his. "Good things, I hope?"

"Glowing. They sang your praises." He smiled again and shifted his gaze to Emma. "They told me all about your little miracle baby, too. May I?" He held out his hands. "I haven't held a baby in what seems like forever."

Kate hesitated only briefly, then handed her daughter over. Any concerns she had were immediately alleviated—he handled Emma like a pro.

He held her up, admiring her. "She's beautiful."

"Thank you." She smiled. "I think so, too."

He talked softly to her, making her grin and squeal. Kate watched them. "I see you've spent a lot of time around children."

"I was the oldest of a brood of six."

"Do you have children of your own?"

"Me? No way. Growing up with the responsibility

of helping care for five siblings was enough.'' He indicated one of the tables. "Come sit with me and chat a moment, if you have time?''

She glanced at Tess and Blake—they seemed to have everything under control. "All right. I'd like that.''

They sat at a table by the window. He bounced Emma on his knee as he sweetened his espresso. "Tell me about yourself, Kate Ryan.''

"What's to tell?'' She lifted a shoulder. "I'm married and a mother. I make stained glass art as a hobby and am addicted to coffee. So addicted, in fact, that I opened my own coffeehouse. Pretty ordinary stuff. You, on the other hand, lead a very different and exciting life. I understand you've become a kind of nomad.''

He ignored her reference to his life. "That smacks of false modesty to me. I look at you and see a beautiful, accomplished and talented woman.''

Kate was a bit taken aback by his blunt and rather forward compliment. She felt herself blush, something she realized she hadn't done in years. "Well, thank you.''

"Take your stained glass. You call it a hobby, yet the love you put into it is more than evident. They're exquisite.''

She laughed lightly. "Today seems to be my day for compliments. Thank you. Again.''

His lips curved up, and he trailed a finger down Emma's velvety cheek. "What I don't understand is, why are you wasting your time running a coffeehouse? You should be making art full-time.''

She gazed at him a moment, uncertain if she should

be flattered or insulted. ''I'm too practical a person to count on sales of my art to make a living.''

''But some things are more important than money. You have a gift, you're wasting it.''

She stiffened as much at his audacity as at the fact that his words expressed the private battle she had waged with herself for years. ''You're entitled to your opinion, of course.''

''Now I've offended you. That wasn't my intention. I'm sorry.''

''Not at all. But duty calls, and I must get back to work.''

He followed her to her feet and handed over her daughter. She took Emma and started off, only to stop and look back at him when he called her name. ''I enjoyed our talk very much,'' he said. ''I think you're an exceptional woman.''

Kate felt herself flush again. She didn't know how to respond, so she just smiled and returned to the counter area, face on fire.

''What was *that* all about?'' Blake asked, his voice low.

''What was what all about?''

''You and Nick Winters.''

''I don't know what you mean. We were just talking.''

''You don't know what I mean? You're still blushing, Kate. I think the guy has a crush on you.''

''Don't be ridiculous. He doesn't even know me. Besides, I'm a married woman.''

''Which doesn't have a thing to do with whether he has a crush on you or not.''

Kate shrugged off her employee's teasing about Nick Winters that day and every day for the next week, though secretly she wondered if Blake wasn't right. Every day Nick asked her to join him at his table, and every day he engaged her in conversation. They discussed their views on marriage and parenting; they discussed such hot-button issues as capital punishment and prayer in the classroom; and he encouraged her to talk about Emma and share her feelings about being an adoptive mother.

She had to admit she was flattered. Besides being an extremely attractive man, Nick Winters was highly intelligent, well-read and worldly.

It had been a long time since any man but Richard had so openly admired her and it felt nice, she decided. Very nice.

52

Kate took the following weekend off to recoup from her first two full weeks back at work. Emma needed the rest, too, and slept away most of Saturday and a good part of Sunday.

By Monday morning they were both refreshed and eager to begin the week. Kate carried Emma into The Bean, taking her directly to her play area. After two days away, the infant was more than ready to play with her Bean toys, and she squealed with delight when she saw them.

"Morning," Blake called from behind her. "Have a good weekend off?"

"Great." Kate made certain Emma was situated, then turned to Blake. "And how was your— Oh, my God, where is it?" Her favorite piece of stained glass was gone. Oversize for a large picture window like The Bean's, it depicted egrets roosting in the gnarled, winding branches of a centuries-old live oak tree.

"It sold. Saturday."

"Sold?" she repeated. She loved that piece, and had been certain it would never sell—at five thousand dollars, the price had been exorbitant. "Who bought it?"

"Nick Winters."

Nick had paid five thousand dollars for a piece of her work?

Kate stared at Blake, not quite believing her ears,

uncomfortable with this turn of events. "You're sure?"

He laughed. "Of course I'm sure. I have the check stashed under the cash drawer." He popped the register open, lifted the drawer, dug the check out and handed it to her.

She made a sound of surprise. "This is a cashier's check."

"Yeah, I know. I figured the register was the safest place for it. Thank God we weren't robbed. I almost told him to wait until you— Speak of the devil, here he is now."

Kate turned. Nick Winters stood just inside The Bean's front door, his gaze upon her. She mustered a weak smile. "Hello, Nick."

"I see you got the money," he said, crossing to the counter where she and Blake stood.

"Yes." She looked at the check, then back up at him. "I'm overwhelmed."

"I'm sure." He smiled, ordered a double espresso, then moved toward one of the tables. "Sit with me."

It seemed to Kate not so much an invitation as an order, and she wondered if he thought that buying an expensive piece of her art was the same as buying a piece of her, or that she owed him something now. Some people were like that. If he was one of them, she would set him straight, fast.

"Did I surprise you?" he asked, as they sat.

"You could say that. I almost had a heart attack when I looked up and saw the empty window. It was my favorite piece."

"I don't doubt it. It was the best of the lot." He sweetened his espresso, then brought the demitasse cup to his lips and sipped. "Did you know, in some cultures they believe the artist gives up a little piece of his soul with each act of creation?''

She narrowed her eyes. "No, I didn't know that Nick."

"Interesting, don't you think? Ceremonies are performed to cleanse the objects of any negative spiritual residue, as if an inanimate object could possess a life force."

She was uncomfortable with this conversation, and she sensed he knew it. Sensed he was getting pleasure from her unease. "You know what that means, don't you?" he continued.

She shook her head.

"That I own a little piece of your soul."

Something about his expression, something in his eyes, chilled her to her core. She fought to keep her feelings from showing. "If one bought into that sort of thing," she said.

"Exactly." He brought the demitasse cup to his lips and sipped, the motion oddly feminine and disturbing. He set the cup carefully on its saucer. "It points to how personal, how private and unique the act of creation is. Some artists call it a bloodletting, some an act of the subconscious, others one of sheer will. What is it to you, Kate? How would you describe it?"

She wasn't about to discuss her personal creative pathos with this man, wasn't about to describe the joy and frustration, the fear or passion. It was none of his business, and she didn't know why, but she had the feeling that whatever she told him, he would find a way to twist it to his own liking.

How had she ever thought him attractive and interesting? she wondered. How had she allowed herself to preen under his attention. The thought made her sick.

"I find it relaxing," she answered. "Enjoyable."

"You're a poor liar."

"The thing is, Nick," she said, working to keep her tone light, "I'd like to buy that piece of stained glass back from you. You see, I...I feel a little silly about this, but at that price I never thought it would sell. It holds a special place in my heart and—"

"I'm sorry, Kate, but that won't be possible."

Her stomach sank. "May I ask why not?"

"It's no longer in my possession. I had it crated and shipped to my home in Ohio."

"I see." She tried another tact. "But surely, since you travel so much and won't be home to enjoy it, you—"

"I'm sorry, Kate." He smiled, the curving of his lips conveying anything but regret. "You're too late."

53

"Hello there, Kate," Old Joe called, stopping at her gate. "Beautiful evening, isn't it?"

"Just gorgeous." Kate turned off the hose and ambled over to talk to her neighbor. "It's been dry, though."

"Good thing you're getting some water on those pansies. I've been worried you were going to lose them. Almost stopped by to tell you so yesterday." He squinted. "Figured you might not have noticed."

Kate fought a smile. "Thanks for your concern, Joe. These days it's hard to find time for everything that needs to be done. I've been meaning to ask you if you're still having problems with your phone line? Mine's still crackly."

He frowned. "Phone troubles? Mine's been clear as a bell."

It was her turn to frown. "I've been having problems for several weeks. A guy from Bellsouth stopped by one morning, took a look at my equipment. Said the entire area was having problems. Something about damage incurred when Lakeshore Drive was widened two years ago."

"There you have it," he said. "The problem must be limited to the customers on Lakeshore Drive."

"I'm sure you're right," she said. "I'll just give them a call in...the morn..."

She let the thought trail off and brought a hand to her mouth. *Steve Byrd. That's where she knew him from. The phone repairman, the one who checked her equipment.*

She recalled that morning, the man standing at her door, and frowned. No, that wasn't right. The two men looked nothing alike. Now, why had she thought that?

"Kate? Are you all right?"

She blinked, and felt herself flush. "Sorry, Joe, the sun must be getting to me."

He nodded and squinted up at the sky. "Weather's sure been strange. Can't remember another October this dry." He shifted his attention to Emma, sitting in her bouncer seat in the shade. "She's getting big. Pretty little thing, too."

"Thank you." Kate looked at her daughter, smiling. The infant swung her arms and burbled as if in response. "She's a joy, that's for sure."

"By the way, Kate, your little mystery's solved. Turns out she is a friend of yours."

"Excuse me?"

"The girl you were asking about, the one from the swing. I saw her earlier today, with Richard. Beauregard and I were taking our noon walk. I called out and Richard waved."

Kate frowned, confused. "Are you sure it was the same woman?"

"Sure, I'm sure." Beauregard tugged on his leash, then looked back at his master and barked. Joe sighed. "No rest for the wicked, I guess. Nice talking to you, Kate."

Kate watched her neighbor walk off, a fluttery sensation in the pit of her stomach. Joe had seen Richard

with the young woman from the swing? Who could
she—

Julianna. Of course.

Kate hadn't thought of it before, but Julianna was
youngish, like a college coed. She had hair the cut and
color of Kate's.

But if her neighbor was correct and the woman he
had seen on the swing was the same one he had seen
today, what had Julianna been doing at their house
weeks before Richard had hired her?

And what had Richard been doing home, with his
assistant during the middle of the day?

The tap of a horn startled her out of her thoughts.
It was Richard, turning into the drive. Kate forced a
smile and waved, not liking the direction of her
thoughts. Richard, she was certain, would have a perfectly reasonable explanation for all of her questions.

He climbed out of his car, slamming the door behind him. "Hi, gorgeous," he called, starting across
the lawn toward her. "What are you up to?"

"Saving the pansies." She thought again of Joe and
her smile faded. "How was your day?"

"Busy." He picked up Emma, seat and all, while
Kate rewound the hose.

"Joe said he saw you home around noon." She
hung the coiled hose on the rack mounted to the side
of the house and together they walked around front.

"I forgot my notes on the Miller case."

"He said Julianna was with you."

"She was. We were on our way to a luncheon with
Mothers Against Drunk Drivers. Since we were passing, I stopped in to get my notes."

So, it had been Julianna. What did that mean?

Kate held the door open for Richard. He carried

Emma to the kitchen, then set the bouncer seat on the floor. He ignored the child's attempts to get his attention and crossed to the counter and opened a bottle of wine. "Want a glass?" he asked.

"No, thanks." Kate went to Emma, bent, unbuckled her and scooped her up. "Could you fix me an iced tea instead?"

"Sure." As he poured the wine, he made a sound of amusement. "Nosy Old Joe. You'd think he could find something better to do than spy on his neighbors."

"He wasn't *spying*, Richard. He was walking Beauregard and happened to see you."

"Then ran straight to you to report what he saw. Sounds like a spy to me."

Kate rummaged in Emma's diaper bag for a pacifier. "He only mentioned it to me because a couple weeks ago I asked him again about the girl he saw on our swing."

Richard drew his eyebrows together as if trying to figure out what she referred to, then nodded. "Oh, that. But what would that have had to do with today?"

"Richard, Joe said the girl he saw you with today is the same one he saw on our swing. He's certain of it." When her husband simply stared uncomprehendingly at her, she let her breath out in an exasperated huff. "Don't you see how odd this all is? Why would Julianna have been on our swing, weeks before you had even met her?"

"This is ridiculous." He made a sound of disgust. "You're going to listen to some old geezer instead of your husband?"

"But what does this even have to do with you? We're talking about Julianna."

"And I'm telling you, Joe was mistaken."

When he tried to take his wine and walk away, she stopped him by stepping directly in front of him and forcing him to look at her. "How can you be sure? I told you, something about Julianna isn't as it seems. I don't trust her, I don't think she's honest."

"Oh, for heaven's sake. Now you're talking crazy. Julianna's smart and sweet and a damn good worker. I trust her completely and don't believe she has a dishonest bone in her body."

"What if she was on our swing? And why are you defending her?"

"Why shouldn't I be? I think you're jealous."

"Jealous!" She made a sound of shock. "Why would I be jealous of your assistant?"

"Why do you think? She's young, attractive and unencumbered."

Kate caught her breath, his words hitting her with the force of a blow. "Unencumbered, Richard? Is that what you think I want to be?"

"That's not what I meant."

"Then what did you mean? Maybe it's you who longs to be free?"

"I'm not going to listen to another moment of this." He pushed past her, some of his wine sloshing over the rim of his glass and splattering on the hardwood floor.

"Feeling guilty, Richard?"

He stopped and turned slowly to face her. "What's that supposed to mean?"

"Just what it sounds like." She sucked in a deep, fortifying breath. "Are you...cheating on me with Julianna? Is that what all the flowers and gifts and 'I love yous' have been about?"

"Thanks a lot," he said stiffly. "After all these years, it's nice to know what you really think of me."

She tipped up her chin, unwilling to back down or hide from her horrible suspicions, though she longed to. "Are you, Richard? Cheating on me with Julianna?" A brittle laugh bubbled to her lips. "Or anyone else, for that matter?"

"I can't believe what I'm hearing. I can't believe it's you saying this to me." He took a step toward her. "What's happened to you? Ever since Emma...you've changed, Kate."

"I haven't." She shook her head. "You're the one who's—"

"I'm not the one who never wants to go anywhere. I'm not the one who's tired all the time, or the one who thinks people are sneaking into her house and stealing photographs but leaving the jewelry behind. I'm not the one who's calling a perfectly innocent and hardworking kid dishonest and manipulative. And I'm certainly not the one who just accused my spouse of more than ten years of being unfaithful."

He started toward the living room. She stared after him, tears blinding her. He was right, she realized. She was paranoid and suspicious and acting every bit the possessive, jealous woman he accused her of being. The kind of woman she had always looked at with pity and had promised herself she would never become.

"Richard," she called, taking a step toward him, "wait, please."

He stopped and looked back at her. "You used to be fun, Kate. You used to feel good about yourself and our life together. You used to feel good about me. About *us*. What's happened to you?" he asked again. "I don't even know you anymore."

54

Kate awakened to the sound of thunder. Rain slashed against the windows and pounded on the roof, and as she dragged herself into a sitting position, a flash of lightning illuminated the gloom.

Richard was already up, she saw, though she hadn't been aware of his rising or leaving. She reached out and touched his pillow; it was cold. She sighed, wondering if he would even speak to her today. Wondering if their marriage would survive another week, let alone a month.

She had slept poorly, and now felt every moment of the wakeful night. She had tossed and turned, tormented by her and Richard's fight. Horrified by the accusations she had hurled at her husband. By what had become of her life and marriage.

The night before, Richard had lain so stiffly beside her. Several times she had reached out to him, whispering her remorse, begging his forgiveness. Each time he had pulled away, rejecting her.

It had hurt almost more than she could bear.

Kate climbed out of the bed, heading for the bathroom. No sleeping in today. Even though Richard's mother had insisted on taking Emma for the day and had picked her up late the evening before, Kate was scheduled to open The Bean. Rainy days, far from keeping customers away, seemed to draw more in.

What better way to spend a rainy morning, than inside with a friend or book and a good cup of coffee?

Kate passed a hand wearily across her eyes. Thank goodness she didn't have Emma to contend with this morning. Exhausted and heartsick as she was, she didn't think she could have handled both her daughter and the Saturday rush. Not competently, anyway.

Aware of time slipping by, she showered, dressed and went down for coffee. There, she discovered that Richard was not only up, but gone as well.

He hadn't left a note.

Her eyes filled with tears. That small omission spoke volumes. Suddenly, the house was too quiet, the sound of the rain agitating rather than soothing, the thunder disturbing.

Deciding she would get her coffee at The Bean, she grabbed her purse and raincoat and hurried out into the storm.

Minutes later, Kate drew to a stop behind The Uncommon Bean. She made no move to leave the car, instead choosing to wait a few moments for a momentary break in the downpour. The wipers flew back and forth across the windshield, unable to keep up with the driving rain, and Kate squinted, visibility so poor she could hardly see The Bean's back door though she was nearly on top of it.

The lull came—she threw open the car door and keys in hand, made a dash for it. Her foot landed smack in a puddle, soaking her shoe and the bottom of her pants leg. Swearing, she reached the door, but as she went to fit the key in the lock, it swung open.

Kate froze. Not only had the door been left unlocked all night, it hadn't even been fully shut. She frowned, working to recall who had been scheduled to close the night before.

Tess, Kate remembered. The young woman had been complaining about it the previous afternoon and trying unsuccessfully to con Beanie into switching shifts with her.

Kate made a sound of annoyance and stepped inside. On a Friday night, in her eagerness to hit the bars, Tess had compromised The Bean's security. What if someone had tried to break in? What if the wind had blown the door open? In this rain, the storage room would have been flooded.

Kate shut the door behind her, checking to make sure it was latched. She was going to have to have a talk with her employee. Usually Tess could manage her ditziness, but this was too much.

As she stepped farther into the storage room, Kate made a sound of dismay and brought her hand to her nose. *What was that awful smell?* Like a garbage can left open in the sun. Or sewage.

She made her way toward the front of the café, the smell becoming stronger as she went. She peeked inside the bathrooms and her office, looking for the source of the odor but finding nothing amiss in either place.

Frowning, she pushed through the louvered door that separated the dining room from the other parts of the café, then stopped, a cry slipping past her lips. Every piece of her stained glass had been yanked from the windows and smashed. The colorful fragments littered the tile floor like an obscene mosaic.

She rushed forward, tripping on something in the aisle. She lowered her gaze. A scream flew to her throat. Tess lay in a crumpled heap on the floor, wedged behind the counter area, arm jutting into the walkway. Her head was twisted in an unnatural angle—her mouth and eyes gaped open. As with surprise. Or terror.

Kate's stomach lurched to her throat. She brought a hand to her mouth to hold the sickness back. From behind her came a stirring. A footfall. She whirled around, the scream ripping from her, shattering the stillness.

It was Blake. Thank God.

Sobbing, Kate fell into his arms.

The police came. The coroner. The forensics team. They questioned Kate and Blake, The Bean's other employees. Eventually, the regulars. They ruled out a bungled robbery as the motive; a careful search revealed nothing missing but Kate's Rolodex.

Tess's neck had been broken, they said. She had died instantly. Judging by her injury and position on the floor, her attacker had come up from behind, taking her by surprise. They surmised that she never even knew what hit her.

At least she hadn't suffered, Kate thought, grabbing on to that one, small comfort. At least she hadn't lain dying, alone and afraid, praying for help that never arrived.

The hours, then days, passed in a sort of waking nightmare for Kate. She closed The Uncommon Bean indefinitely, then managed to go through the motions—talking to the police and the press, listening to the condolences and reassurances of friends, caring for Emma and even managing to eat and sleep occasionally.

She couldn't believe such a terrible thing could hap-

pen at her coffeehouse, to someone she had known
and cared for. That such violence could occur so close
to her shattered her every illusion of safety.

At night as she rocked Emma to sleep, she gazed
down at her beautiful and sweet face and struggled to
come to grips with it all. She longed to feel safe again.
To have her cozy illusion of indestructibility back.

Through it all, Richard was a rock for Kate. Un-
wavering in his support and sympathy, understanding.
She felt closer to him than she had in months, their
fight and her ugly accusations forgotten in the midst
of their tragedy.

Kate was relieved when, a week to the day she had
discovered the body, Tess's sometime boyfriend Matt
was arrested for her murder. Witnesses had seen them
together that night, arguing bitterly. Tess was last seen
getting into his car. The coroner determined that she'd
had intercourse shortly before her death. Preliminary
lab tests revealed the semen most probably to be
Matt's. Even without the final DNA test results, the
police felt they had enough evidence to make an arrest.

It wasn't until Matt was in jail that Kate could bring
herself to reopen The Bean. And even then, it was to
a hush of grief. Everyone who knew Tess was devastated by her death. The regulars, those who hadn't
disappeared like Steve Byrd and Mr. Military, expressed their condolences, each commented on the
tragic loss of the vibrant and funny young woman.

All except Nick Winters.

He ambled in a couple of days after Kate reopened.
He ordered his double espresso, then stood at the
counter sipping it. "Business is slow," he commented.

"It's been that way," Marilyn murmured, "ever
since…you know."

He lifted his eyebrows. "The murder."

"Yes." Marilyn's eyes filled with tears, and she looked apologetically at Kate. "Excuse me a minute."

Kate watched her hurry off, then turned back to Nick Winters, expecting some comment, some expression of remorse or condolence. Instead, he brought his espresso to his lips, then set it down and met her eyes. Something in his gaze chilled her. "Do you feel violated, Kate?"

"Excuse me?"

"By the destruction of your work? It's such a personal, intimate part of yourself."

"I've barely thought about my glass work," she said stiffly, offended.

"How could you not? It looks naked in here now. Colorless."

"Compared to Tess's death, the loss of my work means nothing."

"You don't have to pretend with me, Kate. We're like souls. I know you." He brought the coffee to his lips once more, then sighed. "I'm certainly glad I bought mine when I did. If I hadn't, it'd be garbage now."

She stared at him disbelievingly. He returned her stare, a smile tugging at the corners of his mouth. "Come now," he said, reproach in his voice. "Tess was a pretty girl, but she wasn't like us."

"What do you mean, not like us?"

"She didn't understand loyalty or commitment. She didn't understand fidelity. We both know that." He leaned toward her—Kate instinctively shrank back. "She had the loyalty of a whore."

Kate sucked in a sharp breath. "How can you say these things? She liked you. She was nice to you."

He lifted a shoulder. "Because they're true. You know they are, Kate. You can admit it to me."

"I don't know any such thing." She backed away from the counter, sickened by him. "This conversation is over, Nick. I suggest you take a seat at one of the tables like everyone else."

He reached across the counter and caught her hand. "What would you do, Kate? If you discovered your husband was cheating on you? Could you forgive him? Would you? I'd really like to know."

Emotion choked her, his words striking uncomfortably close to her heart. "Let me go, Nick."

He tightened his fingers instead. "I admire you. You're strong. And honest. Most people aren't, you know. Tess wasn't."

His words, their tone, crawled over her like maggots. She shuddered and tugged against his hand. From the corner of her eyes, she saw Marilyn emerge through the louvered door and stop dead. "I said, let me go."

"You're too good for him, Katherine McDowell Ryan." He released her hand. "It's too damn bad. It's all too damn bad."

55

Kate sat at her desk, staring at the drawing on the far wall. Done in pastels—it depicted her and Richard's house in the springtime, the gardens in full bloom. She had commissioned a local artist to do it in celebration of their first anniversary in their dream home.

She brought a hand to her temple and rubbed at the knot of tension that had settled there. Several hours had passed since her disturbing conversation with Nick Winters, and try as she might, she had been unable to put the things he'd said out of her mind. She hadn't been able to shake the way they had made her feel. Disquieted and on edge. Suspicious.

And angry. At him for saying them—at herself for letting him get to her.

Kate dragged her gaze from the drawing, turning her attention instead to the portable crib where Emma slept. She caught her bottom lip between her teeth. Richard had been away from home a lot lately. Every weekend. Several evenings a week.

The question was, had he been gone more than at other busy times during their marriage? She thought back, trying to recall. It had never been this bad, she decided, even right before the Gary Seneca trial, and that one had been a doozy. High profile, lots of witnesses and complicated medical evidence.

But, she assured herself, he had never been preparing a political campaign before.

She frowned. But the election was still a year off. And he had already secured considerable support, including the *Times Picayune* and the St. Tammany Parish Sheriff's Department. How much more could he and Julianna have to do?

Hating herself for her suspicions, she grabbed her purse, checked on Emma, then headed out front. She would put her mind to rest once and for all.

"Marilyn, Blake, there's something I have to do. Can you watch Emma until I get back? It's important."

"No problem," Marilyn said, meeting her eyes. "What's up?"

"I can't...there's something I need to check out, and I have to do it now." Marilyn frowned, and Kate ignored the question in her eyes. "She's asleep and should be for a while. There are two bottles in the refrigerator and diapers in the bag beside the crib." She set the baby monitor on the counter. "I'll be back as quick as I can."

Leaving before either employee could question her, Kate hurried home to retrieve her car, then drove to Richard's firm, reassuring herself the entire way. Richard would be there, chin-high in paperwork, just as he had said he would be. She would feel like a fool, make some excuse for being there, and head back to The Bean, promising herself she would never distrust her husband again.

But Richard wasn't there. Several associates were, and Kate asked but no one had seen him. Using his office phone, she called home. The recorder picked up. She tried his car, then the club. Both without luck.

Hands shaking, she hung up the phone. She would run home; perhaps he was napping. Or in the yard. His car hadn't been there when she'd retrieved hers, but they could have passed each other on the way.

Kate darted into the hallway and ran smack-dab into one of the secretaries, her arms piled high with copies. The papers flew.

Kate made a sound of dismay, squatted down and began helping the young woman collect the papers. "I'm so sorry," she said, embarrassed. "I wasn't looking where I was going."

"That's okay, Mrs. Ryan. It happens."

"Do I know you?"

The woman flushed. "We met last year. At the firm's Christmas party. Sandy Derricks. Mr. Bedico's assistant."

Kate smiled. "Of course, Sandy. It's good to see you again." She scooped up the last of the papers and handed them to Sandy, her expression apologetic. "It's not bad enough having to work on a Saturday, but now I've gone and made your job more difficult."

"Don't think anything of it, really. I work every Saturday." She drew her eyebrows together. "Can I help you in some way?"

Kate laughed. "Actually, maybe you can. I'm looking for my husband. Have you seen him today? It's rather urgent that I speak with him."

For a moment, Sandy gazed blankly at her, then a small, sly smile curved her lips. "Not today," she said softly. "Of course, he's been out of the office a lot recently." She paused as if for effect, her smile broadening, becoming almost triumphant. Kate's stomach sank, fearing what was coming next. "Perhaps if you find his assistant Julianna, you'll find your husband."

Kate's hands began to shake. She understood what Sandy was telling her. And that doing so was giving her great pleasure.

Kate took a step backward, working to get a grip on her emotions. Her hurt. Her fury and embarrassment. The urge to hotly defend her husband, to tell this young woman that it wasn't true. Her husband would not be unfaithful to her.

Instead, quietly and with as much dignity as she could muster, she asked Sandy to get her Julianna's address.

She did and within twelve minutes, Kate pulled to a stop in front of Julianna's apartment. Richard's Mercedes was parked in the drive, wedged in behind a bright blue Miata.

Kate sat for a moment, breathing deeply, trying to calm herself. She flexed her fingers on the steering wheel, acknowledging fear. And cowardice. She could just drive away, she thought. She could stick her head in the sand and pretend this wasn't happening, pretend that her husband hadn't taken her love and trust and thrown them back in her face.

As if he hadn't broken her heart.

Oh, Richard…how could you? She bent and rested her forehead against the steering wheel, numb with the truth, with the impending betrayal. *We had everything. We had each other.*

Firming her resolve, Kate drew in a deep breath, threw open the car door and climbed out. She strode up the walk; climbed the two steps to Julianna's porch and crossed to the door.

She knocked. When there was no answer after a moment, she pounded.

A moment later the door cracked open. Through the

sliver of space, Kate saw that Julianna wore a slinky, silky robe. Her hair was tousled; her face flushed.

There went her last hope—that they really were working.

Fool. Naive, trusting idiot.

"I want to see my husband," she said, voice shaking. "Now."

"I don't know what you're—"

"Cut the crap. His car's out front." Kate shoved at the door and pushed past the other woman.

Julianna cried out. "How dare you! How—"

Richard appeared at the bedroom door, hurriedly zipping his pants. "Julianna, are you all ri—" He stopped when he saw Kate, his face falling. It would have been comical if it weren't so tragic. "K-Kate," he managed to stammer, his voice thick, "what are you doing here?"

Her eyes flooded with tears. "More to the point, husband, what are *you* doing here?"

"This isn't what it looks like."

"No? Then what is it?"

"It—" He glanced at Julianna, who was wringing her hands and whimpering. The vulnerable, innocent act made Kate want to puke. "We...I spilled coffee on my shirt and...and I took it off to..."

His words trailed pathetically off. As he stood there half-dressed, scrambling around for some lame excuse for being half-naked in his assistant's bedroom on a Saturday afternoon, Kate saw him in a way she never had before. As weak. And shallow. And completely self-absorbed. Did the man she'd thought she loved for so long even exist?

"Kate," he murmured, holding out a hand in supplication, "I can explain."

She thought of their fight of a few weeks ago. Of the things he had said, of the way he had made her feel—as if there was something wrong with her. As if she was the problem, the one who was letting them down. She folded her arms across her chest, battling the hurt that threatened to tear her apart. "You can explain, Richard? How? By telling me I'm a jealous, possessive shrew? Or by telling me *I* don't believe in you? Or that I'm not fun anymore?"

He simply stared at her. A first, she thought, the slick lawyer at a loss for words. She looked away, then back, shaking with sudden rage. "You son of a bitch. I trusted you. I—" Tears choked her, and she fought to clear them. "Don't come home, Richard. You're not welcome there any longer."

56

That night, Kate stood beside Emma's crib and watched her daughter. She slept the deep, untroubled sleep of only the very young; she had no sins to regret, no fears to stalk her, no betrayals to steal her peace of mind.

Kate's eyes welled with tears. She fought the urge to reach out and touch the infant, though she longed to. It wouldn't be fair to wake her only because her mother needed someone to hang on to.

She was so beautiful, Kate thought. So perfect and sweet. She had brought such joy into their lives. No, not *their* lives; not Richard's. Only hers. Obviously. Richard's betrayal had proved that. If he had cared one whit about being a parent, about being Emma's parent, he wouldn't have thrown her away.

Kate brought a hand to her mouth, working to hold back a cry of despair. How could Richard have done this? How could he have betrayed her this way? How could he have betrayed them?

She spun away from the crib and hurried from the nursery. In the hours since she had discovered Richard's betrayal, she had alternately paced and raged and sobbed. She hadn't answered the phone, though it had rung a dozen times. After the first couple, she had unplugged the recorder. She had been afraid Richard was calling, and she neither wanted to talk to him nor take his message. Not ever again.

Kate brought the heels of her hands to her eyes, furious at her tears. He didn't deserve them, the lying, cheating SOB.

Her husband. How could he have betrayed her this way?

She sank to the couch. How long? she wondered. Had he started the affair after he hired Julianna? Or had he hired his lover? She brought a hand to her mouth. Dear God, was Julianna the first?

A month ago that thought would never have occurred to her. But then, only a matter of hours ago, she'd had a good marriage. Perfect, she'd thought— even with the few rough patches. A loving husband, a happy life.

Now she— Her tears spilled over once more. Standing, she went in search of a tissue. Finding it, she blew her nose, tossed the used tissue in the trash, then grabbed another. Had Richard ever loved her? Or had he married her out of competition with Luke? Or because she, stupid, doting fool, had always given him everything he wanted?

Because she *had* always given him what he wanted. Before Emma, she had been happy to cater to him, to his needs, desires and plans. She had been so *grateful* to be Mrs. Richard Ryan.

Selfish asshole, she thought, suddenly furious. He hadn't wanted to share with Emma. Richard had always needed to be number one. Always had to be the center of attention. She knew that about him, had always known it. But she had thought he would be man enough, adult enough, to share with a child.

Apparently, she had been wrong.

But then, she had been wrong about a lot of things lately.

The doorbell pealed. Startled, she swung toward the door. Through the beveled glass panel she saw the figure of a man. He turned slightly in her direction, as if spotting her, then lifted a hand in greeting.

Nick Winters, she realized, both surprised and dismayed. What was he doing here?

Pulling herself together, she crossed to the door. She cracked it open. "Hello, Kate," he said, smiling. "I'm sorry to bother you so late, but I was hoping to buy another piece of your stained glass."

She shook her head, gripping the doorknob more tightly. "I'm sorry, Nick, but tonight's not good. Maybe tomorrow?"

"Kate, please." He placed his hand on the door. "It's for my mother. Her birthday's the day after tomorrow and..." He met her eyes. "Please, Kate. She'd love your work."

She glanced at her watch, then back at him. The last thing she wanted was a visitor. Especially Nick Winters. "This really isn't a good time. Couldn't it wait?"

"It can't." He lowered his voice to a soft plea. "Please, Kate. It would mean the world to her."

She hesitated, then relented and opened the door the rest of the way. "It'll have to be quick. I'm not feeling too well tonight."

He stepped inside, his expression sympathetic. "I see that. I'm so sorry, Kate."

She swallowed against the feeling that he knew exactly why she didn't feel well, and led him downstairs to her glass studio. Many of her pieces were hung, but she had others stored in a flat file. He flipped through them without speaking.

His silence began to make her nervous. Something about it felt wrong—too quiet, too intense. Too...full.

She glanced at her watch again, suddenly realizing what she had done—let a man she knew virtually nothing about into her home when she was alone. A man who had shown no remorse at another's death, one who had upset her just that afternoon.

The hair on her arms and at the back of her neck stood up, and she cleared her throat. "Do you see one you like?"

He didn't answer, and she took the tiniest step backward, hoping he wouldn't notice, wondering if she made a run for it how far she would get.

"I'm really not feeling well tonight. Could we please cut this short?"

He looked at her. In his pale gaze she saw something akin to pity. "I know what it's like to be betrayed, Kate. To have your love and trust thrown back in your face." He lowered his voice to a silky caress. "I know how much that hurts."

She swallowed hard, unsettled. By the intimacy in his tone, the way he was looking at her. "It's late, Nick. I think you'd better go."

She took a step back from him—he followed. "Richard's sleeping and...and I told him I'd be right there. He'll be down here any minute to check on me."

Nick shook his head, pity in his eyes once more. "I saw them together. I know." He cupped Kate's face in his palms, forcing her to look at him. "I like you, Kate. I do. I wish things could be different."

She tried to pull away; he tightened his grip. It felt as if her face were caught in a vice. "Do you think about revenge?" he asked. "About making him pay?"

A sound slipped past her lips, a small squeak of terror. The sound amused him, she saw. Pleased him. The smile that touched his lips sent a chill clear to her bones.

"Loyalty is all, Kate Ryan. You and I know that. When trust is broken, all that remains is vengeance. 'For vengeance is mine, sayeth the Lord.'"

He relaxed his fingers slightly and drew his thumb across her mouth, the gesture almost absentminded. Kate stood frozen in his hands, barely able to contain her shudders of fear. Who was this man? *What* was he?

A monster, she thought in horror. She had let a monster into her home.

Emma. Asleep in her crib, alone, defenseless.

Oh, God. Don't let him hurt my daughter, she silently begged. Please, not my baby.

"I like you," he said again, softly, his tone laced with regret. He bent toward her. His breath stirred against her ear. "It'll be all over soon. Sooner than you can even imagine."

He dropped his hands, then turned and walked away. Kate watched him go, frozen to the spot, shaking so badly her teeth chattered. He climbed her stairs; she heard him cross the floor above her head, heard her front door snap shut.

That final sound penetrated her fear, galvanizing her to action. With a cry of pure terror, she raced up the stairs. To the nursery. Emma was there in her crib, asleep, her chest rising and falling with her breathing.

Kate said a prayer of thanks; it played over and over in her head, even as she left Emma and ran to the front door. She locked it, then looked out the glass panel.

Nick stood beside his car, gazing up at the house. Up at her. Kate brought a trembling hand to her mouth. Her fear amused him. Her attempts to protect herself and her child. She sensed that if he wanted to hurt her, he would. If he wanted to hurt Emma. A door and dead bolt wouldn't keep him out.

Nothing would.

Quickly, she snapped off the foyer light, leaving her in darkness and him in light. He lifted a hand, as if in acknowledgment of her terror, then climbed into his car. A moment later he backed out of the drive, his headlights cutting through the darkness, the twin beams bouncing crazily through the branches of the oaks, the effect like carnival lights.

She turned and hurried from window to window, checking them, locking the ones that weren't, dead-bolting the doors, her panic growing.

Sobbing now, she retrieved Richard's hunting rifle from their bedroom closet. She loaded it, her hands shaking so badly it took her three tries to slip the shells into the chamber. Taking it and the cordless phone, she went to Emma's room. Clutching both to her chest, she sank to the floor beside the crib.

57

Richard took one last glance at Julianna's front door, then started across the porch. He hated to leave Julianna while she slept, but he couldn't stay. It wouldn't look right for him to be here overnight; he had his reputation to think of, the firm's, his campaign.

He hadn't been able to sleep anyway. Every time he'd closed his eyes, he had seen Kate's face, her wounded expression as she had told him he was no longer welcome in his own home.

God forgive him, he hadn't gone after her. He had stayed with Julianna. She had held and comforted him; she had understood his confusion and pain. Comforting had become passion, then urgency. She had taken him into her hands, then mouth, and when, finally, she had taken him inside her, Kate and his ruined marriage had been far from his thoughts.

They weren't now. How was he going to face her? he wondered, looking up at the starless sky, feeling small and gutless. Hardly half a man, let alone a whole one. He'd had the perfect life, the ideal marriage. He had blown it all to hell.

No. He hadn't blown it. If he wanted her back, their marriage back, by God, he would have it. She was his wife; she would forgive him. He deserved that much from her. After all the things he had given her and the way she had shut him out these past months, she owed him this one little mistake. She owed him forgiveness.

He took his cellular phone from his pocket and punched in their home number as he angled across the small patch of lawn to his car. She answered on the first ring, her voice gravelly with sleep or tears, he wasn't sure which.

"Kate, it's me. Don't hang up, I—"

"I've got nothing to say to you."

The phone went dead as she hung up on him. He made a sound of surprise. And anger. She was his wife, by damn, and she *would* talk to him. He pressed redial, but before he hit Send, a figure separated from the shadows beside the house.

"You've taken something that belongs to me," the man said softly. "And I want it back."

Richard strained to see the man's face, still cloaked in shadow. What he could make out didn't strike a chord of recognition in him. "You're confused, buddy," he said, annoyed. "Get lost."

The man took a step closer, emerging from the darkness. "You took my sweet flower and soiled her. Now you have to pay."

Richard expelled a sharp breath. "I don't know you. I didn't take this 'flower' you're talking about. I'd suggest you go sleep it off. Now, get the hell away from me."

Instead, the man came closer, his movements nearly soundless. Richard saw that he had light hair and eyes as flat and cold as death.

A prickle of unease moved over him. "Didn't you hear me? I said to get the fuck away from me before I—"

"What?" The man laughed. "Call the cops? It'll

be all over with before they get here." He eased closer. "Let me tell you a story. About a beautiful young girl. And the man who loved her. She was the world," he murmured, glancing toward Julianna's door. "His everything. He protected and cherished her. He taught her about loyalty and trust. In return, he gave her all that she desired.

"But she was susceptible to evil, to outside forces, ones intent on extinguishing her sweet, bright light. Ones who would turn her into a common whore."

Julianna, Richard realized. He was talking about Julianna. This must be the man she had told him about, the one she feared from her past.

Richard narrowed his eyes. "If you're talking about Julianna, I'm telling you now, it's over between you two. She doesn't want to see you. Not ever."

This time it was Richard who took a step closer, hoping to intimidate. "Leave her alone. If you don't, I'll have you slapped with a restraining order so fast it'll make your head spin. You got that, you freak?"

John smiled. "Self-righteous son of a bitch, aren't you? I look at you and I see the slime of the earth, a man without honor. Without loyalty." He swept his icy gaze over Richard, his contempt all but palpable. "What of your beautiful wife and baby daughter, alone in that big old house? Who's protecting them while you're off fucking my Julianna? Who's taking care of them?"

Richard's blood ran cold at the implied threat to his family. This man knew about his family, where they lived, that they were alone and vulnerable.

Fear choked him, and he took a step backward. "I'm calling the police," he said, punching 911 on his cell phone. "If I were you, I'd—"

Richard heard a loud pop, like a firecracker exploding, then felt a burning sensation in his chest. He lifted a hand to the spot, then brought it away wet.

Blood.

Dear Jesus, Kate.

Head swimming, he lifted his disbelieving gaze to the man's. The man smiled. And pulled the trigger again.

58

Kate opened her eyes slowly. Her head pounded; her eyes burned. She glanced around her, momentarily disoriented. Then she remembered. Richard's betrayal. Nick Winters' frightening visit. Curling up beside the crib, shotgun clutched to her chest.

The pounding in her head became louder, more insistent. Kate realized someone was at her door. She eased herself into a sitting position, then stood, wincing as her joints and muscles screamed in protest. Her entire body ached from sleeping on the nursery's wooden floor. She felt like a prize fighter's punching bag.

"I'm coming," she muttered, peering at her wristwatch, wondering who would be calling so early. It wasn't Richard, she knew. Not only did he have a key, he was arrogant enough to think using it would be okay.

Emma stirred, but didn't waken. Thank God. She would take care of whoever was at the door, then make herself a pot of strong, black coffee. Maybe then she would feel halfway human.

She reached the front door and glanced out the sidelight. Two men she didn't know stood on her porch. Both wore suit jackets and dark sunglasses. Like a couple of guys out of a bad TV show.

She cracked open the door. "Can I help you?"

"Mrs. Ryan?"

"That's right."

"Mandeville police." The man on her right held up his shield. "I'm Detective Owens. This is Detective Dober. Could we have a few minutes of your time?"

Kate moved her gaze from one to the other of them, heart in her throat. She swallowed hard, past the fear. "What's this about?"

"May we come in?"

She shook her head. "Not until you tell me what this is about."

The men exchanged glances. "Mrs. Ryan, do you know where your husband is?"

A half an hour later, Kate was on her way to the morgue to identify her husband. She sat in the back seat of the detectives' Ford, silent, shaking hands clasped in her lap. Emma was with the next-door neighbor. The woman had taken one look at Kate and had agreed without questions to watch the child.

Kate turned her face to the window and watched the world go by, the sights familiar but foreign. She struggled to keep from falling apart, struggled to come to grips with what the detectives had told her. It looked like a robbery, the police had said. Richard's wallet, watch and wedding band were missing. He had been found beside his Mercedes, cell phone in his hand. He had been shot twice, at point-blank range.

The police had questioned her extensively about the last time she had seen her husband, about his whereabouts and the last weeks of his life. Did she know of anyone who might want him dead?

As humiliating as it had been, she had been completely honest with them. About discovering his infidelity. Their fight. That she had told him not to come home.

She had seen their expressions change as she talked, sympathy becoming suspicion. She had a motive, she realized. No alibi. A hysterical laugh passed her lips, and she saw the detective who was driving—she couldn't remember whether he was Owens or Dober—glance at her in the rearview mirror. Dear God, her husband had been murdered, and she had to deal with finding a lawyer.

As if in a waking nightmare, Kate followed the detectives into the morgue. She was aware of a strong odor, like apples fermenting in a cellar. An antiseptic, she realized. Or formaldehyde. Masking the scent of death. Mixing with it.

One of the detectives slid out the refrigerated drawer. She stood dumbly by, waiting for him to lift the white sheet, sweat beading on her upper lip and slipping between her breasts. Down her spine.

He did. A cry rose to her throat. She brought her hand to her mouth, holding it and her sickness back. She nodded and spun away, breath coming in short, shallow pants.

The detective with the gentle voice led her out of the room, then the building and into the bright fall day. There, she sank to a step, dropped her head into her hands and wept.

The next forty-eight hours were a nightmare for Kate. She had Richard's family and their grief to deal with, her and Richard's friends and colleagues to tell, their shock to contend with, The Bean to run and funeral arrangements to make. Emma to care for. The shadow of suspicion hanging over her, the detectives' seemingly endless questions.

Her own grief. Her guilt. She couldn't help wondering—*knowing*—that if she had been more forgiving, if she had allowed Richard to come home, he would be alive.

How was she going to go on? How was she going to live with that?

She was eliminated as a suspect only after Richard's cell phone records were received. That call he made to her, as well as Old Joe's midnight stroll with Beauregard, cleared her.

Blake, Marilyn and Beanie were godsends. They took over the day-to-day running of The Bean. In truth, Kate wanted nothing to do with it.

First Tess. Now Richard. Nothing meant anything anymore.

Except Emma. If not for her daughter, Kate feared she would curl up and die, too. That's why, when family and friends offered to take the child until Kate had a chance to find her footing, she refused. Without her daughter, she told them, she would never find her feet. Emma was all that anchored her to this world.

59

Richard was interred in his family's vault in New Orleans. The November day was cold and damp, the air heavy with moisture. Julianna stood outside the circle of mourners, neither family, friend, nor colleague. An outcast. The way she had always been.

Without Richard, she was alone now. Alone again. Tears stung her eyes and she fought to keep them from falling. She didn't want them to see her cry, didn't want them to think her pathetic. As pathetic as she thought herself.

The firm had closed for the day so that the employees could attend the funeral. They all snubbed Julianna. Somehow they had discovered Julianna's part in Richard's last hours, that the two of them had been embroiled in an affair.

Somehow. Julianna shifted her gaze to Sandy, huddling with the other secretaries, suddenly one of them. Suddenly accepted.

Not so suddenly, not a surprise.

Chas Bedico had called her the day after the murder and coolly reminded her that she had been an employee of Richard's, not the firm's. He would appreciate it if she would remove her personal items from the office before regular hours began Monday morning. As a courtesy to Kate, he would pay Julianna anything that was owed her.

It had been obvious that he had known about her and Richard, too.

Just then, Sandy looked up and their gazes met. Her lips lifted in the smallest of smiles, but in that smile Julianna saw triumph. Payback. In that moment she knew with certainty what she had only suspected— Sandy had made sure everyone knew about her affair with Richard. No doubt complete with all the sordid details she could manufacture.

Payback.

Vision blurring with tears, Julianna dragged her gaze away. She hugged herself, losing the battle with her tears. They spilled over and rolled down her cheeks. Sandy didn't understand. None of them did. She and Richard had been so much more than lovers. They had been each other's destiny. Soul mates.

And now he was gone.

Julianna hugged herself tighter, struggling to keep from completely falling apart. She had nothing now. No lover, no job. She looked toward Kate, cuddling Emma in her arms, holding her tightly.

No baby.

As she contemplated the mother and infant, Julianna longed to hold her child, so badly her arms and chest ached. If only she could hold on to her the way Kate was, seeming to draw strength and comfort from her tiny body, her unconditional love. With Emma, she would never have to be alone and unloved again.

She had nothing. Nobody.

No, she amended, not quite alone. John was out there. Waiting, though she wasn't sure for what. Since she found the obscene package he had left for her on her bed, she'd heard nothing from him, though she had known he was near. She had felt his presence, like the charged quiet of a storm still an hour off. Watching. Biding his time.

Richard's parents opened their home for the mourners to pay their respects after the funeral. Julianna didn't attend. Instead, she drove aimlessly through the city before heading back across the Causeway, working to gather her scattered thoughts, to plan what she would do next, where she would go.

She had allowed herself a false sense of security; she realized that now. She had allowed herself to believe that some stranger had been in her home and had violated her things; had allowed herself to believe that Richard could protect her from John.

Instead, Richard was dead. Julianna's hands began to shake, and she gripped the steering wheel tighter. No one could protect her from John. No one but herself. She had to run—she would have already but she'd felt compelled to attend Richard's funeral. For herself and because she owed him that.

By the time she returned home, the sun was beginning its descent. The humidity of the day had lingered, lending the approaching evening a wet cold that penetrated clear to her bones. Los Angeles, she thought as she climbed out of her car and started for the porch. Palm trees, ocean breezes, moderate temperatures. Surely she could get lost in a city that size.

She unlocked her front door and stepped inside. She stopped dead, a cry of terror crossing her lips, coming out as a strangled whimper. John sat in a straight-backed chair facing the door, a gun laid across his lap.

He smiled, the curving of his lips bloodless. In that instant, Julianna knew that John had killed Richard. He meant to kill her next.

"Hello, Julianna."

She took an instinctive step backward, hand behind her, searching for the doorknob, though she knew he would never allow her to escape.

He picked up the gun, and motioned with it. "Move away from the door, please. After all, we wouldn't want to disturb the neighbors."

She did as he asked, heart beating so wildly she could hardly breathe.

"What's the matter, my sweet? Aren't you happy to see me?" He smiled again. "You can't be surprised. I know you got my gift."

"You...killed...Richard."

"I did. He took what was mine, Julianna. He *had* what was mine. That was unacceptable." He waved her forward. "Come here."

Eyes filling with tears, she did as he instructed. Her legs shook so badly she could hardly walk. She stopped before him, head bowed.

"Look at me, Julianna." She lifted her gaze. "I want you to get on your knees."

Her tears welled and spilled over. She didn't want to die on her knees, but followed his orders anyway, wondering when the bullet would come, where he would place it.

And she wondered whether death would be mercifully quick or agonizingly slow.

He stood. "I'm disappointed in you, Julianna. Very disappointed." He lowered his voice. "After everything I taught you about love, about loyalty and commitment, you do this? You let me down this way?"

"I'm sorry," she whispered. "I'm so sorry."

He shook his head. "Sorry isn't good enough. You disobeyed me. You stole from me. You took my love and threw it back in my face. How do you think that made me feel?'' When she didn't answer, he nudged her with the gun. "How, Julianna?''

"Bad,'' she said, voice faltering. "Awful.''

"That doesn't begin to cover it.'' His voice thickened, as with emotion. "You broke my heart.''

She swallowed past the knot of tears in her throat. "Forgive me, John. I didn't mean to. Please…don't hurt me.''

He ignored her pleading and circled to stand behind her. "I could kill you now.'' He bent and she felt his breath against the back of her neck, his lips against her ear. She shuddered. "It would be easy. Almost pleasurable after the way you've betrayed me.''

A sob rose to her throat. How could she have been so stupid to believe Richard could protect her from John, that anyone could?

"There,'' John murmured, his voice warming, "you're getting it now. You're starting to understand my power. The power of right, of justice.'' He laughed, and the merciless sound ripped along her nerve endings. "Those responsible must pay. Loose ends must be tied up. Like Clark Russell. Like your mother.''

She lifted her eyes to his, and he laughed again. "That's right, my sweet. They interfered in my business, they told you things you weren't meant to know. They had to be punished.''

"No,'' she said, her voice lifting, then cracking. "No!''

"I'm afraid so.'' He placed the gun's muzzle under her chin, forcing her head so far back that her neck began to ache. "It wasn't pretty, love. But it was quick. For you, she didn't suffer.''

Julianna began to cry, deep wrenching sobs of despair. Richard was dead because of her. Her mother. Clark Russell. *What had she done?*

"Stop that." He shook his head, frowning. "She doesn't deserve your tears, she wasn't a good mother. She wasn't there for you. I was there for you. I'm the one you should cry for. Me, Julianna. Only me."

He released the gun's hammer and tucked the weapon into the waistband of his pants, then squatted in front of her. He cupped her face in his palms, his fingers digging into her flesh, demanding she look at him. "You're young and foolish. Susceptible to those who would ruin you. It's not your fault, I know that."

He spoke slowly and patiently, the way he would to an errant child. "Because of your youth, I might allow you this one mistake. I *might*," he repeated. "Just this one."

She caught her breath. He was offering her a chance. A way out of a bullet. She swallowed her fear, her grief. She focused on what he was saying, on what he was offering her. "What…how can I make my mistakes up to you? How, John?" She covered his hands with her own. "Tell me what to do, please."

He smiled and trailed his thumbs softly, tenderly across her cheekbones. "I want my little girl back. My special one. I miss her, Julianna." He brought his face closer and brushed his mouth against hers. "I want what we had before."

At his words, their meaning, vomit rushed to her throat, threatening to strangle her. She choked it back by sheer force of will. Dear God, how could she give him what he wanted? How could she go back to the girl who had innocently loved John Powers with all her heart when now she saw that he was a monster? Dear God, how?

For a moment, she thought of telling him the truth, of telling him that she hated him, that he repulsed her. That she would rather die than be with him again.

She couldn't. Because that, too, would be a lie.

She didn't want to die. She wanted to live. And this was her only chance.

She leaned forward and rested her forehead against his chest. "I've missed you so much." The falsehood tripped easily off her tongue, sounding not only natural but rich with emotion. She lifted her face to his and smiled tremulously. "I've missed being your little girl. I've missed being special."

Beneath her hands, his trembled. That small display of his excitement sickened her. She fought to keep her true feelings from showing as he helped her to her feet and led her to the bedroom. To the bed.

There, he undressed her, his movements faltering. He laid her on the bed, then stripped and lay beside her. She lay unmoving as he fondled and petted her, knowing what he expected, what aroused him most. Knowing that if she fell out of character, even for a moment, she would be lost.

She squeezed her eyes shut as he slid his hands over her body, stroking and petting, unable to quell the shudders of distaste that rippled over her, unable to stop the tears that trickled from the corners of her eyes and rolled down her cheeks.

She was a lost soul.

John caught a tear with the tip of his finger and brought it to his mouth. "Are you frightened, Julianna?"

"Yes," she whispered, voice trembling.

"You needn't be, my sweet." He thought her answer, her trembling and tears a part of the game, she knew. She knew also that they pleased him. "I'll be gentle, you know I will. So gentle."

He brought her hand to his erection. As he had hundreds of times before, he instructed her on how to hold and stroke him. As she followed his instructions, guttural sounds slipped past his lips, ones more animal than human. Hearing them made her physically ill. She wondered if a bullet wouldn't have been a better choice.

He rolled her onto her back and entered her. She cried out. In despair. And humiliation. Instead of a deterrent, her cries served as an intoxicant. He arched his back and with a shout of triumph, climaxed.

He collapsed against her, perspiring, his breath coming in short, quick gasps. "My angel," he murmured after a moment, his lips against her neck. "My sweet, sweet, angel. I knew you'd come back to me. I knew it."

She didn't trust herself to speak without revealing her true feelings, so she said nothing.

At her silence, he raised himself up on an elbow and gazed down at her, tears in his eyes. "Happy?"

She forced what he wanted to hear past her stiff lips and frozen smile. "So happy. I love you, John."

He studied her expression, as if deciding whether she was telling the truth. If he decided she was not, he would kill her. Julianna knew this to be a fact.

One moment became several, still he gazed assessingly at her. Her heart began to race, her breath to come in shallow gasps. Her cheeks felt hot, her pulse quick.

After several seconds, he nodded. "I forgive you. But understand, you must be punished for your disobedience. You must pay for that disloyalty. Now there are loose ends to be tied up. Now it's messy.''

Her mother had been a loose end. So had Clark and Richard. Who was left? She searched his gaze, dread settling in the pit of her gut. "I don't understand."

"The baby, of course." He trailed a finger down her cheek, following the path of her tears. "She has to die."

Julianna's heart stopped. *Emma? No!*

"Yes," he said, as if he had read her thoughts. He shook his head regretfully. "You should have gotten rid of it when I told you to. Now it's more difficult. Now Kate's involved."

Fear rose up in her, grabbing her by the throat. Not fear of her own death, but of another's. She pictured Emma, the way she gurgled and kicked her legs, the way her smile lit up her whole face and made you feel glad to be alive. And she pictured her in a pool of blood, her head blown off or throat slit.

She had to find a way to stop him.

"But why?" she whispered. "She belongs to Kate now. She's not a part of our lives. She—''

He placed a hand over her mouth, hushing her. "Loose ends," he said. "They can come back to haunt you, they must be tied up."

He dropped his hand, swung his legs over the side of the bed and sat up. He reached for his gun, checked the clip, then lay it on the bed beside him. "I'd like to spare Kate, but that might not be possible. It probably won't be."

Julianna stared at his back, sickened. He spoke of killing Kate and Emma with no more emotion than he would talking about lunch. Or the weather. How had she not seen him for the monster he was? How could she have believed herself in love with him?

She wouldn't let him kill Emma. She couldn't.

She darted her gaze over the room, considering her options, scrambling for a way out of this, for a way to stop him. For something she could use to stop him. She needed to get his gun. But how? He never let it out of his reach. Her gaze landed on the hideously ugly ceramic lamp on the bedside table. It would have to do.

Julianna crawled out of bed, snatched up a T-shirt and pair of shorts from the floor beside the bed and pulled them on. "You're right, of course. But I...I should help."

He stood and looked over his shoulder at her in question. "It's my mess," she said. "I should help...clean it up."

He thought about it a moment, then inclined his head. "What do you propose?"

He bent to retrieve his pants from the floor, stepped into them, then reached for his gun.

Julianna saw her opportunity. Her last opportunity. She grabbed the lamp and swung. It connected with the back of his head with a sickening thud. The gun slipped from his fingers.

He straightened and looked at her, his expression registering surprise, then understanding. She swung again, as hard as she could, grunting with the effort. The lamp base exploded against his head. Pottery shards and blood flew in every direction.

As if in slow motion, John fell to his knees, then toppled face first to the floor, square on top of the gun.

Julianna stood above him, shaking, what was left of

the lamp dangling from her hand. She couldn't tell if he was breathing; no way was she going any closer.

She let the lamp slip from her fingers. "That's what I propose, you sick bastard."

60

Kate awakened with a start. She sat up and looked around her, disoriented. She'd come home from the funeral and after getting Emma down for the night, had poured herself a big glass of wine and sat on the couch. She must have fallen asleep.

She glanced at the baby monitor to make sure it was on. The power indicator light glowed; a comforting, red beacon in the otherwise dark room.

Kate stared at it a moment, listening. No sound came from her daughter's bedroom. Reassured, she sank back against the cushions. She brought her hands to her face, acknowledging fatigue. Despair.

It was over. The funeral had marked the end. Not only to Richard's life, but to her own as well. The one she had known for more than ten years, the one with Richard, the one in which she had been a happily married woman. Content. And confident. Of her place in the world. That she was loved.

Suddenly, Emma whimpered, then cried out, the sound sharp and frightened.

The monitor crackled, then went dead.

Kate froze momentarily, then alarm exploded inside her. She scrambled from the couch. Her foot knocked into the glass of wine, toppling it, sending red liquid spilling across the white rug. She ran for the nursery.

She reached it in moments. A cry ripped from her

lips. A figure stood beside her daughter's crib, bent over it. At her feet sat the diaper bag, stuffed to overflowing.

"Get away from my baby!"

The woman spun around. She had Emma in her arms, a hand pressed over her mouth to quiet her.

Even in the minimal illumination cast by the sole night-light, Kate recognized the woman. "Julianna? What do you think you're doing?"

The woman removed her hand, and Emma's cries shattered the quiet. "This isn't what it looks like, Kate."

Kate inched carefully toward the younger woman, uncertain what she would do, afraid for Emma's safety. "Give me my baby."

The infant heard her mother's voice and turned toward her, her cries becoming frenetic howls.

Julianna took a step backward. She shook her head. "You don't understand. He's coming! He means to—"

"Give her to me!" Kate stopped before her and held out her arms. "You're scaring her."

Julianna hesitated. In that moment, Kate saw her grip slacken and she snatched the infant from the other woman's arms and spun away from her. She held Emma to her chest, rocking and cooing. The infant quieted, her cries becoming distraught, hiccoughing whimpers.

"Haven't you done enough?" Kate asked, her voice low, vibrating with emotion. "You stole my husband and now you want my child, too?"

"You don't understand," she said again, wringing her hands, glancing nervously at the Pooh Bear wall clock. "John's coming. He—"

"I don't know any John. How did you get in here?"

"The key in the false rock. Beside the side door."

Dear God, that's how she had gotten in before.
"I'm calling the police."

Julianna grabbed her arm, stopping her. "Don't do that! You can't. You have to—"

"My husband is dead. He wouldn't be, if he'd been home." Kate shook off her hand. "Get out of my house. I want you away from me and away from my child."

Kate left the nursery, hurrying toward the living room. When she reached it, she flipped on the overhead light. The phone lay on the floor beside the toppled wineglass and ugly red stain.

"Emma's life is in danger."

Kate stopped dead. She looked back at Julianna, taking in her tear-streaked face and stained, rumpled clothing. Kate focused on the stains, suddenly realizing what they were. Blood.

Kate widened her eyes, suddenly truly afraid. For her daughter's safety, for her own. "Oh, my God."

"John's coming. He means to kill Emma."

Tightening her grip on her daughter, Kate took a step backward. "Get away from us."

Julianna held a hand out. It, too, was splattered with blood. "I have to protect her."

Kate shook her head, heart thundering, mouth dry. "You're crazy. Unbalanced. You're—"

"I'm Emma's birth mother."

Julianna's words hit Kate squarely in the gut. She stared at the other woman, stunned, numb, her world rocking. "What...did you—"

"I'm Emma's—"

"Shut up!" Kate shouted. "You're lying. You have to be!"

"I wanted to have an abortion," Julianna began, voice shaking. "But I waited...too long. One week and three days too long.

"The doctor," she continued, "he showed me pictures of babies at my stage of development. They were...they—" She looked at Kate, eyes pleading for understanding. "I didn't know. I promise I didn't."

Julianna drew in a shuddering breath and dragged her gaze away from Kate's. She crossed to the couch and sank heavily onto it. "The doctor asked me to consider adoption. He told me about Citywide. It seemed a perfect solution. My only way out."

Kate lowered her gaze to her daughter, tears flooding her eyes. Richard had been sleeping with Emma's biological mother. The thought made her sick.

"Did he...know?" she asked, tears choking her. "Did Richard know you were—"

"No. I didn't tell him." She looked at her hands, then back up at Kate. "At first I thought I'd surrender Emma and disappear. But then I...I read your profiles. Richard's...profile. I fell in love with him."

Kate stared at the other woman, not believing what she was hearing. "You fell in love with my husband from his...because of what he had written?"

"Yes." Julianna hugged herself. "He was everything...everything I'd always dreamed of. But I didn't just fall in love with him." She lifted watery eyes to Kate. "I fell in love with you, too. With your marriage, your lives."

"So...you decided to steal them? Instead of making your own life, you decided to steal ours?"

For a moment, Julianna hung her head. Then she

lifted it and squared her shoulders. "I gave you Emma. You wanted to be a mother more than anything. You said so in your profile. In return for Richard, I gave you Emma."

What could she say to this young woman? Thank you? She looked at her as if Kate should not only understand, but that she should even approve. "How did you find us?" she asked. "Ellen assured us that no identifying information would be exchanged without our consent."

"I stole it. From a file on her desk. She doesn't know."

Dear God, Kate realized, she had been right. About the break in, the missing photograph, the girl on the swing. All along, it had been Emma's birth mother.

"So you followed us," she murmured. "Found a way into our lives, Richard's life. And you seduced him."

The younger woman leaned forward, her expression earnest. "He didn't want to be unfaithful to you, Kate. He wasn't that kind of man. But we were meant to be together. We were each other's destiny. Each other's soul mate."

Kate looked at her daughter, quiet now and gazing up at her with unblinking blue eyes. Eyes only for her. Her mother. Kate's heart swelled, love momentarily chasing away the anger and betrayal she felt, chasing away the ugliness of the past days.

"Leave now." She returned her gaze to Julianna. "If you do, because of Emma, I won't call the police."

"I can't do that. I...there's more, Kate. Something I...have to tell you."

Kate stilled, something in the other woman's tone scaring her more than anything she had said so far.

"There's a man. He killed Richard and he...he means to kill Emma."

"Why are you saying this?" she cried, beginning to tremble. "Why can't you just leave us alone? Haven't you hurt me enough? Haven't you hurt my family enough?"

"He's Emma's father."

Kate gazed at the other woman in horror. The nightmare that had become her life had just taken another bizarre turn for the worse. She went to a chair and sat on its edge. Julianna was a deeply disturbed young woman; this story so far-fetched as to be ludicrous. And yet...something about it rang true. And if it were, Emma's life was in danger.

Kate looked up. "But why? I don't understand."

"Because of me. Because he's crazy. Obsessed."

"I'm calling the police," Kate said, standing.

"No!" Julianna cried, jumping to her feet. "They can't protect you from him! He's a professional. An assassin, trained to do wet work for the government. Killing means nothing to him. It's a job, a way of life."

"This is ludicrous!"

"You have to listen! The police can't help. John will wait them out. Or slip in and out without them being any the wiser. And he won't give up. Emma's a loose end. He told me so."

Kate strode past her and snatched up the phone from the floor. Julianna grabbed her arm. "I saw pictures. Of people with their throats slit. My mother——" her voice cracked "——she knew about him. I wouldn't believe her, so she had a friend of hers from the CIA tell me everything. He's the one who…who showed me the pictures.''

Tears welled in Julianna's eyes. "That man, from the CIA, he's dead now. So's my mother. It's all my fault. Don't you see…he'll kill Emma.''

Kate sank onto the chair, the cordless phone slipping from her fingers. She brought a hand to her mouth. "Oh, my God. If what you're telling me is…if it's true, what am I going to do?''

Julianna squatted down in front of Kate. "We have to run. Now. I hit him over the head with a lamp, but I don't know if I…if I killed him. I'm afraid I didn't.''

"We have to run?" Kate made a sound of disbelief. "I'd sooner accompany a viper into a snake pit than go anywhere with you. I'll take my chances on my own.''

"But I know him, how he works, what he looks like.'' She caught her hands. "You need me. Without me, you'll be sitting ducks.''

"I don't need you. I—''

The phone rang. They both turned toward the unit, though neither made a move to pick it up. It rang again. Then again.

The machine answered. Kate's cheery message floated through the silent house, followed by a man's voice, deep and silky smooth.

"Hello, Kate. Pass this message along to Julianna, please. I have your answer now. You've betrayed me for the last time.'' He sighed heavily. "You and Emma are dead.''

61

The highway stretched endlessly before Kate, the blackness of the night broken only by the illumination of her headlights and those of the other motorists, and even they had become few and far between.

She had been driving for hours, without a destination in mind, simply attempting to put as many miles between them and John Powers as possible. Kate clung tightly to the steering wheel, holding on to it like a lifeline, certain that if she eased her grip on the wheel, the grip she had on her emotions would slacken as well.

To protect Emma she had to stay alert. Calm and focused. If she fell apart... Kate refused to let her mind wander to the *what ifs*. This man, this monster, wouldn't win. He wouldn't have Emma. She wouldn't let him have her.

Kate glanced over her shoulder, at the back seat. Emma was asleep in her carrier; she had been for the past couple of hours, lulled to sleep by the motion of the car. Julianna slept in the seat beside Kate.

The silence was both a blessing and a curse. Blessing because she had neither the energy nor emotional reserve to deal with either female; a curse because it allowed her time alone with her thoughts, with the disembodied voice from the message machine, his words, his threat—*You and Emma are dead.*

Kate drew in a deep breath, keeping hysteria at bay through sheer force of will. After the message machine had clicked off, she and Julianna hadn't spoken. Kate had taken a minute to throw together a bag for Emma, taking only the essentials—diapers, formula and bottles, a change of clothes—most of which had already been in the diaper bag.

She frowned, trying to remember if she had even locked the front door as they left. Try as she might, she couldn't. She recalled the breathlessness of fear, recalled running from the house to the car, climbing into it and backing out of the driveway, nearly running down poor Old Joe and Beauregard. Luckily, she had thought to grab her purse. In it were her credit cards, checks and one hundred dollars cash.

Her eyelids fluttered down, and she forced them up again. She couldn't go on much longer without rest. And food. In back, Emma stirred, and Kate caught her bottom lip between her teeth. Emma would be waking soon. She would need to be fed and changed. Eventually, she would need time out of her car seat, time to play.

She would have to start looking for a place to stop for the night.

A motel, she thought. Fine for tonight, but what about tomorrow? And the day after that? Would her and Emma's life become a string of days on the road and nights sleeping in cookie-cutter rooms? That was no life for a child.

Tears burned her eyes. Tears for Emma. For herself. Her beautiful home, The Uncommon Bean, Mandeville—would she ever see them again?

She fought back the tears, gripping the wheel tighter. Until now, her only thought had been to put as many miles between Emma and John Powers as she could, as fast as she could. But now, she had to decide where they were going. Driving aimlessly would be counterproductive and depressing; a destination would give her something to focus on. Something to achieve. But where should they run? And to whom?

Running to family had been out of the question, though the thought of loving arms had been tempting. It had seemed to her that family—then local friends— would be the first places John Powers would look for her.

A semi roared past, so close her Jeep rocked. As the truck cleared her, he cut back into her lane, then exited. She looked at the sign, realizing with a sense of shock where she was.

Houston.

Luke. Of course.

Luke had not been a part of her life for so long, John Powers couldn't know that they were friends. They would be safe with him. A whimper of relief rose to her lips. Luke would take them in, at least for the night. Surely, he didn't hate her so much he would turn her away, not now?

She steered onto the next exit, pulling into the first gas station she came upon. She stopped the car beside a pump and unlocked her door.

At the sound, Julianna stirred, then opened her eyes. She looked at Kate, still half asleep. "Where are we?"

"Houston." Kate opened the car door. "Is there anything you want from inside? I'm going in to make a call."

62

Luke sat on his front steps, waiting for Kate. He hadn't turned on his porch light; the sounds of the night surrounded him. The buzz and hum of insects, the lonely howl of a dog left chained outside, the distant roar of traffic from a city too big to ever really sleep.

He leaned back, resting against his elbows. He had been working feverishly when Kate called, on a creative streak that had lasted several hours. Totally immersed in his characters' world, he'd had to ask who was calling three times before her answer had penetrated.

Kate. His beautiful Kate.

Luke frowned and tipped his face up to the starless sky, bombarded with second thoughts. He had heard the fatigue in her voice, the desperation. She had said only that she was in trouble, that she, the baby and a friend needed a place to stay, even if only for the night. It was an emergency, she had said.

A matter of life and death.

No had been on the tip of his tongue along with a dozen questions. Ones like "What kind of trouble?" and "Where's Richard?" Instead, he had given her directions to his house.

Luke passed a hand across his face, rough with his morning beard. Kate had never been given to exaggeration or melodrama. If she said something was so, it was. So what could be so urgent it was a matter of life and death?

Luke stood as a vehicle turned onto his street and proceeded slowly down, as if checking the house numbers. He cracked open his front door, reached inside and flipped on the porch light, then closed the door and stepped fully into the circle of light.

The vehicle, a Jeep Cherokee, pulled into his driveway and stopped. The driver's side door flew open. Kate appeared. Their gazes met and with a cry, she ran to him. He met her halfway and enfolded her in his arms, holding her trembling body close. She clung to him, cheek pressed to his chest, shoulders shaking with her tears.

"Thank you, Luke...thank you for taking us in."

"Kate...Kate..." He buried his face in her hair, breathing in her familiar scent. He drew slightly away so he could look into her eyes. "What's going on? Where's Richard?"

The front passenger door opened and a young woman stepped out. "Kate," she said softly, hesitantly, "the baby's awake."

Kate nodded, but held him a moment more before pulling away to retrieve Emma from her car seat.

The infant looked and sounded anything but happy. "Take her inside," he said. "I'll get your bags."

"There aren't any."

He looked at Kate. "No luggage?"

"No. Just Emma's diaper bag."

"I'll get that, then." He motioned toward the front door. "Go on and get Emma inside."

He grabbed the bag, locked the car and followed the women inside. He found them waiting for him in the foyer, both looking exhausted and more than a little lost.

Emma squirmed in her mother's arms, making short, high sounds that weren't cries but definitely sounded unhappy. "Is she all right?" he asked.

"She needs to eat. And be changed, probably."

He nodded and led them into the kitchen. One of the reasons he had bought this house was the open floor plan. The entire downstairs living area—with the exception of the bedrooms and bathroom—was open, one room flowing into the other. The other reason he had bought it was the spacious, third-floor room he used for his office. It had wall-to-wall built-in bookcases and an arched picture window from which he could see the entire street and beyond.

Kate propped Emma on her hip and went to work filling a bottle, then warming it in the microwave. He turned to the other woman and smiled. "I'm Luke."

Before her friend could respond Kate said, "I'm sorry, this is Julianna."

Something about the way she said the other woman's name suggested they were anything but friends. He arched his eyebrows and held out his hand. "Hello, Julianna."

She took it, returning his greeting. Only then did he see the red splatters on the young woman's shirt and shorts. He stared at them, thinking they couldn't be what they looked like. They couldn't be blood.

He returned his gaze to hers. She watched him, something akin to terror in her shadowed eyes. She crossed her arms over herself, as if to hide the telltale splatters from him.

Not only could they be blood, he'd bet money they were.

He turned to Kate. "We have to talk."

She shook her head. "Later. Okay?"

It wasn't okay. He lowered his voice. "Where's Richard?"

Kate looked at Julianna, then back at him, a bitter-sounding laugh spilling from her lips. "Dead. He was murdered four nights ago. Today was...today I buried him."

Luke stared at her in shock. "Jesus, Kate. My God, I...I don't know what to say."

"I need to use the bathroom," Julianna said suddenly, struggling, Luke saw, not to cry. "Could you tell me where it is?"

"I'll show you." He turned back to Kate. "I'm going to get Julianna settled in upstairs. While I do, make yourself at home. I'll be right back."

Luke ushered Julianna to one of the guest rooms. "The bathroom's connected, if you want to shower, help yourself. There are towels on the rods and soap, shampoo and stuff in a basket on the counter. Do you have a change of clothes?"

She shook her head. "That's what I thought. I'll get you one of my T-shirts and a pair of sweats. I'll leave them on the bed."

He did as he'd promised, then headed back down to Kate, mulling over the strangeness of this whole thing. Kate showed up in the middle of the night, scared out of her wits and accompanied by a woman she didn't like and who was splattered in blood. Richard, he learned, was dead. Buried today.

More than odd, he decided. Unsettling. It was definitely time to get some answers.

Kate had found her way into the living room and was sitting on the couch, feeding her daughter. As he entered the room, she lifted her gaze to his. He realized then how whipped she was, how physically and emotionally drained. She was pale, her eyes deeply shadowed, and it looked to him like a good breeze could do her in.

"Been a rough one, huh?"

Her eyes welled with tears. "You could say that."

"Hungry?" She shook her head. "How about a glass of wine?"

"That would…yes. That would be wonderful. Thank you, Luke."

He brought her the wine, then sat with her while she finished feeding her daughter. He didn't push for answers, didn't attempt to coax her into conversation. Instead, he waited, satisfying himself with looking at her, with watching the loving way she interacted with her daughter.

They could have been his family. Emma could have been his daughter.

The thought, the realization raced into his head, along with it a hunger he hadn't expected. To be a part of that closeness they shared, to be a father.

He looked away, uncomfortable with his thoughts, with the feeling of loss that accompanied them.

"Luke?"

He looked back to find her gaze upon him. He cleared his throat. "Yeah?"

"Thank you for this. For not turning us away."

Julianna appeared then, freshly scrubbed and wearing the clothes he'd left for her. She ate a turkey sandwich, then went to bed, barely speaking a word.

Luke watched the two women together, noticing that they never looked at one another, that Julianna kept several feet between herself and Emma, and that Kate never asked for Julianna's help with the baby.

As if they were adversaries, he realized. As if they were two dogs, circling the same bone. But where he sensed a wariness in Julianna, he saw distrust in Kate. And anger. The emotion burned in her eyes every time the other woman came near.

More curious by the moment, as soon as Julianna had retired for the night and Kate had gotten Emma to sleep, Luke handed her another glass of red wine. "Now," he said, "I want to know what's going on."

She nodded and sank wearily to the couch, hands curved around the bowl of the red wineglass. "I don't know where to start, it's been...everything's been so awful for so long."

Awful, he thought, judging by her tone and expression, didn't begin to cover it.

He decided to help her out. "Who's Julianna?"

"No one. Everyone." Kate lifted her gaze to his. "She's Emma's birth mother. I only found out today."

"Ouch."

"Yeah," she muttered, "ouch. And you don't even know the half of it."

"So, tell me."

She nodded, took a swallow of the wine, then set the glass on the coffee table. She dropped her head back against the couch's deep, soft cushions and gazed up at the ceiling. "Richard was unfaithful to me."

"I'm sorry."

"But not surprised?"

"No." He paused, a thought occurring to him. "Was Julianna—"

"Yes." She brought the heels of her hands to her eyes for a moment, then lowered them to her lap.

"That day at Tulane, what you said…you were right, I think. About why he—" her voice broke "—why he married me."

Luke swore under his breath, making a sound of regret. "Kate, the things I said…I said them in anger. Because I was hurt. Because I wanted to hurt you. I didn't mean—"

"Yes, yes you did. Even in anger, they contained a kernel of truth. Maybe not the whole truth, but a kernel of it."

She took another sip of her wine. "It all began with Emma's adoption."

Luke listened as Kate told him about the past few months of her life—about their being chosen by a birth mother, about Emma's arrival and her own joy at becoming a mother.

"I was so happy, so in love with our baby, I didn't notice what was happening with Richard. Not at first, anyway."

She sighed, stood and crossed to the picture window that looked out over his backyard. She gazed out, her thoughts inward. "He wasn't happy. He never held Emma, not voluntarily, anyway. He didn't even look at her, let alone play with her. Turns out, he was jealous of the time and attention I gave her."

She sighed again. "He did it for me, I see that now. I wanted a child—we couldn't conceive, so he agreed to our adopting one. But he never felt good about it, about taking another's biological child and accepting it not only into our family but into our hearts." She shook her head. "I should have seen what he was doing, how he felt. But I didn't want to think about him or what he wanted. I was too hungry to be a mother."

"Kate," Luke said softly, "you don't know, he might have been the same way with a biological child. For whatever reason, some people aren't meant to be parents."

"I wish I'd known."

"Do you? Would you send her back?"

"No." She laughed, mocking herself. "I can't imagine my life without her. Being a mother's the best thing I've ever done."

"Then, there you have it."

"I guess so."

She turned, wandered back to the couch and settled into the corner, drawing her legs up underneath her. "I should have seen Richard's infidelity coming. He and I began to fight, he began seeming more like the boy I had known in college than the man I had been married to for ten years. Arrogant and self-centered. Petulant when he didn't get his way."

She went on, seeming to Luke, to ramble. She told him about how their relationship became strained, then began to unravel, about sensing someone had broken into her home and about how her neighbor, Old Joe, had seen a strange woman on their swing. She told him, too, how she had discovered Richard's unfaithfulness. About how, less than twenty-four hours later, she had learned of his murder.

She hugged herself. "It all seemed to happen so fast. One minute I have a great marriage and am basking in the delight of being a new mother. The next, I'm a widow."

She squeezed her eyes shut, struggling, he saw, to get a grip on her emotions. "How do you deal with that? How do I deal with him being...dead? I'm still back at finding him in bed with another woman."

She looked at him through tears. "And I feel so guilty. I look back and I think, if I had just done one thing differently, he would be alive. If I hadn't wanted a child so badly. If I had seen his real feelings about adoption. If I had given him what he needed or forgiven him when he strayed."

Luke shook his head, not following her reasoning. "Freak twists of fate happen, Kate. Somebody's in the wrong place at the wrong time. That doesn't have anything to do with what you did or didn't do."

"This wasn't a freak twist of fate. It wasn't a robbery gone bad." She met Luke's eyes. "Richard's murder was premeditated. He was singled out by a lunatic and killed. Because of Julianna."

Luke frowned, thinking of the blood spatters on Julianna's clothes. "What do you mean?"

She went on to explain things she said she had only learned of today. About how Julianna had found them through the adoption agency, how she had fallen in love with Richard from his profile, then set out to seduce him.

"She followed us. She learned about us. About me. Dear Jesus—" Kate brought her hands to her face a moment, using the time to collect herself, then dropped them to her lap. "She modeled herself after me. Tried to become like me, so Richard would trust her. So he would be attracted to her." Kate made a sound of pain. "Like me, only better. Younger. Sexier. Unencumbered."

"No one's like you," Luke said softly. "Trust me on this, I've been looking for ten years."

For a moment, Kate simply stared at him, then her eyes flooded with fresh tears.

"The story gets better." She relayed to him what

Julianna had told him about John Powers. That he had killed Richard, Julianna's mother, a family friend connected with the CIA who had tried to help her.

"And you believe her, Kate? Come on, this is not a stable woman. She probably fabricated the whole—"

"No, I didn't, not at first. Until he called. He said Emma was...he said she was dead."

Luke sat back against the couch, stunned. "He said that? Those exact words?"

"Yes. There was no mistaking his meaning. So, you see," she finished, "there's a madman after us. A professional killer. He means to kill Julianna and Emma. If I get in the way, he'll kill me, too. If he finds out you've helped us—" Her voice broke. "I shouldn't have come here. I shouldn't have involved you."

"You didn't have a choice."

"Yes, I did. I could have just kept driving. But I was afraid. And I knew...I knew you'd make me feel safe." She began to cry. "Now, because of me, you're in danger, too. I'm sorry. So sorry."

He went to her and took her in his arms, holding her while she wept. She pressed her face to his shoulder, and curved her arms around his middle, clinging to him.

After a time her tears subsided, and she drew away. "We won't stay long," she murmured, wiping the tears from her cheeks, "we have to keep moving, be sure to stay a step ahead of him. I just need a little time to figure out where we're going. To make a plan."

"You can stay as long as you like."

"No." She shook her head. "I don't want to involve you any more than I already have. The sooner we're gone, the safer you'll be.''

"I can take care of myself, Kate. It's you who I'm worried about. And Emma.''

She laid her head against his shoulder once more. He felt her exhaustion in the way she sagged against him, as if she hadn't the strength to even hold herself upright.

"If only I could think clearly," she whispered. "There's got to be a way to beat John Powers. There's got to be.''

He curved his arms tighter around her. "In the morning," he murmured. "We'll talk some more. Between the two of us, we'll figure something out. I promise we will.''

63

Luke couldn't sleep. Long after he had told Kate good-night he sat at his computer, staring at the glowing screen. He'd thought his story would crowd Kate and her situation out of his mind. His writing had always taken him out of himself, away from the world of flesh-and-blood people and into one of his own making.

Not tonight. The last hour and a half had been futile. As much as he'd tried, his story in progress had been crowded out by hers.

Luke shut off his computer in disgust, stood and crossed to the window. He stared out at the darkened street, mulling over what she had told him. Her story was more high drama than real life, like something from one of his novels.

But it was real life. Kate's.

He was frightened for her.

From the research he'd done for his books, he knew this guy. John Powers was like Condor. At the truth of that, Luke's blood ran cold. He recalled the loving way Condor had held the gun at the range that day, thought of the things he had said about life and death. About killing.

John Powers was like Condor, he thought again. But without the honor. Without the code of ethics.

He was a walking, talking killing machine.

Fear grabbed Luke by the throat. With his mind's eye, he saw Kate lying in a pool of blood. He saw Emma beside her, face contorted in death. The images took his breath away.

Luke turned his back to the window. John Powers could have followed Kate here. From what she'd told him, there had been time. He could have been parked outside Kate's home, calling from a cell phone. He could have been there waiting, watching, laughing at their pitiable effort at escape.

Heart thundering, he crossed to his desk and retrieved the .44 Magnum from the bottom right-hand drawer, recalling his conversation with Condor. He smiled grimly. Right now he was damn glad to have the Magnum's firepower. Up against a man like John Powers, he would be lucky to get off one shot—he would want that shot to do as much damage as possible.

Luke snapped open the cylinder, checked to make certain it carried a full round, then strode for the stairs. He took them two at a time to the second-floor landing, paused a moment to listen, than started for Kate's room.

It lay at the end of the hall. He closed the distance between him and it, opened the door and stepped inside. He crossed to the bed. Kate was there. Asleep on her side, her face pressed deeply into the feather pillow. Crescent-shaped shadows stained the delicate skin beneath her eyes, and her dark lashes stood out in stark contrast to her pale cheeks.

Luke reached out to touch her, then drew his hand away and shifted his gaze to her daughter. Emma slept beside her on the queen-size bed, nestled in the bassinet they had fashioned out of bed pillows. He tipped his head, studying the child. She was small and sweet and pretty, her face angelic in sleep. Her chubby arms were thrown above her head in total relaxation; her chest rose and fell with her deep, even breathing.

No wonder Kate loved her so desperately, Luke thought. No wonder she would sacrifice herself to save her. He drew his eyebrows together. How could Richard not have felt the same? Emma Ryan would be easy to love. Easy to grow attached to. Too easy.

Sweet Jesus, he had to help Kate. He had to help them both, had to stop this man.

"Luke? Is everything all right?"

Kate's eyes were half-open. Regret that he had awakened her skittered through him. "Fine," he whispered, thinking again of John Powers. He forced an easy smile. "Just checking on you. Go back to sleep. Everything's going to be fine."

Her lips lifted slightly even as her eyelids fluttered shut. She mumbled something he couldn't make out, and he realized she was already asleep.

He watched her for a moment, then exited the room, leaving the door ajar. After checking all the doors and windows to make sure they were locked, he brewed himself a pot of coffee, poured himself a cup and took post on the couch.

Someone had to stand guard. Tonight and every night until John Powers was stopped.

And he seemed the most likely candidate.

64

Kate awakened to the smell of coffee and bacon. She stretched, breathing deeply, taking a moment to savor the luxury of being pampered. She smiled. How long had it been since she had awakened to those smells? Since the baby, of course. But how long before then? Somewhere along the line Richard had begun to refuse to make coffee—he said she made the process too complicated—and he considered bacon toxic waste, unfit for human consumption.

Thoughts of Richard brought the present crashing in on her. She didn't think of him in the past tense, she realized. Tears flooded her eyes, and she shut them tightly. She couldn't. Not yet. It hurt too much.

Tears squeezed from the corners of her closed eyes and slipped down her cheeks. She missed him. Not the man he had become in the past few months, the one whose frailties and flaws had surfaced to overshadow his many fine and admirable traits. She missed the Richard who had carried her over the threshold, the man who had made her laugh, who had encouraged her to open her own business; the man who had taught her about love.

She didn't have time for this, she thought, brushing the tears away. She couldn't give her energy to grieving for Richard. She had a daughter to protect; a madman to outrun.

The events of the day before and the gravity of her situation thundered down on her, in an avalanche of fear and helplessness. She glanced at the bedside clock, noted it was after ten, then dragged herself into a sitting position. She brought her hands to her face, working to center herself. She had to stay strong and focused. She, Julianna and Emma would be on the road again in a matter of hours. Between now and then, she had to come up with a plan.

Suddenly, the lateness of the hour sank in, the quiet of the room. Kate twisted to face the bed she and Luke had created for her daughter.

It was empty.

It took a split second for the realization to register, then with a sound of terror, Kate leaped out of the bed and raced for the door. She yanked it open and darted into the hall, stumbling slightly. "Luke!" she cried. "Luke! Where are you?"

He called that he was in the kitchen, and she ran in that direction, heart thundering, hysteria rising up inside her. John had found them. He had slipped into the house during the night and had stole Emma away. She brought a hand to her mouth, a horror of images unfolding in her head.

She stopped dead in the kitchen doorway. Stunned. Speechless. Luke sat at the kitchen table, cradling Emma in his arms while he fed her a bottle.

He looked up and smiled. "Morning, Kate."

"What are you doing?"

He looked down at Emma, then back up at Kate. "Giving Emma her bottle. She woke up hungry, and you needed to sleep. That was about six-thirty, by the way. This is her second bottle."

He had slipped into her room and out with Emma,

and she hadn't heard a thing. Unsettled, Kate moved fully into the kitchen, legs shaking. "But how...how did you know what to do?"

He smiled, the small lopsided smile that had always made her heart go pit-a-pat. "It's not all that technical, Kate. Take bottle, fill, warm and offer to baby. Simple."

She laughed then, a high, nervous sound. He moved his gaze over her, eyebrows drawn together in concern. "Are you all right?"

"Yes, I—" She brought a hand to her chest and let out a long breath. "I woke up and she was...gone."

She crossed to the table, legs shaking so badly she must have looked like an epileptic having a seizure. She sank onto a chair. "I thought...I thought the worst."

His smile faded. "I'm sorry, Kate. I didn't think about that. Considering the circumstances, I should—"

She held up a hand, stopping him. "No, don't apologize. I appreciate you letting me sleep. Richard never—" She bit the words back, forced a smile and held out her arms. "Now that I'm up, I can take her."

"Actually, I'm rather enjoying myself. Do you mind?"

She said she didn't, swallowing hard. "Coffee?" she asked.

"In the carafe. Cups are in the cabinet right above."

"Thanks." She crossed to the cabinet and selected a mug. Obviously a promotional item for *Dead Drop*, the mug's handle was shaped like a gun grip. Luke's name, the book title and release date were printed in red on the gunmetal gray exterior of the mug.

"Nice cup."

"Thanks. Publisher premiums."

She filled it with coffee, added cream, then sipped, murmuring a sound of pleasure. "This is Kona, isn't it?"

"It is." He grinned. "I got hooked on it while I was in Hawaii researching *Last Dance*. There's bacon under the paper towel. And a loaf of homemade raisin bread on the cutting board. Help yourself."

She did, suddenly famished. "When did you become Mr. Betty Crocker?" She carried her plate and mug to the table and sat down.

"Live alone long enough and you get pretty sick of Big Macs and Domino's pizza." The lopsided grin made another appearance. "My repertoire's pretty limited, but I figured you'd be hungry."

"Starving." Kate ripped off a hunk of her bread and took a bite. "I love homemade bread. You have a machine?"

"Mmm-hmm." Emma squirmed in his arms. He popped out the bottle, eyeballed what was left, then popped it back in. She began to suck voraciously. "My kid sister gave it to me for Christmas last year."

Kate couldn't believe they were sitting here talking about such mundane things as bread machines and coffee beans. Only minutes ago she had been sure John Powers had stolen Emma away.

"Sleep well?" he asked.

"Surprisingly well." Sometime during the night her nightmares had retreated and she had been left with a feeling of peace. Of being safe and protected. "And you?"

"Great. Like a baby."

Emma noisily slurped down the last of her bottle, the now empty liner making a wheezing sound as she continued to suck on it. Luke popped out the bottle, brought the infant to his shoulder and began patting her on the back.

Kate watched his movements, astounded by how assuredly he handled the child. She told him so. "I have five younger siblings. And now three of them have children of their own. I've spent a good part of my life burping babies."

"I'd forgotten you come from such a big family."

Emma let out a deep, wet burp, one a sailor would be proud of. Luke and Kate looked at each other and laughed. "Nice burp, sport," he said. "Very lady-like."

Kate laughed again and held out her arms. "Spend a bit of time around her, that's nothing. And she has absolutely no shame about where—or how—she breaks wind. Speaking of which, I'd better change her diaper. She must be soaked by now."

"Done," he said, settling the child in her arms.

"Done," she repeated, astounded.

"Mmm-hmm. Changed her right before you got up." He went to the carafe and refilled his mug. That done, he met her eyes, the expression in his serious. "We need to talk, Kate. I've been thinking about your situation, and I've come to the conclusion that you and Julianna are going about this all wrong."

"You do?"

"Mmm." He brought the coffee mug to his lips and sipped, as if using the time to collect his thoughts. Kate waited, heart pounding, hoping against hope that during the night he had come up with a miracle.

"Seems to me," he said, "if you start running, you'll never stop. There has to be another way."

"And what is it?"

"I don't know. Yet." He returned to the table and sat down, his gaze never leaving hers. "I know this guy who's after you, Kate. Not personally, but from research for my books. He's a hunter, above the law because of skills that keep him there. He has no compunction about taking a human life, to him death is merely an extension of life, the act of killing no different than that of taking out the trash. Necessary. Warranted."

"Thanks for cheering me up," she whispered. "I needed that."

"There's more," he said grimly. "And it's worse, so hold on. What you're contemplating's not a hiatus until things cool down, it's not disappearing for a month or two or a year, then returning to your regular life. It'll never cool down, Kate. This guy's on a personal mission. He'll hunt you down. Even if it takes years, he'll find you. And when he does—"

"He'll kill us."

"Yes." He went to her and squatted in front of her, forcing her to look him dead in the eyes. "We have to find a way to stop him. It's the only way you'll be safe."

"We, Luke?" She shook her head. "I've already put your life in danger by involving you this much. I can't—"

"Yes, you can. I'm not going to abandon you to this monster, Kate. Not you or Emma."

Kate struggled for an even breath, fought to control the fear that had her in a death grip. Fighting, too, the urge to lean on him and to completely fall apart. It wasn't fair or right. It could get him killed.

"I can't let you do this, Luke. You don't understand what you're getting yourself into."

"Yes, I do." He brought a hand to her face and cupped her cheek. "You don't have a choice in this, Katie-girl, you've involved me, now you're stuck with me."

He'd used her father's pet name for her. Tears flooded her eyes and she covered his hand with her own. "What do you think we should do?"

"I have a couple of contacts with the Agency. Let me get in touch with them, ask their advice. In the meantime, you and Julianna crash here. Rest, get healthy—"

"No."

They looked up to find Julianna standing in the kitchen doorway, her expression panicked. "Julianna—"

"No!" She shook her head. "You don't know what he's capable of! You didn't see—"

"I do know, Julianna." Luke stood. "That's why I'm convinced running is futile."

"He's right. We have to have a plan. We have to find a way to stop him." Kate glanced at Emma, asleep in her arms, then back up at Julianna. "You can do what you think's best for you, but I'm staying with Luke."

The younger woman stared silently at them a moment, as if considering her options, then turned and left the kitchen. She returned a moment later with her purse, a backpack-style tote. She set it on the table, opened it and rummaged inside for a moment. She pulled out a Ziploc plastic bag that appeared to contain three items.

She handed it to Luke. "Maybe this will help."

He opened the bag and retrieved the items, a small, black leather binder, like an address book; a used en-

velope and an airplane ticket stub. "What are these?"
Luke asked.

"They're John's. I took them after I talked to my
mother, when I left D.C." Luke flipped through the
black book. "It's in some sort of code," she offered.
"John never spoke of what he did for a living. I was
never to question him about it. I got curious."

"And you began to snoop?"

"Yes." She pulled out a chair and sank onto it, her
expression at once defiant and defeated. "The black
binder was hidden in the freezer, sandwiched between
two packages of frozen meat. So I figured it must be
really important."

"This is good," Luke murmured. "It could be very
good."

Kate came up behind Luke and peered at the items.
"What do they mean?"

"See this ticket stub?" He held it up. "The ticket
was issued to a Wendell White." He held up the envelope. "This was sent to David Snow. But both were
in our man's possession. Why? Because they're both
aliases of John Powers'. And this address is to one of
his dead drops."

Julianna drew her eyebrows together. "How do you
know?"

"Don't. But I'd bet money I'm right."

"Dead drop?" Kate asked, amazed that Luke knew
this stuff. "Like your book."

"Yeah, that's right." His lips lifted slightly. "A
dead drop's a dummy address. Used for correspondence and deliveries but untraceable back to a real
person, in this case John Powers. At any time an agent
might have a dozen—or more—of them scattered
throughout the country. Or countries."

"So they can conduct business without fear of being discovered," Kate murmured.

"Exactly. I know a private investigator, a good one. He helped me with some research a couple years back. I'll give him a call, see what he can dig up on these names."

"What about the other?" Kate asked. "That... book?"

"He wants it back," Julianna offered. "He told me he did. He was really angry that I'd taken it."

"That's good."

"Good? That he's angry?" Kate drew her eyebrows together. "Why am I not reassured by that?"

Luke smiled. "That means it's important. It means we're going to be able to use it to get this asshole."

"But how?" Kate asked, heart thundering, afraid of the relief flowing over her—she feared if she relaxed, even just a bit, that would be the moment that John Powers struck.

Luke rubbed the side of his jaw, rough with morning stubble. "I don't know that yet. I'll meet with my contacts, ask their advice. They'll be able to give us some direction. I know they will."

"Thank you, Luke," Kate said, voice quavering. "I don't know what we would have done without you."

"Not so fast." He flashed her a quick grin. "Wait until we've gotten this bozo taken care of. *Then* you can thank me."

65

Condor responded to Luke's message within forty-eight hours. The man agreed to meet him, choosing an all-night diner near the Hobby Airport.

Luke arrived early. He made his way to the rear of the diner, taking a booth against the far wall. He slid onto the vinyl seat, the upholstery cracked and peeling, held together in places by clear packing tape.

A waitress of no less than sixty took his order of a cup of coffee. The fluorescent lights tinted her gray cap of curls a vague, disturbing green and turned her skin sallow.

She brought the coffee immediately, plunking it onto the table, then without saying a word, walked away. A burned, bitter odor wafted up from the cup, and Luke wondered how long the brew had been sitting on the burner. An hour or two? Three, even?

Possibly, he decided, perusing the room. The diner's only other patrons were a burly man in overalls and two twenty-something girls who were wolfing down patty melts, French fries and colas.

Condor arrived, walking through the door exactly at the arranged time. He made his way to the booth and slid into the seat across from Luke, angling his back to the wall.

They exchanged pleasantries; the waitress brought another cup of the bitter brew, then Luke cut straight to the matter at hand. "A friend of mine's in trouble. I need your help."

"You know the business I'm in, Luke. Exactly what form do you wish this help to take?"

"The form of advice."

The barest of smiles touched the mechanic's mouth. "Go on."

Luke laid out the entire story for him. "The man's name is John Powers," Luke finished. "Do you recognize the name?"

For long moments, Condor remained silent, his steady gaze giving away nothing of his thoughts.

Finally, he nodded. "I know of him."

"But you've never met him?"

"No." He took a sip of the coffee, not seeming to notice its taste. "They try to keep us guys away from each other." Again, that small smile touched his mouth. "The last thing they'd want is us sitting around the clubhouse swapping stories. But I have heard of him."

"What have you heard?"

"That he was one of the Agency's best and most lethal mechanics. Specialized in the most, shall we say, delicate wet work."

"Delicate," Luke repeated. "You mean sensitive, politically charged?"

"Yes. The man is an expert in the use of all manner of weapons, as well as in hand-to-hand combat, poisons and explosives. An outstanding career until he went solo a few years back."

"Solo? What do you mean?"

"He's a renegade. Went out on his own. Hits for hire, no matter the government or cause."

"And the Agency allows that?"

"Up to a point."

"And what point is that?"

Condor ignored the question and continued. "Code name was Ice. For obvious reasons. Rumor has it he killed a Colombian drug czar's six children, disemboweled them while their mother watched."

"Holy shit." Luke felt sick. "And our government sanctioned that?"

"Let's just say that Ice was sent in to negotiate. He was told to use whatever means necessary to get our point across." Condor steepled his fingers. "Of course, that story's only a rumor."

Rumor, his ass. It was true, Condor knew it. And Luke did, too.

Up until that moment Luke had hoped that Kate and Julianna had been exaggerating John Powers' abilities. The threat he posed. He saw now that they had not.

The two drunken girls stood and started for the door. Condor watched them until they had exited the diner, then returned his attention to Luke. "Your friend is in a very bad situation. And now, so are you. I suggest you bow out of this."

"I can't do that."

"That's your choice, of course."

"There must be a way to beat him? A way out of this. If we went to the police, laid it all out for them—"

Condor shook his head, confirming what Luke already knew. "Going to the police will do nothing but make you sitting ducks. You'll be dead before the local boys get their heads out of their asses."

Condor leaned slightly forward, his gaze intent. "The police couldn't find him, let alone pin a murder on him. You know how it works, Luke. No weapon, no witnesses, no arrest.''

He was right. Luke knew he was. What would he tell Kate? She had been so hopeful when he'd left. So positive.

"There may be a way, however. But it won't be easy."

"Go on." Luke waited, pulse hammering. He didn't care how difficult, a slim chance was better than none at all.

"It sounds to me like Powers is losing it," Condor said softly. "Making killing personal. That's dangerous. It crosses the line." He looked away, then back. "It'll make him sloppy. Because it's personal, because it matters so much to him, he'll take chances he never would otherwise. He might have already."

"It'll also make him go to lengths he normally wouldn't to succeed," Luke muttered.

"True. But therein lies your chance." Condor lowered his voice. "The Agency won't get involved unless they believe Powers is a danger to them, their operations or national security. He's one of their own, after all. They can't have him running around the country indiscriminately killing people. Not publicly, anyway."

Condor spoke carefully, his tone even, words measured. Luke tried to read between the words, certain the man was telling him something *beyond* their literal meaning.

Luke took a stab. "They wouldn't want their handiwork exposed, would they?"

Condor acted as if Luke hadn't spoken. "If you could prove Powers is out of control, if you could prove he's a threat to the United States government or the CIA, the Agency would bring him down.''

Condor laced his fingers together. ''They'll need proof, of course. Physical evidence. Names and dates. If you can produce a convincing enough paper trail, that would do it.''

The book. Dear Lord, they had the proof.

''I can do that,'' Luke said. ''Right now. I've got the proof.''

Condor straightened. ''Tell me.''

Luke did, explaining about Powers' black book and how Julianna had come to have it. ''It's in some sort of code, but I'm sure it contains the names and dates you're looking for.''

The other man's expression changed subtly, became sharper, more intent. ''Have you broken the code?''

''No.'' Luke leaned forward. ''Help us do it. It's our only chance.''

''I like you, Dallas. But I can't do that.'' He glanced toward the diner's front door, then back at Luke. ''I don't want to know what's in that book. If I did, I'd be a mark. Maybe not today or tomorrow, but someday. Besides, messing with Powers' book crosses the line, and I won't do that.''

''Then tell me how to break it.''

Condor hesitated a moment, then nodded. ''Make one of the entries, use what you learn to break the rest of the code. Meet with Tom Morris. He's going to play dumb about Ice, but he's in Operations so he'll be familiar with Powers' file. Lay it all out for him, the way you did me, then get the Agency's commitment to take Powers down in return for proof of his activities. It's important that you get a commitment from him.''

"Or we'll be shit out of luck, is that what you're telling me?"

"This is the real world, Dallas. Not one of your stories. The good guys don't always win."

Luke laughed, the sound tight and humorless. "And the line between right and wrong is rarely clear."

"I didn't make the rules, Dallas. I only play by them." Condor laid several dollars on the table and stood. "The coffee's on me."

They left the restaurant. Outside, the cold, wet night curled around them like a snake.

"You never saw me tonight," Condor said. "I'm out of this."

"Agreed."

"One last piece of advice. Don't let that book out of your sight. If Morris or the Agency gets their hands on it, they'll break Ice's code. Once they have what they need, you and your friends will be left high and dry. And if Powers gets it back, you'll have no bargaining chip at all."

"And we'll be dead."

"Yes." Condor turned and looked him straight in the eyes. Again, Luke had the feeling the man was saying much more than what his words conveyed. "Morris will ask for the book. Expect that. But don't give it to him. No matter what he promises you. That's important, Luke. Don't give it to him. That book is your life. Do you understand?"

Luke said he did; in the next moment Condor was gone.

66

Kate and Julianna were awake and waiting for Luke when he got home. They met him at the door, their expressions so hopeful it hurt to look at them. If they expected a miracle, they weren't going to get it.

"We have a chance," Luke said. "Not easy or without risk, but a chance nonetheless."

They went to the kitchen. Kate made coffee while Luke relayed the details of his conversation with Condor. As he spoke, Kate's expression went from hopeful to uncertain.

"Decipher one of the entries?" she said when Luke had finished. "But how do we do that?"

"I've given this some thought already and it might not be as hard as it sounds." Luke stood and went to the coffeepot and poured himself a cup. "Since the dates entered in the book are not in code, the way I figure it, if we can find something that positively ties Powers to a place on a certain date, we can do a search for murders committed in that locale on that date."

"And if we're lucky," Kate murmured, "we'll find something."

Luke met her eyes. "If we're very lucky."

"This isn't going to work," Julianna said, looking from him to Kate. "It's not. And then where will we be? Trapped? Dead?"

"Where will we be?" Kate repeated, bright spots

of angry color staining her cheeks. "I know where I was, Julianna. Before you decided to steal my husband and ruin my life. Before you invited this...this killer through my front door."

"I didn't know!" Julianna cried. "I never thought he would hurt you. Or Emma or Richard. Me, yes. But not you." Her eyes filled, and she looked pleadingly at Kate. "Why would he? You never did anything to him."

"That's just it," Kate snapped, "you didn't think. Not about anyone or anything but yourself."

"I'm sorry," Julianna whispered, tears slipping down her cheeks. "I didn't know." She brought her hands to her face. "I'm so scared. I just want to go home."

"And you think I don't?" Kate rounded on the other woman, shaking with the force of her fury. "I'd love to go home, Julianna. But because of you I can't. Because of you, my husband is dead. Because of you a psychotic kil—"

Luke laid a hand on her arm, stopping her. "I know you're angry, Kate. You have a right to be, but fighting with each other isn't going to do anything but make us more vulnerable to Powers. If we're going to beat him, we've got to work together." He met Kate's eyes. "You know it's true."

She spun away from him and crossed to the picture window that looked out over his backyard. She stood stiffly, arms curved across her middle; Luke saw that she struggled to get a grip on her emotions.

After a moment, she took a deep breath and turned back to the younger woman. "Just running is out of the question. Because we can't outrun him. You know we can't. But if that's what you want to do, you have my blessing. But I'm taking this route with Luke.''

"What's it going to be, Julianna?'' Luke asked. "You have a choice. Are you sticking with us or not?''

"With you,'' she whispered, wiping the tears from beneath her eyes. "I'm staying with you.''

"Then I need your help. We need your help.'' He crossed to stand directly in front of her. "Is there anything you haven't told us about Powers? Anything at all, no matter how insignificant you might think it to be. It could be something you observed or overheard and thought nothing of at the time. Or maybe something he told you in the heat of the moment or mumbled in his sleep.''

"No.'' She shook her head. "I've told you everything.''

"Think, Julianna. It's important.''

"There's nothing.'' She shook her head again. "We had an…agreement. He never discussed what he did, who he worked for. When he went on a trip, he never told me where he went. And I wasn't allowed to ask.''

She looked away, then back. "Until the end, not knowing what he was doing or even where he was didn't bother me. I never questioned him.''

"Then you got curious,'' Luke prodded. "And you started snooping around.''

"Yes. That's how I found the book.''

"What about gifts?'' Kate asked, swinging away from the window once more. "What kinds of things did he bring you? Was there anything that you recall being specific to a place? You know, like chocolates from Switzerland or perfume from Paris?''

Julianna brought her hands to her ears, to the diamond studs that twinkled when they caught the light. Luke had noticed them before; the size of the diamonds had made them hard to miss. "Nothing like that," she murmured, sounding frustrated. "He brought me these. Sometimes he would bring me a…a doll or a hair ornament. He'd bring me books. Flowers he picked up at the airport shop. Everything was generic."

She looked at Luke, then Kate, her expression earnest. "You have to believe me. Even his apartment was plain. So without…identifying features. There was furniture, and stuff for the kitchen and bathrooms, but nothing else. Do you know what I mean?"

Kate looked at Luke. "Are you thinking what I am?"

"Powers' apartment?" When she indicated yes, he turned back to Julianna. "Do you still have a key to his place?"

She nodded. "Though I don't know why. I'm never going back there."

"Never's a long time, kid." Luke smiled and rubbed his hands together. "The last thing Powers will expect is for us to take the offensive. I say we have a place to start."

Julianna looked sick; Kate determined. "Are you certain the Agency will make the commitment to take Powers down?" she asked.

"My contact thought so. If we can deliver the goods on Powers." He looked from Kate to Julianna. "And I don't see that we have another choice."

"I agree." Kate turned toward the other woman. "How about you, Julianna?"

The girl hesitated a moment, then nodded. "Agreed."

"All right, then." Luke checked his watch, saw that it was after 2:00 a.m. and smiled grimly. "We leave for D.C. today."

67

Kate forced herself to rest, though she couldn't quiet her mind enough to sleep. She lay in the bed, listening to her baby daughter's gentle breathing, alternately praying for the best and imagining the worst.

Some minutes were better than others. During the bad ones, the worst ones, fear smothered her. She imagined her beautiful Emma dead, her life force obliterated in all manner of gruesome ways. She imagined Emma crying out, helpless and in pain. She imagined herself, unable to reach and comfort her daughter, unable to save her. If it came to it, Kate had decided, she would beg John Powers to kill her instead.

Someone tapped lightly on her door. Kate glanced at Emma, then climbed out of the bed and crossed to it. "Yes?" she whispered.

"It's me," Luke said. "May I come in?"

She opened the door and held a finger to her lips. He nodded and stepped inside. "I just wanted to make sure that you and Emma...that you're all right."

"We're fine." She glanced again toward the bed and Emma. "I'm frightened out of my wits, but what else is new?"

"It's going to be all right," he said, keeping his voice low. "I'll do everything I can to protect you and Emma. I promise."

She searched his gaze, thinking of Richard's promises. His assurances. And in the end, what had they really been worth?

"I'm not Richard," he said as if reading her mind. "I'm not, Kate. Know that."

He wasn't, Kate acknowledged. Luke Dallas was the man Richard had wished he was.

The truth of that made so many things suddenly clear—like Richard's competitiveness with Luke, his resentment and jealousy. Richard, she realized, had seen Luke's success as his own failure.

She swallowed hard. "Thank you, Luke. For not deserting us. For being here for me even after...after everything."

He brought a hand to her face, tracing the curve of her cheekbone. Without thinking, she turned her face to it, moving her lips against his skin.

He sucked in a short, quick breath. "Kate, I—"

She lifted her gaze to his. She saw longing in his. Longing and regret. She opened her mouth to say something, though she was uncertain what. Before she could, he dropped his hand and took a step back from her.

"Try to get some sleep," he murmured. "Tomorrow's going to be an exhausting day."

And then he was gone.

The next day did, indeed, prove to be an exhausting one. To make the trip, Kate and Julianna needed clothing, cosmetics and other personal care items; Emma needed everything from clothes to diapers, toys to formula and baby food. Combat shopping, Julianna called it as they raced through the drug and department stores, pulling garments off racks and dumping items into carts.

Luke insisted on paying for everything with the cash he had withdrawn from the bank that morning. Credit cards and checks, he told them, left a paper trail even an amateur P.I. could follow.

And John Powers was anything but an amateur.

For that same reason, he suggested they drive to D.C. Despite what commercial airlines assured the consumer, flight manifests were easy to get ahold of. Flying also presented the problem of either renting a car at their destination or relying on taxis; in terms of stealth, neither of those options worked.

It was nearly three that afternoon before Kate had their things packed in Luke's Tahoe and was ready to go. She went in search of Luke, finding him in his office, on the phone. He waved her in. "Doing good, Frank." He covered the mouthpiece. "The P.I.," he murmured, then dropped his hand. "Thanks, I'm glad you liked it.

"Look, I've got a job I need you to do for me. Three names. John Powers. Wendell White. David Snow." He spelled them for the man. "I believe Wendell White and David Snow are both aliases for John Powers. Get everything you can on all three. Addresses, phone bills, credit card summaries, travel destinations. If anyone going by one of these names has so much as burped in the past three years, I want to know about it."

Luke listened to the other man, then nodded. "Two. And a travel agency's name." He took the envelope and ticket stub from his jacket pocket. He gave the investigator John's address in D.C., the address on the envelope and the travel agency's name and address. "That's it," he said. "All I've got."

He smiled, met Kate's eyes and gave her a thumbs-up. "I'm leaving town for a while, I'll drop your retainer in the mail before I leave." Luke laughed. "Sure I'm sure I'm good for it." His amusement evaporated. "No number where I can be reached. I'll check in with you from the road."

He hung up, and Kate suddenly realized she was holding her breath and let it out in a rush. "You amaze me, Luke. How do you know all this stuff? I feel like I'm hanging out with James Bond or something."

"My work." He grinned. "I've basically spent the past ten years immersed in the world of spies, criminals and cops. I've been in the heads of cold-blooded killers and madmen, heroes and even the occasional damsel in distress."

"Now you're a real hero," she said softly, smiling.

"Then that would make you the damsel in distress."

"I guess it would." Her smile faded. "Heroes get killed, Luke. I don't want...I couldn't bear to..."

She couldn't bear to lose him.

She cleared her throat. "Just be careful, okay? No heroics."

"You don't need to worry about me, I've outsmarted guys like John Powers dozens of times."

But that was the beauty of fiction, being able to write the ending of your choice. The one where good triumphed, evil fell and everyone who deserved to lived happily-ever-after.

But this was real life.

"Stop it, Kate," he said. "I know what you're thinking." He lifted her chin with his index finger, forcing her to look directly into his eyes. "We're going to beat this psycho. I really believe that."

She gazed at him a moment, heart thundering. "I

wish I had your confidence. I wish I wasn't so scared.''

He slipped his arms around her and eased her against his chest. She held herself stiffly a moment, then sagged against him, curving her arms around his middle, holding him tightly, half afraid that without his support she would fall.

He passed his hand over her hair, stroking. Comforting. ''You can lean on me, Kate. I'm here for you.''

She drew in a deep breath. He smelled of spicy soap and the sunny day. It would be so easy to do as he offered. Fall apart. Give in to her fear. Lean on him, let him hold her up and take care of her.

She couldn't do that. John Powers was too smart and too deadly to allow her that luxury.

Kate drew regretfully away. ''I have to stay strong, Luke. For Emma. She's counting on her mother to keep her safe, and I can't turn that job over to anybody. Even you.''

He gazed into her eyes a moment, his filled with respect, then bent and brushed his lips against hers. ''Time to go.''

Twenty minutes later, they were on the road. Kate tried to focus on Luke's confidence, on the reassuring things he had said to her about beating John Powers. She worked hard to put on a positive face, to keep her mood upbeat. Not only for herself, but for the others as well.

Even so, she was afraid. For all of them. She glanced repeatedly over her shoulder as they put mile after mile between themselves and Houston, all too aware that each one of those miles put them that much closer to a confrontation with John Powers.

At least they traveled well together. For Kate, being with Luke felt as natural as breathing. They talked and laughed together, often anticipating the other's need for rest or food or quiet.

Being with Julianna, on the other hand, was discomfiting. Kate still couldn't look at the woman without a rush of fury sweeping over her. Without remembering how it had come about that she was running for her and her daughter's life. Without remembering Richard.

Several times, Kate had caught the younger woman gazing at Emma, naked longing in her eyes. Those times Kate had felt anxious and vulnerable. Frightened in a way that had nothing to do with John Powers' threat on her life. She feared Julianna wanted Emma back. She didn't trust that she wouldn't simply snatch the child in the middle of the night and disappear.

Consequently, Kate never strayed far from her daughter's side; she never allowed Julianna to hold or touch her. She wasn't about to take any chances.

By the middle of the second day, Kate saw that the two-day trip would have to become three because of Emma. The hours confined to her car seat began to wear on the infant—she was unhappy and fussy, well on her way to being inconsolable.

"We're going to have to stop," Kate said, dangling Emma's favorite rattle in front of her. Instead of batting at it as she usually did, she turned her head away, screwing her face up with frustration.

Kate met Luke's eyes in the rearview mirror. "Emma's had it. If we don't give her a little downtime, she's going to make our lives very uncomfortable."

As if on cue, the infant began to cry, her cries quickly escalating to earsplitting howls. Kate began to rock the car seat and sing softly, trying to calm the infant. It took a few moments, but it began to work. As Emma's cries lessened to whimpers, Kate slipped a pacifier into her daughter's mouth.

"How do you do it?" Julianna asked suddenly. "How do you put up with her and stay so...calm? I think I'd lose it."

"Because I love her," Kate said simply. "And because I'm her mother."

"Next exit," Luke announced, reading a sign, "two miles ahead. Food. Lodging. Gas. Sounds like just the ticket."

They made it to the exit and into the first motel without another crying jag from Emma. The motel, a very nice La Quinta Inn, had no two-bedroom suites available. So they booked a regular suite, complete with a bar and minifridge. Julianna offered to take the fold-out couch—Luke, Kate and Emma would take the bedroom.

The motel, Kate was delighted to learn, had an indoor pool, one that included a kiddie pool. They spent the late afternoon splashing in the water, laughing at Emma's antics and drinking frozen margaritas from the motel bar.

The hours out of the car did everyone good, especially Emma. The unhappy baby Kate had hardly recognized disappeared, replaced with the contented one Kate knew and loved so well. As for Kate, by the time evening rolled around, she was so relaxed she was practically liquid.

Kate curled up on one end of the couch, watching Luke play with Emma, Julianna on the other, watching a pay-per-view movie. Flat on his back on the floor, Luke lifted the infant high above him. As he did, she stiffened her arms and legs so both stuck straight out.

"Airplane baby," he said, making a motor sound and moving her forward and back until she squealed with laughter.

A tingling kind of warmth moved down Kate's spine and outward, all the way to the tips of her fingers and toes, enveloping her in a rosy-feeling glow. She smiled to herself. Did other women find something sexy about a man playing with a baby the way Luke was with Emma? Did they find all that strength and masculinity channeled into gentle, loving play as irresistible as she did?

She moved her gaze, taking in the way the muscles in his upper arms flexed as he lifted Emma up and down, noting the flatness of his abdomen and the dusting of golden hair across his tanned forearms, admiring, growing aroused.

Luke caught her gaping at him and grinned. "What?"

She hesitated, feeling an embarrassed flush stealing up her cheeks. "I'm just...happy."

"Happy?" he repeated, arching an eyebrow, still holding Emma above him. "Is that why your cheeks are so pink?"

She glanced at Julianna. The other woman seemed engrossed in her movie and oblivious to them. "Too much sun."

"Indoor pools have been known to—" Just then a fat dollop of Emma's saliva hit his nose and cheek. "Oh, man." He sat up, tucking Emma under one arm. "She slimed me."

Kate laughed, stood and crossed to the bathroom.

"Her Grace, Princess of Drool. Actually, I'm starting to suspect she's more Saint Bernard pup than human baby." Kate grabbed a hand towel and tossed it to him. "Don't worry, though. It's just baby spit. Completely harmless."

"Easy for you to say." He wiped his face, then tossed the towel back.

"Sure you want to get rid of this? You may need it." She looked pointedly at him. Emma was blowing bubbles; they were dribbling down her chin and onto his shorts.

"Geez." He laughed. "Throw me that thing again."

Kate checked her watch. "Actually, it's getting close to her bedtime, I'd better get her into her pajamas and feed her. I bet she'll be sound asleep before she even finishes the bottle."

Kate was right, and by the time the adults called it quits for the night Emma had already been asleep for a couple of hours.

Luke helped Julianna unfold the couch, while Kate made certain the door was locked and chained. She propped the desk chair under the knob for extra security.

"Good night, Julianna," Luke said. "If you need anything, we're right here."

"Thanks." She looked hesitantly at Kate, opened her mouth as if to wish her good-night, then shut it without speaking.

Luke closed the door between the two rooms, leaving it open a crack so they could hear Julianna if there was trouble, then turned to Kate. "I'll make a bed up on the floor," he murmured, crossing to the closet and taking the spare blanket from the top shelf.

"Don't be silly," she said, holding out her arms for the blanket. "I'll sleep on the floor."

He frowned. "I'm not being silly. You're not sleeping on the floor. Period."

Kate placed her fists on her hips. "Look, you're doing most of the driving, you need your rest."

"You do, too."

"You're not going to budge on this, are you?"

"Nope."

She made a soft sound of frustration and threw up her hands. "This is stupid. The bed's a king. We'll share it." When he started to protest, she stopped him. "Don't you trust me not to make a pass?"

He gazed at her a moment. "It's not *you* who I don't trust. Can you live with that?"

"Of course," she said airily. "We're old friends."

"Of course we are."

She ignored his sarcasm and climbed in. Ten minutes later, Kate lay stiffly beside Luke, listening to his breathing, knowing sleep was as far out of his reach as it was hers. Knowing why.

Suddenly, unexpectedly, a giggle rose up in her throat. She tried to hold it back, but couldn't.

He turned his head. "What's so funny?"

"Us." She met his eyes. "A professional killer is after us and we're here worrying about who's going to sleep on the floor or if someone's going to make a pass."

He smiled. "Are you? Worrying if I'm going to make a pass?"

Emma stirred in her crib, and Kate lowered her voice even more. "Worrying wasn't quite the right word. Wondering, maybe."

He turned more fully toward her. "And if I made the pass, would you receive it?"

She held his gaze. "I don't know. Maybe." She looked away, then back at him. "Luke?"

"Yeah?"

"You know that night back at Tulane, the one when we...made love?"

"I remember."

"I didn't use you. I didn't plan it." She reached out and laid her fingers against his lips. "I promise you I didn't."

He caught her fingers and curved his own around them. "I know. I was hurt. Disappointed."

"I'm sorry."

"It's in the past."

"Is it?" She searched his gaze. "I know how some hurts are. They never quite heal."

"For a long time it was like that. It's healing now, Kate."

He released her hand, and she drew it away. "I made a lot of mistakes back then. Did some stupid things." She sighed, remembering. "You were right, what you said that day, after your book signing. Not just what you said about Richard, but about me as well. About why I married him."

"Why did you marry him, Kate?"

"Because I loved him." At Luke's expression, she shook her head. "I did, but not for the right reasons. I didn't see it then, but I loved Richard because he made me feel safe. And secure and cared for."

"And I didn't?"

"Not hardly." A smile tugged at her mouth. "You made me feel out of control. Uncertain. Of the future, what it would hold." She turned her gaze to the ceiling, remembering. "You made me feel like I could do anything, if only I'd try. If I would just go for it."

"I always believed in you, Kate. I still do."

Tears flooded her eyes. In all their years together, Richard had never said that to her. "That's just it. It wasn't you, Luke. I believed in you. In your strength and character. In your talent. It was me who I didn't believe in."

He opened his mouth to comment, and she laid her fingers gently against it to stop him. "I wanted to be an artist, but I was afraid. That I'd end up like my parents, scrambling to pay the rent, sacrificing my children's comfort for my art. I went to school wearing other people's castoffs and shoes with cardboard stuffed into the soles to cover the holes. I promised myself I wouldn't do that to my children. Or myself."

"Oh, Kate..." He threaded his fingers through her hair, fanned across the pillow.

She caught his hand and brought it to her mouth. "I was scared," she whispered. "Too scared to go after what I wanted. And too scared to give my feelings for you a chance. I'm sorry for that. And I'm sorry I hurt you."

Luke lifted himself up on an elbow and for one long, electric moment simply gazed at her. Then he brought his mouth to hers and kissed her, once, then again.

With a sigh, Kate returned the pressure of his mouth, the exploration of his tongue. He tasted like a fine wine; the taste went to her head until she grew drunk on it. She felt alive and whole and like a woman, not a mother or business owner, not like a rejected wife or widow. But like a woman, and the feeling was heady, indeed.

She slipped her arms around his neck and drew him closer. He murmured her name, and she heard the arousal in his voice, felt it in the hard length of him, pressing against her.

Suddenly, she thought of her husband. Of the last time they had made love. Of the way his mouth had felt against hers, the way her name had sounded on his lips.

And just as suddenly, what had felt so wonderful only moments before, felt wrong. As if she were being unfaithful.

Guilt replaced longing, and Kate stiffened in Luke's arms. She took her hands from behind his neck and pressed them against his chest. "I'm sorry, Luke. I just, it's—"

"Too soon."

"Yes." Beneath her fingers she felt the wild beat of his heart. She searched his gaze, pleading for understanding with hers. "Richard and I...we were together for so long. I want you, but it feels wrong. I feel like I'm cheating."

"I see."

But he didn't, she saw. Not really. "I don't want our being together to feel wrong. I don't want any regrets this time, for either of us."

He met her eyes. "You and me, Kate, that was the one thing that always felt right to me." He made a small sound of frustration. "It feels too soon to you, and I've been waiting more than ten years."

Emotion choked her. She didn't know what to say. A part of her wanted to ignore her real feelings, submerge them under the flush of passion. She wanted to be with him. To grab the sexual oblivion he offered. To forget the nightmare of her life, even if only for a short while. But most of all, she didn't want to lose him.

"Don't look at me that way." He cupped her face in his palms, kissed her hard, then rolled onto his back. He let out a long breath. "I've waited ten years, I suppose I can wait some more."

68

Luke didn't waste any time. As soon as they had arrived in D.C. and checked into a hotel, he called Tom Morris. Luckily, the man was in town and available; they arranged to meet at a neighborhood park in the Virginia suburbs at four o'clock that afternoon.

Luke deliberately made Morris wait, not so long he angered him, but long enough to get his point across. He wanted to begin their meeting with the upper hand. He wanted the man to understand, even before Luke said a word, that Luke was the one calling the shots. That he would not negotiate for anything less than what he wanted.

There could be no question as to whether he would pull this off, Luke knew. He had to.

Luke smiled grimly as he made his way across the park's thick green carpet of grass to the small duck pond where the other man waited. Morris sat on a bench, tossing crackers into the water and watching as the ducks dove and fought each other for them.

"Hello, Tom."

The man looked up. "Luke. Nice to see you again."

"Thanks for taking the time to meet with me. Why don't we walk?"

The man's eyebrows lifted slightly, as with surprise, but he nodded and stood, pocketing the remainder of the crackers.

They strolled in silence for a moment. "Pretty day," Morris said after a moment. "I like this time of year, the nip in the air, the approaching holidays. Beats the hell out of the heat and humidity of summer." He met Luke's eyes. "But I don't suppose you're here to discuss the weather."

"No, I'm not." He cut directly to the reason he had come. "One of your men killed the husband of a dear friend of mine. And now he wants to kill her and her infant daughter."

"I find that hard to believe."

Tom Morris didn't miss a beat, and Luke sensed the man already knew why he was here and everything he was about to tell him. "Do you? Ever heard the name John Powers?"

"John Powers," he repeated thoughtfully, then shook his head. "I can't say that I have."

"Let's cut the crap, Tom. I don't have time for it. Code name's Ice. Wet work specialist for the Agency. A renegade."

A flicker of something passed over the other man's face. Surprise, maybe. A grudging respect. "I might have heard of him, though not in connection with the CIA."

"Before you decide to stick with that version of the truth, let me tell you a little story." As he had with Condor, Luke laid the chain of events out for Morris, beginning with Richard's murder and ending with Kate and Julianna at his front door.

Tom Morris slipped his hands into his pockets. "Assuming what you're telling me is true—I say assuming because I find this whole story highly unlikely—what do you want from me?"

No culpability. Pass the buck.

Asshole.

"I want your assurance that if I get you proof that your man is not only out of control but a threat to the Agency, that you'll take him out."

"Take him out?" Morris's eyebrows shot up. "My God, Dallas, you're starting to sound like one of your characters."

"Look, Tom, I don't have the time to play a game of who's-on-first with you. If I get the proof, will you take him out?"

"How do you propose to get this…proof?"

"I have, in my possession, a journal. Powers' journal. It contains all the juicy stuff. Names, dates, locations."

"I presume it's in code."

"Or we wouldn't be having this conversation. You presume correctly."

"And you and your friends plan to break this code?"

"Correct again."

The man's eyes narrowed almost imperceptibly. "Save yourself the trouble, Luke. Give the book to us, we have people who specialize in this type of thing."

"I'm sure you do, but fat chance. You'll get the book when Powers is out of the picture."

"But how do you even know if you have anything of value?" Morris asked, his tone mild. "If you handed it over, I could evaluate its worth. My people could—"

"Now you're starting to piss me off." Luke stopped walking and swung to face the other man, head-on. "I may be new to this game, but I'm not stupid. Without that book, we have nothing. You know it and I know it. And that's not a position I or my friends care to be in."

He held out his hand. "Do we have a deal?"

Tom Morris paused, then took Luke's hand. "Not that I'm admitting any knowledge of this man or his activities, but yes, if you bring me something solid on this Powers, something that proves he's a threat to the Unites States or to the Agency, we'll get him off the street. That's a promise."

69

"Complimentary champagne, Mr. Winters? Mimosa?"

John smiled at the flight attendant. "Just the orange juice, please."

"Of course." She retrieved a glass from the galley and brought it to him. She set the glass on the center console table, then straightened. He was one of only three passengers in the first-class section of the 747, and she didn't appear in a rush to move on. "Going to D.C. for business or pleasure?" she asked.

"A bit of both." He smiled again and took a sip of the juice. "What time are we due to touch down? There are some people I need to catch up with, and I don't want to miss them."

"Ten-forty. If you need anything else, just call."

"I will. Thank you, Allison."

She smiled at his use of her name and walked off. John watched her go, then leaned his head against the rest. The timing was perfect. Though, in truth, he wasn't in a hurry. Tracking a target was not about speed, but about accuracy. About precision and timing. He would find them and at the right moment, he would kill them. Cleanly and quickly.

It was better than they deserved. Better than *she* deserved.

John brought a hand to the back of his head and the

ridge of fifteen stitches there, ones received courtesy of Julianna's betrayal. He drew in a long, deep breath, working to calm himself. Since that incident, he'd had to call upon all his self-control, all his training and self-discipline to remain focused. To push back the rage, the betrayal and even hatred, pulsing through him and concentrate on the job he had to do.

He had Julianna and her band of compatriots in his sights already. He smiled to himself, amused. It had been easy to locate them. Pathetically so. They had run to Kate's friend in Houston, the writer Luke Dallas. He had learned that by listening in on Blake and Marilyn's hushed conversations at The Bean. From Kate's Rolodex he had found Luke's address and phone number. The trip from New Orleans to Houston's Hobby airport had taken less than an hour, the trip from the airport to Luke's address in Kingwood another forty-five minutes, including the time it had taken to rent a car.

Unfortunately, he had missed them. John brought the juice to his lips. No problem there, Luke's editor had been only too happy to help him out when she had learned he was from *People* magazine and interested in doing a feature on the author. She had directed him to Luke's agent.

The *People* magazine gambit had worked again, like a charm. The man had fallen all over himself in his eagerness to get the interview. At first he had claimed not to be able to contact his client, then to prevent losing the interview, had confided that Luke was on vacation in D.C. but would be checking in.

Then it had only been the nuisance of discovering where they were staying. A couple dozen calls later he'd had a name—the Holiday Inn—Capitol Hill.

Luke Dallas had made room reservations in his own name.

So easy. John shook his head slightly, almost feeling sorry for them. The choice of D.C. had been the only surprise of the chase so far, and he found a sort of perverse rightness that Julianna's end should come there, where she first betrayed him.

John turned his gaze to the window and the blue sky and billowy white clouds beyond. Luke Dallas should not have become involved in his business. Now John had no choice but to kill him. Kate's involvement he could understand—she would protect her child, no matter the cost to herself—though he regretted deeply having to end her life. He admired her courage and loyalty, her honesty and commitment.

Perhaps, if they had met under other circumstances, he might even have fallen in love with her.

For that, he would not make her watch her child die.

John took a last drink of the juice, holding the cool, sweet liquid on his tongue a moment before swallowing. Savoring it. The way he would savor killing Julianna and her little group of misguided supporters.

He could hardly wait to see the look of shock on their faces when he showed up. Could hardly wait to see *her* shock. John closed his eyes and imagined a bullet blowing the back of Julianna's head off.

70

Julianna's description of John's apartment had been disturbingly accurate. Naked, Kate thought, taking a step farther inside. Bloodless and cold. Like the man.

She moved her gaze over the room before her, taking in the leather couch and wine-and-forest print side chairs, the perfectly appointed and organized bookshelves, the generic prints on the walls. John Powers didn't live here; no one did. It was a shell, like a furniture store display, decorated with expensive and classic items, yet with none of the human touches that made a dwelling a home. The only exception was a framed photo on the sofa table.

"Julianna," Luke said, turning to face her, "you've done this before. Any ideas where we should start?"

The young woman stood just inside the front door. She shook her head.

"What should we be looking for?" Kate asked, setting Emma's carrier down, her daughter sound asleep in it.

"Correspondence," he answered. "Phone bills, credit card receipts, or anything else that might help us link him to a place, date or event. Of course, the big find would be the key to his code, though I'd bet he carries that around in his head." Luke turned to Kate. "Why don't you and Julianna search here and in the kitchen. I'll start in the master bedroom."

Kate nodded. "Sounds good to me." She glanced at Julianna—the younger woman hadn't moved from her position just inside the door. She looked as if she might bolt at any moment.

"You okay?" she asked.

Julianna looked at Kate. "What?"

"Are you okay?"

Julianna blinked, her gaze suddenly focusing on Kate. "Fine. Ready?"

"I'll start in here, why don't you take the kitchen?"

Julianna nodded and made her way past Kate. Kate watched her go, her eyebrows drawn together in concern. The other woman's movements were halting, as if her legs weren't completely cooperating with her brain, and her cheeks were pasty, as if she might be sick at any moment.

It might not be such a good idea for her to be here. Kate glanced toward the bedroom, wondering if she should discuss it with Luke. She shook her head, deciding that she was overreacting. The best thing to do was get busy so they could all get out. Being here gave her the creeps, too.

Kate started with the piece of furniture closest to her, one of the print side chairs, a wingback. She checked under the cushion, then turned the chair over, inspecting the bottom lining carefully, looking for a gap in the stitching, a flap that could be pulled away and some small item tucked inside. Finding nothing, she went to the next chair, then the built-in bookshelves.

While she worked, she heard Julianna in the kitchen, opening cupboards and drawers, rummaging through the freezer. Every so often, she would say something to herself, though Kate couldn't make out what.

Luke emerged from the master bedroom, crossing to her. "Take a look at this."

It was a copy of the New Orleans *Times Picayune*, dated two months before. Kate stared at it, a queasy sensation in the pit of her gut. She met Luke's gaze. "This means that—"

"Two months ago he had discovered Julianna's whereabouts and was planning his trip to New Orleans."

Kate sucked in a sharp breath. *How long had he been watching them? Stalking them, waiting for just the right time to strike?*

Gooseflesh crawled up her arms, and she rubbed them. "Anything else?"

He shook his head. "Unfortunately not. This guy makes spartan look cluttered. How about you?"

"Nada. Let's check with Julianna."

They did, but she'd had the same results as Kate.

Luke made a sound of frustration. "You're checking inside containers, aren't you? Pulling things out to look behind them?"

"What there is to check behind and inside, I am. Take a peak." She swung open one of the cabinets. It was empty save for a half dozen plates, glasses and bowls. "Check out the fridge." Except for a bottle of champagne, it, too, was empty. "Same with the freezer and pantry."

"Was it always like this?" Kate asked, moving her gaze over the room, taking in the white cabinets, walls and tile floor. The surfaces were all so clean they gleamed.

"Not so empty, no. I mean, he always had to have things just so. John hates any kind of dirt or clutter, won't tolerate them, but he used to have food in the refrigerator and pantry.''

"Even the trash cans are empty," Luke murmured, checking the one under the sink. "I wonder what it means?"

"Maybe he thinks of this as a kamikaze mission," Kate offered.

Luke considered that a moment, then inclined his head. "Or maybe this is a further sign of him coming unglued. A compulsion gone haywire."

"Interesting," Kate murmured, "he can't stand a mess but kills people for a living. What does he do when he gets blood on his hands?"

For a moment, the three were silent. Then Julianna sighed. "We're not going to find anything here, are we?"

"We don't know that," Luke said. "We're here, let's finish what we started."

They agreed and returned to their respective rooms. Kate finished the bookshelves, disappointed when her exhaustive and painstaking search yielded nothing out of the ordinary. Frustrated, she turned toward the sofa. Her eyes landed on the framed photo. Perhaps John had hidden something between the photo and the frame's back? Maybe even the key for his code?

She went to the photo, bent and studied. It was a picture of a much younger Julianna, standing beside a man she presumed to be John Powers. He was wearing a baseball cap; his face was partially in shadow. Still, he looked familiar. She tilted her head, studying the man, certain they had met before.

And then she knew.

John Powers and Nick Winters were the same person.

Kate took an involuntary step backward, her mind spinning with the ramifications of it. As Nick Winters, John had been stalking her and Emma for weeks now. He had flirted with her and bounced Emma on his knee.

He had been in her home. She had invited him in. The night Richard had been murdered. The night *he* had murdered Richard.

It all made sense now, the way he had acted that night, the things he had said. Horrified, Kate brought a hand to her mouth. *It'll all be over soon, Kate. Sooner than you can imagine.*

He could have killed her then. He could have killed Emma. Easily. They had been alone, defenseless.

Obviously, he had known that. *Obviously.* She brought the heels of her hands to her eyes. Why hadn't he? He'd had them both where he wanted them.

Because he didn't work that way, she thought, dropping her hands. He was a methodical bastard. Everything in its time and place, first things first. Oh, yes, the John Powers she had come to know through Nick Winters always crossed his *T*s and dotted his *I*s.

With hands that shook, she picked up the photo. Gazing at his image, she recalled other things he had said—about loyalty and trust, about honor.

Tess.

She wasn't like us, Kate. She wasn't loyal.

Kate sank to the couch. Tess's boyfriend had always proclaimed his innocence. He and Tess had been arguing, he'd said. He had dropped her at her car, parked behind The Uncommon Bean, then furious with her, he had torn off without waiting to make sure she had gotten safely into her vehicle and on her way.

That, he had sworn, was the last time he'd seen her.

Kate, like everyone else, had thought him lying. Even though she had always wondered why he had smashed her stained glass. To her, that had seemed such a personal act of rage, one directed at her, not Tess.

That afternoon, Kate remembered suddenly, she had asked Nick Winters if she could buy back her piece of stained glass. She remembered their conversation about artists and the act of creation and how creepy he had seemed, how uncomfortable his words had made her feel.

"How do you feel knowing I own a piece of your soul?"

That's the way he had wanted her to feel. He had been toying with her. Enjoying his game of cat and mouse, enjoying that the poor little mouse didn't have the first inkling she was about to be eaten.

John had killed Tess; she knew it without proof. He had destroyed her stained glass. But why? Kate wondered, searching the photograph as if it would yield a clue. What could he have had against Tess? Why would he have wished her ill?

Maybe her employee had been in the wrong place at the wrong time. Maybe she had caught him snooping around and...

Her Rolodex. Dear God.

Kate leaped to her feet. The photo slipped from her fingers. It hit the floor; the glass shattered.

With her address file, John knew everyone Kate knew. He knew where they lived, their phone numbers and from the notations beside each listing, whether they were friend, family or business associate.

Luke's address was there, she realized, panic taking her breath. John knew about Luke. And as Nick Winters, he had not only access to her employees, but to their trust as well.

She squeezed her eyes shut, trying to remember exactly what she had told Blake and Marilyn when she'd called from Luke's that first day. She had talked to both her managers; she had told them she was in Houston. Visiting a friend. That it had been too painful for her at home, so she had taken Emma and gone. She had asked them not to discuss her whereabouts with anyone.

A hysterical laugh rose from her throat. When had Marilyn and Blake ever been able to keep quiet about anything? How long until John Powers discovered who she was with, then her whereabouts?

Or had he already?

She swung to face the door, heart thundering, half expecting the man to walk through.

"Kate?" Julianna came in from the kitchen, her expression concerned. "What's wrong?"

Kate wheeled around to face the other woman. "I think we're in trouble."

"What do you mean?"

"He might know where we are. He might know we're with Luke."

Julianna frowned and came around the couch. She saw the picture frame and stopped short. The blood drained from her face.

"We need to get out of here, quick." Kate dragged a shaking hand through her hair. "Have you finished the kitchen?"

Julianna didn't answer, and Kate frowned. "Julianna? Are you all right?"

"I gave that to him," she murmured after a moment, her voice curiously flat. "I wanted to make this house nice. Like a real home."

"I'm sorry," Kate said softly. "I didn't mean to break it."

Julianna knelt and with her bare hands began sweeping the shards of glass into a pile. The fragments cut her fingers, and they began to bleed.

"Julianna, you're hurting yourself."

She acted as if she didn't even hear Kate. "He would bring me here. Mama said it was all right. She didn't know."

Kate squatted beside her, reaching for her hands. "Julianna, stop. You're bleeding."

She knocked Kate's hands away, and reached for the crystal frame. Though it had cracked in half, Julianna carefully opened the back, slid out the photograph then set the frame gingerly down. She passed her hand over the photo, as if brushing away the splinters of glass, leaving a red smear in its wake.

Kate jumped to her feet and took a step backward. "Luke," she called softly, afraid to raise her voice. "Could you come here, please?"

"I was pretty, don't you think?" Julianna studied the picture, head cocked as if trying to remember something. "Was I ten or eleven here?" She lifted her face to Kate's. "Do you know?"

Ten or eleven. Dear God. Not trusting her voice, Kate shook her head.

"It doesn't matter, I guess." She touched the photo again, this time with the tip of her index finger. "But I was pretty?"

"You were beautiful," Kate murmured, pressing a hand to her stomach, sick with what she suspected had been the true character of Julianna's relationship with John Powers. "You still are."

"No," Julianna said, her tone taking on a singsong quality. "Mama's beautiful and Julianna's pretty. Be a good little girl, mustn't forget." Her voice cracked slightly. "John's good little girl."

"Luke," she called again, louder this time, not taking her gaze from the other woman. "You'd better get out h—"

"I'm here." He laid a hand on her shoulder and bent close to her ear. "Take Emma to the bedroom."

Kate looked over her shoulder at him, uneasy. "Why? What do you—"

"I don't know. Do it, just in case."

She nodded and went for the car carrier and Emma, skirting wide around Julianna. She needn't have worried. The other woman didn't even notice her.

Kate set the carrier in the bedroom, then shut the door partway. She didn't know what Luke feared was going to happen but she wasn't about to take any chance of her daughter getting hurt.

When she returned to the living room, Julianna had the photo clutched to her chest. Her hands were riddled with cuts and bleeding; she had rubbed blood across her face and onto her khaki trousers. She was humming under her breath and rocking.

Kate met Luke's gaze. "We have to do something. That glass is tearing her hands to pieces."

He nodded and squatted down beside her. "Julianna, honey, come on. You're hurting yourself."

"It's me," she said, showing him the picture. "And John."

"I see that." He cupped her elbow. "You can bring it back to the motel, if you like."

"I don't understand." She lifted her gaze to his—Kate saw that her eyes were filled with tears. "How could he do that to me? I was just a...just a child. A little girl."

"I know, sweetheart. But it's over now. It's okay."

He took her elbow, but she shook off his hand, turning her gaze back to the photo. She dragged in a shuddering breath. When she released it, it came out as a high, thin wail of grief. Another one followed. Then another.

She drew her knees up and hugged them to her chest, beginning to cry, wracking sobs that seemed to come from the very center of her being. When they eased slightly, Luke bent and scooped her up. "Come on, honey. You're hurting yourself."

At first she lay limply in his arms, crying softly. Then, suddenly and with a roar, she fought him, squirming, kicking, trying to claw. He lost his grip on her, and she broke free.

With a howl of rage, she grabbed the lamp off the end table and flung it. It hit the wall and shattered. "I was just a baby!" She screamed. She took the phone and yanked it from the wall. "How could he do that to me! How! I loved him!"

Her gaze landed on the photograph and she fell on it, ripping and tearing at it until she could no longer grasp the pieces, they were too small. "I trusted him!" Panting, grunting with exertion, she ran, stumbling, to the bookshelves and began tearing the volumes from the shelves, flinging them as far and hard as she could.

As suddenly as the rampage had begun, it ended. She collapsed to the floor, spent, whimpering like a wounded animal.

Kate went to her. Kneeling beside her, she took the

younger woman into her arms, holding her as she would Emma, rocking and murmuring sounds of comfort.

Julianna turned her face into Kate's chest, clinging to her. "I was just a little girl. How could he do that to me? How?"

"I don't know, baby. But you're safe now." Kate stroked her hair, and lifted her gaze to Luke's, her heart breaking for the younger woman. "We won't let him near you, not ever again."

71

Luke finished the search while Kate comforted Julianna. She helped the younger woman clean her wounds, carefully washing and drying her hands, picking out slivers of glass, then disinfecting each cut with the rubbing alcohol she found underneath the sink in the master bath.

Julianna sat unmoving on the couch while Kate applied the alcohol with a cotton swab, not even wincing though Kate knew how much it must burn. It was as if she had spent one hundred percent of her emotional energy, leaving her a shell, disconnected and empty.

Kate's heart hurt for her, and she wished she could say or do something that would make everything all right, repair the damage John had inflicted on the mind and spirit of the trusting little girl Julianna had been.

But there was no such thing, Kate knew. The damage was done, and it ran deep.

She capped the alcohol and set the bottle on the coffee table. "Why don't you lay back and rest a moment," she said. "I'm going to check on Luke."

Julianna did as Kate suggested, though she didn't close her eyes. She stared blankly at the ceiling, her expression devoid of emotion. Kate gazed at her a moment, wishing again that she could do or say something to help her, then went in search of Luke.

She found him in the kitchen. He looked over his

shoulder at her when she entered. "Find anything?" she asked.

"Nothing."

"We've got a problem." She told him about the photograph, about realizing that John Powers and a regular patron of The Bean's, a man named Nick Winters, were one and the same person. "If, as I suspect, he's the one who murdered Tess, he has my Rolodex. Your name and address were in it."

"Son of a bitch. That means he could have figured out we're together."

"Yes."

"Then we do have a problem." Luke swore again. "The motel, Kate. I registered under my own name. I thought it would be safe, I assumed he wouldn't know we were together. Dammit to hell, that was stupid. I put us in jeopardy."

"I thought the same, Luke. That we would be safe. I never would have dragged you into this if I'd known who Nick Winters was."

"I'm glad you didn't know."

Their gazes held a moment, then he made a sound of frustration and looked away. "We're going to have to change motels. As soon as possible."

"I don't know if Julianna's up to it. She's pretty traumatized."

As if cued, Julianna began to whimper in the other room. Luke's jaw tightened. "I hate this man, Kate. If he had walked through that door earlier, I swear I could have killed him. With my bare hands. I—" He drew in a steadying breath. "I never thought I could say something like that and really mean it. But I do mean it. I could have done it."

She laid a hand on his arm, and he covered it with

one of his own. "How old do you think she was when he...when he began molesting her?"

"I don't know," he murmured. "Really young, I think."

She thought of her own daughter and of the girl Julianna might have been and tears stung her eyes. "Do you think she's going to make it? She's lost so much."

"The human spirit is resilient, Kate. With therapy she might overcome the damage. People have bounced back from worse."

"I suppose." She turned her gaze toward the living room. Through the doorway she could see part of the couch and Julianna. "I feel so...bad for her," she murmured. "Twenty-four hours ago, I couldn't have said that. After what she did to me and Richard, I would have sworn I could never say that."

"She gave you Emma."

"Yes."

They both fell silent. After a moment, Kate cleared her throat. "Even with everything, I always felt grateful for that. Someplace inside me, I was always thankful to her." She looked at Luke. "What does that say about me?"

"That you love your daughter very much."

"Or does it mean I didn't love my husband enough?"

"Don't do this to yourself, Kate. It's destructive. Counterproductive. Let it go."

He was right; she knew he was. But she couldn't let it go, as much as she longed to. "Julianna told me that in return for Richard, she gave me what I wanted most in the world." Her eyes filled with tears. "Did I want to be a mother no matter the cost?"

The tears spilled over, and she swiped impatiently at them. "I've asked myself that question a hundred times. I've asked myself, if I could bring Richard back to life, if I could have our lives as they had been before, and all I had to do was hand Emma back—" Her throat closed over the words, guilt and grief and shame choking her. "I can't honestly say I would, Luke. I love her too much."

Luke turned her into his arms. She laid her face to his shoulder, her tears spilling over. "I hate myself for that, Luke. I feel so guilty. So disloyal."

"You are not responsible for Richard's death, Kate. You didn't cause it. And neither did Julianna. John Powers murdered Richard. He's the one you should blame, the one who should be punished. Not you."

"I hate him," she said softly, fiercely, tipping her face up to Luke's. "He's not just a monster. He's the devil. And God help me, I want him dead."

"The Agency will take care of him, Kate. We have to focus on getting what we need to make that happen."

She nodded and drew away from him, wiping the tears from her cheeks. She dragged in a shuddering breath. "What next?"

"Let's shake this bastard up a little bit, that's what." Luke smiled grimly. "Do you have a lipstick?"

Kate went to her purse, dug one out and handed it to him. "Very Berry okay?"

He uncapped it and rolled up the stick, admiring the color. "Perfect."

"What are you—"

"I'm going to leave him a message, that's what."
He rolled up the lipstick and crossed to the white cabinet directly in front of him. "Let's just see how Mr.
Powers likes being the hunted."

72

John surveyed the carnage, shaking with rage. How dare they violate the sanctity of his home? How dare they touch and destroy his things.

Didn't they understand who they were dealing with?

John picked his way through the wreckage of his living room. When he reached the kitchen, he stopped short. They had left him a message, scrawled in red across his virgin white cabinet fronts, like a wound.

We're going to get you, asshole.

John stared at the words, the blood spinning crazily in his head. His hands began to shake and his breath came in short, angry bursts. He flexed his fingers, any semblance of control and self-discipline gone. They would pay for this, he vowed. They would suffer.

If it was the last thing he did, he would make certain they died like pigs.

73

"Good morning," Kate said as Julianna appeared at the connecting door between their rooms. It was just after 8:00 a.m. The other woman had slept through the night—Kate knew this because, unable to sleep, she had checked on Julianna a half dozen times.

Julianna met Kate's eyes, then slid her own gaze uncomfortably away. "Morning."

Kate finished diapering Emma, resnapped her pajamas, then scooped her up. Julianna hadn't moved from her position in the doorway. "How are your hands?" she asked.

Julianna held them out; they looked awful, like they had gotten caught in a meat grinder. She tried to bend her fingers, wincing at the effort. "They hurt."

Emma propped on her hip, Kate crossed to the trash and dropped the used diaper in. The infant began to fuss and Kate shifted her from her hip to her shoulder. She motioned Julianna in from the doorway. "Come talk to me."

Her expression wary, she crossed to the double bed closest to her and sat on its corner. "Where's Luke?"

"He went for coffee and rolls." Emma cried out and squirmed in her arms, and Kate adjusted her hold again. "We're going to check out after we eat."

Julianna curved her arms across her middle. "He found us another place?"

"This morning. It's not going to be very nice, I'm afraid. Most places require a credit card to register, for security purposes. Problem is, Luke's registering us under an alias. He called around this morning."

The younger woman eyed Emma, a frown creasing her brow. "What's wrong with Emma? I never heard her make that sound before."

Kate glanced down at the child. She held her in a cradle hold, body tipped slightly toward her. She was, indeed, making a different sound, a cross between a whimper and a whine.

Kate frowned, unsettled by the fact that Julianna had noticed it and she hadn't. "She's a little fussy today. She didn't sleep well. Babies get like this."

Awkward silence stretched between them. Julianna broke it first. "I'm glad I gave her to you. And that I couldn't have the...you know."

The abortion. Kate shuddered at the thought of how close Emma had come to not being. "I'm glad, too. She's a very special little person."

Julianna reached up and trailed her fingers across Emma's downy head, then drew her hand back, eyes bright with tears. "I'm sorry I freaked out like that yesterday."

"You have nothing to be sorry for."

Julianna bowed her head. "I don't know why I...I never saw before. I must have known how... wrong...how sick..." She lifted her gaze to Kate's, her expression anguished. "I allowed it. I'm as much to blame as he is."

"That's not true." Kate crossed to her. "Listen to me. You were a child, he was an adult. He preyed on your innocence and trust. On your helplessness. What he did to you was a crime, Julianna."

"But why didn't I stop him?" She balled her hands into fists. "Why didn't I fight him or tell someone? And when I was older, why did I stay with him? I think about it and I want to curl up and die."

Julianna was silent a moment before continuing. "I knew," she said softly. "Deep down. That's why I—" Her throat closed over the words and she cleared it. "That's why I got pregnant. I wanted a normal relationship. The kind other women had."

A normal relationship. Like her and Richard's.

Even as a wisp of anger speared through her, Kate laid a hand on Julianna's shoulder, hurting for her, hating John Powers with a ferocity that stunned her. "A psychiatrist could help you deal with what John did to you. He could help you understand your feelings, why you did what you did. He would help you feel better."

She stood, struggling, Kate saw, to keep from falling apart. "I better go get cleaned up, Luke will be back any minute."

"Julianna, wait." Kate caught her wrist. "Promise you'll think about it, seeing a psychiatrist, I mean. When this is all over."

Julianna extricated herself from Kate's grip, a ghost of a smile touching her mouth. "All right, Kate. I promise."

74

Luke arrived back at the motel just as Julianna emerged from her room, her duffel bag packed and slung over her shoulder. Her hair was wet from the shower, her eyes red and puffy from crying.

Luke noticed, Kate was sure by his subtle double take at Julianna, but he didn't comment. "Macs was the best I could do in a hurry," he said, setting the McDonald's bag and beverage tray on the dresser. "I got sausage biscuits and fat-free muffins. Take your pick."

Kate propped Emma on her hip and reached for a coffee. The infant squealed in protest, and Kate made a sound of exasperation. "What is wrong with you today, Emma?"

"If you want to eat now, I'll hold her," Julianna offered. "I mean, if that's okay?"

Kate hesitated, but only a moment. She needed a break. She had been walking, jiggling and bouncing a fussy baby for hours and she'd had it. "Okay," she said. "But don't say I didn't warn you."

Kate handed her over with only a twinge of misgiving. The fear that Julianna was going to run off with Emma had all but evaporated. In truth, as Julianna took Emma awkwardly into her arms, she looked more nervous than Kate.

New arms momentarily distracted the infant and

with a sigh of relief, Kate helped herself to a coffee and a biscuit.

"I called the P.I. while I was out," Luke said, folding back the plastic tab on his coffee's lid. "From a pay phone. He found both addresses and travel records for Wendell White and David Snow. The addresses were useless, mail drops and answering services. But the travel records could prove to be a gold mine."

Luke took a sip of his coffee, then smiled. "White and Snow visited some pretty exotic locales in the past couple of years. Colombia. Mexico. Israel. The U.K. I asked my guy to do a search on Nick Winters as well as to continue with the other names."

Kate set aside her biscuit, too anxious to eat. "So how does that help us?"

"We need to prove Powers is a loose cannon, right?" Kate and Julianna nodded. "The book will give us the information we need. All we have to do is break the code. The travel records will help us."

At the two women's blank looks, he explained, "In theory, once we make one of the book's entries, we can use it to decipher the rest. Like an alternate alphabet. I already did a little checking. According to my P.I., David Snow traveled to Mexico on June fourth last year. He returned on the fifteenth. There's a coded entry in the book, dated June fourteenth."

"Then we have him," Kate said.

"Maybe. Maybe not. What if the dates are a code, too? Twisted in some way? Or what if Snow was in Mexico on legitimate business? We've got to do this right. I say we go a step further. We find a library and using these travel dates as a guide, we search the back issues of newspapers on microfilm looking for reportings of deaths of government officials or any other important or prominent person. Then we put the two together.

"It's a long shot." Luke looked from one woman to the other. "But it's the only one we've got. And in my book it beats the hell out of sitting around waiting for Powers to strike."

The three exchanged glances, then leaped into action, a sense of urgency pressing in on them. They had to move fast. Time, they knew, was one thing John Powers was not going to allow them.

They checked into the new motel—a dismal affair done in a medieval knights theme, as if medieval castles had been papered with red-black-and-silver foil, flocked wallpaper. The woman manning the front desk hadn't had a clue where the nearest public library was, let alone the main branch, but offered the motel's yellow pages.

The Martin Luther King Jr. Memorial Library, they learned, was located at 901 G Street N.W. in the old downtown business district. The library had both the *Washington Post* and the *New York Times* on microfilm.

The day was long, their search tedious. Exhausting and frustrating. As the hours slipped by, Kate became more convinced that they were on a wild-goose chase, more aware that with each minute they searched, John Powers got that much closer to them.

Their progress was slowed even more by Emma. Her crabby mood only worsened as the day progressed. Kate and Julianna took turns walking the halls with her. They bounced her, sang songs and read to her. Nothing worked. At times the infant was almost inconsolable.

When they finally called it quits around two that

afternoon, Kate had a screaming headache. Her eyes and shoulders ached and for the first time since arriving at Luke's, she felt hopeless.

She wasn't alone in her feelings. Julianna was subdued and retreated into her own world the minute they reached the hotel; Luke on the other hand, paced. He was frustrated and uncommunicative, and the one time Kate had tried to talk to him, he had all but bitten her head off.

Kate watched him pace for a moment, then returned her gaze to Emma, worried. "What's the matter, sweetie?" She tickled her daughter's lips with the bottle's nipple. "Come on, you've hardly eaten anything all day."

To her great relief, Emma latched on to the nipple and began sucking. A moment later, however, she jerked away and started to cry, the sound high-pitched and hurting.

A thread of panic wound through Kate. *Something wasn't right.* This was more than Emma being a little fussy because of lack of sleep or her schedule being disrupted. Kate laid a hand on her forehead; it felt hot.

Luke stopped pacing. "What's wrong?"

"I don't know. I think she has a temperature." Kate bent and pressed her lips to her daughter's forehead. "She's definitely hot."

"Let me check." Luke came over and laid his hand on her forehead. "She does feel a little warm. But maybe she's just hungry? Or sleepy?"

"I tried to feed her, but she wouldn't take the bottle. I'm worried, Luke. She's never been sick before."

"You don't know that she's sick, Kate. It could be she's just...upset."

"Her pediatrician's in Mandeville, all my child care

books, I—" She dragged in a shaky breath. "This whole thing's been too hard on her. I never should have subjected her to it."

"What would you have done instead?" he asked, impatiently. "Stayed put in Mandeville so she could be murdered in her crib?"

Tears flooded Kate's eyes at his blunt words, and she swung away from him, clutching Emma, struggling not to cry.

He put his arms around her and Emma from behind. He bent and laid his cheek against her hair. "I'm sorry, Kate. I shouldn't have said that. It was wrong."

"No." She shook her head. "It wasn't wrong, it was true. We're just going to die later rather than sooner."

He turned her in his arms so they faced one another. "Don't say that. We have—"

"Nothing, Luke. We have nothing. We're no better off now than we were in Houston."

"We knew from the beginning that it wasn't going to be easy. We need a little more time, that's all."

"And time's just what we don't have." A sob rose in her throat. "It's impossible, like looking for a needle in a haystack. And now Emma's sick. I can't keep dragging her from one place to another like this. It's not good for her."

"Look at me, Kate. We don't even know for sure that John has made the connection between you and me. And even if he has, almost no one knew we were headed to D.C."

"He has made the connection. Somehow, he'll find us." She broke away from his arms. Emma began to cry, and Kate held her to her chest, trembling. "I *feel* him, Luke. He's watching us now, this minute. Nip-ping at our heels, laughing at our feeble efforts. And now Emma...something's wrong with..."

"Calm down, Kate." Luke closed the distance she had put between them and cupped her face in his palms. "I'll call the front desk, they'll know where the nearest Ready Med is—"

"What then?" she asked, tears welling. "Change hotels? Run forever? You know as well as—"

"Stop it!" Julianna leaped to her feet. "I can't take it anymore!"

Kate and Luke swung toward her, surprised. Even Emma was momentarily startled into silence.

"Don't you see?" she implored them. "We've got to stick together. If we're going to beat him, we've got to stick together. We've got to stay positive—"

She stopped suddenly. She brought her hands to her mouth, her expression stunned. "Oh, my God. That's it. I know what we should do, how we can get John. I can't believe I didn't see it before."

She turned to them. "Senator Jacobson. Clark Russell. We've had the answer all along."

"Senator William Jacobson?" Kate asked, drawing her eyebrows together. "Didn't he die last year? Wasn't he murdered?"

Julianna nodded. "I read about it in the paper, but it never made sense to me. The newspaper account reported that he had been found dead in his Washington hotel room. But whenever he stayed in the city, he stayed with my mother."

"Your mother?" Luke murmured, frowning.

"She was his mistress."

"I see what Julianna's getting at," Kate said, turning to Luke. "John told Julianna that he'd killed her mother. If she and the senator were together that night—"

"He would have killed him, too." Luke nodded. "That would mean the true facts of the murder were concealed to protect the senator and his family. It could be. It happens all the time."

"Billy was married," Julianna said. "Mother mentioned his wife a bunch of times. She came from big money, I think."

"She did." Kate nodded. "I read something about that. She came from some important family. Really important, with political ties."

"You're right," Luke said, excitement edging into his voice. "You mentioned two names, Julianna. The other was—"

"Clark Russell. He was with the CIA. Investigative branch, I'm pretty sure. He and mother had been lovers, a long time ago. He's the one who told her what John did for a living. Until then, even though they had been together for years, she hadn't known the truth. When I didn't believe her, she called Clark. He showed me some classified photographs, ones of...of John's victims. I believed them then. And I ran."

"Clark Russell made it personal," Luke murmured. "He crossed the line."

Kate drew her eyebrows together, something suddenly occurring to her. "Wait a minute, you're telling us that all three of these men were at one time or another your mother's lover?"

"Yes."

"And now, two out of the three are dead."

"Yes. John admitted to me that he killed Clark."

Luke sat. "If we can prove Powers killed a United States senator, I think we'd have it."

"Don't we have enough now?" Kate asked, sounding breathless to her own ears. "Couldn't we go to Morris, lay it all out for him and—"

"I don't think so. We don't have anything solid to tie Powers to the murders."

Kate made a sound of disbelief. "Even though all three were at one time Sylvia Starr's lover? Even though two of the three are recently dead and now John Powers is after Sylvia's daughter? What do they want, it delivered wrapped in a gift bow?"

"Yes, actually. That's just what they want. They want us to give them Powers, lock, stock and barrel. Right now, all we've got is speculation and coincidence." He frowned. "But I'm thinking, if we could prove there was a cover-up in the senator's death, maybe, just maybe they would make a move. It's worth a shot.

"We start with the police." He shifted his gaze to Emma, sleeping finally but fitfully, in Kate's arms. "After we get Emma to the doctor."

75

The homicide division of the Metropolitan Police Department, or M.P.D., was located downtown in the Henry J. Daly Municipal Center. Besides police headquarters, Luke learned, the Daly building housed several other entities, including the Department of Motor Vehicles and the parole board. Interesting choice, combining paroled convicts and police officers in the same building. He wondered what genius had thought that one up.

Parking downtown D.C. was a nightmare so Luke had taken a cab. He paid the driver, then made his way into the building and past the uniformed guards and metal detector. Homicide was on three, accessible only from the main lobby elevators. Every police department he had ever been in possessed its own distinct character. Some were rough, some sleekly modern, some carnival-like.

But the officers themselves, as a group, varied little, whether small-town cop or big-city law enforcement. A breed unto themselves, tough but never reckless, unified. He supposed it was because they lived differently than regular folks, on an invisible edge. Seeing death changed a man. As did facing it.

If he made it through this, Luke hadn't a doubt that he would be changed, too.

He stepped onto the elevator, checking his watch as he did. It was nearly five. Emma's trip to the Ready

Med had taken longer than he had anticipated, though it was a good thing they had gone. By the time they'd gotten in to see the doctor, the child had gone from feeling a little warm to downright hot.

And no wonder. Emma had had a temperature of 102.5, brought on by a severe ear infection in both ears. The doctor had prescribed an antibiotic, infant's Tylenol for the fever and discomfort and plenty of rest.

The elevator glided to a stop; the doors slid open and Luke emerged from the car. The homicide division lay straight ahead, through doors that could only be accessed with a key code. He turned right and headed down the hall to the desk lieutenant's office, pausing beside a trash receptacle.

On the way downtown, Luke had had the cabbie make a quick stop at a bookstore. He'd run in and bought a copy of *Dead Drop*. He took it out of the bag, which he tossed in the trash, then tucked the volume under his arm.

He hoped his so-called celebrity status and a free, autographed book might encourage somebody to talk. The guys at the Houston P.D. had adopted him as one of their own, letting him into their closed circle. They filled him in on cases, their theories, why and how things went down—even when they went wrong. They did so because they knew they could trust him, because he always took care to get his facts straight and give an acknowledgment when warranted.

He didn't fool himself that the M.P.D. officers would be so welcoming.

The desk lieutenant was a woman. Luke sent her what he hoped was a winning smile. "Hi, I'm Luke Dallas. The novelist." Her expression didn't change. "I'm in Washington to research my new book, and I was wondering if I could speak with one of the detectives.''

"You'll have to see Detective Peterson in Community Relations. He's on four.''

The Community Relations officer was not about to give him the information he needed. Those guys always played it by the book.

Luke tried again. He flashed the woman another smile, though he could tell she wasn't impressed. "I'm only in town for the day, and I was really hoping to talk to someone currently working cases.''

"Sorry.'' She frowned. "Department policy.''

He shifted the book under his arm. Her gaze flicked to it, then back up to him. "Who'd you say you are?''

"Luke Dallas. *Dead Drop.*'' He held up the book and recognition lit her features.

"I saw you on the 'Today Show.' Isn't that Matt Lauer to die for?''

Luke's lips lifted in self-directed amusement. *Some claim to fame.* "I wouldn't know about to die for, but he's a great guy. A good buddy of mine, actually.'' *When all else fails, lie your ass off.* "I could get you an autograph.''

"Really?''

"Oh, yeah. We play tennis together every week.''

She thought for a moment, then leaned slightly toward him. "I tell you what, I'll let you talk to Detective Sims. I think he'll be able to help you out.''

Five minutes later, Lieutenant Arlene Larson's full name and address in his pocket, Luke sat across from Detective Sims. Luke immediately understood why the lieutenant had chosen this detective to speak with him. He was young, bright-eyed and bushy-tailed. A preppy-looking, go-by-the-books kind of guy. Definitely not the kind who would spill department secrets.

"So, you're a writer?" the detective said.

"That's right. Luke Dallas." He handed him the book. "For you, signed."

The kid stared at the book, his jaw going slack. "Holy shit, not *the* Luke Dallas?"

Luke smiled and relaxed slightly. "The very one."

"I love your books." Sims leaned forward, lowering his voice. "I'm a writer, too. Not published yet, but I will be. Maybe you could take a look at my manuscript?"

First Matt Lauer. Now this.

"I'm only in town for the day," Luke murmured, trying to sound disappointed. "I tell you what, you help me out with this and I'll give you my agent's name and put in a good word for you. Agreed?"

"You got it." The detective looked about ready to bust, he was so pleased with the deal. "Want to hear what my story's about? It's really good. Fast-paced. Lots of action."

"I'd love to, if I had the time. I'll just have to trust that it's great."

The detective looked crestfallen, but nodded. "Okay, so what do you need to know?"

"The scenario I'm currently working on involves the cover-up of the murder of an influential man. An important man."

"Influential? How so?"

"He's a U.S. senator."

The detective nodded. "Go on."

"Our senator is a respectable married man. He has kids. A pillar of the community, country and church. He also has a mistress."

Sims nodded. "This is good. I like this."

"He's in bed with his mistress. An assassin enters

and kills them both. Pop, one shot to the chest and the senator's history."

"Oh, wow. What's the twist? I know your stories, there's always a twist."

Luke's lips lifted. "The assassin's not after him, he's after the mistress. The senator is simply in the wrong place at the wrong time. The wife has family connections that go all the way to the president and the feds—"

"Cover up the true circumstances of the murder to save the wife, kids and country public humiliation."

"Exactly." Luke smiled. "I can tell you're a born writer." The detective beamed at him, and Luke leaned back in his chair. "You ever seen anything like that before, Detective?"

"Personally, no. But it could happen."

"What about Senator Jacobson's murder? Anything like what I described?"

The preppy detective's face fell. "Senator Jacobson?"

"The very one." Luke leaned forward. "I have reason to believe Jacobson was neither in a hotel room nor alone when he was killed. I need to corroborate."

"I didn't work that case."

"You could look up the report." Luke met the other man's gaze straight on. "It's important, Sims. I'd consider it a personal favor."

"This isn't for one of your novels, is it?"

"No, Sims, it's not. But it's life and death, I promise you that."

The young detective hesitated, then looked nervously over his shoulder. "You didn't hear this from me?"

"I didn't hear it at all."

He nodded, glanced around again, then murmured.

"I don't have to look that one up, it's not every day a senator gets whacked. Something was definitely off about Jacobson's death. About the scene." The detective shifted in his seat, his chair creaked. "From the get-go it was hands off, feds only. They examined the scene, collected and processed the evidence. Some of the guys were really ticked off."

"Couldn't that have been because of who the victim was? Like you said, it's not every day a United States senator is murdered."

"Could be. But I doubt it." Sims leaned forward. "I heard some talk. Speculation that something different went down than what was officially reported. The scene didn't look right. Captain told us to put a lid on it."

"What happened then?"

"We did as ordered. Who has time to worry about yesterday's stiffs, no matter how important a person they were, we got today's, you know what I mean?"

Luke agreed that he did, indeed, know what he meant. "Sylvia Starr, ever heard that name?"

Sims thought a moment, then shook his head. "Who is she?"

"Murder victim. Could you look her up for me?"

"Sure. What do you need to know?"

"Date and time of death, circumstances. Whether she was found alone."

He swung toward his PC, typed in the appropriate combination of letters and numbers; a moment later the information came up. Sims scanned it. "Murdered on November 16, last year. Estimated time of death 3:00 a.m. Lover beside her, a John Doe. Gunshot to the head, close range. Blew her brains out. Unsolved."

"That's it?"

"That's it, though there should be more." He

frowned, rereading the information on the screen. "I don't see anything about evidence collection, witness interviews, or a case pending. It must have fallen through the cracks. You want me to look her up in the hard file?"

"No, that's okay. Could you check one more thing for me?"

"Sure. Shoot."

"Jacobson, the date and time of his murder?"

Sims turned to his PC once more. A minute later he frowned. "November 16, last year. Estimated time of death 3:00 a.m. Think there's a connection here?"

"Maybe."

"The mistress, right?"

"Yeah." Luke smiled grimly and stood, thinking ahead to the conversation he would have with Morris. "You got a card, Sims?"

The detective handed him one, and Luke turned it over and jotted down his agent's name, address and telephone number. "Send him your manuscript, tell him I said he should read it. When I get home, I'll call him, put in a good word for you."

The man flushed with pleasure. "Thanks, Mr. Dallas." He held out a hand. "Thanks a lot."

"Thank you." Luke shook his hand. "I appreciate your help."

He started to walk away, stopping and turning back after a few steps. "Sims?" The detective looked up. "A moment ago you said the scene was feds only. Happen to know which Agency that was?"

The younger man thought a moment, then shook his head. "Can't recall. You want me to find out? It'll take a few minutes."

"Yeah, I would," Luke said, turning back toward the desk. "I'll wait."

76

Kate sat beside Emma's crib and watched her sleep. Exhaustion and guilt pulled at her. How could she not have acted on the change in her daughter's behavior sooner? All the signs of illness had been there, crankiness, loss of appetite, sleeplessness. Instead, it had taken a 102.5 degree temperature to galvanize her into action. What kind of mother was she?

Kate passed a hand wearily across her forehead. The doctor had called ear infections a common childhood malady. If treated properly and promptly they posed no long-term health threat, if not, the child's hearing could be affected. He'd also tried to assure Kate that nothing she had or hadn't done had caused it.

As much as she wanted to, Kate didn't buy that. Emma had gone six months without so much as a sniffle; now, her life and routine in chaos, she had a raging infection in both ears and a temperature.

She squeezed her eyes shut. *Please find what we need, Luke. Please.*

The phone jangled and Emma stirred and moaned, her face puckering up in reaction to the sudden, shrill sound. Kate dove for the offending instrument, catching it a moment before it rang again.

"Hello?" she said softly, her gaze on Emma.

"Kate, it's Luke."

"Luke?" She pressed the receiver tighter to her ear,

straining to hear above the din on the line. "I can hardly hear you."

"I've run into a little trouble down here."

"Trouble? What—" The line crackled, then faded. He was saying something, but she couldn't quite make it out. "Luke, speak up. I can't understand what you're saying."

Julianna came to the door between their rooms. Kate glanced at her, and she mouthed, *"What's wrong?"*

Kate lifted her shoulders to indicate she didn't know, then turned her attention back to Luke.

"I think we've got him, Kate," he was saying, his voice fading in and out. "But we need to act quickly. How fast can you get down here?"

"Down there?" she repeated, her heart beginning to pound. "I don't understand—"

"Kate, I can hardly hear you now." The line crackled again. "—need you down here. Three hundred Indiana Avenue, N.W. The Henry J. Daly Municipal Center. Third floor. Quickly. Got that, Kate?"

"Got it. But, Luke, what—"

"You'll understand everything when you get here. Hurry," he said, "we don't have a minute to waste."

The line went dead.

Julianna came into the room, eyes wide, the expression in them worried. "What's going on?"

"I don't know." Kate stared at the receiver a moment, then returned it to its cradle. "Luke says he got what we needed, but there's some sort of trouble and we have to act quickly."

"He got the proof?"

"That's what he said. He asked me to come right down."

"But why?"

"I don't know." Kate snatched up the diaper bag

and carried it to the crib. "It was an awful connection, I could hardly hear."

Kate gazed down at her sleeping daughter, doubt plucking at her. The Tylenol had brought down her fever and relieved her pain, making it possible for her to finally rest. "I hate to wake her up," she murmured. "Poor thing just got to sleep."

"Don't." Julianna came to stand beside her. "You go, I'll stay with her. It'll be much quicker, and she can get some rest."

Kate hesitated. Julianna was right. It would be quicker without Emma. She would have to change Emma's diaper, make sure the diaper bag had plenty of spares and make a bottle. Plus the doctor had prescribed rest.

"She'll be fine. I bet she won't even wake up."

Kate caught her bottom lip between her teeth. She hated this. It felt wrong. But Luke had sounded almost desperate, and Kate knew her daughter—Emma did not like her sleep disturbed. If awakened now she would doubtless scream for the next thirty minutes. Kate didn't suppose that was what the doctor had meant by her getting plenty of rest and quiet.

"You can trust me, Kate. I wouldn't do anything to hurt Emma."

Kate realized it was true. If Julianna didn't care about Emma, she would have high-tailed it out of Louisiana after disabling Powers. Instead, she had put herself in harm's way to save Emma. Besides, how long would she be gone? Surely not more than forty-five minutes?

Kate acquiesced, though still torn. "Okay, but lock the door. Don't answer it for anyone."

Julianna laughed. "Are you kidding? There's a chance I won't even let you guys back in."

On impulse, Kate gave the other woman a quick hug. "I'll check in when I get there. You know where the formula and—"

"And bottle and diapers and wipes are? Yes. Now, go."

Kate grabbed her coat and hurried to the door, unlocked it and stepped out into the cold evening air. She stopped and looked back at Julianna, a knot in the pit of her gut. "Take care of my baby, okay?"

As she said the words she realized how strange they were, considering their relationship. In the beginning it had been Julianna who had entrusted Kate with the care for her baby.

"I will. Don't worry about a thing."

With one last glance backward, Kate hurried out to hail a cab.

77

Twenty minutes later the cab dropped Kate off in front of the Daly building. She paid the fare and hurried inside. She scanned the busy lobby, looking for Luke; when she didn't see him, she went through the metal detectors, heading toward the elevators.

She reached them just as one finished emptying out; she stepped inside and punched the third-floor call button. She lifted her gaze to the floor numbers above the door and drew in a deep breath through her nose, vacillating between being anxious and excited, hopeful and fearful.

Luke had said he'd gotten what they needed. But he'd also said he'd run into some sort of trouble. What could he have meant?

The elevator stopped on three and the doors opened. The hallway was empty, the door to the homicide division locked. Kate turned right and headed to the desk lieutenant's office.

The woman, a capable-looking brunette, looked up when Kate entered. "What can I do for you?"

"I was supposed to meet a friend here, Luke Dallas. He was interviewing one of the detectives."

"Detective Sims." She nodded. "But I'm afraid you've missed him."

"Missed him?" Kate repeated, her stomach falling. "Are you sure?"

"Positive. Detective Sims left on a call about ten minutes ago."

Ten minutes ago. An eternity.

Something was wrong.

Kate began backing out of the office, heart pounding. "He's probably waiting for me in the lobby. Thanks for your help."

She turned and ran for the elevator. This time she had to wait for a car; each moment seemed a lifetime. An elevator arrived. She hurried on. The car was already occupied by two uniformed officers. She eyed their sidearms, cuffs and radios, oddly reassured.

The taller of the two caught her gaze. "Everything all right, ma'am?"

She gazed at the officer. *She could enlist their help. Tell them the whole story and beg them to help her.*

She opened her mouth to do just that, then shut it, remembering what Julianna had said about John and the police. That they would make her a sitting duck, that John would outwit them easily. She pictured herself explaining the story to them, then their superior officer or a detective; could hear their questions, their skepticism.

By the time she convinced somebody to accompany her back to the motel, if she ever did, Emma, Luke and Julianna could be dead.

"Everything's fine," she said, her voice too high.

"You sure?" He narrowed his gaze on her, and she felt her cheeks heat. "You seem a little agitated."

"I'm fine." She cleared her throat and forced a smile. "I was supposed to meet a friend here and missed him. That's all. Thank you for asking."

They reached the lobby and the elevator doors slid open. Kate rushed off, frantically scanning the lobby for Luke. Once, then again.

He wasn't there.

Heart in her throat, she made her way out of the building. She stood in the center of the sidewalk, scanning up, then down. She had a sick feeling in the pit of her stomach. That something bad had happened to him; that John had followed him. That she'd been had.

Stepping up to the curb, she signaled a cab. It veered over two lanes, nearly causing an accident, pulling to halt at the curb in front of her. She yanked the door open.

"Kate! Wait!"

She spun around. Luke was emerging from the Daly building, and she ran to him. "Luke! Thank God!" His arms closed around her. "I got here as quickly as I could. When I couldn't find you I thought the wors—"

"I didn't call you, Kate."

She eased out of his arms and lifted her face to his, searching his expression for the *Gotcha!* She didn't see one and struggled for an even breath. "What are you saying?"

"I just talked to Julianna." He tightened his grip on her. "That wasn't me on the phone. I wouldn't even be here if I hadn't called the motel."

Kate felt the blood drain from her face, like an icy hand passing over her, stealing both her blood and her warmth.

John. Dear God. She brought a hand to her mouth. *She had left Emma. Julianna couldn't protect her from John. Kate wasn't even certain she would try.*

As if reading her thoughts, Luke held her at arm's length and looked her straight in the eyes. "Don't panic, Kate. I just talked to Julianna. Everything's fine. She's got the door locked and chained, she won't open it for anybody." He lowered his voice. "And I told her where my gun is. It's loaded."

"Gun?" she repeated, light-headed with fear.

"So she can protect herself and Emma if need be."

The cabby she'd hailed tooted his horn. "You need a cab or what?"

Luke grabbed her hand and they jumped in. The rush hour traffic was a snarl, and the ride to the motel seemed interminable to Kate. She struggled not to cry, not to completely fall apart, but all she could think about was Emma and John and what he might do to her if he got to her.

How could she have been so stupid? So gullible? She had never even questioned whether it was Luke on the phone, even though she had been unable to hear him clearly.

John knew everything, she realized, despair welling up in her chest. Where Luke had gone and probably why. That Emma had been to the doctor; that Kate would leave her and Julianna alone.

Tears flooded her eyes. If anything happened to Emma, she would never be able to forgive herself. Never.

Luke reached across the seat and covered her hand with his own. She curled her fingers around his, holding tightly. "Hang in there, Kate. She's going to be okay."

She glanced at him, then away, tears swamping her. "I'm trying, Luke. I really am."

"I found what we were looking for." She met his eyes. "Julianna's mother and Senator Jacobson were both murdered on the same night at approximately the same time. Apparently, the local boys' hands were slapped by the feds, who came in and took over. Some of the M.P.D. guys' noses were seriously out of joint.

There was talk. Speculation about a cover-up of some sort.''

She worked hard to concentrate on what he was saying. "So, we have what we need? You can go to Morris now?"

"Not exactly. Two problems. One, Powers killed Jacobson after Julianna stole his book, so we still don't have anything concrete to link him to the senator's murder. Second, Detective Sims did a little checking for me. Guess what Agency those feds were with?"

She swallowed hard. "CIA?"

"Bingo." Luke frowned. "I think we're being used."

"I don't understand. Why—"

"They already know about Jacobson, Kate. And Powers is still on the street."

She sank back against the seat, defeated. "What are we going to do? We have no place left to go."

"Oh, yes we do." Luke's jaw tightened. "If Morris doesn't give me what I want, I'm going to the press. We have enough to shake a few trees over at Langley. Think about it. A dead senator. A cover-up. A government assassin running amok. A little black book filled with nasty secrets. At the very least we can make Morris's life damn uncomfortable. That was what Condor was trying to tell me, they don't want the attention."

"Who told you?"

"A contact." Luke shook his head. "A friend."

The cabby pulled to a stop in front of their motel. Kate threw open the door and ran for the stairs that led to the rooms on the second level, ignoring Luke's shout to wait. The metal stairs shuddered as she pounded up them, Luke only steps behind her.

She landed on the second level. Their adjoining

rooms were located at the far end of the row; the door to their's stood ajar. Kate stopped, her life passing before her eyes. She opened her mouth to call out, but Luke grabbed her arm, silencing her. He bent his head close to hers. "Stay behind me."

She nodded, stepping back slightly to allow him in front, although her every instinct screamed in protest. He proceeded slowly, inching toward the pair of doors.

He reached them. A finger to his lips, Luke eased the door open.

The interior of the room was dim. The curtain had been drawn tight, the lights were off. Luke reached inside and flipped up the wall switch. Light flooded the room.

It was empty.

Emma! Kate rushed to the crib. It, too, was empty. A cry flying to her lips, she spun toward Julianna's room. Luke was already there. Kneeling on the floor, bending over something. Or someone.

He looked over his shoulder at her. At his expression, a cry ripped from her lips. She raced to his side.

Not Emma, she saw. Julianna. She lay in a crumpled heap, naked, her pale skin bruised. Blood trickled from her nose and mouth.

She opened her eyes.

She was alive, thank God.

Kate knelt by her side and Kate took Julianna's hand into her own. The younger woman looked into Kate's eyes, her mouth working but no sound coming out.

"When, Julianna?" Luke bent close. "When did John come?"

Her gaze shifted to Luke's. "Here already...when you..." A spasm of pain shook her, contorting her features. Her fingers convulsed against Kate's. "I...fought...too...strong...I—"

Kate swallowed hard, fighting panic. "Where is she, Julianna? Where's Emma?"

Julianna coughed, spitting up blood. "...be like you. Wish I..." Kate had to bend her head close to hear. "...please...forgive..."

She coughed again, the sound frighteningly weak, wet as she bled internally. Kate gathered her in her arms. "Don't die, Julianna," she whispered, tears slipping down her cheeks. "Please, hold on."

Her body convulsed again, a shudder rippling over her, as if the last of her life force fought to survive against outrageous odds. Her eyes shut, and Kate tightened her arms. "No, dammit! Open your eyes. You're not going to die, I'm not going to let you! Open them!"

Julianna did as Kate commanded, the once vivid blue irises pale now, dull with approaching death. Kate could see her fight to pull away from the darkness, struggle for consciousness. She plucked at Kate's shirt, her mouth working. Kate bent close to her again.

"Please...believe...I... Save my...save Em..."

A breath shuddered past her lips. Her muscles went slack, and her head lolled back against Kate's arm.

For a moment, Kate simply held her, a kind of numbness stealing over her limbs. Then Julianna's words, their meaning, sank in. Kate lifted her gaze to Luke's.

"He can't have her," she said. "He can't!"

She got to her feet and stumbled to the adjoining room and empty crib, tears blinding her. She gazed down at the small bed, at the rumpled blanket and the soft, bright-colored stuffed bear. Emma's favorite.

"Why didn't he bring it for her?" Kate whispered.

"Who's she going to hold on to? When she's scared, who's she going to hold on to?"

Kate picked up the toy and brought it to her face. It smelled like Emma. She breathed deeply, her heart breaking, her despair yawning, unimaginable.

The phone rang. They both swung toward it. It rang again, and Kate lunged, grabbing the receiver before it jangled a third time.

"Kate, love, it's John. Or as you know me, Nick."

"Where's my baby?"

He ignored her. "Surprised? Or did you figure it out?" He paused. "You did, I suppose. When you saw that photograph." He paused again. "What you did to my home, that wasn't nice. It made me very angry, Kate."

"You sick bastard. I want my daughter."

Luke came up to stand beside her. He bent his head close to hers to try to hear what John was saying. From the corners of her eyes, Kate saw that he had laid the bedspread over Julianna. She saw, too, that he had a gun.

"I like that about you, Kate. Your single-minded loyalty. But I've told you that before." He sighed. "I'm sorry I've had to involve you and the people you love. Julianna left me no choice. She was young and impulsive. And like most disobedient children, she didn't take my warnings seriously. And you were made to suffer."

Kate gripped the receiver tighter, her stomach rising to her throat. "What about Tess?"

"She was in the wrong place at the wrong time. Just like the good senator. Sylvia always did have a penchant for paunchy old men with power. Go figure."

"But why?" Kate managed, voice quaking. "What did Tess ever do to you?"

"She caught me stealing your Rolodex, Kate." He made a sound of pain. "Your glass work was an impulse. One I deeply regret. That I destroyed works of art...it haunts me, Kate."

He was a monster. And he had her baby. "I don't care about that, I just want my daughter back."

"She's with me. Her *daddy*." He laughed then, the sound flat, without warmth or life. That a human could make such an emotionless sound frightened her to her core. She fought to keep from crumbling, from simply falling to pieces. The only thing that kept her from doing so was knowing that Emma needed her.

"Such a shame about Julianna," he continued. "Though I think you'll agree, she had it coming. She betrayed me, Kate. *Me.* I gave her everything, and she betrayed me."

"You didn't give her everything," Kate said, unable to contain her revulsion. "You took everything from her, you son of a bitch."

"Such language." He clucked his tongue in admonishment. "Kate, you of all people should understand betrayal. After the way Richard treated you? I would think you'd be thanking me."

"What have you done with Emma? I want her back."

"Funny you should say that. Because you have something that belongs to me. Something I want back." In the background she heard an infant begin to cry.

Emma. Kate brought a shaking hand to her mouth. *She would recognize Emma's cry anywhere.*

She was alive.

"And now I have something that belongs to you.

Something you want back, rather desperately I believe."

"Don't hurt her," Kate begged. "Please don't hurt her, I'll do anything you ask. Anything!"

"Just what I was counting on, love. But please, let's save the pleas and histrionics. This is a business arrangement. If you want your item returned intact, you and Dallas meet me at 2:00 a.m. at the Bay Harbor Yacht Club in Annapolis, pier twelve. Call the cops or the feds and the little baby bitch dies."

78

Annapolis, Maryland, was located on Chesapeake Bay, about an hour from Washington, D.C. Founded in 1646, the town was known to most Americans for the navel academy of the same name. Historic and quaint, the capital of Maryland was also the sailing capital of the nation and sported no less than four yacht clubs—including Bay Harbor.

Kate and Luke arrived at Bay Harbor ten minutes early. Luke drew to a stop in the empty parking lot, shifted the car into park, but left it running. Beyond the parking lot lay the marina with its fingers of piers lined with boat slips.

The winter night was cold, quiet and impossibly dark. Kate huddled deeper into her coat, feeling small, vulnerable and afraid. The last hours had been a horror for her. Before leaving the hotel, they had called 911 and reported Julianna's murder. Then, though it had felt wrong, they'd just walked away. Quickly, not looking back. They'd had no choice.

Kate rubbed her arms. She couldn't close her eyes without seeing the image of Julianna in those last moments, as her life had slipped away. Without remembering that the man whose handiwork had caused her death now had her daughter.

Emma was in the hands of a madman.

Fear clutched at her and for a moment, Kate couldn't breathe. She squeezed her eyes shut, wishing she could stop the images unfurling in her head. Wishing she could stop imagining Emma's cries. Ones of fear. Cries for the safety and security of her mother's arms.

Only her mother didn't come.

If Emma was still alive.

A soft sob escaped her. Kate brought a hand to her mouth, the thought of it almost more than she could bear.

As if reading her thoughts, Luke turned to her. "She's alive," he said softly. "John wants that book. He knows he won't get it if she isn't." He reached across the seat and covered her clasped hands with one of his own. "We're going to get her back, Kate. We are."

Tears flooded her eyes. She didn't trust herself to speak, didn't trust herself to meet his eyes. Because she didn't believe it, not in her heart, no matter how desperately she wanted to.

"Look at me, Kate."

She shook her head. "I can't."

"I need you to look at me while I say this. It's important."

So she did. She turned her gaze to his, her tears welling and slipping slowly down her cheeks. He brought his hand up, cupping her face, catching her tears. "I love you, Kate. I always have."

His words felt like a goodbye. She recoiled from them, tears choking her. "No, don't. Please, Luke—"

He laid his hand gently across her mouth. "We both know this guy has no plans of letting us go, book or no book, but I promise you, I'll do everything I can to save her. To save you both."

Even if it meant sacrificing his own life.

She heard the words he left unsaid, as clearly as if he had spoken them aloud.

"If the opportunity comes for you to run, I want you to do it, Kate. I want you to take Emma and go. And don't look back. Promise me."

"I can't." She shook her head again. "I won't leave you behind, Luke. And I won't say goodbye."

"Then don't." He trailed his thumb across her cheekbone, his lips lifted in a bittersweet smile. "I'll love you forever, Kate. Nothing could change that. Not even death."

She turned, pressing her lips into his palm, sobbing. "I love you, too, Luke."

"Come here."

He held out his arms and she slid across the seat and into them. She clung to him, aware of the time ticking inexorably past, her dread growing with each second.

"It's time."

He was right, she knew. But she held back, clinging to the moment and to him. To life. She realized how precious and perfect it was, now that she faced the real possibility of death.

She closed her eyes and said a silent prayer—of thanks for all that she had been given, and one for the safekeeping of her daughter.

And then she was ready.

She met his eyes. "Let's go get Emma."

They climbed out of the vehicle, the sound of the doors slamming shut reverberating through the night, echoing on the sea air. Kate paused, her senses assailed by the smells and sounds of the harbor: of halyards pinging against aluminum masts, of the rhythmic slap of water against wooden and fiberglass boat hulls, of mast flags flapping in the wind; the smell of fish and salt and the day's sun that had warmed both.

Kate sucked it all in, savoring the corporeal sensations, holding on. Last times were like that, she mused. Superreal. Exaggerated. Perfect.

Luke caught her hand and laced their fingers. "Pier twelve," he murmured. They angled toward it, passing a group of storage sheds and a rest room.

As they reached the pier, John called softly from behind them. They turned. He stepped out of the shadows not twenty feet away. He had Emma. She lay limply in his arms, a piece of silver duct tape over her mouth.

"Emma!" Kate cried in anguish, fearing the worst. At the sound of her mother's voice, the infant began to stir, then squirm, in John's arms.

She was alive! Thank God!

Kate rushed forward; John stopped her by bringing his gun to Emma's head. "I don't think so, Kate." He smiled, his lips stretching obscenely across his teeth. "The gun's cocked, Kate. It's a semiautomatic. I could put twelve bullets into your little princess in twelve seconds. Or less. Would you like that?"

A sob rose in her throat. "Don't hurt her. Please. I'll do anything."

"I know you will." Again he flashed her that horrific smile. "And I admire you for it. Such love and loyalty." He made a clucking sound with his tongue. "Richard was a fool for not appreciating you." His gaze slid to Luke. "Somehow I don't think Dallas here has the same shortcomings. Such a shame."

"Let her live," she pleaded. "Please, Nick...John, I beg you. She's innocent in all this. She didn't ask to be conceived."

He ignored her plea, turning his attention to Luke. "Where's my book?"

"I've got it," Luke answered. "And I'll give it back as soon as you hand over Emma."

John stared at him a moment, then laughed, the sound hollow, cold. "So, hero, what did you think you were going to do with that book? Decipher my code and cut a deal with the Agency? Let me clue you in, my friend, they'd have screwed you. They're a bunch of disloyal, dishonorable pricks."

"Funny, those are the adjectives they used for you." Luke moved his gaze between John's face and Emma, waiting, hoping, for an opportunity. He motioned their surroundings. "What's your plan, Ice? Kill us and sail off into the sunset?"

"Give the man a gold star. I've already got the GPS set for Bermuda."

"You really think you're going to get away with this?"

"I know I am." He laughed. "He motioned to the sleek Gulfstar fifty-four parked in the slip two down on the right. "Pretty, isn't she? I named her *The Julianna.*"

Kate brought a hand to her mouth. He felt no remorse over killing Julianna, no guilt. *John Powers wasn't even human.*

"You've got snakes in your head, you know that Powers? You're pathetic."

The killer's expression tightened. "You need to show me a little respect, Dallas. I could have killed you all a dozen times over, but I didn't. You know why?"

"I'm sure you're going to enlighten me."

"I wanted to see the whites of your eyes when I did it. I wanted to smell your fear, hear you beg for your life." He moved several steps closer. "You see, then I'd be certain you were being punished for your crimes."

Luke laughed suddenly, the sound contemptuous. "You're not a very professional killer, are you? Making it personal is for psychos and street thugs. Why, the deadly Ice is nothing more than a jealous boyfriend."

A muscle began to twitch in John's jaw. The gun slipped a fraction, as if he'd relaxed his hold on Emma.

Kate held her breath, more afraid than she could have imagined possible. All it would take was the wrong word from Luke, and Emma would be dead. Kate held her tongue, knowing that unhinging John might be their only chance for survival.

"Is that why you killed Senator Jacobson?" Luke asked. "In a jealous pique? How about Clark Russell?"

"Jealous of Jacobson or Russell? Get serious." John's lips curled with derision. "Jacobson was in the wrong place at the wrong time, and Russell stuck his nose in my personal business. He had to die. He had to be punished."

"You keep saying that. We all need to be punished, right? Because little Johnny's feelings were hurt? Because his girlfriend dumped him as soon as she got old enough to see that he was nothing but a sick son of a bitch and a child molester?"

"Shut up!" John shouted, his face screwing up with rage. "Shut the fuck up and give me my goddamn book!"

"This book?" Luke asked, holding it up. "No problem. Just hand over Emma."

"You want the little bitch? It'll be a pleasure. Almost as much of a pleasure as putting a bullet in your brain.''

As if in slow motion, Kate watched as John tossed Emma into the air. Luke rushed forward. A scream ripped from her lips as she dove for the infant, hoping at the very least to put herself between Emma and the ground.

Kate caught her, then went down hard, twisting to take the brunt of the fall and protect Emma. She skidded on the gravel; it tore at her arms, elbows and legs.

A blast rent the air.

''No!'' Kate cried as Luke stopped dead, his body convulsing as the bullet slammed into him.

Suddenly the night went from dark to light as spotlights from the boats on either side of the pier snapped on, pinning John in their bright circles. Men with guns appeared as if from nowhere, at least a dozen of them, their weapons trained on John.

''Drop your weapon, Powers! CI—''

With a howl of rage, John swung toward Kate, leveling his gun on her and Emma.

Kate's life passed before her eyes. She lurched sideways, clutching her daughter to her chest, shielding the infant with her body, saying one last, silent prayer as she awaited the bullet's impact.

The agents opened fire. John's body jerked and twitched as round after round blew into him—blood, fragments of bone and bits of flesh flew as the shots pitched him side to side, forward and back in a grotesque dance of death.

As abruptly as it had begun, the explosion of sound that shattered the night ceased. But still, John stood. He hung there, gun clutched in his hand, blank gaze on Kate. In that moment, hysteria pulling at her, Kate wondered if John Powers couldn't be killed. If, monster that he was, he needed neither blood nor bone nor breath to survive. She wondered if it would ever be over.

Then, like a puppet whose wires had been suddenly severed, he went down, folding in on himself, hitting the ground without a sound.

79

Luke opened his eyes slowly, squinting against the bright light. His mouth was dry; his head felt as if it had been used as a battering ram. He moved his gaze, taking in the I.V., the bed rails, the TV mounted from the ceiling. A hospital, he realized. He was in a hospital.

He turned his head. Kate slept in a big chair beside the bed, Emma asleep in her arms.

They were alive. They were all alive.

He shifted slightly and winced as pain shot through his shoulder. With the pain, the events of the evening came rushing back, though in a confusing and disjointed blur. Kate's scream. The intense burning in his shoulder and the sensation of being propelled backward by a force beyond his control. The warm stickiness of blood, then the realization that he had been shot, that he was most probably going to die.

But he hadn't died. None of them had.

"I thought I'd lost you."

He turned his head toward Kate. His lips lifted. "I thought you had, too. Hanging out with you is damn hazardous, lady."

She smiled even as her eyes flooded with tears. "I'm sorry, Luke. I'm so—"

"Don't be. I'm not." He shifted his gaze to take in Emma. Only then did he see the angry red welt across her mouth and cheeks.

From the tape, he realized, fisting his fingers, impotent rage swelling inside him. "That son of a bitch. How could he?"

"It'll heal," Kate said softly. "She's alive and that's all that matters."

"Thank God for the cavalry. If not for them—"

He bit the words back. They both knew where they would be right now if not for Tom Morris and his men. Luke's hunch had been correct. Apparently, they'd had their suspicions about John Powers for some time. They'd used Luke and Kate to get them confirmation.

Kate shifted Emma so she lay in the crook of one arm, propped against her side. With her free hand she reached for his. She curled her fingers around his. "No," she whispered. "Thank God for you."

"For me?" He shook his head. "Some hero. I didn't even get my gun out of my pants."

Kate laughed and brought his hand to her mouth. She kissed his knuckles, then his hand. "Without you, Emma and I would be dead. I believe that, and I'll be forever grateful to you."

He laced their fingers. "It's over now, love. You're safe."

"I know. But it doesn't feel that way. If I hadn't seen him die, if I hadn't—"

"I know." He tightened his fingers. "But you did see it, we both did. He can't hurt you anymore."

The door to his room swung open and a man in surgical scrubs entered. "Morning, folks." He crossed to the end of the bed, lifted Luke's chart, scanned it, then turned to Luke.

He smiled. "How are you feeling this morning, Mr. Dallas?"

Condor. Luke narrowed his eyes. He must have

been in on the Agency's plans, all along. "I feel like shit. How are you?"

Beside him, Kate made a sound of surprise. Luke glanced at her; she was staring at Condor, a look of confusion on her face.

"And here I thought you'd be happy to be alive."

"I am that." Luke motioned him closer, as if he had something to say that he didn't want Kate to hear. Condor bent slightly, and Luke grabbed a fistful of his scrub and jerked him down, so that they were eye to eye.

"You bastard. You could have helped us, but instead you stood back and let Morris use us as pawns to get Powers."

Condor closed his hand around Luke's wrist, his grip like steel. "I had a job to do, Dallas. It wasn't personal. We needed confirmation that Powers killed the senator and Russell, we needed to know why— you got us that. We needed his book to confirm his involvement in other activities. You got us that as well. We thank you."

"And I suppose you guys knew where we were meeting Powers because you tapped our phone?"

"That's generally the way it works."

Luke searched the man's gaze. Condor felt no remorse about having used them that way, at having put them in harm's way, no guilt or regret.

With a sound of disgust, Luke released him. "Fuck you."

"I helped you where I could." Condor straightened, automatically smoothing the front of his scrub. "I warned you to hold on to Powers' book. Hell, Dallas, I could have taken it that day. You would have given it to me."

"And I should be grateful?"

"Frankly? Yes. I could have let you die."

"And what about Julianna? You could have prevented her death."

His expression didn't change. "My loyalty is to the Agency, Luke. And to my country. For me, there was never a question of whose interests came first. I'm sure you can understand that."

"Powers talked about loyalty, too. About honor and commitment. And he was a psycho."

Condor smiled, the curving of his lips emotionless. "We all walk a fine line, don't we, my friend?"

He crossed to the door, stopping and looking back at Kate when he reached it. He smiled. "See you around, Kate."

As the door snapped shut, Kate turned to Luke in disbelief.

"That man was a customer of mine, a Dead Head. Only he looks completely different now. I wouldn't have recognized him, but for his eyes." She drew her eyebrows together. "My phone...the repairman. That man was in my house."

"He's with the Agency, Kate. He was probably sent to watch Powers. Take him out if need be. He probably tapped your phone. The Bean's, too."

She shivered, and Emma moaned and shifted in her sleep. Kate gazed at her a moment, then back up at Luke. "I don't want to talk about him or the Agency or Powers anymore." She smiled and reached for his hand. "I want to talk about you."

"Me?"

"Mmm. The doctor thinks you're a lucky man. The bullet hit a fleshy place in your shoulder. Half an inch to the right or left and the damage would have been much worse. But you know what I think?" She curled her fingers tighter around his. "I think I'm the lucky one."

One spring morning,
Summer Shepherd disappeared...

THE DISAPPEARANCE

JASMINE CRESSWELL

Ordinarily the FBI refuses to negotiate with terrorists. But Summer is the daughter of the U.S. Secretary of State—so they clearly have to make an exception.

Why Duncan Ryder received the ransom demands remains a mystery. Yet it is Duncan who orchestrates Summer's release, helps her convince the authorities she didn't stage her own kidnapping and helps rescue her friend from the same captors. And, in the end, it is only Duncan who can help her expose the shocking truth behind her disappearance.

On sale mid-March 1999 wherever paperbacks are sold!

MIRA